A JOYOUS CELEBRATION

Love and laughter, joy and happiness, pomp and circumstance—the season of love is upon us and what better time to celebrate than during the month of June. As the warmth of summer gently erases all traces of winter cold, so too does love warm the heart and the soul. Bouquets of brightly colored flowers, the gentle swell of voices raised in song, the solemn exchange of rings—the chapel is ready, the bride and groom have arrived. We now invite you to share in this joyous celebration of wedded delight.

And these charming stories of June romance by six of Zebra's favorite Regency authors help set the scene for our wedding festivities. Monette Cummings, Marissa Edwards, Lynn Kerstan, Rebecca North, Cynthia Richey, and Jeanne Savery present brides in the full flower of the season, each discovering the excitement and charm of everlasting happiness in the arms of her one true love.

A Memorable Collection of Regency Romances

BY ANTHEA MALCOLM AND VALERIE KING

A June Betrothal

Monette Cummings • Marissa Edwards • Lynn Kerstan
Rebecca North • Cynthia Richey • Jeanne Savery

ZEBRA BOOKS
KENSINGTON PUBLISHING CORP.

ZEBRA BOOKS are published by

Kensington Publishing Corp.
475 Park Avenue South
New York, NY 10016

First Printing: June, 1993

Printed in the United States of America

CONTENTS

The Runaway Bride
by Lynn Kerstan

"I," John Corbett informed the world at large, "am a happy man."

Ricco, having listened to similar declarations for the past several miles, expressed his indifference with an inelegant snort.

John's good humor remained undiminished. "Your time will come, old boy. I'll see to it myself. Prime English stock, no expense spared, and you can make the choice yourself. Meantime, it's my turn, so pick up the pace, will you? Fifty miles to London . . . and the woman of my dreams."

The grin, permanently carved across his face since he had met Penelope, widened at the thought. He'd seen enough of war and death to appreciate his good fortune, and was so busy counting his blessings that he nearly turned from a side road into the path of a thundering coach.

"Back, Ricco."

The enormous bay, battle-trained and smarter than most men John knew, retreated several yards.

A youngster with more capes on his coat than wits in his head had taken up the ribbons, snapping the tommy at the straining wheelers' flanks until they lurched into a gallop. John swallowed his anger. Reckless boys, lathered horses, and irresponsible coachmen were none of his business. As the stage hurtled past, his keen eyes picked out the legend *Blazing Star* on the panel and lifted with casual interest to the open window. His heart skipped several beats.

Conditioned to action, he moved without thinking, chucking Ricco after the coach at a slow trot. "Looks like a slight detour," he advised the horse.

What the devil was she up to? In ten days and twenty-two hours, on the thirty-first of May, Penelope Wright was to marry him at St. George's in Hanover Square. It was all arranged, signed, and delivered. He'd advanced her repugnant father several thousand pounds to cover expenses, including the bridal trousseau and an elaborate ceremony and reception. The baron had insisted that only the best would do for his cherished firstborn child.

Now the firstborn was taking herself out of London on a common stage, for unmistakably that had been Pen's face in the window. John swore fluently. A family crisis was the only explanation he wanted to acknowledge, but she'd no relations beyond her father and sisters and thus could not be rushing to the bedside of an expiring uncle.

One hellishly cold winter, when his regiment was forced to bivouac in an open field, he had wakened to find his hair frozen to the ground. That same fierce cold gripped him now, as he considered the two reasons Pen might bolt days before her wedding.

He, of course, was one of them, but she had seemed to like him well enough. If she objected to the marriage, why the devil hadn't she said so when he proposed? Or the next day, which was the last time he'd seen her until a few minutes ago.

A lot could happen in a month, he reflected. He should never have given her a chance to think things over and change her mind. But what the hell did he know? All his friends had advised him to get out of town and stay out of sight until the last possible moment. Females in the throes of wedding preparations would trample any man bacon-witted enough to wander underfoot.

Besides, he'd not seen Walford since his last extended leave more than six years ago, and his predecessor rarely parted with a shilling for repairs. Surely duty required him to make certain his new home was fit to welcome a bride.

10

The trouble was, John had little experience of civilian life and none at all as a peer of the realm. The youngest of four sons, he always figured to end his days a crusty bachelor officer, entertaining subalterns with war stories at regimental dinners. But his brothers fell like duckpins, the heir in a hunting accident, his successor of influenza, and Edgar by strangling on a hunk of tough mutton.

Suddenly plain John, the military boy who played with toy soldiers before he could walk, was Viscount Walford and heir to a sizable fortune. Even so, he declined to sell out until Bonaparte was stowed on Elba, but everything went at full speed after that. Less than a week after returning to England he met Penelope Wright and tumbled head over ears in love.

Pen was everything he'd fantasized about during the long years in Portugal and Spain and France. Once, on a ride into the countryside while recovering from a minor wound, he'd come upon huge fields of sunflowers that seemed to stretch as far as the horizon. They stood tall and bright, frank and open, blazing with light. Mesmerized, he sat for hours, watching the flowers swing slowly as they tracked the sun across the sky. That day was the happiest of his life, until the first time he saw Pen.

Like the sunflowers, she was magnificent. Her wide smile lit up the ballroom. Her thick hair, every shade of sunlight from pale dawn to amber sunset, made his fingers burn to uncoil the heavy knot clamped at the back of her neck. Even her freckles reminded him of sunflower seeds.

She was three-and-twenty, on the shelf everyone said, on the town only to chaperone her incomparable sisters. He thanked his stars London men were blind, deaf, and dumb. He could scarcely believe his good fortune in finding her, and the little time he managed to spend with her confirmed his every wish. Pen was intelligent and witty, hot tempered and sensible, and given to odd flights of fancy that intrigued him.

She'd been wary, which hurt him, although he could not be surprised. He'd bought his first commission at sixteen,

11

and spent all his adult life in the army. His manners showed it. When he spoke to her, words came out that bore no resemblance to those in his head and he kept looking over his shoulder to see who was saying them. He'd shed his uniform, but the professional soldier was not so easily cast off and that soldier had no address whatever.

Fortunately, Pen never ran short of words. She filled his aching silences with bright chatter, and he longed for the day when his tongue and brain joined forces to produce something intelligible in return. Meantime he was stiff as a post and dull as cabbage soup. No wonder she kept pushing him at her sisters, three nearly identical hothouse orchids he scarcely noticed once he'd met his sunflower.

Never one to bide his time, he approached her father and found him more than ready to part with any of his daughters—for a price. The baron assumed he meant to offer for one of the other girls, and there was some confusion while that was straightened out. Then, with a vulture's instinct for easy prey, Burnwich demanded and received an outrageous marriage settlement. Money changed hands, the date was set, and John left to ready a home for his wife.

Certain of his own feelings, he never thought to question Pen's. Young women of his class married for advancement or money, and he could give her both. She would be a viscountess, wealthy, pampered, and wed to a man who adored her. What else could she possibly want?

Whatever it was, he thought grimly, she was on her way to find it. And that led to the second, the unthinkable, reason for her to bolt. Another man.

Turning off the road, he urged Ricco to a gallop across the fields, taking hedges in smooth jumps until he came to a fenced pasture enclosing at least fifty horses. Nearby, a busy posthouse was servicing a private carriage. Mr. Bowles, owner of the Notched Arrow, confirmed that London-to-Stroud coaches always stopped to change cattle at his excellent inn. The *Blazing Star* was due within the hour.

John spent nearly ten minutes giving orders and paying

handsomely to see them carried out. Then he settled himself in the best private parlor with a bottle of good claret to wait for his runaway bride.

Not long after the horn announced the coach's arrival, John heard Pen's voice in the hall.

"I can't *afford* a private parlor," she wailed as the door swung open. "You don't—"

When Penelope saw the tall man across the room, her mouth dropped. "Oh no," she muttered, staring at him from huge tawny eyes.

Mr. Bowles nudged her inside and beat a quick retreat.

John bowed. "Hullo, Pen. I've been expecting you."

"Oh no," she said again. Her freckles blazed like pumpkins in a snowpatch. "How can *you* be here?"

He shrugged. "Good reconnaissance. Come inside, will you? The other passengers are gaping at us."

Pen entered on stiff legs, dropping her bandbox and giving it a kick for good measure. "How did you know which direction I'd gone? I never said in the note."

"Ah, the note." John propped his shoulders against the wall and folded his arms across his chest. "I must confess I didn't understand a word of it."

She glared at him. "How did you get to be a colonel if you can't read simple English? It was plain as day."

"Not to me. Would you mind going over the details again?"

"Oh, this is beyond *everything!*" She began to pace off her frustration, careful to keep a distance from him. "No wedding. Gracious, you can't have misunderstood *that*. I cried off. Papa got a note too, and I sent a notice to the *Times*. You jilted me." Her lashes fluttered. "I did apologize. That part took hours to write, but I meant it. I really am sorry for embarrassing you, and for the money Papa spent. He won't pay you back, I'm afraid."

Glad of the solid wall at his back, John sifted through the disjointed explanation to the one bit he understood clearly. "I never jilted you, Pen."

13

"Of course not. But I couldn't make it sound like I'd run out on you, when you were the . . . the one run out on. From what I know about men, that would certainly have been insulting, so I made it seem that you called it off."

"Pen, whatever causes a wedding to be canceled, in public release it is always the bride who jilts the groom. Always."

"I got it backward? Oh dear." She nibbled on her lower lip. "Maybe Papa will know the proper form, and straighten things out."

"Never mind that. From your note, I could not decipher exactly why you did not wish to marry me."

"Well, that's because I didn't say. Pinfeathers! One would think you'd not even read the thing. We should not suit, Colonel Corbett. That is perfectly obvious, and I can't imagine why either of us let things go so far as they did."

Pen always spoke a beat ahead of her mind, which was a thing he'd delighted in, but now she seemed weeks ahead of logic, somewhere in the realm of totally incomprehensible female reasoning. He knew he'd never find her there.

And she was exhausted. Her straw bonnet angled over her left eye, and her forehead was moist with perspiration. John lifted himself away from the wall, took her elbow, and led her to a chair. "Sit," he commanded.

With a mutinous glare, she obeyed. He untied the ribbon at her chin and lifted away the sad bonnet. Her thick hair was matted underneath. It must have been hot in that coach, he thought, wanting to kiss her.

Pen stretched her legs in a distinctly unfeminine gesture and wriggled her feet. After seven hours crammed like a sausage between a pig farmer and a hard wooden panel, all her muscles ached. And she badly needed to use the necessary, although she'd been forestalled by that brute of an innkeeper. Crossing her knees, she curled onto her side in the large padded chair.

She was mortified, but that was nothing new. It seemed that wherever she went she was out of place, and no one who met her family could credit that Penelope was half sister to the Three Graces. As fate had it, she'd not been granted even a quarter of their slender loveliness. They were graceful and petite, she was long legged and gangly. They had creamy, flawless complexions, whereas she was blotched with freckles no amount of lemon juice could diminish. They were gifted with sleek mink-dark hair, while her wild mane of unruly curls was the color of dirt.

She stared at her clenched hands, unable to look at John again. How had she ever imagined this handsome man might really want her? His hair and eyes were brown as roasted chestnuts and he was wonderfully tall, with shoulders so wide they made her feel graceful instead of big and awkward. He'd been awkward when they danced, she remembered, stumbling over his enormous feet every time the figure brought them together. For all her great size, one of the few things she did well was dance, and he offered to take lessons so as not to shame her.

She remembered a great many things from their few meetings, and had been granted a month to think them over when he left "on business." Enough time to realize she could not marry him.

Why in perdition was he here, and how in blazes did he know where to look? She'd thought him miles from London, unlikely to read her note for several days, yet he'd managed to beat the *Blazing Star* to this remote inn. It never occurred to her that anyone would follow or care where she'd gone, but men were damnably reluctant to let females escape while they still had a use for them.

She heard the clink of ice and looked up. John was holding out a tall glass of lemonade. Her mouth felt dry as wool, but she dared not swallow any liquid. "I can't," she murmured, feeling heat rise to her cheeks.

He studied her for a moment and left the room abruptly. When he returned, a buxom serving maid followed, gazing at him with patent admiration. "Pen, I've requisitioned a private billet for you. While you wash up and catch your breath, I'll order dinner."

She stood. "Yes. Thank you. But I can't stay for dinner.

The coach only stops here a few minutes."

He gave her his "colonel" look. "On no account will you continue your journey on a public coach, young lady. The driver has been instructed to go on without you."

Pen grabbed her bandbox. "He can't do that! I paid for my ticket, and I'll be on that coach when it leaves."

"Not," he said mildly, "past me."

In spite of his threat, he made no move to stop her as she vaulted out of the room.

"All ready, outside and in," called the guard as he swung to his place.

"Let 'em go, then," the coachman shouted. Postboys jumped out of the way.

Pen watched helplessly as the *Blazing Star* rumbled out of the yard. A cloud of dust billowed over her.

"*Ten* minutes, to be exact," John commented in a pleasant voice when she stormed back into the parlor. "It's a matter of pride, for coachman and innkeeper alike, to be precisely on time."

Pen wanted to hurl her bandbox at him. "My luggage," she informed him, "is on that coach. I hope they're proud of *that*."

"Relax, Pen. Your bags are upstairs, and the hot water I ordered for you is getting cold."

His deep voice was perfectly calm, but she recognized a command. "This is only a temporary delay," she warned. "Coaches stop here all the time, and I'll board any one of them I choose."

"We'll talk about it over dinner," he said firmly. "This young woman will show you to your room."

From the set of his jaw, discussion was over. Weariness settled over her like a heavy cloak as she stumbled upstairs.

Sure enough, her meager luggage was waiting in the clean, pleasant chamber. Curtly dismissing the maid, who introduced herself as Betty and seemed inclined to stay and talk, Pen hurried behind a wooden screen to use the chamberpot. Then she flung herself on the canopied bed to contemplate the vagaries of fate. The leaf-green curtains and quilted counterpane, crisp and scented with lilac, were the nicest she'd ever seen. This was, she suspected, the best room at the inn, but why such a treat when she could not enjoy it? Drat the man! He should have consigned her to the root cellar, which suited her mood and her crimes.

She banged a clenched fist against the bedcovers. Men never saw things exactly the way one imagined. She'd thought John would be as glad to escape the marriage as she was sorry, but here he was to plague her. And her father had been equally contrary. Instead of being delighted to marry off his unmarriageable daughter, he'd tried to convince her that John really wanted one of her sisters. Men made no sense whatever.

Some few of them did place a large store on honor, though. Especially soldiers. Maybe John thought he was committed to her because he'd shoved a betrothal ring on her finger and muttered something about being captivated by her loveliness and charm. He'd spoken the words by rote, like a multiplication table, but at the time she was too stunned to care. This handsome, dashing man wanted to marry her. *Her!* For the only time since her breasts began to develop, she'd felt shy. He'd had to prompt her for an answer.

John Corbett was her dream come to life, but in the cold light of the next morning her doubts had rushed back. She was awash in them when he called to bid her an awkward farewell, claiming urgent business at the family estate. She'd listened carefully for any hint of sorrow at leaving her or the tiniest enthusiasm about their wedding, but he was gruff as a bear. Didn't want to keep his horse standing, he said, practically catapulting out the door. Her sisters, lurking in the hall to eavesdrop, laughed at her when he'd gone.

Even then she didn't ruffle the waters. Perhaps he would write to her, and they could get to know one another through the mails. She crafted a great many letters to him, not daring to send a one until he contacted her first, but he did not. When a month passed with no word from her betrothed, she was certain he regretted his impetuous proposal.

The truth was inescapable. Colonel Corbett, too long at the wars, sought to marry and breed an heir. Apparently he was in a hurry, or not very particular about bloodlines, because he'd allied himself with the least attractive female member of a thoroughly disreputable family. Creditors were practically beating down the door, not that the Baron of Burnwich would pay a one of them from the marriage settlement. All he really wanted was a stake for the gaming hells.

He didn't get much for his efforts, she thought with some satisfaction. Apparently John Corbett pinched a penny until it squeaked, the way his brother had done. Her father made it clear how little the colonel offered by way of a marriage settlement, and slapped her when she observed that it was considerably more than she brought in dowry.

He'd have paid well, no doubt, for the Incomparable, but Philia wouldn't have him. Pen had listened to the story of that courtship more times than she cared to, with Philia expanding on the colonel's ardor and her dramatic refusal at each telling.

That ardor was noticeably missing when he offered for his second choice. Colonel Corbett had proposed with military efficiency, received her stammered acceptance with a brief smile, and kissed her hand. She was surprised that he didn't salute on his way out. If it were not for a peculiar, almost hot look in his eyes, he might as well have been negotiating for a brood mare.

Which was, she admitted fairly, exactly what he'd purchased, cheaply and with dispatch. Immediately the deal was closed, he left for his estate, where he apparently intended to remain until time to meet his brood . . . bride . . . at the altar.

He'd have recognized her immediately—the freckled plowhorse lumbering behind her three graceful sisters, wearing a homemade dress, trying to hold her drunken father erect. She'd visualized the ceremony a hundred

18

times, and the picture never changed. The real thing would be even worse because John would see it too. She'd spared them both the worst day of their lives by calling the wedding off.

Levering herself off the bed, she splashed cold water on her dirt-streaked face and determined to stop feeling sorry for herself. Facts were facts, and she despised self-pity. Besides, things could be worse. She'd enough money to get by for several months, an excellent if unusual education thanks to her dour grandparents, and a new life to make for herself. Nothing was going to stop her now.

John Corbett had no legal control of her, and if he turned her over to her father, who did, the baron could beat her senseless before she'd willingly jump from one cage into another. She knew all too well how it was to be possessed without being wanted. While she remained free, there was a chance for happiness, but married to the autocratic colonel, she'd be chattel for the rest of her life.

Pen scowled at her reflection in the mirror. Her freckles looked like mold growing on a slab of white bread. Her eyes were bloodshot and felt dry and gritty. She stank of sweat and pigs. Obviously freedom did nothing for her looks.

Her ex-fiancé had come a long way to ring a peal over her head, but men did not like to be thwarted. Once he'd vented his wrath, she could be on her way because men generally went about their business when they were done asserting themselves. Nothing was ever gained by confronting them. She had years of practice ignoring her father's rages and her grandfather's sarcasm while concentrating on subduing her own hot temper, although the urge to fight back almost strangled her sometimes.

She took a long deep breath, summoning every ounce of meekness and self-discipline in her nature. Tomorrow, she'd buy passage on another coach. Tonight, if the price wasn't too dear, she'd treat herself to a bath. This was her one and only great adventure and she meant to enjoy it, but first she had to eliminate a large male roadblock.

* * *

The colonel favored her with a bow, which earned him a false smile, and settled her at a small table laid out with a feast. Suddenly ravenous, Pen eyed a chicken leg with longing before wrenching her gaze to his disturbingly handsome face. This was no time to eat. He stood erect and supremely confident, like a commander preparing to rake down an insubordinate recruit.

Meekness flew to the winds as she launched a surprise attack of her own. "Since we are no longer engaged," she clipped, "you ought not to be in a room alone with me!"

His lips twitched. "If you feel compromised, Penelope, I am willing to do the honorable thing."

Round one to the colonel, she thought peevishly. "Oh, very clever. As if you would, now that I've publicly shamed you."

He shrugged. "In matters of importance, a certain amount of unpleasantness is to be expected. I learned that lesson in the army."

"The war," she reminded him, "is over."

He reached for the pitcher of lemonade. "Not this one, I suspect." Their gazes locked, until Pen broke contact to hand him a glass. "A soldier can always find a war somewhere," he continued briskly, "however senseless the conflict. If my brother hadn't cocked up his toes I'd be on my way to America by now."

Pen took the glass of lemonade with a curt nod of thanks. "So now you have a title instead of a rank. Is that so bad?"

"Too soon to tell." His eyes narrowed. "I've been a soldier all my life, Pen, and God knows I haven't a clue how to be a viscount. Estates, tenants, investments, harvests, distant relations looking for a handout ... ." He grimaced. "I spent the last three weeks trying to evict my brother's wife, who has her claws dug into Walford and refuses to be dislodged."

Pen looked shocked. "You would cast out your own sister-in-law?"

"Damn right I would." He colored. "Apologies, Pen. My language is from the barracks. Estelle is half-vulture, half-shrew, and you would not wish to live with her any more than I do. She's been offered a townhouse in Mayfair, another in Bath, and is welcome to reside at any of several estates my brother accumulated in his career as a miser. What she cannot do is live with us at Walford."

"With *you,*" Penelope corrected sharply. "I won't be there, remember?"

He leaned against the mantel. "Would you mind explaining why? You did accept me, Pen. I remember it clearly. I asked you to be my wife and you agreed."

She took a swallow of lemonade. "I changed my mind. Besides, I never really said *yes.* I said *if it pleases you,* and it does not."

"What in hell makes you think that? Of course it pleases me. Why else would I offer for you?"

"Because you couldn't have Philia, and knew that I was in no position to refuse any offer at all."

"Who the devil is Philia?"

"Oh, you *are* clever." She wrinkled her nose. "But it won't fadge, because she told me all about it. Women talk, you know."

In fact, he didn't. His women had spoken Portuguese, or Spanish or French, and their communication was primarily physical. He couldn't remember the last time he'd actually had a long talk with an intelligent, articulate woman, which was something he'd looked forward to with Pen. "Is Philia one of your sisters?" he asked uncomfortably.

She shot him a look of acute dislike. "Indeed. The one you danced with twice before you were introduced to me. The one you proposed to. The one who thought you too old and too barbaric to make an agreeable husband. Besides, you are only a viscount, and Philia is hanging out for a duke."

"Is she?" He remembered her now, a snippy chit with a

21

creamy complexion and hard, calculating eyes. Had she really told Pen he'd proposed to her?

"Don't take it personally," Pen was saying. "I ought not to have betrayed what she spoke in confidence." She regarded him curiously. "By the way, how old are you?"

He smiled. "Three and thirty. Too old for you too, Pen?"

"When a female is moldering on the shelf," she muttered sullenly, "no potential suitor with one tooth left in his head is too old."

"*Actual* suitor, Pen. I never offered for your sister. Only for you."

She frowned. "No man in his right mind would have me if he could have Philia. I am sorry your hopes were shattered, but you'll have no trouble finding yourself a wife once the gossip has died down. I am also sorry for embroiling you in a scandal, but I couldn't think of any other way and time was running out."

"Way for what?" He regarded her with brooding eyes. "Is there . . . another man?"

She looked surprised, and then her lashes swung down. "Well, now that you mention it—"

"Don't lie to me about this," he warned.

With a sigh, she turned her attention to the food and picked up a chunk of crusty bread. "No," she mumbled. "No other man. Not ever."

"I find that impossible to believe. Every time I saw you in public, you were surrounded by young bucks clamoring for your attention."

She flashed a humorless smile. "I am the friendly sister, don't you know. I talk to anyone. They all like me, and hope I'll put in a good word for them with the Incomparables. But when the music begins, they go off and dance with someone else."

A vast feeling of relief swept over him, followed by a hot wash of rage. He wanted to flatten every insensitive lout who dared to hurt her feelings. But devil take it, he was one of those ratbags. He'd danced with her, yes, but only one time, lumbering around the polished floor like a gut-shot packmule. He'd thought he was sparing her toes and her feelings by not asking again.

Damn. He knew nothing at all about courting well-bred young ladies. Come to think of it, he'd never really courted Pen. He saw her, danced with her, paid one formal morning call, took her driving twice, offered, proposed, and was accepted. All in the space of three days. When the business was concluded, he left town feeling on top of the world. He'd wanted her so badly it never occurred to him that she might not feel the same way.

He watched her spread butter on the bread, place a slice of cheese on top, and bite into the combination hungrily. Her white teeth and open mouth sent a shot of desire through him. He wondered if she remembered that he'd kissed her once, briefly but with more passion than he'd ever kissed a woman. "It's not too late to change your mind," he ventured into the long silence. "Why do you dislike the idea of our marriage?"

She swallowed hard. "If I tell you the absolute truth," she said tonelessly, "will you let me go and not make trouble with my father?"

He poured a glass of claret and held it up to the light. "I will let you go," he lied.

Carefully, she put the half-eaten bread and cheese on a plate and sat back in her chair. "If I married you," she said, "it would be the end of my dream." Her gaze swung to the ceiling. "I would be bound to you the rest of my life. There would be no hope, ever."

His stomach clenched. "What dream is that, Penny? What is it you hope for?"

She closed her eyes. "All women have dreams, Colonel. Philia wants to be a duchess. Antonia and Apollonia want to marry the handsomest men in London. Perhaps my own dream will never come true, but while I am free, anything is possible."

He stared down at the flagstone hearth. "I'm not the answer to any woman's dreams, Pen, but I would do my best to be a faithful and devoted husband."

She mustered a smile. "I'm certain that you will, with the right woman. And that's all I'm going to say, because there aren't any words to explain. I apologize for embarrassing you, and costing you money. I made a dreadful mistake when I accepted you. You need not forgive me, but you must let me go because you promised. I shall take another coach tomorrow."

John took a deep swallow of wine. "Under no circumstances will you ride a public coach again, Penelope. It is uncomfortable, unseemly, and dangerous. If you insist on continuing, I'll see that you have a coach and driver. In fact, I've already sent to my estate, which is only a few miles from here, for a vehicle." He smiled wanly. "I had hoped we could ride back to London together."

She pulled herself off the chair. "I'm not going back to London."

"Then the coach will take you where you wish to go. This is not negotiable, Penelope."

She saluted. "Yes, *sir*."

With a sigh, he crossed to the table and dropped onto a chair. "I've sold out, you know."

"Sorry. It's 'my lord' now." She clasped her arms around her waist. "Will you compel your driver, my lord, to tell you where he left me off?"

He cocked his head. "Would that be so terrible?"

"Let us say uncomfortable. For a great many reasons, I want to disappear."

"In that case," he said smoothly, "the driver and footman will be sworn to secrecy."

She regarded him doubtfully. "You could still hire someone to trace me."

"What are you afraid of, Pen? Do you imagine I'd do anything to harm you?"

"Not," she said after some thought, "deliberately."

He winced. "If it will make you feel better, I swear not to trace you through my servants nor hire anyone to find you. I only want you to be safe and comfortable." He gave her a questioning look. "You do have a place to go?"

"Certainly. I'm not a complete fool, Colonel."

No, she was not. He'd been the fool, letting her out of his sight before the ring was on her finger. Now she'd maneuvered him into promises that would be damnably hard to keep. He gazed at her with respect and no little degree of frustration, wondering if he could salvage anything of the evening.

"Tonight you can sleep well, have a good breakfast in the morning, and be on your way," he said with counterfeit nonchalance. "I'll be long gone before you are awake, and my servants will not disclose your whereabouts." He sat back and crossed his arms behind his head as if putting an unpleasant piece of business to rest. "So, Miss Wright, now that things are settled between us, will you join me for dinner?"

Pen ate in silence, swallowing past a heavy lump in her throat while John played host. He seemed to have found his tongue now that the burden of marrying her was lifted, and told her fascinating stories about life in the army.

"Were you ever . . . hurt?" she asked, when he paused to sample the roasted chicken. It was the first time she'd spoken for half an hour.

With a pleased smile, he carved her a slice. "A time or two, nothing worth mentioning. Unless you count being shot by a farmer who thought I was stealing his piglets."

Her brows shot up. "Stealing?"

"In the army, it's called foraging, but as it happens we were returning the pigs. Some of my men had spent the afternoon supplementing their sparse rations, and when I made the rounds of the camp that night . . . well, pigs make a damnable lot of noise. Wellington had strict rules about pilfering from the locals, so we bundled up the little wretches and took them back. That's when the farmer came out of his house. Everyone else dropped the pigs and ran like hell, but I had three of them wiggling inside my shirt and wasn't fast enough. He got me in the last part over the fence, so to speak."

Pen bent over, laughing until tears streamed down her face.

He regarded her ruefully. "Needless to say, my war wound was not mentioned in the dispatches. Wellington pointed out that I was clearly retreating when shot, and hoped he'd heard the end of the matter. Told me not to get behind in my work."

"I expect," Pen gurgled, "you didn't take that sitting down."

"Not for several weeks," he admitted cheerfully.

She shot him a wry glance. "Much the same thing happened to Sir Lancelot, you know. A huntress shot her arrow at a"—she chuckled—"oh dear, at a hind. She missed, and poor Lancelot wasn't wearing his armor. The wound was *'passing sore,'* and in such a place that he *'might not sit in no saddle.'* "

His brows lifted. "Pen, you are making that up."

"Certainly not," she protested. "Didn't you read Malory at school? *'Ye have mischieved me,'* said Lancelot, as well he might."

Laughing, John refilled her wineglass. "I gather this is not something a man ever lives down."

"The stuff of legends," she agreed solemnly. "You follow an heroic tradition."

"The rear guard," he riposted, sending her into whoops. Then she plastered her hands over her mouth and assumed a guileless look.

"I shouldn't tease you so," she murmured between her fingers. "Pig farmers notwithstanding, you are most certainly a hero. Everyone says so."

"Tease me all you want," he urged. "I like it. So much, in fact, that I am now going to offer further proof of my alleged heroism." Leaning forward, he propped his elbows on his knees. "Three years ago, on a scouting foray, I was caught behind enemy lines by a behemoth of a guard who tried to seduce me."

She blinked.

"Mind you, I was disguised as a woman," he explained with a grin. "And there was no moon."

Pen threw up her hands. "The man must have been blind as a tree stump, because no one in his right mind could mistake you for a female. Not a female human being, anyway."

"Pierre could, and did. He was most importunate." John's deep voice rose several octaves. " 'Ah, my leetle Brussels sprout, *voulez-vouz coucher avec moi?*' "

"What does that mean?" she demanded, her eyes wide.

He bit his wayward tongue. "Uh . . . it's French for *meet me in the barn*. I was encumbered by skirts instead of pigs that night, but I practically flew out of there."

She wagged a scolding finger at him. "Colonel Corbett, you seem to have made a career of running away."

He gazed at her steadily, one eyebrow arched in a reprimand of his own.

Embarrassed, she reached for her glass of wine. "Obviously we have at least one thing in common," she murmured, wanting to kick herself for spoiling the mood.

As if anxious to restore their camaraderie, John launched into one outrageous tale after another until Pen felt she'd been laughing for hours. Deliciously bleary from the wine, she wondered why she had ever thought John Corbett stiff and humorless. When he paused for a moment to open another bottle, she recklessly told him so.

"We never had time," he pointed out, "to become acquainted. I figured that with fifty years of marriage ahead of us we'd come to terms."

"Have you always," she inquired with a snort, "set your artillery to pulling the horses, Colonel Corbett?"

"A serious miscalculation," he admitted after a hefty draught of wine. "I should not have left London when I did, but at the time it seemed imperative to settle matters at Walford House before I brought you there. According to my sister-in-law, the place was practically falling down. That was not the case, although Estelle has filched everything of value against the day I send her packing."

"Well, now there is no reason for her to leave," Pen observed brightly. "Not until you find yourself another bride."

He ignored that. "You'd like Walford, Pen. The house needs work, but it's surrounded by gardens and orchards. There's a river bordering one edge of the estate, and a forest stretches for miles on another. Lots of pasture land, gone to seed now, but ideal for sheep or cattle."

"Did you plan to go there immediately?" she asked curiously. "No wedding trip?"

"I thought we'd spend a few weeks in Scotland."

"Scotland?" She spat out the word. "Well, thank heavens for that. I've always wanted to travel, to Paris and Venice and Florence and Rome, but what a relief to find I'll only miss out on Scotland. Truly, I should have realized you wouldn't be anxious to return to the Continent so soon. After all you've been through, the last thing you must wish is a Grand Tour."

It was, in fact, the last thing he wanted. For him, all Europe was steeped in blood. When he boarded the packet at Cherbourg, he could practically sniff clean English country air wafting across the Channel as if summoning him home. Not once did he consider that Pen might expect a long wedding trip. He'd assumed, stupidly, that she wanted the same things he did.

Now he knew better, but years of dealing with brash young subalterns had taught him when heels were dug in. Pen had made up her mind to leave him, and there was no shaking her. If he ever hoped to win her, he had to let her go.

Checking back over what he'd said, he could not remember promising he wouldn't follow her. No, she'd not demanded that. Obviously she didn't think he would. He gazed at her warmly. She was practically asleep, from wine and weariness, sagging in her chair, batting her lashes to keep her eyes open.

Without warning, the door crashed open and the Baron of Burnwich lunged into the room. He appeared to be stunned at the sight of his daughter, but recovered quickly. "I'll have your hide for this," he thundered.

Pen sprang to her feet, arms clutched around her waist.

In a swift motion, John stepped between them and planted his feet. "Good evening, my lord. Have you had your dinner?" Placing an iron hand on the baron's shoulder, John forced him into the chair Pen had vacated.

Burnwich sputtered. "I say, this won't do." He jabbed a finger at his daughter.

Pen stamped her foot. "Does the entire world know where I am?"

Gripping her elbow, John tugged her across the room. "I think it's time for you to disappear," he whispered.

"Now wait a minute," the baron called. "I've a word to say to you, missie."

John paused at the door. "You look thirsty, Lord Burnwich. Try the claret." He shuffled Pen into the hall and hustled her up the stairs to her room.

"Do you always get your way?" she muttered when they were alone. "I suppose this means you'll turn me over to him."

He shook his head. "On the contrary. I intend to get rid of him. You should go to bed and get some sleep, Pen, but if you like I'll order a bath sent up first."

"Truly?" A smile appeared, only to droop. "It is unkind of you, my lord, to be so considerate when I've caused you all this trouble. Like heaping coals of fire on my head. Shall I pretend to be grateful?"

He grinned. "Will it help if I send you a *cold* bath?"

"Yes," she said weakly. "What will you do with Papa?"

"Stew him in wine and send him home. We shall both be gone by daybreak, and you may continue to your destination in my coach. It's rather an antique, I'm afraid, but there's been no time to replace it." He tapped her nose with his forefinger. "Sleep well, Pen. You are perfectly safe."

He didn't even say goodbye, she thought unhappily as the door closed. Not one sign of regret from the man. He wasn't even angry. Just . . . indifferent, seeing to her departure the way he'd arranged the marriage—with military efficiency.

She crossed to the window and lifted the curtain. Rectangles of light sliced across the dark innyard and were swallowed up by a moonless night.

It was over. Clearly she'd made the right choice, and he had confirmed it by helping her on her way. John was not a man to leave loose ends untied, and had followed her only to make sure the wayward parcel reached its destination. Pressing her forehead against the cool glass, she wondered what to do about her own loose ends. They seemed to be winding themselves around her heart.

She remembered the time he'd drawn her into the shadows of Lady Marchcroft's terrace and kissed her. When he'd licked her lips with his tongue she'd felt as if her dress had caught fire. She'd wanted to climb all over him like a monkey. Indeed, she'd thought of nothing but the eerie, vague promise of her wedding night until the moment she realized there would not be a wedding day.

If only he'd kissed her goodbye. Given her one last taste of him to take with her. It was one thing to relinquish a loveless marriage of convenience and a wedding trip to Scotland, but quite another to realize one would never again be kissed.

All through her bath, which was deliciously hot, and for several hours after that, she tried to concentrate on the future. A bleak, barren, lonely future. And while John remained at the inn, she could only seem to think about what she'd given up, not what waited for her. That was grim enough, for she couldn't expect to stay where she was going more than a few weeks. With luck, which was long overdue, she'd eventually find a position in a genteel household and dwindle into a trusted retainer.

She longed to work with children, but her education was unsuitable for teaching females. She'd never studied languages, was unskilled in music and drawing, and no parent would allow her to instruct little boys in history and mathematics. Most likely she'd wind up as companion to an elderly lady, reading to her and stitching nightcaps. Better that, she reminded herself stoically, than marriage to a man who didn't want her.

Unable to sleep, Pen leaned against the headboard, her favorite book in hand, and tried to lose herself in the adventures of Sir Lancelot. With typical male perversity, the knight was currently bound on an amatory quest. She followed with growing ire as he clambered up a ladder to the Queen's bedchamber, ripped iron bars from the stone windows with his bare hands, and took his pleasure with Guinevere until the dawning of the day.

Pen snapped the book shut. Why was it only men could make advances and go after what they wanted, while females waited like berries to be plucked?

Blast it all, she wanted to be plucked. Why not? What had she left to lose, with her reputation already in shreds and her future a solitary road to nowhere? Tonight she was as ripe and ready as she'd ever be.

Only one man had ever kissed her, or looked at her with a glimmer of desire in his eyes, and whether by sorcery or divine accident, he was here. Moreover, he intended to stay the night. Betty had revealed, with a gleam in her sultry eyes, that John had reserved the room at the end of the hall for himself.

Temptation and virtue wrestled briefly, but Pen faced a lifetime of dismal chastity. She swung out of bed and padded to the door.

As he entered the private parlor, John saw that Burnwich had drained the bottle of claret and ordered several more.

Slouched in a chair with his booted feet propped against the table, the baron yawned widely. "Have to marry her now, y'know," he declared with satisfaction. "Compromised and all. Glad you found her, but I'd have drug her back in time for the wedding."

"Indeed." John propped his shoulders against the wall and folded his arms. "How did you track her here?"

The question seemed to befuddle the baron. "Not her. You. Figured you ought to know she'd took off, so I set out for Walford." He drained his glass in a single swallow and poured another. "Bit of luck there. Showed up right after they got word to dispatch a carriage to this place. Can't say I thought to find Pen, but there you are. My lucky night. Didn't send the notice to the paper, in case you're wondering. Just wedding jitters, y'know. Pen's a flighty female."

John scowled. The man was half gone, his big nose glowing like a Yule log. "Flighty is one way to put it," he observed. "She doesn't want me."

"What's that to the point? I'm here now, and the chit will do as she's told. Not likely to get another offer, with her looks, and I won't stumble on a second chance to fire her off. Tell you what, though. You can have Philia, or one of the others. Don't matter to me which one you take."

John forced himself to relax. Burnwich was Pen's father, and his own relatives were nothing to brag about. Repellent in-laws, he supposed, would be a lifelong cross to bear for the both of them. Meanwhile, this was a good chance to pump his future father-in-law for information before the old sot passed out. "I'll stick with Penelope," he said, trying to sound pleasant, "but I couldn't help noticing that she looks nothing like her sisters."

"Gel takes after her mother, more's the pity." The baron burped loudly. "Maude was a chit, a big gallumphing woman with spots all over her face, but I needed the money. All I could do to bed her, but I wanted a son. After Pen there were three boys, all dead when she dropped 'em, and the last one wore her out. Died trying, I'll give her that. When I married again, Eleanor didn't want anything to do with Pen so I sent the chit to her grandparents." He reached for the claret. "Bristol merchants, with vinegar in their veins. They didn't want her either, but a dotty old aunt said she'd move in and see her reared properly."

"Where do they live?" John suspected Pen was headed there again.

"With the devil, I warrant." Burnwich filled his glass.

"Dead, the lot of them, and good riddance. Invested a fortune in some idiotish steam engine and went broke. Not a penny did they leave m'darlin' Penny. Anyhow, I brought her home when Eleanor stuck her spoon in the wall. She left me with three more daughters, thoroughbreds this time, and I figured Pen could take care of them." He stared owlishly at the glass in his hand. "Not a bad chit. Works hard and don't complain. But you can have Philia or one of the others if you'd rather."

With massive constraint, John reined in his temper. It was a wonder Pen hadn't run away years ago.

"Made her own wedding dress," Burnwich bragged. "No point wasting the ready on goods already sold off, I told her. Better to spend on the other girls so they'll make a good impression. I expect offers on all three of them once they've been on parade at St. George's."

Fists clenched, John staunchly kept the distance of the room between his knuckles and the baron's bulbous nose. "The wedding is postponed," he said coldly. "You will return to London and inform the guests. Give any story you like so long as it does not damage Penelope's reputation."

Burnwich gazed at him from bleary eyes. "Postponed? You're still going to marry her?"

"Certainly." If she'll have me, he amended silently. "But we'll be wed when, and where, and how she chooses. I expect you to cover up this delay and stifle any gossip. Should you fail, I'll tie the marriage settlement in the courts so long you'll be in your dotage before you get a farthing."

"Well, she ain't leavin' here until I get the money she cribbed from me last night!" Burnwich staggered to his feet. "The chit went through my clothes and made off with a . . . five hundred guineas. Damned cutpurse is what she is. I'll have m'money or see her in Newgate." He stumbled to John, who regarded him with disgust in his eyes. "You can pay me and collect from her later. 'Spect you'll be collecting more than that tonight, eh?"

That did it. John's right fist slammed into a flabby jaw and the baron dropped like a rock.

* * *

Pen leaned against the door, nearly asleep on her feet, listening for the colonel. There was no mistaking his deliberate stride, and she murmured a silent prayer as he advanced up the creaky stairs and past her room to the end of the hall.

John was fitting his key into the lock when she wrenched open her door. He swung around and his dark brows shot up.

She felt him staring at her as though she were stark naked. Over taut white lips, his eyes blazed as if he could see through her heavy cotton nightrail. She backed away as he stalked into her room and closed the door.

"What the devil do you think you're doing?" he gritted. "This is a public inn."

"I knew it was you." She wrapped her arms around her waist. "What . . . what happened with Papa?"

"We came to terms." His voice softened. "Your father understands the situation, Pen. He'll not trouble you again. My word on it."

"Did he tell you that I took money from his pockets?" Her voice shook. "Almost a hundred pounds."

"He only wished it could have been more." John looked past her, to the bed. "You should be asleep," he said huskily. "The coach will be here before eight o'clock."

With a bow, he turned to leave, but her fingers closed on his wrist. He went absolutely still.

She moved closer, pressing her forehead against his shoulder. "Stay with me," she mumbled.

He could not believe he'd heard her right. Stay? Dear Lord, had she changed her mind? He turned, his arms trembling as they wrapped around her. It was a miracle. Pen wanted to marry him after all.

She spoke again, her words almost smothered by his lapel. He strained to hear. "I . . . wedding . . . don't mind . . . Scotland . . . want . . . remember."

He fastened on the one thing he understood. "Of course

34

we can go to Scotland, sweetheart."

Her head jerked back, clipping his jaw. "Blast it, John Corbett, Scotland can sink into the North Sea for all I care."

Bewildered, he stared at her.

"If you don't want to, just say so!" Impossibly, her blush deepened. "This has been another terrible mistake, hasn't it? The thing is, I was informed that men always wanted to."

"Wanted to what . . ." His voice faded. She couldn't mean? He looked at her closely. Her lashes fluttered, and she bit her lip. By God, she did mean it. This was a damned seduction.

"You know very well what!" She pulled away and spun around, her back rigid. "There is no end, it seems, to my foolishness. When you looked at Betty that way, I assumed you were interested and not very particular. But a man must draw the line somewhere."

"Who —" He closed his mouth with a snap. Betty, whoever the hell she was, didn't figure in this, but Pen, for all her bluster, was fragile as a snowflake. He wanted to hug her. He also knew what would happen if he did, and called a retreat on pure instinct. How could it be right, when they were both so confused, to make love for the first time? "Pen," he said carefully, "the only line I want to draw is a circle around the two of us."

Her shoulders lifted as she breathed a heavy sigh. "You must think me mad," she said with a brittle laugh. "First I run away, and then I throw myself at you like a starving puppy. I feel perfectly ridiculous."

"Never that," he muttered, feeling ridiculous himself. His body surged with a primitive urge to claim her even as he took a disciplined step back. Maybe it was the baron's foul assumption that he planned to bed her that night, or his own suspicion that she would leave him in the morning no matter what he did, but he held himself in check with preternatural self-control. "You . . . astonish me. I never expected this."

"Nor did I," she confessed in a haunted voice. "In fact, I never thought to see you again at all, but when you appeared from nowhere it seemed a pity to waste the opportunity." Her lips trembled. "Leaving you was not altogether a simple thing, my lord. I've had a great many regrets, most of them selfish, as I thought of what I was giving up. Then I saw . . . thought I saw . . . a chance to claim something I'll never experience unless you share it with me now. I cannot marry you, but for a few hours, so I'll have something to remember, I'd very much like to be your bride. Is that possible, John? Will you give me a wedding night?"

He closed his eyes. Was there anything he could say or do that would not hurt her?

He heard a rustling sound, and looked up to see her climbing onto the bed. She leaned against a bank of pillows, her hair a thick wash of brandy against the white linen as she gazed at him. To his surprise, she seemed utterly composed.

The silent invitation floated across the room. Now or not at all, she dared.

His gaze slid away. "Pen," he said somberly, "the first time you take a man into your body . . . and every time after . . . he must be the man you love."

"Does he have to love me too?" she asked after a strained moment.

His reply was a ragged whoosh of air. "Yes."

She leaned over to extinguish the table lamp. "In that case, my lord, I bid you good night."

On the whole, John decided, knight-errantry suited him to the nines. He'd a gallant charger between his thighs, a sunny spring day to begin his quest, and a fair maiden for the claiming. Already he'd slain a dragon for her . . . well, drawn his cork, but the baron would think twice and then again before baring his rotted teeth to his daughter. Pen didn't know it yet, but she had herself a champion.

He leaned back in the saddle, enjoying the fresh breeze

on his face. As campaigns went, this was a piece of cake. He only needed to keep himself well behind the heavy coach, which lumbered at a steady pace half a mile down the road. The driver, Davy Morgyn, was regarded as eccentric by the staff at Walford, but John had years of experience judging men and considered him reliable. He had left a detailed letter of instructions for Morgyn at the Notched Arrow, along with money to pay for horses, meals, and the best rooms in the finest hostelries. The coach was to travel no more than eight miles an hour, and Pen was to be treated like royalty.

Midmorning, the horses were changed at a posthouse in Lechlade. Concealing himself behind a row of drying sheets, John watched Pen scurry inside and emerge with a basket of pastries. She took one for herself, passed the basket to Davy Morgyn, and strolled toward a small herb garden not twenty yards from where John was hiding. He held his breath, cursing the slight wind that plastered damp muslin against his body, but she was preoccupied with her breakfast. White teeth flashed as she bit hungrily into the thick crust, and he heard her sigh with contentment. He released a sigh of his own when she turned away.

John waited until the coach was out of sight before dashing into the inn for some pork pies of his own and a carrot for Ricco. Really, this was all too easy. Even Ricco was bored. Except for the occasional pause to let a curricle or post chaise whip by, there was little for the knight-errant to do but reflect on his sins and consider how to redeem himself.

He'd been shot three times in his career, not counting the incident with the pig farmer, but nothing had ever hit him like Pen's announcement that she'd cried off. The bone-deep pain, unlike anything he'd experienced on the goriest battlefield, resonated again as her words came back to him. *No wedding. . . . We should not suit.*

Caught by surprise, he'd tried to take his cues from her, but Pen was a tangle of contradictions. She kept him off balance, fighting him one minute and laughing with him the next, determined to leave him but not before a farewell tryst in her bed.

If he'd swept her back to London, or made love to her, and God knew he wanted to do both, he'd have won her consent to the marriage. Forced her consent, he reminded himself, because the part of her that felt trapped, even threatened, had not run itself out. The baron had showed up just in time to keep him from making that mistake. Pen would never again be compelled to do anything. Outmaneuvered, yes, with every advantage he could seize, but never forced.

He patted Ricco affectionately on the neck. Years ago, when he'd bought the half wild bay, Ricco had thrown him a dozen times before realizing he wouldn't give up. Then he'd soared over the fence with John clamped on his back for a wild ride clearly designed to break both their necks. Only when the horse had run himself to exhaustion had they made peace. It would be the same with Pen, he thought. Like Ricco, she was brave, stubborn, and reckless.

She was also soft, feminine, and vulnerable. Pen must have been desperate to steal money from her father's pockets and set out alone on a public coach. The only thing that spoiled his otherwise splendid day was reflecting on her unhappiness.

And worrying that he'd added to it. Leaving her last night was the hardest thing he'd ever done. He'd spent hours pacing his narrow room, changing his mind a hundred times, haunted by all the mistakes he'd made when he'd arranged the marriage and afraid he'd compounded them by seeming to reject her. How must she have felt?

And yet . . . Pen had asked him to make love to her. She'd not run away because he repelled her, which had been his deepest fear. Were he truly convinced she wanted no part of him, he . . . Damn, he'd have tried to change her mind. Change himself, if it came to that. He could make himself over. No woman dreamed of a battle-weary, callus-hard soldier without two poetical words in his vocabulary.

Lancelot had mastered the art of courtly love, and so would he.

John whiled away a pleasant hour rehearsing his next proposal, fully prepared to deliver it on his knees. He mustered exactly the right words, lined them up in strategic order, and drilled them again and again. His heart went into that speech, and he was congratulating himself on its effectiveness when he suddenly realized Ricco was limping.

With an oath, he swung from the saddle to examine the bay's right foreleg. A twisted nail barely held the shoe in place. He looked ahead to see the carriage emerge from a dip in the road and lurch up a steep hill, pausing at the crest while the footman chained a back wheel for the descent.

A lizard darted into the middle of the road, shooting him a malevolent glare before disappearing into a hedgerow. The fine hairs at his nape tingled. Beware of dragons, the lizard seemed to be warning him. He swore again, violently, as the coach vanished from sight.

There was no question of going on until the horse was re-shod. Grumbling all the time, he led Ricco for nearly two miles before he spotted a farmhouse. As he turned off the road, a man driving a recalcitrant mule stopped his plowing to stare curiously. John waved to get his attention, but the man lowered his head and went back to work.

In all the books, a questing knight was immediately offered a meal, a bed, and a comely wench, but apparently the Code of Hospitality hadn't reached this backwater. John traipsed sullenly to the farmhouse and was continuing around its side to the barn when he heard a cheerful whistle. The plump woman scattering grain to the chickens greeted him with a smile which turned to a frown when he explained his problem.

She shook her head. The itinerant smithy, with his box of tools, could generally be found at one of the posting houses. She'd send her son to fetch him, but most likely the business would take two or three days. John drew out a handful of money, but nothing could buy a swift repair for Ricco, or even a nag to replace him. The only large mammals on the Baldwin farm were three milk cows and one mule. His lordship was welcome to rent the mule.

That was when being a knight stopped being fun.

Donkey Oatie set new standards of obstinacy for his breed, swaying along at his own halting pace with frequent stops for a roadside snack. John could have walked faster, and tried, but Oatie objected to being led. He refused to budge an inch, and expressed his displeasure by chomping off a hunk of blue broadfine from John's riding coat. Short of abandoning the beast, which he was sorely tempted to do, there was no choice but to stay on its back.

Oatie will trot right along, Mr. Baldwin had told him, if you shout tally ho. John shouted until he was hoarse. One time in ten the mule picked up its pace, from a slow amble to a lurching trot, but there was no question who was in charge. Donkey Oatie went when he wanted to, and he rarely did.

They spent long minutes sideways across the road while the mule nibbled at blossoms twining through the hedgerows. When a coach bore down, Oatie waited with seeming deliberation until the last possible moment before snailing out of the way. Then he twisted his long neck and favored his rider with a mocking bray which John interpreted as Scared you that time, eh? The unholy glint in the beast's round brown eyes spoke of possession by the devil.

John remembered a cold winter in the Pyrenees when the troops were forced to slaughter and eat their packmules. Those were the good old days.

Three hours and fewer miles later, he spied a private gate leading to a squat house nearly concealed in a copse of trees. The elderly resident, a retired naval officer, knew the Baldwin family and would gladly see the mule returned, but the only horse he kept was a small mare his granddaughter rode when she visited. John regarded the horse with displeasure. She was not up to his weight, except for short stretches, and came equipped with a sidesaddle.

40

"Just rid me of that blasted mule," he instructed Captain Pickins, forcing several coins into his hand. "I'll go back to the road and wave down a coach."

Without a word, the captain led him inside and stood him in front of a mirror. In dirt-streaked trousers and frayed jacket, he looked like a man with highway robbery on his mind. No one would pick him up.

"Take Florabelle," the captain advised. "Ride bareback, and walk some of the way. She'll get you to the posting house before dark."

John set out again with his toes practically dragging on the ground. He'd not ridden bareback in years, and there was little to choose between blistered feet when he walked and battered rump when he rode. He slugged along for hours before encountering a small public house where he was able to replace the mare with a swaybacked gelding. It wasn't long before he regretted his choice. If he relaxed his guard for a moment, the gelding immediately lunged for home at an astonishing speed. At this rate, John calculated grimly, Pen could be all the way to Scotland before he made the next town.

He had better luck at sundown. The Duck and Drake supplied a decent mount, a quick supper, and news of another hostelry five miles down the road. With a clear night and a full moon to light the way, John wearily continued on. The roan was big, dullwitted, and refused to stir above a halting trot when clouds obscured the light. Barely able to see the road, the knight-errant reflected that "errant" pretty well described his quest so far. Near midnight, he collapsed on a narrow bed in the small country inn and dreamed of mule-faced dragons wearing sidesaddles.

Pen thought once that she saw her jilted fiancé. She stuck her head out the window as the carriage topped a hill, looked back, and imagined it was John crouched beside an enormous bay in the middle of the road. It must have been a mirage in the dust, because she hung out the window

41

most of the afternoon and never spotted anyone that resembled him again.

For one thrilling moment, she'd thought he'd followed her. It took hours to suppress that fierce hope and convince herself she never wanted to see him again. Not after she'd humiliated herself, practically thrown herself at him, and been rejected. Were she his wife, he'd have bit the bullet and done his duty to sire an heir, but he didn't want to make love to her. Any doubts she'd had about running away were squelched by his calm refusal. She had offered her body, and not incidentally her heart, but he wasn't interested.

For all she knew, he'd made a deal with her father. Probably he was on his way back to London, this time with a proposal for another Wright sister. Apollonia would jump at his offer, if only to beat Philia to the altar, and there was always Antonia waiting in the wings.

Or maybe he'd come to his senses and find himself a wife from a reputable family. Pen hoped so, for things were bad enough without John Corbett as her brother-in-law. After what happened last night, she could never face him again. Never.

A few miles later, when the coach stopped to change horses, she approached the driver, a bright smile pasted on her face. Beyond offering him a pork pie, she'd not spoken to the man, who struck her as rather odd. For one thing, the large limp vegetable he wore in his hat attracted flies.

He lit a cigar as she drew near, and grinned at her over yellow teeth. "They do love the leeks," he said, batting the insects away. "Always smoke unless we're movin'. Hope ye don't mind."

"Not at all," she fibbed. "You haven't told me your name."

"Davy Morgyn," he replied with a swaggering bow. "Welsh-born, Welsh-bred, and proud of it."

She laughed. "Well, that explains the leek, anyway. I did wonder."

"It's m'trademark," he boasted. "Took to wearin' it when

I come to work for his lordship. His other lordship, that is. Edgar Corbett thought Welshmen good for nothin', so I made sure to sport a leek in m'hat whenever we drove out. No reason now he's in the ground, but everybody knows me fer it."

"Like Fluellen," Pen observed with a curtsy. She loved Shakespeare, and *Henry V* was one of her favorites. " 'There is occasions and causes why and wherefore in all things.' "

Davy's mouth opened. "His new Lordship said them same words not a week ago," he told her in amazement. "Said the Welsh regiments were damned fine soldiers and I should wear m'leek with pride."

She wasn't surprised. Fluellen was a master of the disciplines of war, like John. A soldier through and through.

Davy broke into her thoughts. "Don't suppose you'd care to tell me where we're goin'? I'll stay on this road 'til you say otherwise, but we'll have to turn off at Cirencester."

"Not that far." She pulled a battered envelope from her reticule, opened the much-read letter, and studied the crude map drawn on the back. "You'll need to take a side road before Cirencester. I'll bang on the ceiling when it's near time. Will you report back to the colonel when you've left me off?"

Davy puffed on his cigar. "Don't know what he wants. I got my orders from the innkeeper. Said I was to take you where you wanted to go, and return to Walford."

She sighed, deliberately quashing a flimsy hope that John planned to come after her. Of course he did not. He'd given his word, after all, and without a second's hesitation. If he'd wanted to marry her, he'd have carried her back to London. He'd have made love to her last night. He'd have followed her. He'd have arranged with the driver to tell him where she'd gone. He'd have done *something,* damn him. But he'd done nothing at all, except make sure they parted amicably.

If only he'd cared, just a little, that she was leaving him.

Pen thought she'd abandoned her hopes in London, or at

43

the inn, or on the road, but now she knew that all along she'd really been screaming for reassurance. Why had she suddenly become so demanding, wanting the impossible, when she held in her hands more than she'd ever expected to have? She should have taken John Corbett, on any terms. What if he didn't love her? He'd have given her children to love.

Too late now. Even her father would never take her back, not after he'd passed out drunk in the parlor and she'd rifled his pockets to finance her journey. She'd been lucky to find him so flush. He'd been gambling with most of the funds given him to pay for the wedding, which would have been a cheese-paring affair except for her sisters' expensive dresses. No flowers, no music, and a cold collation of cheap wines and cheeses and fruits at the celebration afterward. She'd been so embarrassed to think of facing John over cucumber sandwiches and stale cakes in her home-made wedding gown while her sisters preened before his friends.

She had a hundred reasons for running away, none of which she could put into words because each one sounded so petty, but all together they had overwhelmed her. As she settled herself in the coach to continue her journey, Pen resolved not to look back again.

It was when he paid his mark the next morning that John realized he was nearly broke. Something had to be done about that, unless he found Pen today. She'd set out on the London to Stroud coach, so he was fairly certain she'd go that far, but he eyed every crossroad with misgivings. Who was to say she hadn't turned off on any one of them? He inquired at every inn he passed and was relieved to find that Morgyn changed horses at the Golden Lion. At least he was still headed in the right direction, but he badly needed to hire a suitable mount, and even a knight had to eat. Questing was damnably expensive.

He made Cirencester at midday, and spent the afternoon

cooling his heels in a banking establishment while three whisper-thin gentlemen debated whether they should advance him funds with no collateral but his signet ring and an honest face. Sir Lancelot, John thought sourly, never applied for a loan.

Fortunately, it was discovered that one of the bankers had a grandson in the army. John was acquainted with the boy's commanding officer, and after entertaining the men with a few war stories he left with funds enough to mount a small crusade.

Midway to Stroud, astride yet another recalcitrant jobhorse, he eyed the scudding clouds with misgivings. They opened within the hour, and he slogged from posting house to posting house in the driving rain, inquiring for his coach without luck. After a while, he realized that Davy would have changed horses long since. More than likely he'd turned onto one of several roads that radiated like spokes from Cirencester. Lord, Pen could be headed anywhere. He began to suspect it would require real sorcery to ferret her out, but at the least he needed Ricco and a good map. Reluctantly, he turned around.

The next day, armed with an old surveyor's map, he made his way back to the Baldwin farm. Donkey Oatie brayed a cheerful hello from the pasture, kicking up his heels as if welcoming an old friend. John replied with a raised finger, wondering how Oatie would look turning on a spit.

To his great relief, the smithy had come and gone. He greeted Ricco with a kiss on the muzzle, to the astonishment of Mr. and Mrs. Baldwin, and left them enough money to buy a decent mule. They seemed offended at that. Donkey Oatie was unaccustomed to the ways of Quality, Mr. Baldwin huffed, and overexcited by the trip. In general, he was the most sweet-natured mule in Christendom.

Which only proved, John thought as he rode away, that everyone cherished fantasies about those they loved.

Ricco, newly shod and anxious for a good run, carried him at high speed along the muddy road. John had decided

45

to start anew, at the last place Pen had been seen—The Golden Lion.

Rain beat down on them both like exploding case-shot, nearly obscuring John's whoop of joy when they turned into the courtyard. There, sheltered just inside the enormous stable, was his coach! Flinging the reins to an ostler, he dashed into the inn, water streaming from his caped greatcoat.

Davy and the footman, sitting near the fire with hands wrapped around mugs of ale, jumped up when he burst into the taproom.

"Don't say a word," John commanded as he settled on the bench across from them and shucked off his coat. "Sit down, men. Drink your ale. I assume you're on your way back to Walford."

They nodded in tandem.

He beckoned to a serving maid. "Has Miss Wright been delivered safely to her destination?" Davy opened his mouth and John shook his head. "Quiet, man! Of course she has, and that narrows things down. She can't be far."

"Nope. We—"

"Dammit, shut up." He ordered a bowl of rabbit stew and ate it quickly. "You stay here," he said between bites, "until I come back, however long it takes. Or I may send for you." He spread his map, damp from rain, on the table. "Where are we?"

Davy, looking at it upside down, eventually pointed to a spot. "About here. We—"

"Fine." John calculated elapsed time and distances. *There*—wherever *there* was—could be no more than one day's journey in this weather. That left a thousand places Pen could be, but he could deal with a thousand. He ran his finger around the stew bowl and drew a circle on the map with gravy drippings. "Thank you, God."

The two men stared at him.

"I'm on a quest," he explained, folding the map. "Surely your Welsh soul can appreciate that, Davy."

The coachman took a long swig of ale. "Not much of

46

one," he muttered. " 'Ceptin' that all these towns got names sound pretty much alike. Easy to get 'em mixed up."

John suspected, as he left the taproom, that he'd just been given a clue, but a careful examination of the map showed that it wouldn't be much help. Most towns and villages were marked with dots instead of names. He decided to ride full speed to Cirencester and choose a route from there.

Knighthood had turned into a royal pain in the arse.

Well into his second week of questing, disoriented in a blinding rainstorm, John redubbed himself Sir Duncelot. It was a wonder he'd survived the Peninsular War, considering his inability to navigate the Cotswolds without losing his way. King Arthur would have drummed him out of the ranks long ago.

The Dunisbourne Valley had seemed a likely spot to investigate, boasting several hamlets with nearly identical names, but every muddy track he followed deadended at a sheep pasture. Then he headed northeast and spent a long time wandering in the dense woodlands surrounding Chedworth. He got to know Chedworth rather well. No matter where he came out of the woods or which way he turned, all roads led to the small, isolated town. He'd become a prime source of entertainment for the citizens, who emerged from their houses and shops to gape each time he rode through.

Probably they thought him deranged, and not without cause. By now he was practically a legend in several counties he hoped never to see again. But for all his efforts, and he asked everyone he met, no young woman remotely resembling Pen had been observed.

For the sake of her reputation he was careful never to describe her, and his story changed each time he told it. If someone knew of a small, light-haired girl new to the neighborhood, he assured them his "cousin" was tall and sallow. Whatever they might have seen, he was looking for

47

something else. The one thing he feared was missing her, so he made sure to stop at every dot on his sketchy map and inquire at every farm he passed. Should the villagers ever compare notes, they'd realize he was pursuing a short, statuesque, pudgy, svelte blonde with dark hair.

Decent inns were few and far between. He spent two uncomfortable nights under hedgerows and three sheltered in barns, but he was accustomed to hard living and his spirits remained high. The memory of his Sunflower, tall and splendid in her white lawn gown as she invited him to her bed, drove him past exhaustion. At night he reviewed the day's events in detail, wanting to remember odd characters and amusing encounters so he could tell her about them.

On his fourth or fifth pass through Chedworth, a gnomelike man bounced into the road, wagging his finger. "Come," he said.

With no reason to do otherwise, John trailed him for several miles, along a track so narrow Ricco could scarcely maneuver. When they came to a thick line of trees, the gnome stopped abruptly and pointed to an even narrower path. "Coln." Without another word, he turned back.

Chedworth's way, John realized with amusement, of ridding itself of a bloody nuisance. He threaded his way to the river, got out his map, and tossed a mental coin. Bilbury.

The rain let up as he followed the Coln south, anticipating the pleasures of a hot bath and a good meal. Both were to be found at the Swan, and he was well into his third fresh trout before it occurred to him that tomorrow would have been his wedding day. His mood soured.

He made his way to the taproom, strangely reluctant to begin interrogating the locals. They eyed him with the aloof curiosity reserved for outsiders while he stood in the middle of the smoky room giving serious thought to drinking himself under a table. Just his luck that all the tables were occupied.

To hell with it, he decided. None of these hostile rustics had seen Pen. Nobody in the world had seen Pen. He'd get a good night's sleep and start fresh in the morning. Except

. . . this should have been his last night as a bachelor. His last night sleeping alone.

A lonely bed was suddenly the last place he wanted to be. Spotting a small round table in the corner, he made up his mind to join the sole occupant, a hearty-looking individual with bushy sideburns and a head balder than an eggplant.

To John's surprise, the man welcomed him cordially. "Harry Harrison, at yer service. Late of the eighty-second." He signaled to the tapman. "Knew you fer a soldier the minute you walked in."

John introduced himself, omitting former rank and current title, and they swapped stories over mugs of dark ale for several hours. Harry, invalided home after the Battle of Alexandria, owned half interest in the Swan. He spent his days tending the bar and his nights drinking up the profits, or so he declared. Considering the amount he put away, John believed him.

"I expect," he said in a voice thick with ale and weariness, "you know everything that goes on around here."

Harry nodded. "I hear the news before it happens. You after somethin' in particular?"

"My ward. She's run away, and gone to ground somewhere in this area." He described the coach and driver, but Harry shook his head.

"No gentrymort come through the last couple of weeks," he said, "and most every wagon stops here to change cattle. I seen nothin' like the one you're after, nor anybody wearin' leeks. I'd recollect that."

"She might have disguised herself," John said. "Maybe as a servant. My cousin is damnably inventive."

"Females!" With accuracy, Harry spat into a battered metal pot near his chair. "Only one gel come new to these parts, but she ain't Quality. Vicar down at Ampney St. Peter's brought her in from Lunnon to take care of his kids. Got eight, with 'nother in the oven. I ain't seen her m'self, but heard tell of her. Big woman, with red-yeller hair and freckles."

John choked on a swallow of ale. With care, he set down

the mug and tried to look bland. "Can't be my sister, then," he managed to say. "Delilah's short. Straight black hair. But maybe I'll ride by the vicar's house tomorrow. He might have heard something."

John set out at dawn, annoying Ricco with his off-key rendition of "Greensleeves." "Penelope was all my joy," he bellowed. "Penelope was my delight, and who but my lady Penelope?" Passers-by began to look at him strangely.

Everyone and his brother seemed to be on the road this fine Saturday morning. John waved to the others, and most waved back. Humoring the madman, he thought genially, but what the hell? After today, he'd never set foot in the Cotswolds again.

When the tower of St. Peter's came into view, he felt blood pound in his ears. Less than half a mile away, his Fair Lady tended another man's children with no idea she was about to be rescued from her drudgery. Hauled away under protest if need be.

He swore aloud. Not hauled. Coaxed. Wooed. Devil take a bit, he'd learned his lesson. Tugging Ricco to a halt, he scaled a high stone fence and collected a fistful of wild-flowers.

Ampney St. Peter's was a small town, and he easily found a house adjacent to the church which fit Harry's description. Sweat beaded on his forehead as he walked up the gravel path lined with geraniums. Two little girls playing with hoops scampered away, eyeing him cautiously from behind a tree.

He paused at the threshold to savor the end of his quest and the prize waiting for him on the other side of the door. A child wailed, and it occurred to him that a year from to-day Pen might well be cradling a babe of her own. The first of many, if Dame Fortune continued to smile as she smiled upon him now. He lifted the iron knocker and beat out the signal to charge.

Seconds later, the door swung open and a tall, freckle-faced girl with an infant on her hip bobbed an awkward curtsy.

He dropped the flowers.

"The vicar's not to home," said the girl in a high, nasal voice. "C'n I help ye?"

John stared at her, unable to speak.

She smiled, revealing two prominent buck teeth. " 'E's doin' a wedding, but ye c'n come in and wait. 'Spect 'e'll be awhile, though. Likes 'is sermons, 'e does."

John glanced over at the church. It looked deserted.

The girl followed his gaze and laughed. "Not 'ere," she said. "The weddin's at Ampney St. Mary's, down that road about a mile and off to the right. Middle o' nowhere, it is, but ye can follow the tracks. All the townsfolk goin' there but me and the littlest babes."

John gathered up the flowers and handed them to her. "You are very kind," he croaked. "Pleasure to meet you." He felt her watch him as he stumbled back to Ricco and mounted clumsily.

Dear God, he'd been so sure.

It had seemed so right, almost heaven-sent, to find Pen on their wedding day. Now all he had was the memory of a girl's bright smile—so like Pen's it hurt to dwell on it—and directions to someone else's wedding. A perverse demon led him down the road to St. Mary's church. What better place to wallow in his misery, he thought as a heavy lethargy settled over him.

For a time he followed the parade of gaily clad celebrants, mocked by their laughter and high spirits. When they turned off the main road, he cut away and guided Ricco in a wide arc through pastures and copses until he saw a tiny ivy-covered church standing in an open field. On either side, weeds and flowers grew among scores of gravemarkers and statues and tombs, as if a village had died and been interred around the honey-gold chapel.

Men, women, and children thronged outside the massive elm door, chattering excitedly. Small boys squabbled for the privilege of minding the animals. John left Ricco to

51

graze and looked around for a viewing spot. The area was flat, so he scaled an enormous oak and settled on a branch with his feet dangling. Concealed by the leaves, he commanded an excellent view and scanned the crowd for Pen without hope. Sure enough, he saw no one who resembled her and his heart sank impossibly lower.

The groom he spied immediately—a tall, lanky boy with a red face and prominent Adam's apple, being baited unmercifully by his friends. After a while everyone drifted into the church except the boys chosen to mind the animals. Then a gaily bedecked cart drew up and a short, portly man assisted his chubby wife and equally plump daughter to the ground. The bride, John surmised. She wore a wreath of yellow and purple blossoms in her colorless hair and giggled loudly.

John became aware his hands were bloody from clutching the scratchy bark. He leaned his shoulder against the tree trunk, sighing as the bride and her family disappeared into the church. Everything was suddenly still, except for the warbling stonechats. He closed his burning eyes.

When he looked up again, the cemetery wavered as if underwater. Grave markers tilted and angled in the high grass, and near the church, almost hidden by a rough-stone crypt, an angel stretched its arms.

He blinked. The angel moved, reaching skyward, throwing back its head. Thick auburn hair lifted in the breeze. He wiped his eyes. For a moment, he'd imagined it was Pen, but when he looked again the angel had vanished.

In his mind's eye he saw her everywhere, since the day they met, but until now she'd never disappeared. Nor did he expect she'd grown wings. He swung to the ground and circled to the rear of the cemetery, moving stealthily past a choir of marble angels to the place where she'd been.

And there she was, seated on the ground, arms wrapped around bent knees, thick hair shadowing her face. He heard a tiny sob, and then another. Dear Lord, she was crying. Anything but that. "Pen," he said softly.

With a shriek, she scrambled on hands and knees behind a lichen-streaked headstone.

Startled, he drew back a few paces and spread his arms. "For God's sake, Penny, don't run away. Please."

Her head lifted, and she peered at him over the tombstone with saucer-wide eyes. To his vast relief, she looked furious.

"Blast it all, John Corbett, I thought you were the devil."

"And I," he said with a bow, "mistook you for an angel."

Frowning, she stood and brushed her hands down her skirt. "Aunt Maritha didn't know where I was going today. How in blazes did you find me here?"

"You've been staying with your aunt? I thought all your relations, except your father and sisters, were . . . that is . . ." He gestured helplessly at the graveyard.

"You mean dead? I assure you she is not planted at your feet, Colonel. Aunt Maritha lives near Ampney Crucis. She is a recluse, or was until I appeared on her doorstep."

"Is that the same aunt that raised you?" When she scowled, he held up one hand. "Your father told me. Actually, I quizzed him, figuring you'd go to her, but he is under the impression she . . ." Again he waved at the tombstones.

"Exactly the impression she intended to give everyone, except me. In fact, Aunt Maritha was my inspiration. She ran away from home too, although she was seventy at the time. When Father brought me back to London, she didn't want to become an unpaid retainer at my grandparents' house so she purloined some silverware, left a suicide note, and disappeared."

"Did she? At seventy, by God." He swiped his fingers through his hair. "I think I am going to like your Aunt Maritha."

"Well, she won't like you," Pen told him frankly. "She has a low opinion of men in general, and you in particular."

Heat rose to his ears. "From that, I gather you have catalogued my faults and reviewed each one in detail."

The corners of her mouth lifted. "There hasn't been time for detail," she retorted. "Besides, we are only to the *I*'s—

53

imposing, insensitive, intimidating, into—" She scuffed her toe in the grass.

He cocked his head. *"Into . . . ?"*

". . . xicating," she muttered. "Well, *intoxicating* is a fault when it goes along with *indifferent* and *imperturbable*. Never mind that. You broke your word to me. That's . . . that's—"

"Iniquitous? Indefensible?" He smiled. "So it would be, but I assure you no one told me where to look, Pen."

"You just happened to wander by this cemetery today? Codswallop. The leek man sent to you Ampney Crucis, that much is obvious, and someone must have seen me coming here." Moving from behind the headstone, she planted her hands on her hips and glared at him. "I have certainly been misinformed about men, Colonel. They don't always want to, and their word means nothing."

"I kept my word, Pen," he said stonily. "But the next time you take the bit between your teeth I'll not be coerced into foolish promises. Let me tell you, it was no picnic following you all the way here."

"You . . . followed me?" she asked in a squeaky voice. "Truly?"

"All the way from the Notched Arrow," he declared with some pride.

"Did you indeed?" She considered that for a moment, and then regarded him skeptically. "I left there ten days ago, Colonel. What, pray tell, took you so long?"

He laughed. "Poor tactics, inadequate supplies, impossible transportation. Wellington would be ashamed of me. In my defense, you put me down foot, horse, and cannon, Pen. I've been stumbling around trying to regroup ever since."

"Coming it too brown, Colonel. When I resigned from your command you saw me transferred out with all due speed. One snap of your fingers and a coach and driver appeared to carry me off. Lord knows how you rid yourself of my father, but I expect he slunk back to London with his tail between his legs."

"Did it seem that way?" He grimaced. "I'm accustomed to taking charge and giving orders even when I'm not sure what the hell to do. In this case, I seem to have mishandled the entire campaign."

"I am not," she informed him caustically, "a military objective."

"I never imagined you were, Pen, although I swept down on you like a cavalry charge. It comes of being a professional soldier. Not much of an excuse, and you will require a good deal of patience, but I am resolved to remake myself into a genteel civilian and model husband."

She moved a step closer. "Genteel and model sound awfully dull, Colonel. Please don't expect those virtues from me, because they are not in my nature."

"Nor mine," he confessed. "At the least, I shall from this day forward cease issuing orders to you as though you were a green recruit."

She took another step. "I doubt that, but never mind. I am nearly as accustomed to hearing orders as you are to giving them."

"That," he said firmly, "will change."

"It need not. The thing is, *I* have changed. These last few weeks taught me several lessons about independence, not all of them good mind you, but I seem to have rediscovered my backbone. Feel free to order away, Colonel. I shall obey . . . when I choose."

"Ah." He put that to the test immediately, in a soft, compelling voice. "Come here, Pen."

She cocked her head, analyzing his tone and the expression on his face. Ramrod stiff, wholly self-controlled, he personified confidence. And yet, the look in his eyes was almost wistful. He seemed pale under his dark tan, and somehow anxious. His arms were rigid, but open wide.

At that moment, she understood what his very presence signified. Between lovers, victory and surrender were one and the same. With a cry of joy, she rushed to his embrace.

His arms shook as they enveloped her, but there was nothing tentative about his kiss. She clung to him, reeling with pleasure, needing his strength to hold her up as he tasted her lips and tongue. So much for genteel and dull, she thought at the edges of her spinning mind. She much preferred this masterful, aggressive male, sweeping away her fears with his passion. Never again would she question that he truly wanted her.

All her muscles felt like jelly when he finally lifted his head and gazed into her eyes. "Would this be a good time to propose again?" he asked. "Tell me if it's not. I have a speech ready, but—"

"This would be an excellent time," she assured him breathlessly.

"Yes. Very well then. Just give me a moment." Stepping back, he stared at a spot beyond her right ear for a long time. Finally he cleared his throat. "Miss Wright," he barked, "you are beautiful. I love you. Knew it right away. Hit me like a cannonball." A hot flush swept up his cheeks. "Devil take it, Pen, I can't do this now. We're in a dashed cemetery."

"Don't stop," she begged. "You were about to say *I love you.*"

He looked confused. "Thought I'd done that part. Let me see. I love you. Knew it right away. Something about artillery." He muttered under his breath, brow furrowed with concentration. "Ah yes. I have money. Title, estates, all that. Laying it at your feet. Heart too." He shook his head. "No, the sunflowers come next. Or is it the children?" He groaned. "Bloody hell! The same thing happened with the letters I wrote you from Walford. They all sounded like dispatches—*inspected pastures, consulted bailiff, requisitioned supplies.* I didn't have the nerve to send them."

"John," she queried with a wide smile, "however did you manage to entice a romantic Frenchman with such pathetic address?"

"Dashed if I know." He slanted her a woebegone look. "Just say you'll marry me, sweetheart. I'll do the speech later, when I'm not so befuddled. It was rather good, until I had to say it out loud."

"I liked the bit about the sunflowers," she assured him. "And I especially want to hear about the children. I presume you mean ours. We'll have a lovely story to tell them, won't we?"

A muscle ticked in his jaw. "Is that a real yes, Pen, or another ambiguous if it pleases you?"

She wrapped her arms around his neck. "With all my heart, a million times, *yes* and *yes* and *yes*."

Dragging her to his chest, he kissed her with such urgency that all her doubts and most of her bones melted. She hung in his arms, toes off the ground, as he swung her around until they were both dizzy. "I love you," he whispered into her mouth.

"Me too," she said giddily when he set her down. "Oh, John, me too."

Cheers and laughter rang from the front of the church as the wedding party spilled out the doors. In silent agreement, John and Penelope moved hand in hand to watch. The short pudgy bride and tall skinny groom hung onto one another, laughing with delight as children made a great fuss of showering them with flower petals.

"This should have been our wedding day," John grunted crossly. "If I'd thought to bring a special license, we could be married right now, in this church."

"Just as well you did not. On the coach out of London, while I was trying to convince myself I'd made the right decision, I kept remembering an old proverb. 'Marry in May, rue for aye.' "

"I'm not sure what that means," he responded, "but those two look perfectly happy to me."

"So they do, but I'm a bit relieved to be a June bride." She squeezed his hand. "Early June, I hope."

"As soon as possible. Shall we set London on its ear with an elaborate ceremony at St. George's? With or without sisters," he amended quickly. "Or should I procure a license?"

"Not London," she said flatly. "Let me think. We should do something splendidly romantic. Have ourselves one last

57

fling before we retire to the farm. Breeding cows sounds rather dull, I must say."

"We shall breed anything you like, Pen, or live in the city if you'd rather. Either way, I suspect life with you will never be dull."

"Maybe not, but I fear that life with *you* will never be precisely wild — and I've a terrible longing to be wild. Once the children come," she added slyly, "we'll not have the chance to run mad."

"Well, I've been running mad for several weeks now and have become something of an expert on the subject," he said with a diffident grin. "However, we shall do exactly as you wish — so long as it doesn't involve mules."

She regarded him quizzically. "I expect you'll explain that one day, but no mules. We ought to include a wedding, though, just in case I truly am a prime breeder. Aunt Maritha says I'm built for it."

"Wonderfully so," he agreed, molding her hips with his large hands. "How about a wild adventure in a warm bed?"

"Yes. Certainly that." Trying to ignore his roaming fingers set on a distracting quest of their own, she concentrated hard. Adventure. Wedding. When the answer came it was so obvious she practically bounced with excitement. "I have it! Oh John, this is perfect. We shall run away *together,* to Gretna Green!"

He looked stunned. "Gretna Green? Dear God, Pen, that's four hundred miles from here." He regarded her sternly. "A man has only so much self-control, young lady, and I squandered every ounce of mine walking out of your room on a certain memorable night."

"Memorable indeed." She punched him in the chest. "So why did you walk out? My heavens, John, I thought you didn't want me. That hurt."

"I'm sorry." He brushed her cheek with his finger. "Another tactical error, but I thought allowing you to retreat before coming after you would prove something. At the moment, I'm not altogether sure what, but the strategy seems to have worked."

"One of these days," she complained, "I hope you'll realize that I am a woman and not Boney's Imperial Guard. Meanwhile, this would be an excellent time to kiss me again."

He obliged, at length, before setting her away. "Self-control," he groaned.

"Blast it, whoever asked you to control yourself? I shall not be at all pleased if you do so all the way to Gretna. Now, what do you say?" She gave him her sunflower smile. "Shall we be impetuous lovers and throw convention to the winds?"

He kissed her nose. "If that is what you want, Pen, we'll bid farewell to your redoubtable aunt, join up with Davy Morgyn, and make a mad dash for the border. Mind you, I won't settle for a havey-cavey affair when we get there. We'll take our vows in a church, with all proper solemnity. Agreed?"

"Agreed." Her smile turned impish. "So what are we waiting for, Colonel? You of all people know how I long to visit Scotland!"

Chlöe's Elopement

by Rebecca North

"Whatever shall I do?" moaned Amaryllis Weymouth, wiping a quivering hand against her damp cheek. "Father is being mulish about me marrying Henry. He refuses to change his mind."

"I shall talk with him." Chloë handed her sister another handkerchief and wished Amaryllis would refrain from being such a wet-goose. Weeping always left her sister's eyes as red as her trembling lips. It was a decidedly unattractive way to be, and Chloë wondered why her sister could not show more pluck.

"He will not listen. When I tried to explain, he chided me for my back-answers." She wrung the lace, threatening it with ruin. "Why has he decided *now* that I cannot marry Henry? The banns have been read. The wedding was to be Saturday next. What will everyone think?"

"Do you really care what *everyone* thinks?"

"Only what my dear, dear Henry thinks," she moaned into the handkerchief. "He must consider me completely beastly. Oh, whatever shall I do? Why has Father taken such a dislike to Henry?"

Instead of speaking the truth, that Henry Moore was dull as ditchwater, Chloë offered her sister a sympathetic pat on the shoulder and went to stand by the window overlooking the back garden. She stared at the June roses bursting forth on the arbor and sighed.

Father had his reasons for not wanting Amaryllis to wed Henry, and Chloë was well aware of them, as her sister should be. When Father had fired both of them off into this Season, he had let them know—from the beginning—that Amaryllis must marry well, bringing a fortune and a title to the family.

Henry Moore possessed neither, for he had had the misfortune of being born the fourth of four sons of a rakehell marquess. While his older brothers had been given the courtesy of one of their mutual sire's lesser titles, none had remained when Henry was born. What funds there might have been for the marquess' offspring had long since vanished in the gaming hells of London.

Chloë sighed again as she crossed the well-proportioned bedchamber to ring for Marsh. Their abigail might be able to convince Amaryllis to stop putting her finger in her eye over this muddle. Looking back at her sister, Chloë wondered why Amaryllis had not been born with wit to match her beauty. With her golden hair and wide, blue eyes, Amaryllis was the pattern-card of their late mother. Not so Chloë. She resembled the dark and mysterious Weymouths, who were rumored to be the offspring of a Gypsy who had cast her wicked spell over Chloë's great-great-grandsire, causing him to forget caution and make her his bride.

Chloë was tall and slender, too tall and too slender for her own liking. She would have preferred to be a petite doll like Amaryllis, but she had accustomed herself to her raven hair and the fiery temper that was a legacy from her father. She did not look forward to unleashing Father's temper with a dagger-drawing.

"Marsh, sit with Amaryllis and soothe her while I speak with Father," she said as the bulbous abigail bustled into the room.

Nodding her gray head, Marsh began clucking like a hen with a single chick as she perched next to Amaryllis and drew the young woman's cheek down onto her generous breast. That Marsh had not asked the cause of Amaryllis' tears was a sign the whole household knew of Lionel Weymouth's decree that the wedding planned for

64

Saturday next was to be canceled.

Blast Father! Chloë's unladylike vexation sounded in her fierce footfalls on the stairs to the first floor. *And blast Amaryllis.*

When she heard a buzz of voices from the ground floor, she did not slow. Yarwood would deal with any callers. Neither she nor Amaryllis had an at home planned for the rest of the week, so that would give the butler an excuse to turn any visitor away.

"Miss Chloë?"

She turned, amazed to see the butler hurrying up the stairs toward her. He came rapidly down the long passage, his black coat contrasting with the cheery gold-striped wallpaper. Yarwood never rushed, and she had thought his ancient bones incapable of any speed faster than a shuffle. His aged voice was rough with emotion as he said, "Miss Chloë, a gentleman requests the opportunity to speak with you."

"I need to talk with Father now. Tell—"

"Mr. Weymouth has left the house to join his companions at his club."

"At this hour?" It could not be more than an hour past midday. Father seldom went to Boodle's before tea.

"He told me to inform you that he had very important business with Lord Sturgis."

"I understand." And she did, for, since the beginning of the Season, Father had been anxious to have the baron call upon Amaryllis. Over a hand of books, he might convince the baron to give his daughter a look-in.

Yarwood held out a card. "Do you wish to speak with this gentleman, Miss Chloë?"

Chloë took the *carte des visites*. She smiled when she read "Lord Abington." Henry Moore had talked often of his friend the earl, but, from Amaryllis' erstwhile *beau's* comments, Chloë had guessed that Gareth Ogilvie, Lord Abington preferred to remain far from the hubbub of the Season, enjoying instead the company of his fellow bachelors. That opinion contrasted sharply with the rumors she had heard at Almack's, for there it was whispered in the corners that Lord Abington was a man who enjoyed the company of any pretty lady, but refused to do more than dangle after any of them. Not once during the Season had she chanced to meet him at any social occasion. Clearly that was about to change.

Was this about the situation with Henry Moore and Amaryllis? She could imagine no other reason the earl might call. A prick of alarm cut along her back as she wondered if Henry had sent Lord Abington to act as his second to challenge her father to a duel. Then she told herself she was being silly. Such a challenge, even if Henry was hotheaded enough to do such a thing, must come from the insulted party himself.

Curiosity urged her to say, "Tell Lord Abington I would be delighted to welcome him in the green parlor."

The butler nodded and scurried down the stairs.

Chloë wondered what Lord Abington had done or said to inspire such speed in the butler. It might behoove her to discover that for herself; so many were the times that she had despaired of Yarwood ever finishing a job on time. Yet the man was so dear and so devoted to the Weymouth family that she could not imagine the house on Hanover Square without him.

Knowing she must not keep the earl waiting too long in the parlor below, she did not pause to check her appearance in the mirror by the table at the top of the stairs. Her dress of sprigged yellow linen was appropriate for receiving callers. She brushed her hands against the bright yellow ribbons dropping from its high bodice and touched the ones strung through her hair. With a grimace, she realized she should be wearing a mob cap to greet a caller at this hour, but she had reached the bottom of the stairs and could not rush back up like a shy child.

Crossing the foyer with its green marble floor, Chloë walked through the double doors which Yarwood had opened for their guest. The pleasing scent of damp roses billowed into the room, past the door leading to a cozy terrace and the compact garden. This was undoubtedly her favorite room in the house. Without the stuffiness of her father's book-room or the pretensions of the ball-room, it invited one to sit and enjoy conversation.

The man she assumed to be Lord Abington was standing by the hearth on the far side of the room. She noted that he must be even taller than Father, which was rare among the *ton*. His dark hair was brushed casually over the high collar of his dark brown riding coat, which he wore above buckskins and Hessians. Clearly he had stopped at Hanover Square on his way for a ride in Hyde Park.

"Good afternoon, Lord Abington," Chloë said quietly.

He turned, and she found herself confronted by a cool smile. It fit perfectly on his severely sculpted face. His brows, which were as black as his hair, seemed darker against his tanned skin, revealing he was a man who enjoyed the out of doors more than a stuffy clubroom. The line of his jaw was broken by a cleft in his chin, but she was not bamboozled by it. The uncompromising glow in his oddly tawny eyes told her that he had come to her home with a goal and would not be waylaid in obtaining it.

"Miss Weymouth?" he asked in a pleasingly deep voice as he crossed the room.

"Chloë Weymouth." Gesturing toward the chair covered in green silk, she said, "Please sit down. I shall ring for something cool to drink. Do you prefer lemonade or iced tea, my lord?"

His smile became self-deprecatory. "I had hoped you would suggest white wine."

"That can be arranged without any trouble."

As she turned to give the request to Yarwood, who was little more than a shadow by the door, she flinched when the earl said, "I have the feeling, Miss Weymouth, that there is little you cannot arrange when you set your mind to it."

Chloë ignored Yarwood's amazement at Lord Abington's impertinent comment. She simply asked him to bring wine for the earl and lemonade for her. As a friend of Henry Moore's, the earl had few expectations of finding a welcome at the Weymouth home. Mayhap he cared little if she considered him a ramshackle fellow.

When she sat on a settee facing the tall man, she folded her hands primly in her lap. She was determined to remain pretty-mannered. A tray was placed on the table between them. Thanking the maid, Chloë reached for the bottle of wine. She pulled back when Lord Abington's broader hand closed around it. His smile metamorphosed again, this time into a challenge as he poured himself some wine. Then, as coolly as if he were the master of the house and she was the unforeseen guest, he filled a glass with lemonade and held it out to her.

"Thank you," she said as she took it. A jolt raced through her as his rough skin brushed against her fingers. She quickly lowered her eyes, not wanting to chance his seeing the confusion that must be on her face. That she reacted so fiercely to such a mundane motion warned her to be cautious. She knew nothing of this man, except what whispers of rumor suggested. They might well be correct, for he seemed unwilling to accede to any canon of propriety.

"Allow me to be plain-spoken, Miss Weymouth, as I speak of what has brought me to intrude on your afternoon."

"Of course, my lord." The gold fire in his eyes forewarned her that he would speak his mind whether she granted him that courtesy or not.

"My ears have been battered by the frustration of my tie-mate, Henry Moore. He is distressed that your father has halted his wedding to your sister only days before they were to meet at the altar of St. George's."

Chloë smiled when she heard the frustration in his voice. "I understand what you have endured. My sister has been a watering-pot all day."

"By the elevens, I fail to comprehend their grief." He set his glass on the table and clasped his hands around the knees of his buckskin breeches.

"You have no love of marriage, my lord?"

He smiled again, the expression adding a dangerous glint to his eyes. Chloë's own smile faltered. So many whispers she had heard about the earl, but until this moment she had discounted them. Perhaps she would have been wise to listen to the poker-talk that Lord Abington surely had signed a pact with the old gentleman in black. She could see the reflection of hell-fire on his face as he dared her to speak the thoughts she feared were too clear on her own visage.

"I suspect marriage is an unnatural institution for most men." He raised his hands and grinned with such boyish good humor that she could almost forgive him his words. "It is a state much desired by most women, so therein lies the *contretemps*."

"For you, my lord, not for others."

"Not for me," he declared stoutly. Picking up his glass, he took a reflective sip. "However, we are not speaking of my opinions on this tedious subject, but of Henry's. He is determined to wed your sister."

"I see but one solution."

"Other than more moaning from your sister and my friend, I hope."

Chloë chuckled, delighted anew by the earl's candid disgust, for she secretly shared his feelings about the two who sought solace in grief instead of seeking a way to resolve their problem. "If you will assist me in a small endeavor, I believe we can reach a solution, which will—in turn—save our ears from suffering more of their grief."

His brows arched as he relaxed against the back of the chair, acting as if she had invited him to run tame through the house. "You have piqued my interest, Miss Weymouth. Please enlighten me."

"It is so simple, I am ashamed to own that I did not think of it earlier." With a furtive glance toward the door to assure herself that Yarwood had set no one to eavesdrop, she lowered her voice and said, "We must convince Amaryllis and Henry to do what any other couple does when they cannot obtain permission to wed."

"Elope?"

She nodded.

Rubbing his forefinger against the cleft in his chin, he laughed softly. "It is an inspired idea, but Henry—I must own—often is pudding-hearted. I doubt he will take to this idea with alacrity. Does your sister have more courage?"

"I am afraid not. She acceded to Father's demands immediately." Chloë pressed her hand to her lips, as heat oozed up her face. "My lord, please understand that I meant no disrespect for Father. He is doing what he perceives is right."

"Just not what you deem right?"

"Amaryllis has a true *tendre* for Henry." She could not keep from smiling. "And my ears have grown weary of listening to her weeping."

With a sigh, he set himself on his feet, and she wondered if his head would brush the ceiling. He seemed that tall when she looked up at him. "We all should be more like your esteemed father, who clearly can see the nonsense of allowing two mouses to marry. However, Henry is my friend, and I have vowed on more than one occasion—foolishly, I can now own—that I would do what I could as his best friend to make his passage from bachelor to spouse as easy as possible."

Chloë was shocked when he took her hand without asking permission. Smiling, he drew her to her feet. He brazenly folded her fingers between the warmth of his palms as he waited for her to speak.

She vacillated between chiding him or simply pulling her hand away, then did neither, for his fingers stroked the back of her hand gently, sending a ripple along her skin. Staring up into his golden eyes, she wondered what thoughts he was hiding. He was not being completely candid with her, in spite of his avowal otherwise.

Gareth Ogilvie could not keep from smiling. This meeting was going far better than he had expected. Although Henry had assured him that Miss Chloë Weymouth would be anxious to ease her sister's broken heart, he had given Gareth no idea that Amaryllis' younger sister was so delightfully needle-witted. And certainly no bracket-faced tabbie, for she was a pleasure for the eyes. Her ebony hair glistened with ruddy highlights as the afternoon sunshine caressed it before sliding along the high arch of her cheekbones and the slender line of her nose. She had a mouth that seemed accustomed to laughter and a chin that hinted at a strong will. Admiring the curves of her willowy form was something a man could enjoy doing for hours, but the exotic tilt of her brown eyes drew his gaze back to them again and again. Definitely this was a woman who would be difficult to ignore.

He chuckled silently to himself. It was just as well that Henry was dangling after the older sister, who was reputed to be a golden angel. Timid Henry would be no match for Chloë Weymouth.

This, however, boded well for what must lie ahead. This Miss Weymouth would be an able ally in what he planned to do. No time would be better than this to make the suggestion he had come to offer to her, so Henry could be brought out of the dismals.

"I suspect, Miss Weymouth," he murmured, as he slid a single fingertip along her delectably soft skin, "that you are correct. Eloping is the only quick solution to this bothersome problem."

"Yes," she answered faintly.

He knew he was overstepping the customs of the Polite

71

World, but he was curious as to exactly how eager Miss Weymouth was to help her sister. If she proved to be—under stress—a straitlaced miss with nary a thought in her head, this peculiar partnership was doomed before it began.

He smiled when she squared her shoulders and lifted her chin. In a stronger voice, she said, "If you will speak with Henry, I shall convince Amaryllis to meet him at a spot that is convenient for both of them."

"Will your father allow her to sneak out of the house alone at night?" He drew her a half step toward him, and she gasped at his boldness. Although Henry's misfortune had taken him from his outing in the park and the enjoyment of a quiet afternoon within it, that did not mean that he should have to abide ennui. He suspected teasing Miss Weymouth, with that stubborn chin and jesting mouth, would be uncommonly amusing.

When she pulled away, he did not try to hold her prisoner. Infuriating Miss Weymouth would not help him or Henry at all. "Of course, Father will not allow Amaryllis to *sneak* out at night. If we arrange a time to meet during the day—"

"She is sure to be seen getting into Henry's carriage. The chase would be on before they were out of Town." He shook his head. "No, I fear, Miss Weymouth, that we must use a bit more imagination in our efforts to ensure their elopement."

"Imagination? I think we would be wise to keep this simple, my lord."

"Simple is what I have in mind."

"What do you have planned?"

This woman was a sharp one, Gareth realized, no simpering chit. He would be wise himself to guard every word he spoke. Otherwise, he would do nothing to help Henry out of this bumble-bath.

"I would as lief ask what you and your family have planned for tomorrow evening," he said, watching puzzlement crease her forehead when he answered serenely.

"Father, Amaryllis, and I have accepted an invitation for Lady Norton's masquerade in Kensington."

"Perfect!"

Her eyes widened at his fervor, but as she listened to what he had devised, they narrowed in a satisfied expression. Then Gareth knew he had been right to approach Miss Chloë Weymouth. With a little luck, this was going to work out just as he hoped.

Henry Moore was sure this was the most sap-skulled escapade he had ever let Gareth Ogilvie talk him into. Since their school days, he had been jobbernowl enough to let his best friend lead him on what Gareth called "merry adventures." He had been a block to let Gareth bamboozle him into playing this game tonight. Eloping with Amaryllis had been a brilliant idea — and he vowed to thank Miss Chloë for it — but it was too important to risk the hand of chance.

Damp air inched beneath his brown hair and through his dark coat before creeping along his back in a clammy caress. Instead of being abroad on this foggy night, he would have preferred to be sitting by his hearth, a glass of warm brandy in his hand. His horse shifted under him. He suspected it sensed his anxiety through the reins.

His nose began to itch. Blast it! Henry Moore as a gentleman of the pad was doing it too much the brown. If his dear, recently departed grandmother had been alive, *this* antic would be guaranteed to make her cock up her toes. He rubbed his gloved hand against his nose, but to no avail. Sneezing, he ignored the glower his companion fired at him and the low laugh that followed.

And no mistake, Gareth Ogilvie was enjoying himself. He had assumed his rôle as a bridle-cull as if he had been born to be a highwayman. With his dark hat pulled nearly to the collar of his ebony cloak, he could have been any conveyancer haunting the night.

"How long?" Henry asked, readjusting himself in the saddle.

"Not much longer, I suspect."

"This is a want-witted scheme. If Weymouth orders the driver to take another road—"

"Miss Weymouth assured me *this* would be their route." Gareth's voice was as steady as the breeze teasing the branches over their heads.

"You do not know that bull-headed man! Weymouth heeds no one but—"

"Silence!"

Henry would have retorted—although he knew that brangling with his friend was a waste of breath, for Gareth was as stubborn as Amaryllis' father—but his ears caught the rattle of approaching carriage wheels. His hands clenched on the reins. This was a skimble-skamble idea. He hoped they did not end up frying in their own grease if this fell apart before he could flee with Amaryllis.

The coach became a silhouette against the trees edging the road. It was traveling at a sedate pace, appropriate for people who suspected no trouble. And why should they? Henry asked himself. Highwaymen seldom struck within the parameters of Town. He swallowed roughly. If Weymouth suspected he was about to be played for the jack, there would be more misery for all of them.

"On my mark," whispered Gareth.

"Mayhap we should—"

"Now!"

Henry's horse leapt forward. He clutched the reins, but his friend plied the tommy to his mount again before bending low over his own. Knowing he had nothing to lose and everything to gain, Henry tried to keep pace with the other man. It was impossible. Gareth was a neck-or-nothing rider.

He heard the earl shout to the brother of the whip who

was sitting in the box. When Gareth brandished something, the carriage came to a sudden halt. Henry drew even with his friend.

"A gun?" he choked as he tried to see what the earl held.

"Cut line!" Gareth returned in a low whisper. "Get what we came for!"

"But a gun could—"

When his friend spat his prayers backward, Henry shut his mouth. Only once had he seen his friend's temper roused, and the bully who had teased Henry that day received a painful lesson from Gareth Ogilvie. Henry had vowed then never to hazard inspiring his friend's fury.

He dropped to the ground and edged toward the carriage. He pulled his hat low over his forehead, then pushed it back up, for he was unable to see a thing. Jerking the door open, he squinted to see into its shadowed interior.

"What is the meaning of this outrage?" Weymouth exploded.

Henry could not see Amaryllis' father's face clearly, but he knew the angry expression all too well. The features that were so lovely on Miss Chloë's face were stronger and unquestionably more fierce on her father's. The tall man's black eyes, which would be sparking with fury, had cowed Henry in the past. They must not tonight.

Ignoring Weymouth's blustering, he looked past him to where the two women sat. He faltered for a moment, for he had forgotten they were en route to a masquerade. Both women wore dominoes to match their costumes. As they reached to remove the masques, he heard Gareth's impatient shout.

But which one was Amaryllis? When a hint of moonlight touched pale curls, he smiled. His sweet, golden angel! He put out his hand to her.

Weymouth knocked his hand away. "Begone, blackguard!"

Henry hesitated, unable to pull his gaze from the furious glare in Mr. Weymouth's eyes. He had been short a sheet when he'd allowed Gareth to talk him into this. Keeping this escapade a secret would be impossible for, as soon as he and Amaryllis returned from Gretna Green, his father-in-law would know they had deceived him.

With a low curse, Gareth reached past him and plucked his fiancée out of the carriage, tying a cloth over her mouth. Henry started to protest such rough treatment, but at a shriek of horror from within the carriage, he raced to his own horse. Chloë was playing her part even better than she had promised.

He mounted. Gareth dropped Amaryllis in front of him. When she struggled, a smile pulled at his lips, as pride swelled his chest. How wondrous it was to be betrothed to a woman who wished to be his wife so much that she was willing to compound this falsehood with such wondrous playacting!

"Let's ride," Gareth hissed.

Henry kept one arm around his fiancée and slapped his horse. The beast raced along the road, but he heard Weymouth shout to his coachee, "Grainger, halt them!"

He laughed triumphantly. Let Weymouth bellow until his throat closed with choler. That doddering coachman could not whip up his team to catch them now. Patting Amaryllis' arm, he said soothingly, "Have no fear, sweetheart. Your father's anger cannot reach—"

A gun fired. When a ball sliced through the darkness, only inches from his skull, Henry choked back a half-shrieked curse. He could not speak so in Amaryllis' hearing. Another shot exploded through the night.

Gareth shouted, "Into the park! Before he can reload!"

Henry slapped his horse again and tightened his arm around Amaryllis. When she stiffened, he silenced his complaint at her needless modesty. Riding would be simpler if she would relax back against him, but she was frightened. Who would have guessed that Weymouth would chance his daughter being killed?

Sweat rolled along his back as they fled into the night. This was supposed to be sport. Gareth had said nothing about them risking death.

He concentrated on following Gareth's flapping cloak, for he had a difficult time seeing past Amaryllis' tall bonnet. Fortunately the park was deserted at this hour, which was too late for outings and too early for trysts.

When Gareth drew in his horse where they had left an open carriage, Henry slowed as well. Gareth dismounted and, whipping the cloak back over his shoulder to reveal its scarlet silk underside, grasped Amaryllis about the waist. Silently, he plucked her from the saddle and set her—rather too forcefully in Henry's opinion—on the seat in the carriage. She tried to protest, but the gag over her masque muffled her words.

"Treat her gently," Henry said as he slid out of the saddle. "We have a strenuous journey ahead of us. There is no need to begin it with Amaryllis suffering a twisted ankle."

Gareth chuckled. "You have your lady fair, Henry. You would be wise to vanish from Town before Miss Weymouth's father discovers our ruse."

"A moment." He reached into the carriage and tried to loosen the knot on the gag. It had caught in her tawny curls which had escaped from beneath her crushed bonnet. Pulling it off, he said, "Sweetheart, tell me you are unharmed by our subterfuge."

When he put his hand on her elbow to turn her toward him, she slapped his fingers away as fervently as her father had. Shock battered him. His delicate Amaryllis was never so spiteful. Stepping unassisted from the carriage, she ripped off the masque. With it came the tall bonnet and the curls that had teased his cheek as they raced through the park.

"Miss Chloë!" Henry stared at her, certain his eyes were playing him false, but he could not mistake her for her

77

sister. With her dark hair falling about her shoulders and her furious gaze meeting his evenly, there was no doubt that a terrible error had been made. "What are *you* doing here?"

"What do you think? *You* abducted me!" Chloë tossed her masque to the ground and was about to speak when Lord Abington's laughter struck her like a blow. She whirled to face him. "You needn't bray like a witless ass!"

"Why not?" He drew his horse from the shadows. " 'Tis seldom I get to enjoy such a travesty. Why did you choose to be a blond shepherdess tonight?"

"I told you I would be wearing this costume." She looked down at the simple, Grecian style gown with its lacing that emphasized the high bodice.

"You said nothing of this." He took the feathered bonnet from her and tapped the fake curls. "How was poor Henry to tell you from your sister when you were wearing this?"

"Does it matter?" she retorted, not wanting to own that his words made sense. If Henry had given her and Amaryllis a moment to remove their masques, everything would have been fine. "My sister is not here. Father is sure to sound the alarm. In short order, he will have his friends searching every inch of the City for me."

The earl pressed his horse's reins into Henry's hand. "If you have an ounce of sense, you will make yourself scarce tonight, Henry. Weymouth would be glad to see you in a sheriff's picture frame."

Henry put a hand to his throat as if the noose already was set about it. "What a chucklehead I have been to listen to you!" he groaned.

"It was a good idea! How was I to know that you would not recognize your own betrothed?" With a derisive snort, Lord Abington held out his hand to Chloë. "May I be your dashing hero, Miss Weymouth?"

"You? I would as lief see no more of you after suffering this shocking mull."

"That is no way to treat the man who is going to return you to the loving arms of your doting papa."

Chloë felt compelled to hurl another insult at him. He had destroyed what might have been Amaryllis' final chance to marry Henry. Anger sharpened her voice. "If we had done as I suggested and arranged a simple rendezvous, Amaryllis and Henry would have been on their way to Scotland by now. Instead the situation is worse than it was before, for Father is certain to watch over her as closely as a *duenna*."

"It was a good plan, Miss Weymouth."

"It was . . ." The rest of her words melted on her tongue as Lord Abington took her fingers and drew them into his arm. His skin was as rough as the dirt beneath her feet when he stroked her hand. Knowing she should scold him for being so bold, she could not bring herself to speak the words that would halt this beguiling pleasure. Her feet, of their own volition, took a step closer to the unyielding strength which the ebony cloak could not conceal.

He unsettled her further as he voiced her thoughts. "Do you approve of our costumes? I thought Henry and I turned ourselves into rather dapper highwaymen."

"You did nothing but prove you both are goosecaps!"

When his hearty laugh resounded through the night, Chloë swept away from him, fearing *she* was the goose for letting his charming words divert her from his true intentions . . . whatever they might be. She let Henry hand her into the carriage. Not that she wished to ride to Lady Norton's party with these two incompetent gulls, but, if she arrived sitting on the knees of one of them, her reputation was certain to be compromised.

"I am sorry," Henry muttered when she was positioned on the leather seat.

Her heart contracted painfully. She must never forget the real reason she had agreed to this idiocy. Thinking how Amaryllis must now be crying, Chloë nearly succumbed to her own tears. Her poor sister did not deserve to suffer another blow to her happiness.

She put her fingers on Henry's thin arm and whispered, "I am so very sorry, too."

When Lord Abington stepped into the carriage, Chloë pulled back quickly.

Coolly, he said, "You need not sound so shocked, Miss Weymouth. My earlier advice to Henry remains sound. He should endeavor to avoid meeting your father tonight." Without giving her a chance to answer, he slapped the reins on the back of the horse.

Although she understood his good sense in regards to Henry, she wondered if he had paused to think that riding like this might cost her her reputation, if it was discovered she was alone with a man she barely knew. How long would it take for every bagpipe to be prattling with the story of tonight's fiasco?

As if again he could hear her thoughts, Lord Abington said, "If we deal with this properly, no one will think the worse of you."

"My concern now is for Amaryllis," she hedged, not wanting him to discover how easily he gauged her emotions.

"Yes, they will be bemoaning their mutual misfortune again." He cleared his throat before adding, "Miss Weymouth, I find it dismally uncomfortable to speak to your back."

Chloë considered continuing her petulant stance, but knew it gained her nothing. After all, she could not blame Lord Abington for the night ending in such a pickle when it had been Henry's mistake.

She faced the earl and discovered he was no more than a broad-shouldered shadow against the darkness. Quietly she said, "You seem unsympathetic to their grief."

"I have great sympathy for them, but they have bungled their chance to elope."

"We must try again." She put her fingers to her mouth,

but the words had escaped before she could halt them.

He laughed softly, the sound rumbling like distant thunder through the night. "You are indomitable in your determination to play Cupid."

She smiled as she relaxed against the tufted seat. "Not Cupid, for his arrows have found their targets already. I wish only to see Amaryllis' dreams come true."

"And your dreams? You are of marriageable age as well."

"Amaryllis must be first to marry. She is older."

His grin flashed in the faint moonlight which sifted through the coiling mist. "So you will do all you can to buckle her to Henry so you may convince some singleton to leg-shackle himself to you. A devious plot."

" 'Tis no plot we have planned." Irritation added an edge to her voice as she said, "And I shall be party to no more schemes with you if you insist on belittling me at every turn."

"You mistake my intentions."

Chloë choked back a gasp as his arm stretched along the back of the seat. He did not touch her, but she could not be unaware of those strong muscles so close to her. When he had seized her about the waist to snatch her from the carriage, she had been impressed with his strength.

Struggling to knit together her frayed composure, she asked, "And what are your intentions, my lord?"

"I am surprised you need to ask, for they are unchanged, as I assume yours are."

"I want Amaryllis to be happy with Henry."

"Very good. Then we still agree on our goal." His finger brushed her shoulder, tracing a lazy pattern along her bare skin. She could not dampen the quiver that coursed through her in the wake of his touch. It flowed deep within her, setting her alight as if the sky were filled with fireworks. Leaning toward her, he whispered, "We do still agree, don't we?"

She closed her eyes, unable to combat the dual assault on her senses. His breath grazed her ear and swirled up into her hair like questing fingers. As his hand curved along her shoulder, he turned her toward him. She gazed into his face, which was lost to the night. Not that it mattered, for their single meeting in the daylight had etched his features in her memory.

His words grazed her face on each breath, telling her that his lips were too close to hers as he repeated, "We do still agree, don't we?"

"Yes," she answered as softly. She was not sure if she could have said anything else when he touched her with such enchantment.

"Good," he said in his normal voice. "Lord Cresmere's ball is two nights from now. Are you attending?"

Chloë shook herself and drew away from him. She did not need moonlight to know that he was smiling. What a blind buzzard she was to let him deceive her with his obviously well-practiced seduction! She had heard the tales of his skill with court-promises that had no more substance than a fading rainbow. She would not allow herself to be taken in again.

"Yes, we are planning to go to the ball," she said coolly, "but—"

"As you yourself have said—not in the most dulcet tones, I must own—your father will play the ever vigilant watchdog for both of you now. Yet, at the ball, we can provide another opportunity for this elopement."

"I am unsure if I wish your assistance in this matter any longer."

"I fear you will need it. I doubt your father will allow Henry within a league of your sister."

"And you think you can arrange that?"

"I do."

She laughed. "Words I thought you had vowed never to voice, my lord."

"*Touché,* for you know well my opinion of the subject

82

of marriage."

"It is solely desired by women and those men who were on the wrong side of the hedge when brains were given away. Do you hate women so much?"

"You mistake my distaste for the married state for a dislike of women. I can assure you, Miss Weymouth, that I find the gentler sex intriguing and delightful company. All in all, you provide a pleasurable pastime for a man who is interested in a bit of fluffy conversation and a warm armful." His voice became serious, giving her no chance to fire a back-answer. "However, you cannot refute the fact that you need all the help available to get Henry and your sister into the parson's mousetrap."

Chloë was about to answer, but halted as she stared at the building appearing out of the mist along the road in front of them. Her eyes widened. Those six columns could belong nowhere else but St. George's Church. "Why are we returning to Hanover Square? Father will surely be—"

"At your house." He chuckled. "You should heed your father's orders more closely, Miss Weymouth. He bid—rather vociferously, I must say—your coachee to return them to your house posthaste. Didn't you hear?"

"How could I have heard?" she snapped back, more irritated than before at his amusement over this debacle. "If you will recall, Henry was squealing like a frightened piglet in my ear."

"Henry is not of highwayman's cut, I fear."

"And you are?"

When Lord Abington did not retort immediately, Chloë glanced at his stern profile. He had discarded the low-brimmed hat and the ebony cape before climbing into the carriage, but she could easily resurrect the image of him mounted so casually and with such pride, the dark wings of his cape capturing the night breeze. He had enjoyed his part in the deception. . . . He had enjoyed it too well.

He lifted her hand from her lap. She swallowed her

gasp of shock at his audacity. She tried to tug her fingers away. It was futile, for his hand closed over them in a trap of flesh. In the light of a passing streetlamp, she saw his smile had returned.

"Are we partners again in this undertaking, Miss Weymouth?"

She sighed. If she had any other choice . . . But there was none. Not if she wished to halt her sister's heartbreak. "Yes," she answered, "we are partners, but, my lord, this time, we must be successful."

"I assure you we will be."

The house was in a complete uproar when Yarwood opened the door to admit Chloë and Lord Abington. She knew the butler must be excused for losing his formerly unshakable aplomb. With a raspy shout, he called up the stairs to her father.

Lord Abington said nothing, although a smile played along his expressive lips.

Fearing the old man would suffer apoplexy if he continued at this pace, Chloë hurried to the butler and tried to calm him. Only the appearance of Weymouth, with a damp-cheeked Amaryllis in tow, soothed Yarwood.

As she smiled up at her father, Chloë could understand why Henry was so intimidated by him. Lionel Weymouth was extraordinarily tall, challenging even Lord Abington's height. Next to him, Amaryllis looked tiny indeed. Weymouth nearly ran down the curving stairs to grasp Chloë by the shoulders. Unsure whether he intended to shake her or embrace her, she was surprised when he did neither, only smiled as he brushed her mussed hair back from her face. The motion nearly undid her, for it told of the love that never needed to be spoken. What an ungrateful wretch she was to deceive him!

Before she could blurt out an apology, her father looked past her, curiosity apparent on his face. Lord

Abington stepped forward and said, "Gareth Ogilvie at your service, Mr. Weymouth."

Lionel Weymouth pumped Lord Abington's hand. "We are forever in your debt, my lord, for saving Chloë. I feared for her very life—not only when the knights of the pad abducted her but when that clod-pate Grainger fired after them. He is a peter-gunner at best and cannot hit a tree from an arm's length. I will own to being frightened that he would hit my daughter."

Seeing the contrition in Amaryllis' tear-filled eyes, Chloë was sure she wore the same expression. What gabies they had been! If their ploy had succeeded, Father would have been prostrate with fear for Amaryllis' safety. Now that they had failed, they should own to the truth.

She started to reveal it, but the earl replied smoothly, "It was my pleasure to be of assistance to your lovely daughter, Mr. Weymouth. However, the debt is mine."

"Yours?" Chloë's father asked, voicing the shock she was struggling to hide.

"How else would I have had the opportunity to speak with her? She has a rare wit that was not dulled, even by her harrowing evening."

While her father continued to gush about Lord Abington's gallantry, the taller man looked over his head to grin at Chloë. He was delighting in this deception. Mayhap they had missed the masquerade ball, but Lord Abington still wore his masque of falsehoods.

Chloë's hands clenched at her sides. Father was wrong to deny Amaryllis the opportunity to marry where her heart had led her. Yet Lord Abington was even more wrong to delude her father. And when she heard the earl say he hoped he might call at a later date to determine for himself that she was unharmed by the night's events, she realized how readily he had orchestrated the conversation. If the man was not the devil himself, he certainly was in league with Old Scratch.

"Of course, you must feel free to give Chloë a look-in

whenever you wish, my lord." Her father patted her on the shoulder. "I am sure she would be delighted to welcome you at any time."

"That is kind of you, Mr. Weymouth," Lord Abington replied.

"Nonsense!" Weymouth's smile broadened until Chloë wondered if his narrow cheeks could contain it. "Please join us for a bit of something to take the chill of the fog from your bones."

"I would enjoy that," Lord Abington said, dashing Chloë's hopes that he would demur and leave her alone with her remorse.

"Chloë, show Lord Abington to the parlor. Amaryllis, if you can stop being watery-headed for a moment, you may sit with us." He turned toward the stairs. "There is a bottle, my lord, that I keep in my book-room, which I think you will concur is of an exceptional vintage. I shall go and ring for it."

Trying not to speculate about how the evening could become worse, Chloë walked between Lord Abington and her sister, who kept dabbing at her cheeks with a damp handkerchief. They had no sooner entered the parlor than Amaryllis asked where Henry was and if he was unharmed.

"Your father is right. Your coachee's aim was fortunately wide." Lord Abington's voice was gentle as he drew his lawn handkerchief from beneath his black coat and handed it to her. "You need have no fears on Henry's behalf. When next we—"

"There should be no next time," Chloë interjected, unable to remain silent when her guilt was strangling her.

"How can you say that?" He flashed Amaryllis a dazzling smile and was rewarded with one in return. "Look at the hope in your sister's eyes when I speak of another venture. Can you refuse her the dream she holds most dear?"

"Chloë, you must help us," Amaryllis chimed in when he paused.

"Us?" she countered.

Amaryllis grasped Chloë's hand. Entreaty widened her blue eyes. "Do say you will help, Chloë. I swear I would die if you turned your back on me now."

A helpless sense, that of being unable to escape an inevitable disaster, sank through Chloë as she looked from her sister to Lord Abington. His smile did not waver, and she recognized the aura of victory he made no attempt to disguise. Lord Abington intended to let no one halt him from abetting his friend in eloping. Not even Chloë Weymouth.

As she heard her father coming toward the parlor, she softly said, "Of course, I will help." She regretted her words as soon as she saw the glimmer of satisfaction in Lord Abington's eyes. This was a mistake. She knew it, but could do nothing to stop what seemed as inescapable as tomorrow's sunrise.

"I like this plan much better," Amaryllis said as she peered into the cheval glass and patted the pink rosebuds twisted with pearls which were artfully arranged in her upswept hair. Her pale pink gown was of the lightest gauze. On her sleeves, narrow strips of white satin glittered in the candlelight.

Chloë ignored her own reflection, which she could see past her sister's shorter head. The gown of unrelieved white was her best, and she had looked forward to wearing it with her favorite petticoat, which was decorated with net at the yoke and with embroidery at the hem. A coronet of white flowers matched the ones in the lace along the ruff rising nearly to her dark hair.

"There is no plan." Chloë tapped her fingers impatiently on the edge of the dressing table.

Her sister turned, frowning. "Do stop that irritating sound."

"I cannot help it." Chloë paced to the window and back

to the chaise longue. "I wish we had some sort of a plan. Lord Abington said nothing in the note he sent this afternoon."

Amaryllis clapped her gloved hands. With a sly chuckle, she said, "He seems quite taken with you."

"He is interested solely in your elopement."

"Is he?" Amaryllis picked up a cut crystal vase from the dressing table. Taking a deep breath of the glorious scent of the red roses, she smiled. "Do not be blind, Chloë. A man who plies you with gifts—"

"A handful of flowers."

"—is anxious for more than a fleeting conversation."

Chloë did not wish to disabuse her sister of misapprehensions by speaking the truth. Lord Abington had been honest with her. He thought marriage was reserved for dolts who did not know better.

"I have just the jolly," Amaryllis said with another gleeful giggle. "Father is intrigued with Lord Abington's interest in you as well."

"I have told you, Amaryllis, the earl is interested only in—"

"My elopement. I know, which is why I am asking you to take Father's attention from me tonight, so I can slip away more easily."

Chloë shook her head. "You know as well as I do that Father will be anxious to watch over both of us."

"Yet Lord Abington is in his best graces. Dance with him, Chloë, and Father will be pleased. He has already asked among the *ton* about Lord Abington. Your dancing with him might divert his eye from me and Henry."

"He has asked about the earl?" Chloë sank to the chaise longue and wondered what else could go amiss. If Lord Abington heard of Father's queries—and he was sure to—he would be even more insufferable than before. Tonight was going to be as horrible as she had feared. It was not an auspicious beginning to what must be a perfect ending, or she feared Amaryllis' smile would vanish for good.

Lord Cresmere's house was one of the grandest on the elegant west side of Berkeley Square. As rain lashed the leaves of the plane trees in the heart of the square, lights from the trio of window bays offered a nebulous welcome. The twilight clung close to the street, leaving the mansard roofs to vanish into the thickening fog.

Stepping from the carriage, Chloë hoped the throbbing in her head would diminish once they were inside the marquess' house. She avoided looking directly at her father, as she had for the past two days. Surely her guilt was visible for him to view. How much easier it would be to act like her carefree sister! No, she corrected herself as she listened to Amaryllis' rapid-fire prattle. Amaryllis was as impatient as she was to have this evening come to a propitious conclusion.

The grand foyer blazed with candles placed on every table and hanging from the brass and crystal chandelier. After she had given her shawl to the major domo, Chloë walked with Father and Amaryllis up the white marble staircase which was broad enough to allow them to climb it three abreast.

The babble of myriad conversations set against the tempo of a waltz swept out of the ballroom to encircle them and entice them into the gaiety. The huge room was chock-full, for the marquess had gained a reputation as an excellent host with a fine cellar. On this evening, Chloë guessed everyone in the Polite World had gathered beneath the trio of chandeliers that were even more glorious than the one in the foyer. Gilt and violet silk covered the walls, which were interrupted by a parade of white pilasters. Perfume and cigar smoke made a smothering combination.

"Very impressive," Weymouth said as he patted his blue striped waistcoat.

Chloë was not certain whether he was speaking of the sumptuous house or the many young men who might be interested in Amaryllis. As she watched him scan the room, she guessed he was looking for one specific person. It was certainly not Henry Moore, who was standing by a door that opened onto a balcony overlooking the garden. A smile spread across Father's lips, and she knew he had found the person he sought.

When a man pushed through the press of the guests to greet them, Chloë recognized him as Lord Islen. He was, without question, the most handsome man she had ever seen. Framed by blond hair, his face was classically drawn, and his blue eyes contained a genuine warmth. His navy velvet coat was in prime twig to match the pristine white of his breeches. Yet she found herself dismissing him as insignificant and looking around the room to see if Lord Abington had arrived.

She was astonished at the thought. The devilment in the earl's smile should not clog her mind when this young Adonis stood before her. Had Lord Abington befuddled her so completely that she could no longer see things as they truly were?

"Lord Islen, my beloved daughter Amaryllis," her father said, putting a halt to her disturbing thoughts.

To keep from thinking of Lord Abington again, Chloë watched the buttons on Father's waistcoat, sure they would pop as pride swelled his belly. When he offhandedly introduced her to the viscount, she was not offended. Father was making it no secret that he had brought them to this party specifically so that Amaryllis might meet Lord Islen.

Her sister chattered prettily and smiled as the viscount bowed over her hand, but she continued to glance about the room. Chloë wished she could whisper that she had seen Henry Moore by the balcony door. His name must not be spoken in Father's hearing, however, for no suspicions must betray whatever plan Lord Abington had conceived. But where was the earl? Mayhap, she thought, he had come to his senses and decided tonight was the wrong time to try whatever he had planned. A heaviness dropped to her stomach as she realized she was hoping foolishly. Lord Abington would not allow a small thing like common sense to intrude on his schemes.

"May I be so bold as to ask you to stand up with me, Miss Weymouth?" asked the viscount. A lisp in his warm, tenor voice gave his invitation a charming candor. "The next dance is about to start, and I would be enchanted if you would let me escort you to the floor."

Amaryllis looked at Chloë, who gave her the slightest nod. Until the earl appeared, Amaryllis might as well enjoy a harmless flirtation.

As soon as the twosome was out of earshot, Father chuckled with satisfaction. "Lord Islen has an income of fifty thousand pounds a year and may be his uncle the duke's heir if the old man fails to produce a male child."

Grimacing at her father's glee, she said quietly, "They have only met, and Amaryllis was honest with you when she says that if she cannot wed Henry, she shall buckle herself to no one this Season."

"Bah! Henry Moore! What is he? The destitute youngest son of a man who let the board of green cloth seduce every farthing from his pocket. What little of value remains in the family estate will go to Moore's older brothers."

"But Amaryllis avows a heart-deep affection for him."

He smiled gently and patted her arm. "Chloë, you surprise me, for I thought you more clear-headed than your sister. I shall not see either of you want for anything. After all, Amaryllis has been touted as the most beautiful woman this Season. Why shouldn't she have the best-looking man? Especially when he can give her a life of luxury."

Unable to argue with such well-meaning intentions, Chloë watched her sister with the viscount. Father was correct. Amaryllis was lovely, and with the tall viscount who was as blond, she looked like a porcelain doll. Heads pivoted as they twirled about the floor in easy unison. No doubt, there would be much chatter about how easily the bride-to-be had set aside her grief to find amusement in the arms of another man.

"Good evening, Weymouth, Miss Weymouth," came a deep voice Chloë easily recognized.

A pulse of warmth, as fast and fierce as lightning severing a summer sky, whirled through her when she saw the sparkle in Lord Abington's mysterious eyes. She struggled to pull her gaze away, finding it easier to stare at the stitchery on the white waistcoat he wore beneath his deep blue coat.

"Abington!" crowed her father. "It is indeed a pleasure to see you again!"

"And under far more comfortable circumstances than our last meeting." Only the slightest arch of his sable brows warned Chloë that Lord Abington was as impervious to her father's gabble-grinding as he was to the ardent feminine eyes turned in his direction as he passed. When she saw her father's broadening and decidedly covetous smile, dismay twinged in her stomach. Lord Abington was, without question, both titled and well heeled, exactly the sort of beau Father was seeking for her sister. If Father chose the earl for Amaryllis . . .

Don't act as if you have no head, she chided herself. Lord Abington had no intentions of marrying anyone. She need have no worry about him overmastering Amaryllis with a wit her sister could not match at the very same time the daring earl was filling Chloë's daydreams with longing.

That twinge became horror. How could she think such things? The only reason Lord Abington should be in her mind was the ensuring of her sister's happiness. Certainly Lord Abington gave her nary a thought except when his devious mind turned to the next twist in their mutual strategy to get Amaryllis and her betrothed to Scotland.

Lord Abington's deep voice jostled her out of her apprehensive thoughts. "I am glad to see that both you and your daughter appear completely recovered from the disturbing events of two nights past." He gave her father his most innocuous smile, but Chloë did not believe it. The man was a chameleon, ready to lather anyone he passed with whatever they wished to hear. When he turned to her, she steeled herself for his double entendre only she could understand, but which would threaten to unnerve her utterly. "I trust you suffer no lasting scars from the experience, Miss Weymouth."

"Chloë is resilient," Father answered before she could think of a suitable response that would not expose the truth.

"Thank goodness it was not her sister who was abducted then, for I suspect your other daughter would not have handled the situation with as much aplomb."

"Amaryllis is a far more delicate creature."

Lord Abington glanced over his shoulder to see Amaryllis laughing with Lord Islen. "I can see that, although she seems quite recovered from her recent heartache."

"I have always felt that a *soirée* with its excitement is the best antidote to any young woman's silly woes."

Father's solemn tones exasperated Chloë, but she must not let him discern that. If he thought his daughter so faithless that she could shunt aside Henry for the viscount, he knew less of Amaryllis than she did of Lord Abington. Again irritation pinched at her as the earl invaded her thoughts.

"Then," Lord Abington said, "I must endeavor to bring the other Miss Weymouth's smile back. Will you shake a toe with me, Miss Weymouth?"

She did not answer as she looked up at him. As the first time she had met him, she was drawn into the abyss of his eyes, which glowed as brightly as the gilt on the walls. So many mysteries waited there to be explored, but she also knew how thoroughly she could be lost, never to escape if she dared to test their depths. She teetered, between daring and desperation, not ready to take the perilous step into trusting him.

She bit her lip at seeing her fingers tremble when she raised her hand to place it on the smooth black wool of his coat. Why was she acting like a schoolgirl who dared not say boo to a goose? Lord Abington was no stranger eager to woo her with court-promises as they danced. He was her partner in this escapade to arrange Amaryllis' elopement. If she wished Amaryllis and Henry success in running away together tonight, she must stop acting moony.

Despite her resolve, her breath caught over her rapidly thumping heart when the earl put his arm around her waist and turned her into the pattern of the dance. He was, without question, an excellent dancer, but that did not surprise her. She suspected Gareth Ogilvie became a master at whatever he set his mind to accomplishing.

His voice resonated through her as he said in barely more than a whisper, "I can see you were smart enough not to hide your ebony tresses beneath those ridiculous blond ringlets."

"Tonight is not a masquerade."

"No?" His ironic tone became less subtle than when he had been talking with her father. "I suspect you are still masking much."

Shocked, she gasped, "You cannot think that I should tell Father—"

"Of course not, but he is not the only one from whom you hide facets of yourself, for I suspect you put on a pretense for *tout le monde.*"

She started to retort, but with an astonishingly vigorous twirl, he halted her protest.

"You appear serene and docile," he continued, "but I vow you are quite the opposite. The man who disregards that wants for sense."

Chloë did not lower her gaze from his taunting eyes. If he thought she would give him a heated answer so he could proceed with his insults, she would deny him that pleasure. Mayhap he should have stayed in his persona of the ill-mannered highwayman. It suited him better than the milieu of the Polite World.

"You have succeeded in filling my father's head with your pap," she said.

"He wishes to know more of my intentions toward you."

She hoped her cool laugh would conceal the increasing warmth bubbling within her as he spoke boldly of matters best left undiscussed. Wanting the soft fire to be caused by nothing more than her anxiety about the elopement, she could not lie to herself. She liked being in Lord Abington's arms, feeling their strength around her, moving with him to the strains of a delightful waltz.

"I think," she said with every ounce of hauteur she could summon, "Father considers you a possible match for Amaryllis."

"That lamb?" He chuckled. "She is the perfect choice of a wife for Henry, if he insists on doing something as want-witted as tacking himself together with your sister." Looking past her, he laughed again. "Poor Henry is moping in the corner, jealousy dripping from every pore of his being, as he watches your sister with Islen."

"You should have pity for him. He loves her."

"I suppose he thinks he does."

Her fingers clenched on his shoulder. "Simply because you dare not feel the glorious joys of love, my lord, gives you no license to denounce others. Each of us would be fortunate to know even half of the devotion Henry and my sister feel for each other. What they have is extraordinary."

"Such an impassioned defense! Spoken, however, as a woman who thinks only of trapping a man into the shackles of matrimony."

Heat seared Chloë's face as she wished she could break the swirl of the dance and leave him standing alone in the middle of the floor. The pledge she had made to her sister this evening muted her exasperation enough so she was able to continue the dance. It was imperative that she keep Father's attention directed toward her until Amaryllis was on her way to Gretna Green.

Her voice quivered, but she raised her chin and took a deep breath as she said, "Mock others' feelings as you wish, but you cannot disclaim that they exist."

"I would never waste wagging my tongue on that, I can assure you. I do, I must own, have a great deal of compassion for your father. He is concerned, as he well should be, when his two daughters are the topic of much talk throughout the *ton*."

"Talk?" she choked. "About—?"

A sharp laugh cut her off. "You worry needlessly about your reputations. I was speaking of the envious lips that flap in your wake. Other women would love to claim your loveliness as their own."

His arm tightened around her to bring her closer. When she raised her eyes, startled anew by the lightning pulse racing through her at his touch, a hint of a smile tugged at his lips. But it was the golden flecks in his eyes that were mesmerizing. They altered with his moods like stars in a night sky, growing brighter when the mists of pretense were swept aside. Now they threatened to scorch her as his gaze roved along her face as eagerly as his fingers were gliding across her back, luring her ever closer to him.

She was certain he must be able to perceive how her heart throbbed ever faster as the conversation and music vanished. She could hear only her frantic heartbeat and the hushed pulse of his breathing. Together they created the most wondrous melody she had ever heard, for it tempted her to think of nothing save its bewitching rhythms.

Her heart pounded harder when he leaned toward her, his lips parting as they descended. If he kissed her before all these people . . . She fought her yearning to sample that pleasure and dampened the small voice which murmured that such a public outrage would be guaranteed to hold Father's eyes. If *this* was Lord Abington's idea of a way to help Henry and Amaryllis, she must urge him to formulate another. She must . . .

Closing her eyes, she let him bring her outrageously near. As his breath grazed her cheek, sending a molten longing through her, she fought the part of herself that cared nothing for Society's dictates.

"The hour is nigh," he whispered against her ear.

"The hour?" Chloë shook the webs of fantasy from her head as she stepped back. She was a worse air-dreamer than Henry Moore if she thought Lord Abington had anything on his mind save helping his friend elope.

"For our plan to unfold."

"What plan?"

He laughed at her sarcasm. "Now, now, you must trust me."

"I have little reason to trust you after you left us at sixes and sevens with your last idea."

"You have every reason to trust me," he murmured as his arm slid nearly imperceptibly across her back, closing the distance between them inappropriately once more. As she tilted her head to look up into his eyes, he gave her a cold smile. "We want the same thing, you and I. We want to guarantee that the people we care about deeply get the happiness they deserve."

"Which they would have obtained two days ago, if you had not higgedly-piggedly taken me from the carriage instead of Amaryllis."

He put his finger against her lips, shocking her. "Hush, for if even a whiff of what really happened reaches your father's ears, he is sure to fly off into a pelter that will end any chances of me protecting *my*

97

ears from Henry's mewling laments."

She put a respectable distance between them again. "I shall not risk Amaryllis' happiness. Tell me what plan you have devised. I trust—unlike last time—it is simple."

"Deliciously simple." His smile sent a flutter through her, which she tried, without any success, to ignore. She fought to concentrate on his words, not his attempt to manipulate her with charm. Knowing she must listen cautiously, for he could talk the hind leg off a donkey, she said nothing as he went on. "This plan is assured to hoodwink your esteemed father completely. Henry and I developed it so well, if I may boast, that nothing can go wrong this time."

"My lord, I urged you before not to arrange any intricate plan. A simple one—"

His low laugh interrupted her. "As we are conspirators together in this *affaire d'amour*, we need not be so formal. You should call me 'Gareth,' and I shall call you 'Chloë,' if you will allow it."

Absently she nodded, not caring what name he used. All her thoughts focused on her dismay. She had asked him not to complicate the situation this time. All they needed were a coach, a team of strong horses, a competent coachee, the prospective bride and groom, and a diversion to give them time to flee Town.

"Is the carriage waiting?"

"There is no carriage waiting." His hand stroked her back as he added in a lower voice, "You dance beautifully, Chloë."

"No carriage? Then how does Henry expect to get my sister to Scotland?"

As if she had not spoken, he said, "It is a rare pleasure to be able to look into a dancing partner's eyes instead of being presented with the sickly sweet aroma of the flowers in her hair, which invariably are directly below my nose."

"Why don't you have a carriage waiting?" Vexation tainted her voice. She had no interest in his Spanish coin now. "I thought everything was set for tonight."

His smile grew wider, and the twinkle in his eyes remained as bright as when he had been hoaxing her father. "It is especially agreeable to look down into eyes as enchanting as yours."

The music came to an end. As Chloë was about to walk away, too piqued by his ridicule to endure more of the conversation, he seized her arm. She faced him, furious that he continued to treat her as if her head was empty of any sensible thought.

Although it was, whispered the tiny voice of truth, when his arms enveloped you.

"Are you preparing to flee like Cinderella," he asked in a taunting voice, "and miss the opportunity to relieve your curiosity about what Henry and I have conceived?"

As his false smile fell away, her sharp retort went unspoken. The candid earnestness on his face was disquieting. Softly she asked, "What do you intend to do?"

"I shall tell you while we dance."

"Dance? There is no—"

As if to prove her wrong, the violins played the first notes of the next waltz. Gareth chuckled, and she smiled in spite of herself. Staying angry at this enigmatic, enticing man was impossible, for he always managed to show her the foolishness of trying to be pompous.

Chloë let him turn her back into the dance. She saw Amaryllis spin by with a short man with a bushy mustache. Her sister caught her eye and smiled. No doubt, Amaryllis considered a second dance with Gareth the perfect way for Chloë to divert Father's attention from his elder daughter.

"I thought," Gareth said, bringing her eyes back to meet his, "that . . . since our little drama failed two nights ago, we would create a more successful one this evening. And for a wider audience, who will indisputably enjoy our talents." Boyish mischief tilted his lips. "Tonight Henry will challenge our mutual friend Jeremy

99

Howell to a duel to protect your sister's honor."

"Have you taken a maggot in the head?" She tried to draw back, but his arm kept her imprisoned against his chest. Instead of struggling, which would bring too many eyes upon them, she said, "Henry is no more capable of defending himself than a pup. Less, for he does not as much as growl."

"You are fretting your gizzard needlessly. There are things that you do not know about Henry Moore. You will be surprised. However, you need not be anxious. He will do no more than throw down the gauntlet to Howell in front of Cresmere's guests. A brilliant idea, I say modestly, for it is certain to enhance Henry's standing at his club, when his clubmates discover he is not the mouse he appears. Then you need only to bring your sister to where the supposed duel will be held. Even your father would not deny her the chance to watch her beloved meet his end at grass before breakfast." When she grimaced, his voice lowered. "Think of it, Chloë. You escort your sister to the park, and off she goes with Henry to Gretna Green."

"Father may insist on accompanying us. Did you give thought to that?"

He shrugged with indifference. "My dear Chloë, I deemed you capable of dealing with that slight complication. After all, don't you wish a hand in making your sister's wedding possible?" His fingers traced a zigzag between the buttons along the back of her gown, again warming her skin with the trickles of heat that rippled outward from his touch. "Just think. After the sun rises, when your father joins you to enjoy a cup of coffee in your breakfast-parlor, you can present him with a *fait accompli.*"

"But if something goes wrong—"

He laughed beneath the joyous music. "What can go wrong?"

As happened too often, Chloë's retort vanished as she

stared up into his eyes. It was easier to imagine dissolving into their gold luminescence than to think of the catastrophe she feared would come of this night.

Chloë did not see any signal between the three men, but she knew the next act of what might prove to be a comedy or tragedy was about to unfold when Henry went to speak with Amaryllis. Gareth played his part by drawing Lord Islen and Lionel Weymouth into conversation near a table where wine bubbled in a silver fountain.

As he walked toward Amaryllis and her beau, Lord Howell gave a smile to a group of dowagers, who had been eagerly prattling, not taking pains to be quiet, about Lord Abington dancing two dances in a row with the same woman. Chloë disregarded them as she watched the red-haired man stride purposefully across the crowded floor. Uneasiness coursed through her, leaving iciness to clamp around her heart. Lord Howell was a thickly built man, easily a mismatch for Henry, if this had been a real confrontation.

Chloë moved next to Amaryllis. She was not surprised when her sister took her hand and gave her a warm smile. Although Chloë's face was surely devoid of any color, Amaryllis glowed with a happiness that would betray them if her sister did not take care.

Looking past Amaryllis, Chloë gave Henry a weak smile. He acknowledged it with a nod, and from his stiff motion, she suspected he was as bothered by this as she was. They were both cabbage-heads to have let Gareth persuade them to trade simplicity for a path fraught with potential pitfalls.

"Miss Weymouth," Lord Howell said in an oddly thin voice, "you have taken a turn about the room with others. It is time for you to stand up with me."

"Thank you for your generous invitation, my lord, but I would prefer not to dance now," Amaryllis answered.

101

Lord Howell glowered at Henry. "You would as lief sit and listen to Moore's opaque babble?"

"Henry knows that when a lady speaks her mind, he should heed it."

Chloë was startled by the uncommon spirit in her sister's voice. She had not expected Amaryllis to take to this game so readily, but clearly she was ready to go to any lengths to make her elopement possible.

"Leave off, Howell," Henry added when Amaryllis gave him a surreptitious poke with her elbow. "Miss Weymouth has made her wishes clear. She has no interest in being plagued by a profligate."

"A profligate?" Lord Howell's voice rose sharply, garnering the ears of all those around them. "I shall allow you a chance to retract that scurrilous word, Moore. Hurry — your apology." He gave Amaryllis a frightful leer. "I want to return to the dancing."

Amaryllis slipped an arm through Henry's and hid her eyes against his shoulder. Chloë almost laughed when the slender man stiffened his spine and jutted his chin in Lord Howell's direction. She had to own that, despite her initial distrust of the plan, this was as amusing as a satire in Drury Lane.

"I see no reason for an apology to come from me," Henry said. "I shall await yours with what little patience I have left."

Lord Howell laughed too loudly, but with the desired results. Heads turned toward them from every corner of the ballroom.

Chloë sensed rather than saw Gareth come to stand behind her, for her gaze settled on Father who was staring with gaped-mouth astonishment at the startling *tableau*. His features took on a sickish pallor when Lord Howell snarled an insult at Amaryllis.

Henry flushed at the coarse words. "Howell, that is too much to take, even from your infernally big mouth. You leave me no choice but to ask you to name your friend —

if you can claim anyone who lives in your pocket—to meet me before dawn in the park."

"No!" gasped Amaryllis with the perfect amount of horror.

"Mayhap," Henry continued with cool composure, "by that time, you shall have come to your senses, Howell, and realized you cannot be such a rough diamond in the presence of a lady who has shown the good taste to refuse you a dance."

Hearing a low hiss of a breath expelled between clenched teeth, Chloë glanced over her shoulder. Gareth's face was taut, shocking her, for he seldom revealed any emotion except easy good humor. His eyes were as cold as Lord Howell's in the moment before—without another word—the stocky man stormed from the ballroom into the card room in the back corner.

"That set up Lord Howell's bristles," Amaryllis said, softly. She had no chance to add more as they were surrounded by the guests who were eager to discover if Mr. Moore would truly fight a duel for a woman who had spent the evening dancing with other men. Her eyes sparkled with excitement as she kept her arm through Henry's while they were the center of everyone's attention.

Father cleared his throat, and Chloë turned to see his dismay clearly evident. Why had she allowed herself to become a party to *this* deception? It was bringing no happiness to anyone but Amaryllis who delighted in knowing she was ever closer to being Henry's wife.

Chloë's eyes were caught by Gareth's. When one closed in a lazy wink, she shivered with a sudden coldness. They were daring much with this ruse. She hoped they would accomplish what they must this time, because she did not wish to think what failure might cost them.

Balancing Amaryllis' small bag on her knees, Chloë stared out the window of the closed carriage. The rain

103

had ended, but fog still roiled along the cobbled street. She sighed. As soon as Amaryllis and Henry were on their way, she would return to Hanover Square and Father. She did not look forward to the moment she had to reveal the truth.

"What did Father say when you told him we were coming to view this duel?" Chloë asked when her sister halted her bibble-babble for a scant moment.

Amaryllis laughed with unrestrained happiness. "I did not tell him we were coming here."

"You didn't . . . ?" Shock strangled her. If Father took it upon himself to follow them, their conspiracy would be exposed. "Amaryllis, you said you would broach the matter to Father and tell him what I told you to say."

Her sister shrugged with a nonchalance that was irritatingly reminiscent of Gareth. "I saw no reason to complicate the situation further."

On that, Chloë had to agree. A simple elopement would have been so much easier than this complex series of goose's gazettes. She did not like having Father on a string.

Shortly thereafter the carriage slowed in the heart of the park. Unlike their ride through Hyde Park during the sunlit hours, there was no sound of conversation and laughter in the early morning darkness. Dew weighed heavily on the grass and flowers. As they were handed down from the carriage, Chloë drew her lace shawl over the skin bared by her gown.

Amaryllis quickly pushed past her to run toward the shadows where another coach waited. It was a unicorn, Chloë noted, for a single horse led the two behind it. Such a team could reach Scotland quickly.

Throwing herself into her beloved's arms, Amaryllis seemed to care nothing for the others who viewed them. Henry swept her to him and kissed her with eagerness.

Chloë glanced shyly at Gareth, who was walking toward her, his tall beaver in his hand. He did not look in her direction as he watched the impassioned embrace. Suddenly an odd emptiness swelled within Chloë, swallowing her in a void of loneliness. The warmth glowing in Henry's eyes when he beheld her sister was so nakedly unaffected that she was almost embarrassed to view it.

A shiver of excitement went through her when Gareth's broad hand cupped her elbow. She looked at him again. It was a mistake, she realized, with a muffled gasp. His gaze riveted her, refusing to let her escape its hold. Slowly his hand slid along her arm, ruffling the lace on her sleeve and setting the skin beneath it on fire. His fingers stroked her bare shoulder beneath the lacy wrap before inching along the sensitive skin of her neck to caress the curve of her ear.

When he whispered her name as softly as the night breeze drifted through the branches above them, she stepped nearer to him, drawn by the beguiling sound of his voice and the promise in his eyes. His arm slipped around her waist, bringing her ever closer, until each breath brought her against the hard plane of his chest. A single finger tilted her mouth toward his, and she watched as moonlight laced shadows across the face that was lowering toward her. She closed her eyes, ready to give all of herself to his kiss, which was sure to be the quintessence of rapture.

Pounding hoofbeats splintered the night's peace. Chloë leapt back so suddenly she would have fallen if Gareth had not put out a hand to steady her. What kind of widgeon was she to go so easily to this man who had professed—from the onset—that he considered women only an enjoyable pastime, nothing to be taken too seriously?

A man rode wildly into the clearing. She shrieked a warning, but Henry pulled her sister out of the way of the madman. The rider leapt to the ground and lurched toward them.

"Moore, where are you?" The slurred words were followed by a drunken laugh.

"Lord Howell!" Chloë clutched Gareth's sleeve and gasped, "You said he would not come, that this was only a jest."

Peeling her fingers off his arm, Gareth stepped past the carriage. "Howell, you are foxed!"

The red-haired baron crowed as he raised a bottle. "I pledged to give this bottle of wine a black eye." He drank deeply and staggered another step forward. "And I have." He tossed the empty bottle to the ground, laughing when it shattered. "Now for the trouncing I promised *you,* Moore."

"Gareth, you had better see your *friend* home," Chloë warned as Lord Howell reached under his coat. What he pulled out flashed in the moonlight. "He is as drunk as an emperor. He will have a fierce case of barrel-fever, if he drinks another bottle—"

"That is no bottle!"

Chloë pressed her hand over her heart which halted in mid-beat. Gareth was not jesting. Lord Howell did not hold a bottle. It was a pistol.

Amaryllis screamed as Lord Howell raised the gun to point it directly at Henry. Her fiancé's face was as pasty as the moon, but wisely he did not move.

"Do something," Chloë whispered as she gripped Gareth's sleeve again. "You started this. You have to end this before someone is hurt."

"What would you have me do? I have no weapon."

"Talk some sense into his upper story!"

"I shall try." Raising his voice, he called, "Jeremy, old friend, have you forgotten what we had planned for tonight?"

"A duel!" Lord Howell shouted. He waved the gun at Henry, who stood as still as the trees around them. "Never let it be said, Moore, that I did not play fair. Get your popper, my friend, and let us settle this question once and for all."

"You have no second, Jeremy," Gareth said in the same

106

calm tone. "Without one, how can you fight a duel?"

The sewed-up man bent over double in a fit of giggles. "True, so sadly true." Straightening, he leveled the pistol at Henry again. "Then I have no choice but to shoot you to redeem my honor."

The cocking of the pistol seemed as loud as Amaryllis' scream. From the corner of her eye, Chloë saw her sister collapse to the ground. She wanted to run to Amaryllis, but could not pull her gaze from the horrible scene before her.

"You will shake a cloth in the wind if you kill Henry like this," Gareth insisted.

The baron hesitated, lowering the gun. Chloë bit her lip to keep from shrieking out her terror. Was the threat of the hangman's noose enough to reach the drunken man?

"You are too in the gun to think clearly. Give me the pistol," Gareth ordered.

"I am not pogy!" He swayed, contradicting his own assertion. With a laugh, he reaimed the gun at Henry.

Gareth leapt forward and seized the baron's wrist, jerking it skyward. The pistol fired. Leaves and branches rained down on them from the trees overhead. Pulling the spent gun from Lord Howell's hand, Gareth swore.

Chloë did not wait for the baron's reply. She ran to where her sister lay on the ground. She knelt and picked up Amaryllis' limp arm. Chafing her sister's wrist, Chloë wished for sal volatile to bring Amaryllis back to her senses.

"I assume you want this."

Chloë choked as an open bottle of smelling salts was held under her nose. Batting Gareth's hand away, she grasped the bottle and carefully wafted it in front of Amaryllis while scowling up at him.

"Henry is unhurt," he said quietly.

"I hope I can say the same for my sister."

His smile was markedly devoid of repentance. "I have found that a swoon—while dramatic—seldom causes any

107

damage to its victim, only to those who witness it."

"Henry could have suffered more damage. How could you be so skimble-skamble as to allow a suck-pint to be part of your intrigue?"

"Howell usually is more prudent when it comes to brandy." Gareth chuckled lowly. "What does it matter? Nobody was hurt."

Amaryllis moaned, but her eyes did not open.

"Get Henry," Chloë ordered. "If she hears his voice, she is sure to waken straightaway."

Calling to his friend, he stepped aside as Henry came to slip his arm beneath Amaryllis' shoulders. Her lashes fluttered prettily against her cheek when she opened her eyes. When Henry whispered her name, she clung to him, weeping.

"More tears," grumbled Gareth under his breath as he walked with Chloë toward the Weymouth carriage.

"Where is Lord Howell?"

"I sent him on his way. Now that his honor is fulfilled, he is probably on his way back to the party to find another bottle to keep him company." He chuckled as he pulled a flask from beneath his coat. Holding it out to her, he said, "You appear to be in need of something to fortify you."

She shook her head. If she drank anything stronger than mulled wine tonight, her stomach was sure to betray her. She was sure she would never get the sight of that gun aimed at Henry from her mind. Furiously she glared at Gareth, but he showed no reaction to her anger. "You should have known he would push about the bottle tonight."

"How was I to guess that Henry—of all people— would infuriate Howell enough so he would make this duel a reality?" Gareth's eyes narrowed as he took a quick drink and made the flask disappear under his coat. "You need not look at me with such shock. I saw your consternation at Cresmere's party. You, too, feared

Henry had taken his rôle too far."

"Then it should have been stopped before anyone could reach the park."

"No," came a fragile voice from behind them. "We had to take this chance to flee from Town."

Chloë spun to see her sister leaning precariously against her betrothed. "Amaryllis, you are going nowhere except home."

"Chloë," began Henry.

"No!" She gave him the same frown she had focused on Gareth. This time she got the desired results, for he nearly cowered as she added, "I shall not condone Amaryllis attempting such a long journey when she can barely stand. If you had the least affection for her—"

Henry squared his shoulders. "I have more than the least affection. She knows that." Wistfulness filled his voice as he looked at his love. "You do know that, don't you, Amaryllis?"

Gareth gave the wobbly woman no chance to answer. "By all that's blue, Henry, which one among us can doubt the *tendre* you have for her? We have lost two nights of good conversation and sleep to trying to help you wed her." He folded his arms over the front of his coat. "However, I must agree with Chloë. Her sister is in no condition to travel. After this *crise de nerfs,* she needs to rest before leaving for Scotland."

"I am fine," Amaryllis argued.

"Nonsense," Gareth returned. Putting his hand under her elbow, he nearly hefted her into the carriage. He silenced Henry's objection by saying, "There will be another opportunity. Mayhap, in the wake of Henry's fervent defense, Weymouth will rethink his dislike for this marriage."

"But Saturday is only two days from now," Amaryllis whispered. "Can Father be persuaded in that amount of time?"

"I leave that to the charms of you and Chloë, Miss

Weymouth." He tipped his hat to her, then handed Chloë into the carriage. Not releasing her fingers, he smiled up into her eyes. "I trust I may call later in this eventful day to determine the next best course of action."

Chloë wanted to tell him that the time for silly schemes was past, but she was caught anew in the warmth of his smile as she imagined those lips against her mouth. When he raised her hand to his lips, her breath caught against her fiercely beating heart. Her eyes closed when he made the common courtesy of kissing her hand a rare rapture as his tongue toyed with the tip of her finger. At his soft farewell, she looked down into his eyes. The flame burning along her skin blazed there, threatening to consume her in its dangerous heat. She wondered if she could resist it much longer . . . or if she wanted to.

"Thank goodness, Lord Abington was ready to come to Henry's rescue," gushed Amaryllis as she sat on the edge of her bed and watched her sister pull the drapes to shut out the brightening light of dawn.

"Yes . . ." Chloë's fingers clenched on the drapes. Gareth *had* been prepared to save his friend. Too prepared it seemed in retrospect, for he had vaulted forward at exactly the right moment to keep Lord Howell from letting the pop fly into Henry. He had hurried the viscount away before Lord Howell could say a word. He even had smelling salts at hand.

She gritted her teeth until her jaw ached. How could she have let Gareth bamblusterate her so completely? It all became clear to her now. He had no wish to see his friend marry up with Amaryllis. In the guise of an accomplice in the alliance against her father, he was doing all he could to play the addle-plot.

And not just this morning! She must not forget that it had been Gareth's idea to abduct her sister as a knight of the pad. So easily he had baffled them—Henry most of all—until Henry had stolen the wrong Weymouth sister.

No, she thought with a pinch of sorrow, Henry had not been the most confused. Chloë Weymouth had.

Gareth had blistered her ears with easy talk while she'd asked questions he avoided answering. Then—and she flushed as she recalled how his touch had elicited such passion from her—he had filled her head with fantasies that meant no more to him than his promise to help his friend.

What a shuttle-head she had been! Gareth had been honest with her from the beginning when he said that he considered marriage an unnatural state for most men. So determined was he to protect his best friend from what he saw as unhappiness, he was undermining every effort to make the elopement a success. She would not swallow Gareth Ogilvie's gudgeon again.

Gareth arrived exactly as the church bells tolled the hour past midday. Yarwood brought him to the garden at the back of the house, where Chloë had sought refuge from her sister's praise for the earl. Standing and brushing her damp palms against her white cambric gown, she raised her head to look past the broad brim of her leghorn bonnet.

Her heart seemed to have forgotten how to beat regularly as she stared at the man who could not claim Lord Islen's good looks or even Henry's sincerity. Yet she found herself admiring how his dark brown riding coat clung to his broad shoulders and how his leather riding breeches followed the strength of his legs into his boots.

She fought the enchantment as she greeted him. When he motioned toward the back of the garden, she nodded. No one else needed to hear what they said, although it mattered little, for she had no interest in what nonsense he might spout today. If only she could stop thinking of how wondrous his lips had been against her hand . . .

Gareth paused on the gravel path and looked back at the house. Tapping his finger against the cleft in his chin, he smiled. "Perhaps we have been making this too complicated."

"Perhaps *we* have."

He chuckled at her sharp answer and put his arm around her shoulders. Although Chloë stiffened, he must not have noticed as he said, "The trite way might be the most effective. Darkness, a ladder, a waiting carriage, and two sweethearts on their way to Scotland." He pointed to the window to the far right. "Your sister's room?"

"The middle one," she answered, then clamped her teeth on her lip to silence the rest of her answer. She was a sap if she thought Gareth was any more sincere now than he had been during the past week.

"Then all it will want doing is to have Henry bring a ladder into the garden tonight. While your father is at his club this evening, Henry can scamper up to retrieve his heart's desire, and he and Amaryllis can sneak away." He offered her a smile. "What can be more simple? And that is what you want, isn't it?"

Chloë lowered her eyes. If she let herself become beguiled by his grin again, she might allow herself to believe he truly wished to see his friend reach Gretna Green. She longed to demand that he explain why he was twisting them all about in this game he so clearly enjoyed. She must not, however, for then she would reveal that she was no longer bamblusterated by his out-and-outers.

"What do you say to that plan, Chloë?" he asked when she remained silent.

Blinking back tears as she heard the enthralling sound of her name on his lips, she squared her shoulders and raised her eyes to meet his. "I think, Gareth, that I can see where this plan may finally succeed where the others have failed."

Her heart threatened to splinter anew when he squeezed

112

her shoulders and laughed. She dreaded what would happen when he discovered that *he* was the one being deluded.

The late twilight of June wafted along George Street, and shadows crept from beneath the portico of St. George's Church. Chloë watched as Henry handed Amaryllis' last bag to his coachee to store in the boot of the carriage that would take them to Scotland.

Amaryllis said, "But, Chloë, I do not understand. I thought Gareth was to bring a ladder to our house, so that Henry could climb up to my room and sweep me away like a knight rescuing his lady in days of yore."

"There has been a change in plans," she said as she looked to where a nervous Henry was wringing his hands.

"But Lord Abington expects us to—"

"Never mind what he expects." Chloë kissed her sister swiftly and offered Henry a feeble smile. "Hurry away, so I can get back to the Square before Father comes home." Tears stung her eyes and anxiety clogged her throat as she whispered, "Have a safe journey, and come back soon."

Henry handed Amaryllis into the carriage, then turned to Chloë. More than once, he started to speak. His lips twisted, but no words emerged.

"Go safely, and hurry home," Chloë said as she stood on tiptoe to kiss Henry's pudgy cheek.

He colored as bright as his waistcoat. Scrambling into the carriage, he pulled the door closed behind him as the coachman leapt into the box. Chloë motioned for the coachee to get them underway, then stepped back on the walkway to watch it roll along the street toward the road north.

She clasped her hands in front of her, suddenly feeling empty. The impossible had been achieved, yet no sense of triumph delighted her.

Too late, she understood why her sister had been weeping the day Chloë allowed herself to become entangled in Lord Abington's insidious plot. Amaryllis had been mourning the loss of her father's trust—something she had thought would never be betrayed. Father had broken Amaryllis' heart as surely as Gareth had shattered Chloë's by playing her for the fool. She would not let him do so again.

The church bells were ringing midnight before Chloë stopped pacing the floor of her bedchamber. No tears dampened her cheeks, for they all had fallen hours before in the fierce heat of her pain. Although she should be joyous, for it was too late for Father to halt Amaryllis from marrying Henry, she had never been more melancholy. She had not realized—until she had vowed Gareth must be put out of her life—how much a part of it he had become.

She climbed into bed for the fourth time and pulled the coverlet over her. Sleep had failed to reach her the previous times, and she harbored scanty hope that she would fall asleep now. What a stupe she had been! Now she must pay the price for believing in a man who had twisted her heart with his easy patter.

Hearing the sound of hoofbeats from the back garden, Chloë jumped from bed and pulled on her wrapper. She could delay telling Father the truth no longer. Although she had hoped he would stay late at his club, she would be glad to have this chore completed. He would rail at her, and she would listen to his temper without comment. She deserved his fury.

She went to the door of her room, then heard something thump against the back wall. Hurrying to the window overlooking the garden, she threw it open. Tendrils of damp fog slipped in, but she paid it no mind as a form appeared from the mist.

"Gareth!"

Silently he climbed over the window with the ease of a lad scaling an apple tree. With the black cloak he had worn when he pretended to be a highwayman swirling about him like malevolent wings, he closed the drapes behind him. The room fell into deep shadow, which emphasized every stern line of his face.

His easy smile had vanished, and she could believe, as she had refused to before, that he and the Dark Prince were one and the same. When his gaze moved over her in a slow, sinuous path that stroked every inch of her, she pulled her wrapper closer to her chin. The corner of his lips tipped as his tawny eyes glistened with the eagerness of a cat about to pounce on its prey.

She took a step back from the window. He countered, and she moved away again, not taking her eyes from him. His very silence was menacing, and she recalled his suppressed fury when Howell had nearly shot his best friend. Lord Abington might enjoy playing the jester, but the real man was as intense as the fire in his eyes.

"What are you doing here?" she whispered, wanting to break the silence, but unable to speak louder. "If someone saw you —"

"To perdition with your blasted reputation. You worry too much about it. I came to help your sister elope with Henry." When she started to answer, he held up his black-gloved hands. "No, you need not tell me more bangers, Chloë. Imagine my surprise when I gave Henry a look-in less than an hour past and discovered that he was gone." He advanced upon her, forcing her to take another step toward her bed, as he drew off his gloves. He folded them over his belt as he added, "Gone to Gretna Green, Henry's man told me."

"No thanks to you," she returned, but her voice quavered when his hand settled on her arm. She tried to shrug it off to no avail. His smile returned as she balked when he tried to tug her toward him.

"No, I assume their flight was due totally to your assistance. You are quite single-minded in your determination to help your sister marry the man of her dreams."

"As determined as you were to see their plans come to naught."

"Henry is my friend," he said as he pulled her to his waistcoat that was cool with the night air. "I would not see him blindly leave his bachelor days behind him."

She took a deep breath to remonstrate with him, but released it in a gasp as the motion caused her to brush against him. Aware of her *déshabillé* and his admiration of it, she said in a strangled voice, "You did your best to give him a chance to change his mind. He didn't."

"Perfect block that he is, he is bent on having your sister for his own." His gaze drilled her. "And that, my dear Chloë, was why I suggested this uncomplicated method of his eloping with your sister. A climb up the ladder to her room, a climb down, and off they go to delight in their soon-to-be wedded bliss."

"You wished to help him? That is amusing, my lord."

He pressed her even closer, until she was sure he must be aware of every inch of her form. "I own to being amazed that Henry took it upon himself to deceive me, but then I realized 'twas you, not he, who conceived this plan to hoax me."

"If you know the truth, then why are you here?"

He shrugged, his cloak slapping her arm. With another rumble of laughter, he untied it from his neck and let it fall to the floor. "I wanted to see if my plan would have succeeded in its very simplicity."

"Amaryllis does not sleep in here." Heat warmed her face as she spoke so candidly of such private matters. Taking a steadying breath, she hurried on, "I told you her room was the window in the middle."

"But yours is the one to the right of the garden. This is where you spend your nights dreaming of the man who would bring passion into your life as Henry has done for your sister. It is time, Chloë, for you to make those

116

dreams come true."

She quivered as his hand swept up her back, pinning her to his firm chest. Boldly his fingers entangled in her hair, and he tipped her mouth under his. She stared up into his eyes which glittered like twin gems and saw the challenge there. Not once, in the few days she had known him, had Gareth made anything simple for her. Not even now when she knew his lips ached for hers. Yet the decision was hers, as it always had been.

She allowed her fingers to rest upon his strong arms, then brought them up along his broad shoulders, till she felt the back of his collar and the nape of his neck. Her breath was shallow beneath her throbbing heartbeat as she touched his skin, which was deliciously damp from the exertion of his efforts to reach her room.

When his finger brushed the half circle of her ear, she closed her eyes to savor the heated whirlwind swirling through her. He whispered her name and captured her mouth. She felt his hunger on his lips, the desperate hunger of a man who has been denied too long and refuses to be denied any longer. His arms cradled her, but lured her from her safe world to one afire with passions she had never known.

"Chloë!"

She started to spin out of Gareth's embrace as she stared at her father's shocked face. Gareth halted her by keeping his arms around her.

"Father, I—"

Fiercely her father snapped, "I welcomed you into my home, my lord, when you saved my daughter."

"And told me that she would welcome me to call any time." Gareth smiled without humor. "I took you at your word, sir."

"You twisted my words to do your bidding. Little did I guess that you safeguarded her reputation from that knight of the pad only so you could destroy it."

"Father, please—"

117

"She was in no danger that night," Gareth said in a tone that was as even as if he was speaking of the day's weather.

"No danger? Those highwaymen could have—" Her father interrupted himself. His hands fisted at his sides as he gasped, "You! It was you and Moore, wasn't it? You thought you could steal both of my daughters from me. Let me give you fair warning. You shall not succeed."

Again Chloë tried to step toward her father. When Gareth's arm slipped around her waist to keep her from moving, she looked from his grim expression to her father's scowl. In a near whisper, she said, "Father, Amaryllis and Henry are on their way across the border to be wed."

"What?" he roared.

"Father, Henry will make her happy. She loves him with all her heart, and he loves her."

"And with the inheritance he receives upon his marriage, Henry Moore will give Amaryllis Weymouth Moore a very luxurious life." Gareth cocked a dark brow as his lip curled in a cool smile. "You had no idea, Weymouth? Henry Moore's maternal grandmother was the Duchess of Mayfield."

"That I knew."

"As you knew that when her daughter—Henry's mother—wed Lord Pennet, who quickly lost every penny brought into the marriage, she disowned her." If possible, Gareth's voice became even more frigid. "Did you know as well that the duchess made certain that the youngest child of her only daughter would have plump pockets once he reached an age where he could be trusted not to gamble it all away as his father did?"

Chloë knew her father's amazement was mirrored on her face. Neither Henry nor Amaryllis had mentioned this inheritance to her. She wondered if her sister was aware of the truth, for Amaryllis found a secret as hard to keep hidden as her love for Henry. Perhaps Gareth had

118

been right. There could be more depth to Henry Moore than any of them had guessed.

"Be that as it may," Weymouth stated, unwilling to let defeat encompass him, "you have gone against my wishes, Chloë, in helping them marry. Worse, you have welcomed a man into your private chambers." He strode across the room and tried to pull her away from Gareth. When the taller man did not release her, Weymouth's eyes grew even more round.

Quietly Gareth said, "It will do none of us any good to stretch Chloë's arms until she looks like an African monkey."

"What does it matter how she looks?" Frustration burned in her father's voice. "Who would have her now when you have assured that she is ruined?"

"I would."

"You would?" gasped Chloë, ignoring her father who echoed her words.

Gareth turned her so that she faced him. His broad hands encircled her face as he tilted her head so her gaze met his. Again the quiver soared through her when she saw the fierce longing in his eyes. "I would."

"I thought you considered marriage a trap for leatherheads."

"It is." A smile quirked his lips. "But the church is reserved, and I have a special license with our names on it in my pocket." He laughed softly as he drew her into his arms again. "And, as caper-witted as it may sound, I love you, Chloë."

"I love you, too," she whispered, delighted to be speaking the truth she had tried to ignore.

"Then say you do want to marry me."

"I do." Chloë smiled as Gareth grimaced when she repeated the words he had vowed never to speak, the words he had uttered only seconds before. With her hand on his arm and his fingers stroking hers as the rest of the marriage ceremony was spoken at the altar of St. George's, she still found it difficult to believe the complex series of events that had brought her to this moment.

Her father had given his blessing on the match once he had discovered Gareth was sincere. Still reeling from the news that both his daughters had made excellent matches, his grin had been nonstop.

The pastor spoke the final benediction and stepped back. Gareth lifted Chloë's veil as he gently pulled her against him. The grand organ burst into song, and his mouth caressed hers, speaking silently of the glorious delights awaiting them. When he drew away—far too soon—she was sure her heart would drown in the flood of happiness.

Together they turned to see their delighted guests. Few people had expected to see the day when Lord Abington would set aside his determination to keep his life uncomplicated by love, so all of his friends—save Henry Moore—had descended on the church to watch. With her hand tucked in Gareth's as they walked past the altar rail to the checkered floor, Chloë gasped when she saw two familiar forms at the rear of the church.

Amaryllis Weymouth Moore stood with her arm through her new husband's. Glittering on her third finger, as she raised it to wipe away the tears rolling along her cheeks, was a jeweled wedding band.

"By all that's blue," muttered Gareth.

"What is wrong now?" Chloë smiled at his fierce frown, which she now knew was only a jest.

"After all we went through to get them leg-shackled so there would be an end of your sister piping her eyes, look at her! Watering her plants as if she was broken-hearted anew." He put a single finger under Chloë's chin and tilted her face toward him as they reached the first row of pews facing the altar. "Promise me one more thing, my love. Do not become a wet-goose like your sister."

"And if I do?"

"I might have to think of some way to put an end to your tears." The mischievous glint brightened his eyes. "Nothing complicated, you must realize. Something terribly simple. Like this." He pulled her into his arms and kissed her with every bit of the love she had dreamed would be theirs.

*Miss Durham's
Indiscretion
by Marissa Edwards*

A couple stood, outlined against the hearth fire in the private parlor of the Dog and Duck, a pleasure gardens located happily enough just outside London and made fashionable of late by those of the *ton* who considered that they set the trends—be they in hats, gardens, or the new plum comfits it was all the rage at present to serve one's guests after dinner.

As is frequently the case, their older and more staid peers had declared the features of this same gardens to be cast in the shade when one compared them to the entertainments of the fashionable Covent Garden or Kew Gardens. These peers went further, if pressed, to describe the Dog and Duck with a distasteful moue and a roll of the eyes. The word *fast* was often also heard to adorn their description.

After desiring to know—impertinently—as the young always do, in what fashion their elders had come by this knowledge had they not stopped at the gardens in question, the younger set was all the more determined to visit the gardens themselves. For all this—the rumors, the moues, the curiosity—had contrived to assure the momentary fortune of the Dog and Duck, basking in the ephemeral favor of the aristocracy, until such time as another unfamiliar, intriguing rendezvous displaced it.

Rendezvous, however, that are entertaining for being risqué in the daytime, frequently cross an indefinable line near twilight and turn from being merely risqué to being decidedly seamy as well as dangerous.

This line Caro Durham had crossed.

She could have gone home when most of her crowd gathered up shawls and hats preparatory to leaving. And *almost* she had gone . . . almost.

But the wine they had all sipped during the afternoon had clouded her thinking and made her feel more daring and rebellious than she might have felt had she been of a more sober mind. Then, too, she had seen what she would be returning to — or, rather, what she would not be returning to — as she had waved off her good friend Sara, concern written plainly on her face, and could not bear the thought of it. At that moment, anything had seemed preferable.

Sara returned to a house full of light and warmth and people. During Caro's stays with Sara's family, she had loved even the arguing and bickering which had broken out at the dinner table at least once each time she had visited, between Sara and her brothers and sisters. On the last visit, Lord Alvinly, Sara's father, had only made her laugh as he had thumped his silver knife handle for quiet, eyed the row of children on either side of his table with exasperation, and asked if all the wits would please confine their remarks to polite dinner conversation — which did not include, the last he had heard, judgments on another person's conduct or appearance. Then someone — Sara? — had whispered, "At least not when they are present!" The children had united in howling with laughter, bickering forgotten; Lady Alvinly had been surprised into laughing aloud, and even Lord Alvinly had had to hide a smile behind his napkin before he thumped his knife again. Just so, when Sara returned from the Dog and Duck — no matter that some of the questions, and answers, might be phrased to goad — people were going to be agog to hear where she had been.

Caro would be returning to her uncle's, the Duke of Seward's, town house to sup with Lady Burton, her companion and chaperone. She was assuredly an attractive, pleasant woman, but one who kept her interests her own. In the face of her aloofness, Caro did not make free with her own thoughts. She would, of course, tell Lady Burton about her day, and Lady Burton would naturally reciprocate. They would maintain a correct, polite, and in the main superficial conversation throughout supper. Then they would remove to the sitting room. With just the two of them in the front of the house, though her uncle did not seem to begrudge them candles, there would be no need—indeed, it would be wasteful—to burn them in any rooms save the dining room and the sitting room. It was so with the fires as well, though certainly her uncle did not begrudge them wood either. Thus, Caro always thought of her own home as dark and rather cold and empty.

For her uncle would be out—at his club or pursuing, late though it were, some business interest. On occasion, he did dine with them at home, but, truth to tell, Caro did not prefer those occasions.

Though she supposed he loved her as his brother's only child, since he had had the care of her he had never manifested any particular affection for her beyond being pleasant and civil to her, exactly as he was to Lady Burton.

Her father had died eight years ago. He had contracted the influenza in Rome on one of the many trips he made collecting and trading the mysterious ancient marbles that were the passion of his life. Her mother had died in childbirth.

One might have supposed the death of her father to make a difference in her life. In fact, she felt her protector, merely, had changed. For her father and her uncle were very like in choler. She saw her uncle about as often as she had seen her father—which was to say, little—and was left by her uncle to the chaperonage and companionship of Lady Burton, as she had been left by her father to the care and instruction of her nanny and later her governess.

She had understood from her father's will that she was to go to her uncle, with whom she was little acquainted—and, in truth, knew little better eight years later—until she married. On her marriage, provided that occurred before the age of twenty-five, she would inherit half of her father's, apparently large, holdings. The other half would be divided between her uncle, in gratitude one assumed for the protection of her until that day the office passed to another, and the British Museum, earmarked for the further excavation and preservation of her father's beloved marbles. Should she remain unmarried on her twenty-fifth birthday, however, the entire fortune went to the British Museum.

Wryly, Caro had concluded that, Roman marbles notwithstanding, her father must have been a great believer in the institution of marriage to so blatantly motivate both herself and her uncle toward her own marriage. Therein lay the point of tension that had developed between her uncle and herself in recent years.

He, she felt, also genuinely believed marriage the best future for her and had called her into his library on the occasion of every offer made her—for she had not been without offers—to coldly deride what he called "the fast set" it looked to him she went about with and to urge her to accept the offer and settle down, her future secured. "My dear, you will end with your reputation in shreds, and then where will you be? Even your inheritance will not make you palatable." This dispassionate pronouncement seemed to Caro to be his favorite end to these unpleasant interviews. But he had not forbidden her to see her friends. Nor had he curtailed her actions in any way. Both of which she was well aware he could have done, and she was thankful and appreciative that he had not. These feelings made her the more uncomfortable for doubting his motivation, but still the doubt was there. She was never certain, on leaving his library, exactly how much, if any, of his concern was colored by an interest in his portion of the inheritance.

Her uncle, however, she acknowledged, had the right of it. Her future lay in her marriage. She did him the credit to believe he would not turn her out into the streets, even if she wished away the inheritance. But the thought of living the rest of her life with Lady Burton for companion and with her civil, dispassionate uncle depressed her so that she could scarcely think. And at twenty-three, she knew her time was flying. Eventually—soon, rather—she would have to choose someone, and, almost, it would not matter whom.

If she had allowed herself to examine why she had not accepted one of the offers made her, she might have discovered that she feared in accepting any of those gentlemen merely to duplicate the household she resided in. What she truly wanted, in some remote, ideal part of her heart, was a gentleman with whom she could feel even the smallest rapport, some bit, some spark of humor or playfulness, on which some sort of a mutual respect and true affection — she did not think she required an Adonis — might be built.

Such a respect or rapport she had yet to feel for any gentleman. And soon, she knew she would choose a cold household in which she presided as mistress as preferable to remaining in such a household as dependent. Hence, she threw herself into the excitement of setting trends, lived for the entertainment of the moment, and tried her best to forget the marriage she was going to have to contract, voluntarily.

Thus, when she had seen, on waving goodbye that afternoon, the contrast between returning to her uncle's town house and returning to Sara's home, which had people — and therefore need of candles and fires — in almost every room in the house, she had turned her back easily on her departing friends with, one might have said, the gayest of laughs and rejoined those who remained. Indeed, the harder task for her at that moment would have been to have departed.

She moved away from the hearth in the Dog and Duck, shaking off the hand of the gentleman who stood beside her. "Don't, Lord Macomb. I asked you before supper to forgo your lovemaking.

"Now please, if you will not call for your carriage, I shall. You know as well as I we should have left before supper, as I suggested. The others have very likely returned home long since."

Lord Macomb, Earl of Rochester, put his foot upon the

grate and remained where he was. "My dear Caro, I fear I have no carriage."

Caro fixed him with an irritated stare. "Please do not be nonsensical, Lord Macomb. I saw you drive up here this afternoon with Lord Meryl, Lady Alison, and Lady Margaret. What were you riding upon then, pray—one of Aladdin's flying carpets?"

Lord Macomb gave a polite cough. "I allowed Meryl the use of my carriage before supper to convey the ladies home."

After a moment of stunned silence, in which Caro realized she had grossly misjudged Lord Macomb's character, eyes flashing, she pronounced, " 'Tis no matter. I shall merely hire a carriage from the owner of this establishment and convey myself home. Please do not exert yourself!"

She swept toward the parlor door, angrily berating herself for being the greatest fool the Lord Almighty had ever created, turned the knob, and yanked the door open.

In the same moment, Lord Macomb's arm grazed her curls as it shot by her head to push the door shut again and hold it so. "I fear you still do not quite understand, Caro," he remarked softly. He bent to place a light, warm kiss on her neck. "Hellraiser's Club and all that, you know."

An icy chill of fear ran down her spine, and her heart began to beat loudly in her ears. "I begin to perceive," she said slowly, feeling his warm breath on her neck and studying the fine-grained pattern in the wood of the door.

In a voice devoid of emotion, she observed, "I thought that tale of you merely a rumor. Is it a bet then?"

He placed another kiss on her earlobe and chuckled. "Lord no, my dear. It took no bet—I've scarcely been able to think of anything else since I first saw you whipping up Harding's grays to race The Ring in Hyde Park."

He removed his arm from the door and pulled her around to face him. "Which you won by a good horse-length, as you well know," he said and took her mouth, pressing her back against the parlor door. The door banged

130

softly as the latch struck what it should have been turned to fit into, but neither noticed.

He released her mouth. "You may have it just as you wish, my dear Caro," he murmured, his dark eyes smoldering into hers. "Without a struggle, as my favorite mistress would have it, or you may fight me every step of the way. I will only gag you then — for I have learned I cannot endure screaming — and we will make a rough, bawdy time of it."

"How could I have been so deceived in you! You are nought but a, a—" Caro shoved him away and delivered a resounding slap.

The parlor door, as her body came away from it, and as old doors are wont to do, fell open a crack.

"Vile toad!"

Miles Grayson, Marquess of Strathmore, passing outside the door at that moment, paused, arrested midstair on his uncertain way up to his room for some urgent reason he could not now remember.

He turned, expecting to see the owner of the sultry, intense voice he had just heard standing at the foot of the stairs, and thought fleetingly of taking exception to the epithet he assumed had been directed at him. Whatever transgression he was guilty of, he did not believe it could have been serious enough to have earned him either "vile" or "toad."

"My uncle will kill you for this, and I shall take great pleasure in watching him do so!"

Wonderfully, for the marquess was decidedly in his cups, he looked around himself and discovered the parlor door as the entrance to a room he had not hitherto noticed and the source of the expressive speaker's voice. "Ah," he told himself wisely, eyeing the crack, and came down a step.

Ponderously, he considered what someone could have done to deserve killing. To his mind, very few transgressions fell into that category of retribution. Illogically, he also wondered if the unseen speaker were half as attractive as her sultry voice led him to believe she might be and came down another two stairs.

"Your uncle, my dear Caro, will merely believe that you have at last gone one step too far with your 'fast set of friends' and landed yourself squarely in the briars."

The marquess heard Caro gasp.

"Oh yes, I know what your uncle thinks. Do you take me for a fool?

"We can speak of this evening after tonight if you like, but I guarantee our stories will not be the same.

"Whose story do you think your uncle will believe?"

He has bet all her pin money on the cock fight and backed the loser! guessed the marquess. No, no, no. He shook his head. Her accents had been those of a lady. No lady would have been at the cock fight he had just witnessed. They did not attend such things. Indeed, he wished he had not been there himself.

He ran a hand distractedly through his chestnut hair and wondered why he had allowed his friends to talk him into coming when he knew he did not care for the sport. "Sport, hah!" he muttered. He wished heartily he had remained at Brooks's to be bored by the shockingly low stakes he had considered them to be playing for that evening. He believed he would rather feel bored than disgusted with himself, as he was now beginning to feel.

That thought made him remember he had been on his way to meet his man, Jeeves, in his room and gather his things and depart, having no desire to see the next cock fight. Let his friends think he had hared off, disgruntled over the size of the bet he'd lost on the last match. If they were better friends of his, they'd know he had never caviled over the loss of a bet or the turn of a card in his life—no matter what the amount. And, assuredly, he had lost more before than he'd lost tonight. That was just the way the wheel of fortune went round: Some nights one lost, other nights one won. In his experience, the sums eventually balanced themselves out. If they did not, one reduced one's gambling and betting accordingly. He was not about to be one of those fools who lost everything to a bet or on the turn of a card.

He realized that the sultry-voiced Caro was speaking again.

". . . walking about like the veriest gentleman, and you are nothing more than the greatest, vilest toa—Oh!"

"Consider how many people saw us together here this afternoon. Whose story do you think they will believe? And you weren't fighting me then, Caro, eh?"

The marquess heard a muffled cry and the tear of clothing. Whether to convince himself he still had noble instincts or merely to assuage his noble instincts outraged by the brutality of the cock fight, or whether to satisfy his curiosity about the attractive voice's owner, the marquess covered the remaining stairs and sauntered through the parlor door.

" 'Tis a pity, I think, to stop such a lovely voice as must, I am convinced, belong to this beautiful lady," he complained. "And, if I may be allowed to note, in such a churlish fashion," he deplored, eyeing the handkerchief that went round the lady's mouth and disappeared into the golden brown tresses that tumbled from what once must have been a neat coiffure. Neither did his eyes miss the sleeve of the lady's dress, torn and dangling from the side of her gown to reveal one smooth white shoulder. "Your servant, my lord, I'm sure," he finished ironically.

It took the couple several seconds to realize his presence and cease struggling. When they did, the gentleman took advantage of the opportunity thus afforded him to force the lady within the circle of his arm, keeping his grip on both her wrists.

"This is none of your affair, sir. The lady is my wife. Be pleased to concern yourself elsewhere!"

Caro shook her head vehemently, her dark blue eyes pleading for the marquess' help.

The marquess' eyebrows rose disbelievingly. His lip curled. There was no question in his mind that if he accepted the lie and left, the slender woman before him, tall though she was, would be no match for the robust brute who held her.

To see such a beautiful woman—even more beautiful than her voice—pinioned thus made the marquess want to grip the man by the throat and pummel him senseless.

With difficulty, he restrained his mounting anger. "The lady does not appear to agree with you," he said softly.

Hope flooded the dark blue eyes.

"Go back to your tankards, man!" snarled the earl.

The marquess' eyes glinted. "I believe I must ask you to release her."

The lady struggled suddenly, surprising her captor, and wrenched herself free with a gasp, whisking herself into the proximity of her benefactor.

Intelligent chit, that, thought the marquess admiringly, as he noted that she stayed outside arm's reach of himself. After all, she does not know that I wouldn't do just what this fellow has done.

Lord Macomb's eyes narrowed. "To be sure, you will meet me for this, sirrah!" he grated.

The marquess inclined his head. "Most certainly."

"I think not," came a cold voice. "If I hear of any duel between the two of you after this night, I will have whoever should live through it, injured or no, shipped into the heart of the French countryside and imprisoned there until he would not be recognized here."

All three heads snapped to see the large, black-caped figure of the Duke of Seward looming in the doorway. He and the heavyset, black-liveried man standing beside him each held a deadly looking pistol, trained on the two gentlemen before them.

"Uncle!"

The Earl of Rochester saw at once that the trap he had so painstakingly set to net Caro had just closed on himself instead. His mind racing with explanations logical enough to buy his freedom, he considered the possibilities of implicating the fool that had allowed his ladybird to struggle free.

The Marquess of Strathmore coolly observed the duke and Caro's unhappy reaction. Satisfied that he had rescued her from her first attacker, he wondered if he shouldn't have to protect her from her own uncle as well, so forbidding did that gentleman appear.

The duke's eyes traveled slowly from his disheveled niece to the supper table, still with the plates from the repast and half a carafe of wine upon it, to Lord Macomb, to the marquess.

"It would seem, Caroline, you have at last found yourself in a rather unsavory situation," the duke remarked, his eyes alighting on her exposed shoulder.

Caro, blushing furiously, ineffectually fumbled to pull her torn sleeve back into place. "Uncle, truly, it appears much worse—"

"I did warn you, my dear.

"Gentlemen." He bowed ironically to Lord Macomb and the Marquess of Strathmore. "Allow me to introduce myself. I am the Duke of Seward.

"I offer you my felicitations, though only one of you need accept them. For, as soon as the parson arrives and my man returns with the information I require, one of you shall wed my niece—"

"No, Uncle!" gasped Caro with a look of horror.

"You're raving!" exclaimed the earl, glancing uneasily from pistol to pistol.

The marquess, noting Caro's reaction with humor, merely raised a surprised eyebrow and continued to regard the duke with interest. Thus far, he had proved high drama.

"I assure you, my lord, I am quite sane."

"How did you know to come, Uncle?" asked Caro, somewhat bitterly the marquess thought.

"You may thank Miss Alvinly for her concern for your reputation."

"Oh, Sara!" Caro grimaced and bit her lip to stop the rest of the words of vexation she might have uttered. She knew Sara had meant well, but she could not see that her friend's good intentions had done anything but harm. She did acknowledge inwardly that she had no idea how she would have prevented the two gentlemen from dueling, nor stilled the resulting rumors and gossip that would have accompanied the injury or—she shuddered—death of one of the two. But, whatever the imbroglio, her uncle's knowledge of it and his arrival, in her view, only worsened matters enormously.

The marquess, observing uncle and niece, remarked their interchange. Its brevity and absence of endearments or compassion spoke volumes. The chit's evident chagrin and annoyance, where he might have expected relief or gratitude, he also found telling.

The earl objected insolently, "This grows tedious, Duke. You really cannot hope to induce me, at least, to marry Caro, delectable though she may be." Attempting to brazen his way out, he started for the door, heard the cocking of both pistols, and halted abruptly.

Forestalling the retort hot on Caro's lips, the duke replied coldly, "Gently, my lord. Should you be her choice, I would hate to make my niece a widow . . . ere she is wed."

Several loud knocks were heard.

"That would be Fields, with the parson, one hopes, for everyone's sake," remarked the duke. "Please see to the door, Caroline."

Caro, awkwardly holding the pieces of her sleeve in place, went to open the door.

"Here we are, here we are. Always happy to oblige for a wedding—yes, always happy for a wedding, even if circumstances seem a trifle peculiar.

"Oh my!" A short, plump gentleman in the garb of a country parson entered, followed by a large man dressed in the duke's black livery. The parson was brought up short as his quick little eyes took in and darted from Caro's disheveled hair and the tatters of her sleeve to the pistols trained calmly on the two gentlemen standing opposite the duke and his man.

Fields, the duke's second man, shut the parlor door with an audible click and crossed to his lord's side, beginning to speak quietly into his ear. Several times he looked in the direction of either the earl or the marquess as he spoke.

"What in heaven's name is going on here?" demanded

the parson. "My lord, this looks very havey-cavey, very havey-cavey indeed! I do hope you do not expect me to marry anyone who does not wish to get married, for I couldn't do that, my lord. Really, I could not!"

He looked dubiously from Caro to the earl to the marquess. "I own, I am a trifle shocked, my lord!"

"One moment longer, Parson, if you please," commanded the duke.

Caro, thinking the little man appeared more than a good deal shocked, despite the gravity of her own situation could not repress a tremulous smile as she followed his outraged gaze from the earl to the marquess.

Her eyes met the amused hazel gaze of the Marquess of Strathmore. He, she gathered, had also been observing the parson's outrage.

In the moment it took them to acknowledge their mutual, and inappropriate, amusement, Caro was struck by the marquess' appearance, which she had previously been too preoccupied to notice. His dark brown hair was attractively mussed, as if he had run his hand through it several times, and his amused hazel eyes held kindness behind their amusement. The dark blue superfine coat and buff breeches fit him to perfection, betraying no flaw or padding in the well-proportioned, muscular physique they outlined.

She thought fleetingly, as she inadvertently compared it to Lord Macomb's physique, beginning to show a slight paunch and a touch of dissolution, that the marquess would have come out the winner of any duel the two fought. Indeed, his whole air of easy assurance, evident in even the little he had said thus far, made her almost certain of it.

She dropped her gaze and, annoyingly, blushed.

Fields stopped speaking into the duke's ear and stood aside, impassive.

"Now, gentlemen, we come to terms. Parson, be pleased to hear and judge that I give a choice of alternatives only and that the gentlemen choose freely.

137

"I shall be brief, and I shall begin with you, Earl of Rochester. I tell you frankly, judging by what my man has gleaned of you and your reputation, that I suspect you of machinations that culminated in my niece's downfall this evening. Moreover, I do not believe it is the first time you have manipulated such a scenario—merely the first time you have, perhaps, been caught out in it.

"Please," the duke held up his hands as the earl started to expostulate. "Spare me your denials. The evening, as you have already remarked, grows overtedious."

He turned to the marquess. "Between the two of you, I believe my niece would do better to choose to wed the Marquess of Strathmore here. He I believe to have some measure of human kindness—sadly lacking in you and your fellow Hellraisers—if my niece can only forbear to interfere with his penchant to gamble and lose."

The marquess' eyes glinted a moment at this before he covered his anger with a lazy smile.

The duke addressed his niece. "More than this to sway your decision, I'll not say, Caroline."

He looked back to the two gentlemen. "As I am fairly certain you know, Earl, and as you, Marquess, may or may not know, my niece will come into a sizable inheritance on her marriage. Naturally, her dowry may be expected to reflect that."

"One wonders if you, Duke, might also be expected to benefit from your niece's marriage?" sneered the earl. "How well are your stocks and investments doing these days, eh?" He laughed.

The duke's only response was a tightening of his jawline. "Choose, Caroline!"

"I will not be bartered or traded, Uncle, like a pound of tea or a good mare! I do not desire a husband!"

"Think again, Caroline—carefully," the duke replied coldly. "If you choose to remain unmarried, your reputation cannot withstand the kind of rumors that will attach to this evening.

"When these rumors become known, as rest assured they

will, you will be accepted in very few houses—you cannot like that."

He sighed with exasperation as he observed the stubborn set of her face and took another tack. He motioned Fields to take up his position and then circled Caro slowly, lowering his voice. " 'Twill be little over a year hence before you must needs make this decision, will it not? You are on the very threshold of twenty-four. Have you any gentlemen in mind?"

Caro's head snapped up, and her dark blue eyes locked with her uncle's black ones.

"No. I thought as much. You will be forced to choose then very much as you are tonight, will you not?"

Refusing to acknowledge his home thrust, Caro averted her face.

"Save that, with the rumor of this night attached to your name, a year hence you will not even have the choice of two, for no gentleman will have you.

"I urge you: choose while you may."

Caro's shoulders drooped, a subtle admission of the truth of the duke's arguments.

She threw up her head and regarded the Earl of Rochester. "Very well, Uncle."

The earl looked back at her stonily.

There could be no question of marrying him after his treatment of her.

Her eyes traveled to the Marquess of Strathmore. Of necessity then, it must be he.

The marquess, having witnessed the earl's brutality, also understood that she had no choice. Indeed, he did not believe he could have left the parlor knowing her about to be shackled to the brute and thus at his mercy for the rest of her life.

He started toward Caro with the idea of taking her hand and raising it to his lips, but hastily stepped back into place as he, too, heard the cocking of both pistols. "Apologies! My apologies, gentlemen." He gave a resigned smile and made an elegant leg where he stood.

Regarding Caro steadily—taking in her luxuriant honey brown hair, streaked with gold, her dark blue eyes, and her well-shaped, slender figure—he said formally, "Your niece would do me a great honor, my lord, if she would consent to become my wife."

He saw astonishment, then gratitude, flash through the dark blue eyes.

"Very prettily done, Marquess," sneered the Earl of Rochester. "One must guess the duns to be close on your heels, indeed!"

The marquess ignored him and continued to regard Caro steadily.

Caro returned his look and remembered their moment of humor. "Thank you, my lord. I accept your kind offer," she answered huskily.

She turned to the duke and the parson. "Let us have it done and over with."

"Fields, Campbell, kindly see that the earl gets safely started on his way home," commanded the duke.

"Don't trouble yourself, Duke. I assure y—"

"Good evening, my lord," interrupted the duke as Fields and Campbell each took hold of one of the earl's arms. "I am certain I do not need to mention to you how displeased I should be to learn you are spreading any type of rumor concerning my niece's precipitate love match—the more vicious because you were yourself enamored of her, and she would not have you."

The earl flushed.

"You take my point, I see. Good.

"I should dislike having to repeat the exceptionally sordid and pathetic little tale of one Lady Jane Courtland's drowning."

The earl started and then paled.

"Yes, just so. Fields. Campbell."

The duke's men roughly hurried the earl from the room.

The duke turned to the parson. "Now, Parson, we may begin, may we not?

"You have the special license, I have your word that you

will not speak of this night's occurrences, and your very commendable scruples about marrying this couple must surely have been set to rest as you heard the gentleman ask and the lady accept."

He fixed the parson with a steely eye.

"Harrumph! Oh yes, very well, since you will have it. But I must say I consider these circumstances peculiar in the extreme and this entire evening highly suspicious!" He brought his Bible out of the folds of his cloak and flourished it to emphasize his feelings.

"Step up before me, my children, and we will start with a prayer. Heaven knows with such a beginning as this, your marriage will have sore need of it!

"All bow your heads, if you please!"

Far too quickly for Caro's peace of mind, she and the marquess had both said I do, the marquess was hesitating and then taking off his large signet ring and slipping it on her third finger, and the simple, country ceremony was ending.

"No." She looked down at the signet ring and shook her hand, feeling the loose weight of it knock and slide up and down on her finger.

"I should not like to lose it, my lord," she said, removing it and handing it back to the marquess. " 'Tis much too big, and 'twill be sure to come off."

She was surprised to see him frown slightly.

But he accepted the ring back, merely saying, "Please, call me Miles." He smiled and teased, "For I shall certainly call you Caro—wife."

Her brows snapped together at that, and she turned her back on him to address the duke. "There now, Uncle," she said crossly. "We've had a lovely June wedding, even if it was a trifle too early to be fashionable. Merciful heavens!" she exclaimed as she watched her uncle draw out his pistol again. "What are you about now?"

The parson and the marquess turned to see the duke aiming his pistol at the marquess a second time.

"Oh my!"

"What the devil!"

"Parson, I thank you once more for your services to-night, and your parish may look to a donation that reflects my gratitude."

The parson brightened and then looked dubious as he eyed the marquess' situation.

"I shan't kill him, Father. I merely require one more service of him, of a rather delicate nature," said the duke impatiently.

Without taking his eyes from the marquess, he commanded, "Please escort the parson to his carriage and then wait outside this room."

The parson glared as Fields and Campbell crossed the parlor to stand at his side.

Then he capitulated, throwing glances behind him and muttering as he left. "Oh, very well. Very well . . . I must say . . . consider . . . of a certainty . . . highly suspicious!"

The duke waited until they heard the parlor door click shut.

"My apologies, Marquess, for the melodrama. I fear I must insist, a trifle indelicately, that the marriage be consummated this night."

The marquess' eyebrows rose.

Caro blushed furiously. "Uncle, surely—"

"I must protect my niece from any thoughts of annulment on the morrow. Tales of a precipitate marriage followed by an annulment would do her reputation little more good than her original predicament.

"For good or ill, you are husband to my niece now. Accept it.

"For my niece's sake, I would advise you to attempt to curb your gambling.

"But do not think to bleed her family. If you go through her inheritance, that will be all you go through. I'll see you in Newgate before I lend you a groat.

"I shall send an announcement of the wedding to the papers.

"Should you like to attend me tomorrow afternoon at, let

us say, two o'clock, the settlements may be arranged then."

The marquess' eyes were snapping and his lip curled sardonically. He bowed and drawled, "But the pleasure is all mine, my lord.

"In truth, 'tis one of my very dreams come to life—to be held at gun point to wed both a beauty and a fortune at the same moment!"

"That I can well believe, Marquess.

"Caroline, you will thank me for this one day."

Caro returned no answer, torn between anger at herself, anger at her uncle, and a rising certainty that she did not want to be married.

The duke motioned with his pistol. "Please step toward the door, my lord, and open it."

Outside, Fields and Campbell turned to receive the duke's command.

"See the marquess and his wife to the room he has taken and remain outside the door all night. No one is to come out."

Caro, feeling as if she might bolt at any second, reached for the bannister and started up the stairs. At her next step, she felt the marquess' hand slip under her elbow and support her.

Surprised, she shot him a grateful look and received a smile in return.

"Good night, Fields, Campbell," said his lordship, shaking his head in resignation at Caro as she passed before him into the bedchamber. "I would not trade beds with you for all the world!"

Both men touched their forelocks and took up a position on either side of the door.

"Lord! What an evening," exclaimed his lordship, closing the heavy oak door and locking it. He rubbed his forehead and ran his hand through his dark brown hair. "I hope to heaven I may never have another like it."

He untied his cravat and pulled it from his neck. "Ah!"

He shrugged himself from his coat and sat down in a nearby armchair and began struggling with his boots.

"Damnation! Don't suppose they'd let Jeeves in, just to help me get these boots off, do you?"

Several minutes of groaning and soft cursing ensued, and the boots finally fell to the floor with two heavy clumps. "Lord! I must remember to thank Jeeves. The man works harder than I guessed!" exclaimed the marquess.

Then he caught sight of Caro, who had sunk down on the foot of the bed and sat staring ahead into space.

"Forgive me, Caro," he said, coming to sit down next to her and drape a brotherly arm around her shoulders.

He gave her a small squeeze. "You must be fagged to death. Here I am standing in the middle of the floor ranting away—and your evening has been far worse than mine. First that brute knocking you about—"

A sob escaped Caro. She stopped staring into space and looked down at her hands in her lap.

Pressing her lips together, she swallowed to keep from sobbing again.

The marquess gave her shoulder another squeeze. "Then your uncle and the pistols.

"Bit of a cold fish, your uncle. Can't say I care much for h—"

Sobbing, and gulping to keep from sobbing, Caro turned and hid her face in the ruffles of his lordship's shirt. One hand crept up to his neck and held on to his collar.

"Then the parson and a wedding on top of all the rest—Caro, Caro, don't do that. You'll give yourself the hiccups." He smoothed the curls away from her hot face and put both arms around her, holding her close.

They were quiet, sitting thus, for several moments.

His lordship stifled a yawn.

After another moment, he asked, "My dear, do you think we could . . . just . . . pull the covers back a little . . . like so?"

She yawned. "No. I don't want to."

"And just . . . You must be worn to a thread. I know I feel like hell. . . . And just . . . lie . . ." He inched his body under the bedclothes, inching hers after him. "Just lie . . .

down?"

"No, no. Please . . ."

"Like . . . so. Shhh. Go to sleep. Mmm, much better. Now, isn't that much . . . better, Caro? Yes." He pulled her against the warm length of him, draped his arm over her, and kissed the mass of curls.

"Just like two spoons. Mmm . . . Say yes, Caro."

"Mm."

The Marquess of Strathmore motioned his man Jeeves from the room and sat down on the bed next to Caro.

He watched her sleep for several seconds, a serious expression upon his face, and then touched her shoulder and shook it gently. "Time to rise, sleepyhead."

"Don't M'tilde. You must know I was up late." Caro shrugged off the shaking hand and snuggled deeper into the sheets.

Then the baritone voice registered, and the feeling of being watched struck her.

She turned over and sat up, clutching the sheets to her chest and exclaiming, "The marquess!" She peeked under the bedclothes and then looked back at the marquess, blushing to have checked but relieved to find that she was still in her clothes. "Of—of Strathmore, is it not?" she finished lamely, striving for a measure of poise.

The marquess laughed at her. "There is really no point, Caro, to my mind, in ravishing a sleeping woman. Miles, if you please, not Marquess."

He patted the bedclothes over her leg. "Now, get up. Jeeves has breakfast coming downstairs, and then we must be off before the world gets up and claps eyes upon you.

"You're going to look a fright after sleeping in your gown all night, and Jeeves was unable to scrounge up another to see you home in." He chuckled. "And *my* reputation, my dear, will not stand walking out with a fright."

He got up and smiled at her look of dismay. " 'Tisn't that bad—I am but teasing, Caro.

"We can always cover you with my cloak. All that will be

145

seen then is your hair. You can do something with that, can you not?"

"Yes!" she snapped. "I am not a simpleton." She did not like in the least being caught at such disadvantage, particularly when his lordship was not.

The marquess quite understood and forbore to laugh again.

She drew herself up beneath the bedclothes. "If your lordship will only take yourself off, I can endeavor to hurry!" she said haughtily.

Smiling only, his lordship replied, "Your water is by the dresser," and did as she requested.

Scowling at the marquess' smile, for she knew he was laughing at her, Caro threw off the bedclothes and set to repairing the damage as best she could.

Fifteen minutes later, having drawn her hair into a relatively tidy, if loose, chignon at the nape of her neck, she gave up upon the dress. "For, faith, what could anyone do with a crushed gown that has one sleeve torn from it?" she asked the reflection in the cheval glass.

She threw up her hands and went to peep out the bedchamber door.

Seeing and hearing no one, she picked up her skirts and flew down the stairs, gave a rap to the parlor door, and entered breathlessly.

Swallowing the mouthful of eggs and mutton he had been enjoying, the marquess rose from the small table and pulled out the chair opposite his. "I am sure, my dear, you would rather I did not wait for you to begin breakfast, as I fear I eat rather a lot and take some time to do it. I thought you would rather be off as soon as possible," he apologized.

Caro slid into the chair he held out for her. "Quite. I feel ridiculous skulking about doorways and sneaking down stairs.

"Lord! I don't believe I've ever appeared this badly dressed in all my life. What Matilde is going to say when she claps eyes upon me I cannot imagine."

Caro smiled to herself. She had a very good idea what Matilde was going to say.

"Matilde, I take it, is your maid?" asked the marquess.

"Yes." She scooped up a small portion of eggs and deposited it upon her plate.

"You will want to bring her with you then when you move your things to my house," he said conversationally.

"Why, yes."

"That would be 22 Crescent Street, my dear. Mutton?" he offered, holding out the dish. "And you may be pleased to engage as much of my staff as need be to get the thing finished today.

"I suspect Matilde could see to most of it, with both staffs to help her fetch and carry, for I don't believe your uncle would tolerate inefficiency in any position in his household.

"She would need one or two initial directions from you, of course," he added, seeing that Caro was regarding him oddly.

"Why, I'm not going to move my things today, ah . . . Miles. I don't have time.

"I shall do it . . . Let me see, oh dear."

The marquess stopped eating in astonishment.

Silently, she went over her engagements for the next several days. "Well, I will try to get it done by the end of the week, or certainly by the beginning of next week."

"Caro, I fear your uncle had the right of it," the marquess explained patiently. "The best course for scraping through such a sudden marriage without a scandal of some sort is for you—and me—to behave as if we are besotted with each other.

"Now, the last time I observed any, and I grant you they're a rare breed, I noted that besotted newlyweds did not wait a week or ten days to begin living together."

"Oh, poo, Miles! Don't be such an old nanny. Who is to know when I start living with you, pray? We will simply act and arrive as if we started out from the same house."

"Old nanny! Act as if . . . !" The marquess almost

147

choked on his mouthful of mutton.

He managed, with effort, to hold his temper in check. "My dear, I believe you are being a trifle naive to credit that we could bring off any such ruse. Even the best servants would find such a start too entertaining to forbear repeating.

"We will need to be seen arriving together, leaving together, and spending time together—for some time to come, I might add!

"Only that way will we scotch the gossip that is sure to come and keep your reputation untarnished.

"Indeed, I had thought we should go for a drive in St. James's Park after I wait upon your uncle."

"I am sorry, my lord. I have said I cannot!"

The marquess scraped his chair back from the table and stood, running his hand through his hair in frustration. "And I say you must."

Eyes flashing, Caro pushed back her own chair and stared defiantly at the marquess.

He fetched his cloak from the settee, where Jeeves had left it. Holding it out for Caro, he said quietly, "We need to get shut of this place in any case."

She allowed him to drape it around her without answer and stood, adjusting its length to her shorter frame.

When she was finished, he escorted her through the parlor door, whereupon she perversely stopped, for all to see if they chose, and turned to look pointedly back at the breakfast table.

"My dear woman, I have never left an outstanding bill behind me in the whole of my life!" he barked.

He then waited for her to precede him, instead of taking her arm again, and appeared, for the first time, so truly vexed with her that she believed him implicitly.

Since it was still too early for any but Dog and Duck servants to be up and about, they met only a sleepy mongrel in the carriage yard on their way out.

Jeeves had the carriage waiting for them and climbed up with the driver as he saw them come out.

They entered the brougham, and the ride to the Duke of Seward's was begun quickly and in silence.

Caro averted her face to stare out the carriage window. Her misfivings about the wisdom of her uncle's solution returned full force.

Though the marquess had appeared pleasant and devil-may-care last night, she was beginning to suspect that, though he might be pleasant, he was not devil-may-care. Possibly, she thought, it would have been better to have taken her chances and waited, hoping to marry someone more malleable.

She turned to regard the marquess' handsome, impassive face and received a bland smile.

Giving a small sniff, she returned her regard to the window, with the uncomfortable feeling that his lordship was still smiling, and kept it there for the duration of the ride.

As he helped her down from his brougham, the marquess politely repeated, "For your own good: I expect you to transfer the whole of your belongings to my house today. Directly I return home I shall dispatch enough servants to see to the task with or without your help. I dislike giving you an ultimatum, Caro, but you've left me no choice, and, again, 'tis for your own good.

"I also expect you to be ready to go for a drive when I have finished waiting upon your uncle."

Reading the defiant expression in her dark blue eyes, he added softly, his own hazel eyes glinting, "And if you are not, I guarantee, sweet wife, you will mislike the repercussions." He bent his head, placed a gentle, demanding kiss on her mouth, and left her standing at her door.

For all the servants to see, no doubt! she thought, putting a finger up to her tingling lips, and was vexed to notice that her heart had quickened a pace.

She refused to look after the retreating marquess, and, when Smiths, the major-domo, opened her front door at last, she stalked through it.

She discovered Matilde, on entering her bedchamber, bent over a trunk and surrounded by bandboxes and piles of dresses, hats, gloves, shawls, slippers, and half boots. "Matilde!"

"Oh, Miss Caro," Matilde told the inside of the trunk, as she finished securing the lining paper and straightened. "I'm glad you're back."

She stopped speaking as her glance fell on Caro. She stared, and one hand rose to her cheek in horror. "What *do* you have on, miss?"

She approached and plucked at the creases and the torn sleeve, apparently bereft of further speech.

"Please Matilde! I will explain another time. What is going on here?" Caro looked around her in disbelief, though she could see very well that her uncle must be of the same mind as the marquess.

"Did you . . . fall, miss?" asked Matilde dubiously, still eyeing the gown and at a loss to account for the state of it.

"Matilde, please!" begged Caro.

"The duke . . . your uncle has . . . asked us to move you to your new husband's house," the maid explained, still eyeing Caro distractedly. "Alice and Cloë, from the kitchen, are to help me—they are in the attic fetching the other trunks now—and I am to have the chatelaine hire temporaries from the Agency if I need more help."

As she heard her own explanation, Matilde remembered the astonishment she had felt at the Duke of Seward's command and forgot the condition of her mistress's gown. "Is it true, miss? You are married?"

Caro stared. She began to take the marquess' point as she watched disbelief and curiosity war to be uppermost on Matilde's face. If it were thus with even her own maid, she might count upon its being ten times worse among her peers.

In the blink of an eye, Caro capitulated. "Oh la, Matilde! Can you doubt my uncle?

"He was not pleased, you may be sure, when I told him. Miles and I wished to be married quietly at the end of June—that was only four weeks away when I told my uncle, Matilde.

"He didn't believe I knew Miles well enough, you see.

"But, 'tis not as if I haven't been on the town an age and met many a gentleman!

"And, from the first moment I met Miles, I vow we knew we were meant for each other."

Caro leaned closer to her maid and lowered her voice. "Matilde. Do you believe in love at first sight?"

Matilde's eyes grew big, and she nodded vehemently. "Oh yes, miss—madame!"

"At any rate," Caro folded her hands over her heart, astonishing Matilde with her uncharacteristic romanticism. "I wished to be with Miles as soon as possible and forever!

"I couldn't wait, Matilde. And Uncle already had the special license.

"So I sent him a note and dragged him away from his club, I fear, and we were married last night.

"You know me, I never do things the way other people do them."

"Indeed you don't, miss—I mean, madame!" said her maid proudly.

"It was so spontaneous Uncle scarcely had time to collect Lady Burton for the ceremony." She could not doubt that her meticulous uncle had apprised Lady Burton of her marriage. "But oh! Matilde! It was all so romantic! Just . . . Miles and me!"

Caro was silent for several minutes, gazing, she hoped, starry-eyed into space.

"Oh, madame, it does sound so!"

Caro came out of her trance. "Oh, Matilde, I do miss him so, every moment I'm not with him.

"Can you see to my bath water? Lord, I want to get shut of this dress! I, I mean I must hurry and get changed and attend to all the packing before he comes to take me for a drive this afternoon."

The maid's eyes fell on her gown again. "And how did your gown—"

"Oh! I nearly forgot, Matilde. My lovely new husband is sending his servants over this morning to help us with the packing and moving, so we needn't bother Mrs. Smiths to send to the Agency."

The maid brightened and forgot the gown. " 'Tis good news indeed, madame, for I'd no idea in this world how I was to get it all done today, I'm sure.

"Temporaries are no better than the shoes they stand in, for all they're an extra pair of hands, if you'll pardon my saying so, madame.

"But the Marquess of Strathmore's people . . . Well! I'm sure we'll finish today and then some, what with their help."

She went off to see to Caro's bath water, and Caro went to her escritoire, moving a pile of folded shawls from the chair to the bed, to sit down.

She penned several brief notes in the space it took Matilde to ready her water.

"I need these delivered immediately, Matilde, or I shall be in several people's black books," said Caro, as the maid came to help her strip off, at last, the gown she had begun to think of ruefully as her "wedding gown," so aptly did it seem to illustrate, with its sad creases and torn and dangling sleeve, what her wedding had been.

"I'll see to it, madame, never fear."

Caro would have liked to linger in her bath, but she didn't dare. The morning was slipping away, and she had an uncomfortable feeling the marquess' people would be arriving soon.

As she had feared, no sooner had she donned her sprigged morning dress and had Matilde brush and coif her hair than Alice knocked and came in with the news that the marquess' servants were belowstairs asking where they might be of service.

"Please bid most of them come up here, Alice," directed Caro. "And take several to the attic to help you and Cloë finish fetching the trunks down."

She sighed and took a deep breath, resigning the rest of the day to the tediousness of packing.

However, by the time she learned the marquess had gone

to her uncle in the library, having instructed Matilde to tell her the moment he set foot in the front hall, Caro had most of her trunks on the carriages and on their way to 22 Crescent Street with instructions to begin unpacking them as soon as they arrived.

She left the gathering of articles that could only be packed at the last moment to Matilde and went to eat a light luncheon.

Then she returned to her bedchamber to change her sprigged morning dress for a walking dress and hat the exact color of her dark blue eyes.

"Thank you, Matilde. Please pack up the remaining articles and collect your things and ride over on the last carriage. Oh dear, when I see you again, we shall be at 22 Crescent Street, for good or ill."

"Madame?" Matilde was surprised. "You surely don't have the fidgets *now?*"

"And why not, pray? 'Tis as good a time as any other, I'll wager."

Matilde hid her smile as Caro flounced from the bedchamber.

Wondering if she would dread returning home to 22 Crescent Street as much as she dreaded returning to her uncle's, Caro went down to wait upon the marquess in the sitting room.

She had not long to wait.

"La!" she exclaimed testily as the marquess was announced. "I felt certain you and my uncle would be closeted all afternoon, and I rearranged my engagements for nought," she observed sweetly.

The marquess grinned and raised her hand to his lips. "Had a change of heart, did we, sweeting?

"Now, I wonder why. Most certainly not to please me, I'll warrant," he remarked seriously.

He continued dryly, "Not at all. Your uncle is not a long-winded fellow."

"No, indeed," she agreed, knowing well how brutally precise and to the point he could be.

She tapped the marquess playfully with her fan. "And why wouldn't I wish to please you, pray?

"Besides, you were right." She had the grace to look embarrassed. "I saw that as soon as I returned home."

The marquess' eyebrow rose disbelievingly.

"And I believe it would be wise, Miles, to come to some sort of agreement with you."

"Ah. Such as?"

"You needn't look so suspicious! I merely thought—to speak plainly—I merely thought that when we have acted the lovers to everyone's satisfaction and laid all the gossip to earth—as *you* suggested . . ." she cried defensively.

"Come, out with it."

"Well, I rather thought we might . . . try to . . . be friends. You know, a modern marriage of convenience—"

"Of whose convenience do you speak, may I ask?"

"Why, both of ours, of course! Each of us could go his own way and do what he likes so long, naturally, as it doesn't reflect poorly on the other.

"I wouldn't interfere with your gambling, so long as you did not bankrupt us, that is; and you wouldn't interfere with my . . . pursuits."

"Hmm." The marquess appeared to consider her proposal.

Caro blushed and looked at the floor. "I understand . . . that you might want children some day—to carry on your title and all that." She gulped. "And I believe, after a suitable time, after we know each other a little better, we might arrange something on that score."

"Friends. Yes, I like that," remarked the marquess, consideringly.

He came to stand unnervingly close to her.

Her pulses quickened. For a moment, she thought he would kiss her again and was surprised to find that she was disappointed when he didn't.

Instead, he lifted her hand and slipped a gold band, which had alternating rubies and pearls across the top, upon her third finger. "This one fits a fair sight better than

154

my signet ring, wouldn't you agree?"

She swallowed and nodded. " 'T-Tis beautiful, Miles."

"Good. For I believe I should be perturbed if you should refuse to wear this one," he remarked, his hazel eyes looking intently down into her blue ones.

"And what if I desire more than friendship from you, Caro?" he asked softly.

He released her hand and ran one large finger gently along her jawline, down the side of her neck, and slowly around the edge of her décolletage. "Hmm? What if I want a marriage of body and soul—a wife in name and in fact?"

She backed away from him. "I-I do not know. I do not offer that at present!"

They stared at each other, his eyes demanding, hers denying.

Then Caro broke the spell, retreating to the sitting room door. "I-I will just go and say goodbye to my uncle, as I presume we will be returning from St. James's to your house."

He bowed. "Our house, Caro," he corrected softly.

She gave him another look and then fled, throwing "I shall have some Madeira sent in!" over her shoulder.

The marquess chuckled and seated himself placidly upon a Chippendale chair.

When Caro returned some twenty minutes later, she had regained her composure. "Shall we go, my lord?"

"What, so soon?" he teased.

She shrugged, astonished still at what her uncle had just told her of her new husband: The marquess had insisted her fortune be tied up in their children. He had arranged it so that he could not touch a guinea of it! "As you say, he is not long-winded."

The marquess set down his wineglass and offered her his arm. "Then let us go."

"Thank you, my lord." She smiled shyly up at him and proceeded to walk out of her uncle's house, very likely for the last time, without a backward glance.

"A high-perch phaeton!" she exclaimed admiringly, as

she saw the marquess' carriage.

The marquess helped her up.

"That was well done of you, my lord."

He grinned at her. "I couldn't imagine driving you in anything less up to the mark, my dear," he said, getting up himself. "Giddap, there."

She grinned back at him. "I don't suppose you would let me drive it?"

"Oh, I might . . . if you were to give me a look that clearly stated you were besotted with me." He gave her a bland smile and turned his attention back to the road.

"And, if you could endure one or two practice drives with me, so I could be sure you wouldn't break your pretty neck."

"Humph!" She tossed her head. "I do not need practice drives, sir, thank you very much. I vow I could drive anything you could hitch a horse to."

"I do believe you."

"But, I shall attempt, for the novelty of it, a besotted look. I am certain I need practice there."

The marquess regarded her besotted look critically. "Quite a lot I should say. You look totty-headed."

"Oh! See if I try it upon you ever again then. Humph!"

"Nonsense. Simply continue to practice. Come, try it again."

Caro laughed. "Yes, you would like that!"

The marquess smiled. "Indeed I would."

She glanced around them. "We don't seem to be creating much of a stir."

They had been in the park for several minutes, both nodding occasionally to acknowledge friends as they passed. No one had behaved in any way out of the ordinary.

"Are you disappointed?" He chuckled.

"Ohh, no. But you would think we were not married at all!"

"Hmm. Perhaps I didn't need to marry you after all."

Caro gave him a sharp glance.

He smiled lazily back at her.

"Oh, pull up, pull up! There is Sara. *She* will be all curiosity."

"Sara, good afternoon!" called Caro as the marquess halted the phaeton. "Miles, may I present Miss Sara Alvinly. Sara, this is Miles . . . ?"

"Grayson, darling. You'll remember it one day," supplied the marquess, with a resigned expression for Miss Alvinly.

Caro blushed and hit the marquess with her fan. "Yes, my husband, Sara—the Marquess of Strathmore."

"Your *husband?*" Sara asked faintly. Only her mother's tireless training kept her from gaping.

The marquess chuckled and, handing the reins to Caro, obligingly got down from the phaeton. "May I give you my seat, Miss Alvinly? I see some friends yonder, and it looks as if you and Caro need a good coze."

He smiled at Sara and helped her up into the carriage.

Sara watched the marquess saunter off to meet his friends and asked, "Are you certain you're married to him, Caro? For, the last time I laid eyes upon you, you were still single, and, if you're not, by heaven, I shall set my cap at him!"

She turned to her friend, wide-eyed. "Don't tell me his pockets are well lined too, or I shall just die of envy!"

"Don't be vulgar, Sara," replied Caro primly, for in point of fact she hadn't the least idea what the marquess' financial status was.

" 'Don't be vulgar'? This from you, Caro! Where are my smelling salts? I vow you are my mother disguised! Come, confess it. Lud!"

Caro laughed. "Besides, you may not set your cap at him, for he is indeed my One and Only." She folded her hands over her heart and rolled her eyes for Sara's benefit. "Only, can you believe it, no one seems to care one whit!"

"I daresay they don't know of it yet, goose. You could've knocked me down with a feather just now!

"And before you burst into some revoltingly sentimental song or the laces of your corset snap under the strain of your swelling heart," asked Sara dryly, "mayhap you could enlighten me as to how you acquired him?"

Turning serious, Sara put one hand over Caro's. "My dear, I was so worried!

"I knew I should not have left you behind with Lord Macomb. I should have made you leave with me. Mama said so too.

"You can have no notion of the reputation he has. Goodness! It gives me chill bumps just to think of it! And those three he drove to the gardens are little better. They frequently run with his crowd.

"I do hope I'm not in your black books for sending a note round to Lady Burton. I imagine the first thing she did was send for your uncle?"

"Yes."

"Oh dear. Did you get in much trouble? Oh Caro, I'm sorry, but, indeed, I was so very worried about you."

" 'Tis all right, Sara. Really, it is. I begin to think everything may work out for the best.

"You know I had to marry in little more than a year for my inheritance at any rate.

"And when Miles walked in upon us, and, and . . ." She hated to fib to Sara. "Well, after Miles walked in, I did not care to see Lord Macomb — or his friends — ever again."

"Tut. I shall have to buy you a ribbon or some such fribble to make it up."

"A ribbon! Sara Alvinly, 'twould be more like a hat, I should think!"

"A hat! How much pin money do you think Papa allows me?"

Both ladies broke up laughing.

"Not enough, as you've told me often enough," said Caro.

"But, Caro, you haven't really told me how you married your marquess.

"Uh-oh, and it appears I am not the only one to ogle him." She looked pointedly at a pretty, dark-haired woman in a very becoming red dress, who had laid one gloved hand on the marquess' arm and was smiling up at him.

Caro followed Sara's gaze and felt her heart contract. "Why, when did she join them? Do you know her, Sara?"

"No, I fear I don't . . . but I'll lay you a monkey that dress came straight from Henrietta Cavendaw's shop! Look at those lines, see how it falls from the bosom."

"Oh, do be quiet, Sara! I do not care a jot about her dress."

Sara turned a surprised face on Caro.

"Or *whose* shop it came from! If it were to be bestowed upon me tomorrow, I wouldn't have it."

"You don't understand, Caro. Henrietta Cavendaw won't make just anyone's gowns. She dresses the Prince's set. For example, she very likely wouldn't make a gown for you or me.

"And Papa near faints every time he hears how much just *one* of them costs.

"Well, of course you wouldn't want it, goose, for 'tis not your color at all—as I'm certain you very well know."

"Bother! I refuse to sit here and watch her hang all over him.

"Come, Sara! We shall go for a ha'penny cup of milk. I see the cows over by the lake, and I'll wager you haven't had a cup that fresh since you came up to London." She slapped the reins. "Giddap!"

"Capital idea! And I vow the stuff they sell you up here tastes as if they put chalk in it," exclaimed Sara.

She immediately thought better of their idea. "Oh, but Caro, you-you're not just going to leave the marquess? I mean, I have his seat, Caro. How will he get about?"

"Am I not? Oh, we'll come back for him, Sara. And I doubt he'll even have noticed we were gone."

"Caro! Caro Durham! Where in thunder did you get that phaeton?" called a male voice.

Caro and Sara turned to see a blond, mustachioed gentleman wave his hat at them and start his gig in their direction.

"Teddy!" both ladies cried, waving back at him.

"Hallo, Sara!" He pulled his gig alongside them and kept

pace.

"Now Caro, let's have it. Did you finally wheedle that carriage out of your uncle, or have you, ah . . . borrowed . . . it from some poor wretch who doesn't know you half as well as I do!"

He frowned slightly. "And by Jove! I've just this moment heard," he nodded toward Lord Meryl and Lady Margaret, just turning their horses down one of the many tree-lined alleys in the park, "you are keeping rather close company with Macomb. And frankly, Caro dear, I wouldn't encourage it.

"Sara!" he teased, "why do you let her encourage him?"

"I? I told her as much, didn't I, Caro?" answered Sara calmly, refusing to be drawn.

Caro nodded. "Besides, Teddy, I'm not encouraging him, for the simple reason that I've a husband who would object."

"Caro! You didn't! I know you did not go and get yourself riveted to some bloke without inviting me!

"Sara! Did you go?"

Sara shook her head, smiling. "I am outraged too, Teddy."

"It was *very* small and very intimate, both of you, just as I wished it. Surely you would want me to marry as I see fit?"

"Oh. Well, if no one else was invited either, I shan't be offended with you.

"Can't be offended with her, Sara. 'Tis just another of her queer starts."

Sara made a great show of sighing. "I know, Teddy."

"Doing it up a bit too brown, both of you," retorted Caro.

"Quite. All right, ladies, what say we stop all this fadging about and give it a race?

"Don't shake your head, no, at me, Caro. I know you've been dying to race that phaeton since you took hold of the reins. Come on!"

Caro laughed and shook her head again. "No, truly,

Teddy, I cannot. You were right the first time. 'Tisn't mine."

"Neither were Harding's grays, but that didn't stop you! What's wrong, Caro? Afraid you can't handle a high-perch phaeton? They can be devilish ticklish to balance on the curves, Lord knows."

"But I had *asked* Harding, Teddy. Faith, I didn't just steal his grays and race them."

"Oh? Just whose phaeton is it you've stolen, my dear? Or, could it be you're simply afraid I'll beat y—"

Caro gave it up, laughing. "Oh, drat you, Teddy! You ever were a thorn, weren't you?"

"Come on! Down to the lake and back to that line of trees! Loser buys ha'penny milk! Hold on, Sara! Giddap!"

"Done!"

Both drivers slapped their reins, and the two carriages bolted down the lane toward the lake.

Those carriages and riders in their path hastened to move out of the way, a few turning to send glances of irritation after them. Many more, however, paused to see the outcome of the race, shouting in their wake to cheer one or the other on.

Several moments later, there was a general outbreak of clapping and cheering as Teddy pulled past the row of trees that was the finish line inches ahead of Caro and pulled up on his horse.

He turned in his seat as Caro pulled the phaeton to a stop next to his gig. Laughing, he cried, "Hah! That's one for me, Caro!"

Laughing herself from the sheer thrill of racing, and groaning at the same time, Caro replied, "Oh, 'tis too bad of you, Teddy. I shall never live it down, either. Beaten in a high-perch phaeton—by a gig! Lord!"

"Caro!" gasped Sara. "That was famous! For a moment, I thought we were going over into the lake when we turned around! I was never so scared in my life! We almost beat you too, Teddy!"

"Lord, don't I know it! I only beat you by a nose-length—and I'd wager the turn did it, Sara. Phaetons are ticklish on the turns. Didn't I warn you, Caro?"

"Yes, you did, and I want a rematch, Teddy," said Caro smiling. "You only beat me because it's the first time I've driven a phaeton," she teased.

"Oh no! I sha'n't let you get away with that! I beat you fair and square, ladies.

"Now, what was it you said we were racing for? I'd like to collect my winnings, if you please."

"I knew he couldn't have heard aright!" exclaimed Sara, beginning to laugh.

"I did wonder at it myself," answered Caro, also laughing.

"Whenever you ladies have finished laughing at my poor expense—"

" 'Twas a ha'penny cup of milk, Teddy," Sara enlightened him. She nodded at the cows standing in the grass near the lake.

"Nonsense, I never touch the stuff," he said, without thinking. "You're funning."

At the shocked look that crossed his face, both ladies began to laugh again.

"I see.

"We shall set the bet well before the rematch, ladies," he said, laughing himself. "Of that, you can be sure. Oh, very well."

In good-natured disgust, he led the way over to the small herd and the girl handing out cups just milked from the cow.

He procured three cups, under protest from the ladies that he must join them, and pointed to Caro when the milk-girl looked to him for payment. "Not I. There's your ticket."

He grinned at Sara and Caro. "It's bad enough my having to drink the stuff. I refuse to be made to pay for my poison as well!"

The ladies laughed, and Caro paid the girl.

They stood, watching the herd and finishing their cups

and trading gossip.

Reluctantly, Caro suggested, "Well, Sara, I suppose we should be getting back."

"Yes. My sister is very likely looking for me by now." She rolled her eyes.

"All right, ladies." Teddy helped them back up into the phaeton. "If I am abominably ill for having imbibed this poison, I shall know precisely whose houses to descend upon for nursing!"

"Oh Teddy!" cried both ladies in unison.

He laughed, doffed his hat, and bowed to them before getting back up in his gig.

"Did you come with Evelyn?" Caro asked Sara.

"No, Jana. She will be having apoplexy by now."

"Always a pleasure beating—er, racing—you, ladies," Teddy called, grinning.

"Coxcomb!"

"Beast!" returned the ladies, rising agreeably to his goading.

"Until our rematch!" Still grinning, he flourished his hat at them and drove off.

"And she may not be the only one," added Sara meaningfully, as Caro set the phaeton rolling.

"You mean the marquess? I sincerely doubt it," she returned dryly.

Several minutes later, Caro remarked, "There is Jana. And she looks as if she has died and gone to heaven."

"Good lord! She is talking to the French count Mama has forbidden her to see," exclaimed Sara. "And by herself too! Wait till I tell Mama!"

Caro laughed. "I wouldn't advise it, Sara dear. For the first question out of your mama's mouth will be: and just where were *you* while she was talking to him!"

"Drat you, Caro, but you're right—ugh," Sara exclaimed as she jumped to the ground and landed. "Nevertheless," she smiled wickedly back up at her friend, "some sort of blackmail is clearly called for here!"

"Sara, you devil!" Caro laughed again.

"I hope your husband may prove as easy to manipulate, Caro." She waved her goodbye and bore down upon her unsuspecting sister, flirting outrageously with the French count.

Smiling at Sara and her sister, Caro turned the phaeton toward the spot where she had last seen the marquess and drove on.

He was there still, leaning gracefully against one of the trees, his arms folded across his chest, talking to only one other gentleman now.

Observing him as she drove up on them, Caro felt something squeeze her heart tightly. He looked ridiculously male and handsome, from the smooth, muscled line of the buff breeches above his Hessians to the perfect fit of his dark brown superfine coat, relieved only by the white lace edges of his shirt.

She heard the deep rumble of his laughter, as both gentlemen laughed and she pulled up on the reins bringing the phaeton to a halt in front of them. He also, she thought with sudden irritation, looked as if he was having just as good a time now as he had been having before she had driven off without him.

Indeed, looking at him, she might have guessed she had only been gone five minutes instead of the nearly forty-five she suspected would be closer to the mark. Her eyes narrowed.

"Ah, here is my sweet wife now, come to collect me, no doubt," the marquess remarked lazily, further giving Caro the impression that he considered she had not been gone long. "The former Miss Caro Durham, now Lady Strathmore, my good friend, Tom Fagan, Earl of Weycote," he said.

"Charmed to make your acquaintance, Lady Strathmore. Your husband and I go back a long way." The earl smiled at the marquess.

"Delighted, I'm sure," murmured Caro.

"Fagan, old man, do you stay?" exclaimed the marquess, slapping the earl heartily on the back. "My sweet wife is beginning to get that long-suffering look women who have been kept waiting too long wear.

"We're still newlyweds, don't you know. I wouldn't want to put her pretty little nose out of joint just yet." He winked blatantly at his friend and got up in the phaeton.

The Earl of Weycote chuckled. "Yes, I see Tarryton over there, and I did want to have a word with him." He gathered the reins of his horse, bowed, still smiling, and began to lead the animal off.

"Miles, you put me to the blush!" protested Caro crossly, slapping the reins and starting the phaeton moving without thinking. "One would think I had been waiting as long as you must have done, if you've even noticed that I left at all."

She cast him a sharp glance. "Oh, I see. That was your point, was it not?"

The marquess gave her a bland smile. "I fear I am not following, my dear. Of which point do you speak?"

"Humph." Glad to see that her absence had vexed him after all, she kept her eyes on the road and smiled to herself.

After a moment of silence, the marquess asked, "Where do we go, sweet wife?"

"Home. To change for Lady Gallworth's rout.

"Merciful heavens, *I* am driving—is that what you mean?" she cried, pulling up on the reins. "I beg your pardon, Miles. I simply did not think."

"No, no!" the marquess laughed, covering her hands with one of his own and pushing the reins back at her. "It was a real question, Caro. Keep driving."

She gave him a dubious look.

"Yes, I mean it. . . . Perhaps, with a little more practice on the turns, you can beat that chap in the gig next time," he added dryly.

Caro started and gasped. "Lord, Miles! How did you know? You must have the eyes of a raven."

"I have been said to have very fine eyes. May I say, I could have wished *you* to have noticed them?" He gave her the full benefit of them, looking at her intently.

"You know very well what I meant," retorted Caro, blushing. "Don't stare, if you please."

He sighed audibly and looked at the road. "Yes, I do know. Left here, my dear."

"Oh! I don't know where I'm going, do I? How stupid of me." She chuckled nervously.

"Turn right onto Prospect Street."

The marquess gave several more directions and said, "Rein in, my dear. Here we are."

He jumped down easily and came round to help Caro.

As he put his hands on her waist and lifted her down, he said, "I had thought we might go to Drury Lane tonight to see the Shakespeare play — *The Taming of the Shrew?* It is a particular favorite of mine." He tucked her arm in his and led her up the steps.

"I would love to go on another night, Miles. But tonight is out of the question. Lady Gallworth expects me. If she discovered I went to the theater instead of her rout, she would have my head! You understand, don't you?" She gave the marquess an anxious look.

"Shall I go with you then?"

Since she had assumed he would go to his club while she attended an engagement made prior to their marriage, she was surprised, and pleased, by his offer. But fearing that he might change his mind after all, particularly if she appeared too pleased, she merely answered, "As you wish."

The front door of the marquess' house was opened at that moment, and Caro beheld two long lines of servants.

"Oh my."

"Oh yes — forgot they were going to do this, my dear. I meant to warn you," apologized the marquess.

"Why, how very considerate, Mrs. . . . ?" Caro said, smiling pinkly at the woman, obviously the chatelaine, at the head of one row of servants and looking to the marquess to supply her name.

"Siddons, my dear."

He introduced the gentleman standing opposite Mrs.

Siddons at the head of the second row of servants. "And this is Mr. Siddons, her husband. The major-domo."

Husband and wife bowed and curtsied and then took Caro down the middle of the two rows of servants, introducing each by name.

At the end of the introductions, the marquess, patiently following the proceedings, said, "We can go for a tour of the house now, if you like, my dear. Or, if you feel you won't have enough time to dress for Lady Gallworth's rout, we can postpone it to another time?"

"Oh no, Miles! I should love to see the house now, even if it delays us a bit," Caro replied quickly, earning the silent approval of Mr. and Mrs. Siddons.

One did not have to be punctual for a rout, Caro knew, as long as one arrived. But she felt it would be rude in the extreme, after the staff's welcome to her, not to reciprocate with an interest in the marquess' home. Moreover, she wanted all to know she expected to oversee every detail of the running of the marquess' establishment, and the best way to convey that message was to start learning about the house immediately.

By the end of the tour, she felt she had established a good rapport with both Mr. and Mrs. Siddons, whom she judged to be cheerful and efficient workers.

Complimenting them, she declared herself pleased with the spotless, well-aired condition of the entire house.

"Which shall continue to be the case with nary a hitch, I'm certain," returned Mrs. Siddons, smiling her good will. "And, as I understand you've plans for this evening, will dinner in two hours' time be convenient?" she asked, before returning to her duties.

"Most convenient, Mrs. Siddons," answered Caro.

"Well, you've made a conquest of her, to be sure," commented the marquess as they walked from the front hall, having finished the tour where they had begun it, back to the door of Caro's bedchamber.

"And of her husband as well, I hope," answered Caro. "A household in which mistress, chatelaine, and major-domo are forever at cross purposes is a household in which one is apt to lie down between musty sheets or discover the dust covers still over the furniture in the music room." She smiled at the marquess. "I shouldn't think you would care for that."

"I shouldn't, but I must admit it would disturb me a sight more if it began affecting my meals." He smiled back.

She laughed. "But of course! I should have mentioned that first.

"Oh, Miles!" she cried impulsively, as they stopped before her door. "Your home is so beautiful! It has such handsome, old things in it, and the windows are so large. They make the whole house so much brighter than my uncle's. I love it!" She almost threw her arms about his neck.

He smiled, genuinely pleased, and leaned over to brush her lips with a kiss. "Our home, Caro."

Throwing "Until dinner" over his shoulder, he sauntered off to his own room.

Caro blushed and smiled after him a moment before turning to enter her bedchamber, beginning to contemplate which of her dresses would make her appear most beautiful in her husband's eyes.

They arrived at Lady Gallworth's rout several hours later, after a good dinner, quite in charity with each other.

Indeed, Caro wondered, as they climbed Lady Gallworth's steps and entered, what it might be like to remain at her own home and have a quiet evening alone with her husband.

Her ruminations were abruptly cut short, however, for by now many had heard of their marriage, and their appearance caused a ripple of constrained exclamations to go round Lady Gallworth's State-Room before the friends of both began to descend upon the pair, congratulating and questioning all at the same moment.

They were thus required to spend the first forty-five minutes of the rout presenting a united front to fend off questions they did not want to answer and telling as little of the tale of their marriage as would satisfy their friends.

Caro adhered closely to what she had told Sara and Teddy in St. James's Park. "I was not desirous of a large ceremony with pomp and circumstance. I wanted my wedding to be very small and *very* intimate."

Here, she cast the marquess such a languishing, sultry look that all of the gentlemen hearing the remark and catching the look silently envied the marquess for what they believed to be his wedding night.

The marquess himself stopped dead in the rendition of Caro's version he had been giving and blinked, bereft of speech. He then winked at her, grinned broadly, and proceeded to embellish their rather spare wedding tale with numerous details about the honeymoon trip—a walking tour of the north of England and some time to go abroad—that they were going to make as soon as an important business investment of his might be settled in a week or, at most, two.

Caro's eyebrows flew up in horror at this out and out humbug, and she sent him a fleeting scowl.

Those listening, however, nodded their satisfaction on hearing of the trip, for it added, to their minds, just the right measure of balance to a wedding ceremony that seemed too small and too quiet by half.

Having satisfied their friends that they had all of the story of the wedding there was to be had, the pair were finally allowed to move on to other topics of conversation and, in a time, even to separate and mingle with the other guests as is more usual conduct at a rout.

They thus, after the first forty-five grueling minutes, passed a pleasant evening seeing and being seen and even contriving before they left to mingle together for a good half hour as if they were a very long-standing couple.

In this fashion, they were successful in leaving Lady Gallworth's guests with exactly the notion of a happy, content couple that they wished to impress upon the *ton*.

"An evening well spent, wouldn't you say, Miles?" Caro asked after the carriage door was closed upon them, and

169

several moments of silence had passed. She assumed that was the reason he had forgone his club for her rout. "Lord Meryl, Lady Alison, and Lady Margaret may tell whatever tales they like. I'd wager none would credit them now."

"And I should wager you'd win that bet, sweeting.

"May I say that you are in looks tonight?"

"Of a certainty you may." Caro blushed, unseen in the darkness of the carriage. She had chosen the light violet silk because she knew it would bring out the blue of her eyes as well as the blond highlights in her hair.

"I particularly like the top of your dress—or rather, the lack of it. I have been admiring your neck and shoulders all evening.

"Come over here, Caro, and sit closer to me."

Unaccountably, Caro found herself nervous and a trifle breathless.

She turned the conversation to less dangerous ground. "Why did you tell that Banbury tale about a honeymoon trip north and abroad? Now that I consider it, it could give the gossip of Lord Meryl and those women more credence."

"Shouldn't you like to take the walking tour, Caro, and travel abroad?" the marquess asked lazily.

The carriage slowed and came to a halt. The door was opened, saving Caro from answering.

The marquess got out and waited to help Caro descend.

"Shall we go into the library and have a cognac brought in?" he suggested as they climbed the steps to their front door. "It isn't so very late yet."

"Why, that would be the very thing, Miles, yes! I confess I am still rather whirling from answering all those questions about our wedding."

"I, too," he returned, smiling ruefully.

Mr. Siddons took their cloaks, and the marquess requested the cognac as Caro strolled ahead into the library.

There were just enough lights and fires burning haphazardly throughout the house, she noted, to give it a warm, lived in atmosphere. She sat down in the armchair nearest the fire, for the early June night had chilled her despite her cloak. And soon, as she stared into the crackling fire and warmed herself, she began to feel . . . cozy.

When the marquess came in a moment later, pausing to close the library doors, and handed her a snifter of cognac before he sat on the couch in front of the fire, the feeling was strengthened tenfold.

The marquess smiled at her. "I waylaid Siddons."

Caro smiled back and sipped.

They were quiet, staring into the fire and listening to its crackling, for several minutes.

A thought occurred to Caro, and a suspicious frown passed over her face. "Miles?"

"Mmm?"

"Taming of the Shrew was not playing at Drury Lane tonight."

"Indeed?"

"No. 'Twas Goldsmith's *She Stoops to Conquer."

"Indeed! Are you certain?"

"Quite. I spoke of it to three different people. Each of whom corrected me," she added dryly. She heard the marquess' deep rumble of laughter.

"It is still a particular favorite."

"Humph. It would be.

"I should have known you were but testing me. To see if I would drop Lady Gallworth's rout to go to the theater with you."

"I think, Caro, you should come over here and sit next to me."

He let several minutes of silence pass and then got up and went to her, reaching for her hand. "Come." He pulled her up and led her back to the couch with him.

"Better, don't you think?" he asked as they sat down and he draped an arm around her shoulders.

Gently, he tilted her head back and placed his lips on hers. "Mmmn. Much better, I should say."

His eyes twinkled. "Come, Caro. You've never been bereft of speech in your life. Say *something.*"

"Very cozy, Miles. Very cozy indeed," she said, smiling.

She settled herself closer to his large frame and laid her head against his shoulder. He smelled faintly of bayberry and cheroot.

He began to trace different parts of her body with one finger—her slim fingers, her smooth rounded shoulder, the line of her cheek. "I thought, Caro, we might really make that honeymoon trip," he murmured into her hair. "If it appeals to you."

He lifted her head from his shoulder so that he could look into her eyes. "We seem to be getting along famously."

He traced her lips with his finger and then kissed her as if he would draw out her soul.

Slowly, he drew the pins from her hair until it tumbled down her back. Then he gathered it to one side to kiss the nape of her neck, the column of her throat, and finally the hollow at the base of her throat.

"Miles, I . . . I think I'll go to b-bed now," she protested, shaken by his intensity. She could feel her heart and her very blood racing to his lovemaking, and it was an unfamiliar sensation.

She would have risen, but he held her a moment longer to kiss her again as if he would settle for nothing less than her soul.

"You're not afraid, are you Caro, love?" he asked softly, letting her go.

"N-No . . . Certainly not!" she cried, then fled, hearing his deep rumble of laughter long after Matilde had helped her out of her dress and into her nightgown and she had blown out her candle and pulled the bedclothes over her head.

The marquess was just lifting a forkful of potatoes to his mouth when Caro entered the sunny breakfast parlor the next morning.

He paused to greet her. "How did you sleep, Caro, love?" He had a fair notion and grinned.

Seeing his grin, she tossed her head and hoped she

172

sounded nonchalant. "Tolerably well, Miles, I should think."

She was not about to tell him she had stayed awake hours after she had gone to bed, trying to quiet her racing heart and unable to stop imagining what might have occurred if she had remained in the library.

"I'm glad to hear it."

Refusing to look at him, she busied herself gathering a pair of scones, butter, and jam from the sideboard and pouring out a cup of tea. "Tea, my lord?" she asked politely.

His eyes twinkled. "No, my dear."

She set down the pot and sat down, pulling her chair up to the table.

"I'm just on my way out to see to our investment so that we may visit as many countries as we like when we take our . . . ah . . . trip."

Caro turned pink and discovered that she had missed a great many places on the top half of her scone when she had buttered it.

The marquess smiled and rose, mercifully changing the subject. "What shall you do today, my dear?"

She wished she were going for another drive with him, but all she said was, "I suppose I must make all the visits I postponed yesterday when you must needs go for a drive in St. James's. No doubt I shall have a deal of explaining and apologizing to do," she said petulantly.

The marquess laughed. "Nonsense, simply tell them all you were indisposed until I dragged you out into the sunshine and thereby miraculously cured you."

"They'll not believe that. I am never indisposed."

"Very well then, fabricate a Banbury tale of your own." He came to put his hands on her shoulders and kiss the top of her hair. "Shall we meet before dinner then, eat, and go to Prinny's ball at Carleton House? He has said 'tis only an impromptu, informal thing, as 'tis before the Season, but I must at least make an appearance."

She rubbed her cheek against his hand and said with dismay, "And I am engaged to attend Lady Hereford's soirée. . . . Perhaps, we could do both?" she asked hopefully.

"Done!" The marquess dropped another light kiss on her hair and strode toward the door. "Until dinner, Caro, love."

She waved and returned to her second scone, feeling suddenly bereft. Then she brightened, turning pink again as she thought of the trip the marquess was arranging . . . when they might spend every day, all day, together for a week or more!

"In that case, we shall allow him to be gone from us all day today," she intoned haughtily, licking her buttery fingers and laughing inwardly at herself.

"I beg your pardon, madame?" asked Mr. Siddons, who was looking in quietly to see if the breakfast plates might be removed.

"Oh!" Caro started, blushing to be caught both talking to herself and licking her fingers.

"Er . . . yes, Mr. Siddons. Please go ahead and clear. I am just leaving."

She wiped her fingers on her napkin and rose hastily to go and collect her gloves and shawl and set out on her day of visiting.

"You will be happy to know, Miles," announced Caro after the footmen had removed the covers from their dinner, served, and left them alone, "that you and I are no longer the latest *on-dit*."

"May I say you look lovely, my dear?

"Tch, tch. Never say so! I had thought we should last at least a week," he teased.

"Thank you, Miles. You look quite handsome yourself.

"No, I fear we have been upstaged by Letitia Greenfeld, who grew so annoyed with Lord Savile for following her about simply everywhere and ingratiating himself to sit next to her on every occasion—he is greatly enamored of her, you know."

"No, I didn't."

"And how should you? You are very likely always off somewhere attending to your 'investment.' "

The marquess grinned. "Did you miss me, sweeting?"

"Don't be ridiculous," she smiled. "At any rate, as I was saying, Letitia Greenfeld grew so vexed with Lord Savile that she overturned Lady Carlow's second course into his lap and knocked his wig askew for good measure! Can you credit that?"

"No. I expect the tale has gained quite a bit in the retelling," said his lordship bluntly. "Poor devil. I don't believe he deserved all that, if it's true, simply for liking the chit."

"No, I suppose not. But then, I expect you're right, and it very likely isn't all true."

"You will be happy to learn, my dear, that I have our trip all set up. We leave the last week in June, so I suppose that means you had best start your packing now," he teased.

"Nonsense!" she retorted. "It took me only one day to pack and move all my things from my uncle's house to ours. I hardly need even think about packing for a mere trip abroad!"

The marquess laughed. "Home thrust, Caro.

"And I would like to point out to you your very natural use—though it's been a long time in coming—of the words 'our house.' "

"I did not say *our house*. I said *ours*," she teased.

"Don't cavil. That's what you meant."

"And so I did."

"No, don't tell me you're going to agree with me. I don't believe my heart can stand it."

"Beast."

They both began to chuckle and had soon passed the remainder of dinner in a similar raillery.

"Lord, Miles, look at the time!" exclaimed Caro as they came out of the dining room into the front hall. She nodded at the grandfather clock. "We're going to be late if we don't hurry."

He took her cloak from Mr. Siddons and wrapped it

round her. "I'll wager no one waiting on the steps will know who was on time and who wasn't."

Caro laughed. "What makes you think we'll have to wait to get in? 'Tis before the Season opens."

"Exactly!" he retorted. "What makes you think we won't?"

Caro gave a mock scream. "Well, come on then! We must hurry!" She picked up her skirts and ran for the front door.

Mr. Siddons, staring straight ahead, opened it.

"Thank you, Siddons!" called Caro as she sped through.

The marquess laughed gaily, shrugging the rest of the way into his cloak, and strode after her.

"Don't mention it," Mr. Siddons told the air at large, closing the door and allowing himself, at last, to smile.

The pair did in fact have to wait, if only ten minutes, before they might enter and make their good evenings to Lord and Lady Hereford.

They suffered their hosts to congratulate them on their marriage and moved with the stream of guests leaving their wraps with the footmen and flowing into the ballroom, where dancing had already begun.

They agreed to mingle and visit for two hours and then seek each other out and depart for Carleton House.

In what seemed to Caro like only five minutes, the marquess was back at her side, indicating it was time to go.

"Lord, but the time did fly," she exclaimed.

"Do you want to stay longer?" asked the marquess.

"Oh, good heavens no! I've never been to Carleton House.

"My uncle might have taken me several times, but . . . Well, you know my uncle. He did not go himself, I think.

"I want to go Miles. I wore this dress especially!"

The marquess grinned at that. "Ah, and I thought you chose it for me!"

"Well, for you too," she said, looking up at him shyly.

"Come on, then. To Carleton House." He took her hand and began towing her through Lady Hereford's guests. "But don't expect too much. He did say it was an im-

TAKE ADVANTAGE OF THIS SPECIAL OFFER, AVAILABLE *ONLY* TO ZEBRA REGENCY ROMANCE READERS.

You are a reader who enjoys the very special kind of love story that can only be found in Zebra Regency Romances. You adore the fashionable English settings, the sparkling wit, the captivating intrigue, and the heart-stirring romance that are the hallmarks of each Zebra Regency Romance novel. Now, you can have these delightful novels delivered right to your door each month and never have to worry about missing a new book. Zebra has made arrangements through its Home Subscription Service for you to preview the three latest Zebra Regency Romances as soon as they are published.

3 **FREE** REGENCIES TO GET STARTED!

To get your subscription started, we will send your first 3 books ABSOLUTELY FREE, as our introductory gift to you. NO OBLIGATION. We're sure that you will enjoy these books so much that you will want to read more of the very best romantic fiction published today.

SUBSCRIBERS SAVE EACH MONTH

Zebra Regency Home Subscribers will save money each month as they enjoy their latest Regencies. As a subscriber you will receive the 3 newest titles to preview FREE for ten days. Each shipment will be at least a $11.97 value (publisher's price). But home subscribers will be billed only $9.90 for all three books. You'll save over $2.00 each month. Of course, if you're not satisfied with any book, just return it for full credit.

FREE HOME DELIVERY

Zebra Home Subscribers get free home delivery. There are never any postage, shipping or handling charges. No hidden charges. What's more, there is no minimum number to buy and you can cancel your subscription at any time. No obligation and no questions asked.

TO GET YOUR 3 FREE BOOKS
FILL OUT AND MAIL THE COUPON BELOW

3 FREE BOOKS

Mail to: Zebra Regency Home Subscription Service
120 Brighton Road
P.O. Box 5214
Clifton, New Jersey 07015-5214

YES! Start my Regency Romance Home Subscription and send me my 3 FREE BOOKS as my introductory gift. Then each month, I'll receive the 3 newest Zebra Regency Romances to preview FREE for ten days. I understand that if I'm not satisfied, I may return them and owe nothing. Otherwise, I'll pay the low members' price of just $9.90 for all 3 books and save over $2.00 off the publisher's price (a $11.97 value). There are no shipping, handling or other hidden charges. I may cancel my subscription at any time and there is no minimum number to buy. In any case, the 3 FREE books are mine to keep regardless of what I decide.

NAME

ADDRESS _____ APT NO.

CITY _____ STATE ____ ZIP

TELEPHONE (   )

SIGNATURE _____

(if under 18 parent or guardian must sign)

Terms and prices subject to change. Orders subject to acceptance by Zebra Home Subscription Service, Inc.

RG0693

GET
3 FREE
REGENCY
ROMANCE
NOVELS—
A $11.97
VALUE!

ZEBRA HOME SUBSCRIPTION SERVICE, INC.
120 BRIGHTON ROAD
P.O. BOX 5214
CLIFTON, NEW JERSEY 07015-5214

promptu affair."

They made their goodbyes to their host and hostess and departed.

A short time later, they descended from their carriage and crossed the threshold of Carleton House.

"Ah, wonderful," breathed the marquess. "If it weren't so late, Caro, I'd wager we would've had to wait again. Look at all the people!

"Prinny's affairs are always a sad crush.

"There, see? He has not even got out of the foyer yet.

"Come on, we'll leave our cloaks with the footman here, and"—he took her hand and drew her toward the Prince Regent—"I shall present you."

The introduction complete, Caro waited until they were well out of earshot to murmur, "Miles, he is . . . he is *portly.*"

The marquess laughed.

"And, if this is an impromptu affair, I should love to attend one that has been planned. Lord, it is magnificent!" she exclaimed, looking about herself.

"Indeed. However, I believe I could discover a better use for the funds that went into this magnificent display," the marquess said dryly.

They entered the ballroom.

"But, as the money has been spent, shall we dance, Caro?" asked the marquess, smiling down at her.

The orchestra struck up a waltz on the heels of the gavotte they had just concluded, and the marquess placed one hand on Caro's waist, lifted her hand with the other, and swept her onto the floor in time to the lilting music.

She laughed up at him, her dark blue eyes sparkling at his spontaneity.

The waltz ended, and a minuet was begun.

The marquess started to lead Caro off the floor.

"Ohh, don't stop yet!" she cried, pouting up at him. She stole a glance at him from under her lashes to see what effect her pouting was having.

"Minx!" he laughed, giving in and sweeping her back

among the crowd of dancers.

The strains of the minuet died away, and a reel began.

"No, no, no, Caro," said the marquess, seeing her face and forestalling her. "I have never been one for the reel! 'Tisn't dignified. Here . . . Fagan, old man," he called, catching sight of his friend and clamping a firm hand upon his shoulder.

"Dance with Caro, Fagan."

"Assuredly. More than delighted to," answered the Earl of Weycote, smiling.

"Come, Caro. You must own I have earned a sedate game of cards," the marquess teased.

"Ah, the cards are calling, are they?" she teased back.

"Relentlessly." He grinned.

She waved him off. "Oh, very well. But mind you don't lose the house—or me. You shan't rid yourself of me that easily!"

He gave her a pained expression. "My dear, I never lose."

She raised her eyebrow in mock disbelief.

He grinned again and bowed. "Well, almost never."

"I do hope you don't mind having me fobbed off upon you, Lord Fagan."

"Not at all, ma'am. My pleasure." He observed that her eyes followed the marquess as he made his way out of the ballroom. "I recall your husband saying you two are still newlyweds, Lady Strathmore?" he asked, his eyes twinkling.

"It is showing, is it not?" she asked, returning her attention to Lord Fagan and smiling ruefully.

He chuckled. "Only a very little, Lady Strathmore, and then, I am rather a close observer, never fear."

"You are very gallant, Lord Fagan. Can you credit that I once swore that I should never behave in such an addle-pated fashion?"

"Time and love, my lady, change everything."

"La, sir!" she cried playfully, "If you are going to wax profound, this reel shall be over before ere we begin to dance!"

"Then not another serious word, Lady Strathmore," he promised cheerfully and swung her, laughing, onto the floor.

When they came off at the end of the reel, Teddy was waiting to dance the next dance with her.

Caro introduced the two gentlemen, and then Teddy led her back out onto the floor.

"And where did you spring from, pray?" teased Caro, when the steps of the minuet they were performing allowed her.

Teddy executed several steps before he answered. "Caro, Caro. You are not the only one in Prinny's circle. I swear, I am hurt—yes, hurt—to think you wouldn't *expect* to discover me here." He gave her a long face.

Caro laughed at him. "Oh, give over, Teddy. We both know, unless there is a very good reason for your being here, you would far rather be in the card room with my husband. Now, confess."

Teddy laughed. "Caro, you're dangerous. You know me too well. M'mother made me hang about in here to partner m'sister, don't you know, and while doing my duty by her I have discovered the prettiest little filly! But I don't know her, and I thought as you did . . ."

The minuet ended, and they came to a stop.

"That I'd introduce you? No, Teddy. I couldn't do that. I wouldn't be able to sleep tonight if I did," she teased.

"Oh, c'mon, Caro. Please. Don't play with me. I'd do it for you." He pointed a young woman out. "There! Know her?"

But she didn't. "I'm sorry, Teddy. I truly don't know her."

A thought occurred to her. "Did you ask your mother? I'll wager you didn't. Teddy, your mother knows simply everyone."

Teddy looked struck. "You're right, she does! Trust m'mother. I'm off, Caro, excuse me. Must find m'mother immediately!" he said, making his escape.

"Loose screw," remarked Caro fondly, shaking her head and chuckling as she watched Teddy dodge in and out among the Regent's guests, hunting for his mother.

"It's another waltz, my dear, and I had ample opportunity only a little earlier to observe that—forgive the cliché—you waltz divinely."

"Lord Macomb!" Caro gasped, turning to identify the familiar voice.

He took her in his arms and swung her out among the dancers.

"Stop!" she hissed. "I do *not*"—she endeavored to wrench her hands from his—"desire to dance with you!"

"But I desire to dance with you, Caro. And I want you to look up at me with that same starry-eyed—positively, it was!—expression that you bestowed upon your . . . ah . . . *husband*."

"Let go! Ugh!" She tried again to pull free. "I despise you!"

One or two nearby dancers turned to stare.

"Will you cause a scene, Caro? Please. We should make Prinny's ball—he would love it!"

She glanced about her angrily and stopped struggling.

"Ah, that's better. Now, come. Let's go out on the terrace for a bit of . . . air."

Still waltzing, he led her over to the French doors that lined one side of the ballroom, then stopped waltzing. He released her hand and, grasping her arm firmly, forcibly walked her through one of the French doors.

It was chilly, quiet, and dark out on the terrace, the only illumination being provided by the tiny white fairy lights so fashionable to hang in one's arbors or gardens.

He dragged her, struggling, toward the steps that led down into the Regent's formal garden, but abruptly stopped to grasp her roughly by the shoulders and try to force his mouth upon hers.

She shrank from him, backing up until she ran up against the stone balustrade that descended alongside the steps into the garden.

"No!"

The cry was cut short.

His mouth covered hers, and he pressed her over the balustrade until she thought her back must break.

"You become exceedingly tiresome."

Four cutting words pierced the cold and the dark, and Caro's pain was alleviated.

The smack of a punch thrown registered belatedly on her consciousness, and she saw the earl fall, sprawling across the middle of the stone steps.

Then the marquess' arms went round her, and she smelled his bayberry and cheroot scent and heard him murmur urgently into her hair, "Caro . . . you are all right?"

She clung to the front of his coat and nodded her head against his chest, stifling a small sob of relief.

"Pick him up, if you please, and remove him to the Regent's sitting room, as I told you," directed the marquess coldly.

Two large footmen emerged from the shadows behind the marquess and went to help the earl up.

When he stood, each footman gripped an arm and started down the steps with him.

The earl began to curse and struggle as they reached the bottom of the staircase and disappeared through the sculpted trees and bushes.

"How do you feel, Caro?" asked the marquess with concern, holding her close and patting her back at intervals.

"Caro?

"You're shivering! Come, shall we go back inside now? You'll catch your death out here . . ."

"N-Not just yet, Miles. Please. It isn't the cold."

"As you wish. But I insist," he said, putting her aside a moment to unbutton his coat and then pulling her back inside it and closing as much of it around her as he could, "on doing *this*."

He chuckled. "Jeeves would have my head if he were to see me now."

"Oh, Miles." Caro hugged him fiercely. "What would I do without you?"

She raised her face to look at him intently. "What would

I have done without you the first time?

"And it occurs to me now that I have never even thanked you for that. I am the greatest beast imaginable!

" 'Tis a marvel you agreed to marry me at all! Indeed, I cannot imagine why you did."

The marquess smiled into her eyes and chuckled. "A loaded pistol, my dear—nay, two!—being waved about under one's nose are ample persuasion, to my mind."

"Gammon. You shall never make me believe that a pistol or my uncle or two pistols or anybody's uncle could force you to do anything you truly did not wish to do.

"You would have fashioned some clever means of fobbing me off on Lord Macomb, or you would have bethought yourself of some perfectly rational point that would truly have deterred the parson. Confess."

"Your uncle suggested I married you to use your inheritance to pay my gambling debts."

"Please, Miles. Don't insult me. I don't believe you've ever had an outstanding debt in your life. And my uncle told me that you had tied all my money up in settlements on our children."

"I had to marry someday, Caro, to pass on the title—very like your own situation."

"Miles, you had scarcely clapped eyes on me! You were going to agree to have some woman who appeared to be entangled in some type of tryst gone bad—for it must have seemed so—as wife, as *mother* to this child who must inherit your lands and title?

"You didn't even know my name."

"Certainly I did. 'Twas Caro from the first!" protested the marquess flippantly.

"And I doubt you must needs marry by twenty-five," continued Caro seriously, shaking her head. "I cannot credit it.

"You aren't going to tell me, are you?"

"I don't know, Caro!" The marquess removed one arm long enough to run a hand through his hair.

"I don't know that I know myself. And, if you don't believe the reasons I've already given you, assuredly you aren't going to believe me when I say I think I loved you — I simply loved you from the first — when I heard your beautiful, sultry voice.

"And then when I saw you, with that absurd kerchief round your mouth and your hair all tumbled, and you were still putting up the devil of a fight, though you must have known you would lose . . . And you could still smile at that poor parson's outrage.

"I just knew, in my bones I guess, that here was a woman I could very likely live with the rest of my life and I'd better marry her while the opportunity offered."

"Oh, Miles, I think I love you!" exclaimed Caro, throwing her arms about his neck and rising on tiptoe to press her lips on his.

She rubbed her cheek against his and then looked into his eyes and, glad the darkness would cover her blush, murmured, "I believe we should make the Prince our goodbyes and go home and have a cognac . . . before the fire . . . in my bedchamber."

"Indeed?" asked the marquess, raising one eyebrow and smiling.

"Indeed." Returning his smile, she allowed herself to slip back down to her natural height.

"I did say we were getting along famously, did I not?" The marquess' head bent after her and found her mouth.

A moment later, Caro stepped outside his coat and began smoothing the wrinkles from it. "But first we must set your coat to rights."

A question struck her. "Where did you have Lord Macomb taken, Miles?"

He began to button his coat. "To the Prince's private sitting room. Where he shall remain until it pleases Prinny to attend him and demand his name, for a lady Prinny took rather a particular interest in is now, I fear, in . . . ah . . . dire need of a husband."

Caro looked scandalized. "Good lord! The Prince Regent!"

She frowned. "The poor chit. I shouldn't wish Lord Macomb on her for all that."

"Nor have I. She shall still reside under Prinny's protection. She merely needed Macomb's name."

The marquess chuckled. "And, I would guess, she is very likely not averse to his money."

Caro laughed at that. "You have him all done up, have you not?"

"I did my humble best." He smiled.

She looked at the marquess shrewdly. "Poetic justice, Miles? For that young woman my uncle told us had drowned herself?"

The marquess drew Caro's hand through his arm and began to walk back to the ballroom with her.

"You begin to know me far too well, Caro, my love. Already, I foresee disadvantages." He smiled warmly down at her, opening a door for her to pass through.

"Wait till I have lived with you twenty-odd years, my lord," she murmured, linking her arm back through his as he stepped in after her. "You shall have no defenses at all!"

They both laughed and, grinning absurdly at each other, made their way back through the ballroom to wish the Prince good night and depart for home.

A Springtime Affaire
by Jeanne Savery

The nastiest part of the raging storm was over, but now it had settled into rain, the heavy fall drumming on the cottage roof. The young widow who occupied the small sitting room thought it an almost soothing sound, when compared to the growls and cracks of thunder which had preceded it. One could, with practice, ignore it, and they were certainly getting practice!

One could not, however, ignore a sudden new and forceful noise. Jessica, Viscountess Knoll, lifted her head from her book, her nose pointing toward the hall very much in the manner of the little dog snuggled against her skirts. When the sound was repeated, that clank of the lion-head knocker hitting the thick oak of the front door, Jessica rose to her feet. She'd reached the hall when, for the third time, the knocker sounded—this time imperatively repeating itself.

"I'm coming. I'm coming," she called and added in a mutter, "If you're a lucky soul, I may even get there before you drown!" A distinct possibility, drowning, if one were fool enough to travel through Walland Marsh in the midst of a spring storm.

Jess struggled with the first of the many bolts and locks which Emma, her housekeeper and one-time nurse, found necessary for peace of mind. As she lifted the final bar and placed her hand on the latch, Emma herself appeared at the back of the hall.

"Don't you dare open that door, Jessica Darling."

"I can't very well leave travelers stranded, Emma, dear, and my name is now Jessica Rippon, as you very well know.

187

Peter would have a word or two to say to you for forgetting."

Emma ignored the reprimand. Brandishing the fire iron she'd brought from the kitchen she said, "Open if you must. I won't let nobody hurt you."

Jessica chuckled. The door swung slowly inward, groaning and creaking. The old house on the marsh hated wet weather and complained mightily whenever it rained for days as was the case now. Jess studied the man before her. A coachman, she decided. A *real* coachee, whose many caped driving coat was the model for those worn by young bucks she'd seen tooling their coaches along the coast road in the summer.

"What may I do for you?" she asked.

The man doffed his dripping hat. "My master and his, er, sister, need a bed, er, *beds* for the night, mistress. The bridge down the road apiece is out. The horses gone a far piece today and too weary to make the ten miles back to Rye, you see.

"How many are you?"

"Master, his, hmm, sister, Roy Groom and myself is all, mistress. John Coachman at your service."

"Well, you and Roy must take the carriage around back. There's a barn of sorts. I doubt your prads—"

"Jessica!" interrupted Emma in a whispered but scolding tone at the cant term her charge should not be using.

"—I mean I doubt your *horses* will find the accommodation up to their expectations, but it will do if you crowd them a bit with my riding mare and carriage horse. When you've settled them, I fear you'll have to bed down in the loft. Emma will find you blankets and have hot mulled cider for you in the kitchen. Take this umbrella. Help your master and his, er . . . sister . . . into the house before you do anything else."

"His, er . . . sister?" asked Emma, mimicking Jessica's wry tone.

"Probably the man's mistress." She put a hand over her old friend's mouth. "Now, don't set up a screech. Have a bit

188

of Christian charity."

"But where will we put her?" wailed the graying woman.

Jessica's eyebrows rose, a mischievous light giving her face a glow. "Well, you always say you hate to sleep alone!"

Emma growled.

"Do stop fretting, Emma. You know we'll work it out. . . . Oh, you poor dear, you!" In the doorway there appeared a small woman tightly holding the arm of a dark man who towered over her. "Do come in out of the wet." Jessica's thin nose almost twitched, and she nearly laughed aloud at the embarrassment the gentleman obviously experienced. She guessed, for him, it was a previously unknown emotion. "Sir? Won't you please come in?"

"I, er, I mean," he corrected himself, with a glance at the woman, "*we* appreciate your aid, miss. It's a bad night and I don't recall another dwelling for miles back."

"There isn't. Not if you mean just off the road. And I doubt you'd find the Grange in the daylight let alone under these conditions — although I can give you directions if you wish to try."

"You mean we passed the turn for it?"

"That was your *destination?*" Jessica frowned. "Deep End Grange?"

"Yes." A perplexed look creased the man's brow. "Is there some reason I should not visit there?"

"With your er . . . sister?"

The man wiped a quick grin off his hard-featured face. "I had no intention of staying more than a few minutes," he explained, "but the whole day has been a series of unforeseen accidents ranging from the loss of a horseshoe to the baggage coming off the back of the coach. This abominable weather has not eased the situation."

Jessica nodded, but wondered why he would stop for even a moment at the Grange. "Emma, find blankets for the men. Let them warm and dry themselves at the kitchen fire before they return to the barn. Warm drinks for all, I think. Come with me, sir and, er, miss."

"Lawks!" said the golden-haired young woman, opening

189

her mouth for the first time. "You'll bump your 'ead for sure and all, m'lord!"

"Shut your bonebox and keep it shut, you fool," hissed the man before ducking the aforementioned portion of his anatomy under the lintel into the sitting room and again, quickly, to miss the first of the beams crossing the room.

A young dog—it had been lying before the merrily burning fire—jumped up, yapping shrilly. "Hush, Amigo." The spaniel bounced toward his mistress, begging her pardon. Jess bent to pat his head and pull his ear gently. "Perhaps we should introduce ourselves. I am Jessica and you?" Jess deliberately omitted a last name. If this man had known Peter she couldn't bear the pain of listening to condolences. And if he hadn't, well, it was unlikely they'd ever meet again anyway. . . .

"I'm Adlington."

Well. Maybe he'd not heard of her, but she'd certainly heard of *him*. A great deal. Whether Peter had mentioned her name to him was another question entirely. Jessica turned to the woman.

Charles Hilbert Adam Dudley Thornton, fourth earl of Adlington, looked more embarrassed than ever. "Oh, yes. My, er, sister. Call her Rosy . . . er, Rose!"

Adlington—and, er, Rose. Peter had talked of Chad—a pet name made from his initials—Thornton ever since he'd returned from his first term at Eton. They'd met as mischief-making equals and, after one rip-roaring round of fisticuffs, become the best of friends. So what had Chad Thornton, Lord Adlington, expected to do at the Grange where Peter's irascible father was trying to wipe out every evidence his son had ever existed?

"Please be seated," said Jess absently, her mind occupied with thoughts of the past.

Rosy complied with alacrity, winding herself down into the comfortable chair near the fire. Jess thought the young woman very like a plump and well-satisfied cat. Chad, however, moved toward the small-paned, bottle-glass windows which ran high along the far wall. He lifted one of the short curtains and peered out. "The rain hasn't eased at all," he said.

"I doubt it will any time soon. We'll be lucky if the weather changes in the next several days." Jessica spoke from life-long experience of the marsh.

"Days?" squawked the girl, raising her head. *"Days?* Oh no. *No.* Chad, m'boy, you promised me a fine old time and I'm not about to—"

Further words were muffled behind a heavy hand. Jessica tucked away the memory of how quickly and gracefully he'd crossed the room and leaned over his, er . . . sister. She studied his broad shoulders, the long well-formed legs shown to advantage in tight buckskins. Muttered words were a barely heard murmur until the young person slumped, her pretty mouth forming into a pout.

"Emma comes," said Jessica, catching their attention. "She'll have hot tea or mulled wine to warm you."

"And you?" he asked.

"I'm fine," she said. I'd better be, she thought. Between you, you and your servants will soon drink up my quarterly allowance of wine and ale from that old screw up at the Grange.

None of her thoughts appeared on her face, however, as she helped serve the man and woman who had invaded her placid existence. When the two had drunk their steaming wine, Jess spoke again. "It is late for this part of the world, my lord. I hope you'll forgive us if we persist in keeping country hours? But before we show you upstairs, if I might have a word with you . . . ?"

Jessica moved out into the chilly hall and waited until Chad followed, closing the door behind him. "Are you," she asked, "going to persist in the fiction that that woman is your sister?" Lord Adlington blinked. "Because," Jess continued before he could reply, her eyes sparkling with suppressed humor, "if you *do* insist, I must take her into my room with me, and frankly I don't wish to do so. I've only the one guest room, you see."

"I see." Strong color reddened his ears. "Do you see why

I tried to pass her for such?"

"I see you are a fool to try to do any sort of business at the Grange with such as she in tow," responded Jessica on a dry note. She tipped her head, wondering if she'd been overly rude.

Obviously she had.

Her guest stiffened, all expression leaving his face. "Thank you for your opinion," he said in a cold voice.

"You're welcome," she responded as demurely as if his tone itself hadn't been an insult.

The lurking sense of humor she was almost certain she'd seen in his tanned face revealed itself in a chuckle. He made the fencing sign indicating touché as Rosy peered out the door to the sitting room. "What are you laughing about?" she asked in such overly genteel tones they hurt the ear. "It isn't fair to leave me all alone in there with that smelly little dog."

Chad ignored her. "If you'll tell me where to take her, I'll see she's tucked in for the night."

"You may tuck yourself in as well, my lord. I'll see the fire is banked and be off to my own bed."

Lord Adlington, holding a well-shaped hand out toward Rose, crossed to the narrow stairs which rose against one wall of the hall. Jess said, "My Lord?" He turned, a quizzing eyebrow arching into his broad forehead. "We haven't room to be fancy here. Meals are served in the kitchen. Breakfast will be at nine sharp. We're not up to your standards, I'm sure, so don't expect a great deal of choice."

"Are you warning me or apologizing?" He didn't allow time for a response. "We are not so top-lofty you need concern yourself, Miss Jessica."

Now was that, she wondered, a royal sort of "we" or did he refer to the both of them? Jessica managed a "Thank you." He nodded and disappeared up the stairs to where an obviously disapproving Emma awaited them.

Emma came down to the sitting room before Jess finished banking the fire for the night. She moved around, efficiently picking up and setting right and, just when Jessica decided she'd get away with no lecture, turned toward her, hands on her broad hips. "He's a right smooth charley," she said.

"He's an old friend of Peter's, Emma. I recognize his name. I wonder why he's visiting the Grange."

"Although it's been awhile since your husband died, perhaps it's to condole with the old man."

"He'll get short shrift if that's his errand," said Jess dryly.

"I know that and you know that, but a stranger would not."

"True."

"If he's an old friend of your husband's, he should know about *you*."

"It was war time. Friends can't always communicate as they'd like."

"So you think he doesn't know of your existence?"

"He thinks I'm Miss Jessica and we'll leave it that way, if you please. Or even if you don't!"

"Why should *you* please?"

Jess raised the curtain and looked out—not that she could see anything. "Why, Emma?" What would she accept? "Oh, because I met his sort in London that one short season with Peter. He'll treat *Miss* Jessica properly. But married? Or worse, by far, that I'm widowed. He'd think a widow fair game." Jess tipped her head, considering. "Perhaps I malign him. As *Peter's* widow, he might *not* see me as available, but I'd prefer to take no chances."

"You mean he's a rake."

"Rogue, more like," said Jess tolerantly. "After all, he was a friend of Peter's, was he not?" Jessica's smile took any possible sting from the words.

A little later she let herself and Amigo into her own room as quietly as possible so as not to disturb her guests. She needn't have worried: the wall between the bedrooms might not have been there, so clearly heard was their argument.

"Why won't you sleep up here with me?" asked a fretful feminine voice.

"A man does not sleep with his sister, Rosy." Chad said that as if he'd said it already—and several times more than he liked.

"Well, I don't like it. I don't see why I need be your sister. I don't think that Miss Jessica believed it for a moment, and I'm sure the housekeeper didn't. She *sniffed*."

"Stifle it Rosy, or you'll sleep in the trundle and I'll take the bed."

"You wouldn't! It's drafty and cold down there, and I'll wager there are rats and mice. You *wouldn't!*"

"No rats," Jessica called through the wall, deciding it wasn't proper to listen to the young person's complaints even if it was all rather amusing. "A mouse or two, perhaps."

Silence greeted her words. A deep chuckle followed the silence. "You see, my dear? No rats. But cold and drafty and, perhaps, mice. I'd suggest you go to sleep where you are because one more word and I'll dump you down here. By yourself."

Jessica heard one more muttered "You wouldn't" before she drifted off. She didn't wake until Emma clattered in with hot water and a hod of coals the next morning. Jessica pushed back into her pillows, yawning and stretching. She felt as if the day held something special but, for the moment, couldn't think why. What a lot of coal Emma has brought up, she thought. That hod was much too heavy for her. Besides, they couldn't afford such prodigal use of their limited supply, and Emma knew that. Jessica yawned again. "Has it stopped raining?" she asked.

"No. You'd better bestir yourself, Mistress Jess. I don't know what to do with that man."

"Man?" Oh. *That* man. The one who had been so ungentlemanly as to invade her dreams last night. And such dreams! Jessica stirred herself right over to her wash stand and tipped hot water into the basin.

"I'll be down immediately, Emma. Just because we've company doesn't mean you're to overdo, now. Remember what the doctor said about your back."

"If you mean the coal," said the old woman with asperity, "your Lord Adlington's man brought it in. I found it at the top of the stairs. And that fine lord, well, *he's* already started fires in the sitting room and the kitchen, been out to the stables, and one of the men, him or another, cooked their breakfast. I haven't a notion what else."

What else turned out to be a survey of the surrounding countryside, which overnight, was knee deep in water. "Do you," asked Adlington mildly, "often find yourself cut off in this fashion?"

"Once or twice a year. My fath—er, my landlord won't spend a halfpenny on the ditches, and he'll be furious he must throw up a new bridge. But he has only himself to blame that it will cost far more now than if he'd repaired the bridge last summer." Jess tipped her head. "Then again, perhaps he won't fix it. There is another, longer, route we tenants may use."

"You don't sound particularly angry with the man."

"It is his property, Lord Adlington, and his money. If he prefers to hoard his funds, I've no grounds for quarreling with him." She looked around the kitchen. "Has Rose not come down to breakfast?"

"She still slept when last I checked." He waved away the subject and continued: "How soon will the road be safe?"

"Three to four days . . ."

He nodded in a resigned way as if it were no more than he'd expected.

". . . once the rain stops," she finished.

He looked up sharply. "And when," he asked in an exceedingly polite voice, "do you think the rain might stop?"

"Any day now."

"Any day now," he repeated. "And a day or two for the water to recede. And then another day or two before you'd dare the roads. Has it occurred to you it is dangerous for you to be so isolated and alone for so long?"

"I don't see why. If I can't get *out,* then no one can get *in.*"

"Is it totally unthinkable that you might become ill? Or that Emma might fall and hurt herself?"

Jessica scowled. That nightmare had occurred to her often, but Emma refused to go when flooding was expected—not without Jessica, and Jessica couldn't go. Not so long as that iniquitous clause existed in her lease.

"You are very quiet. I didn't mean to distress you. I merely thought it better if you and Emma were to visit friends during sieges such as this."

"Our circumstances are such that it isn't possible." Not willing to explain, Jessica turned the subject. "Thank you for your help this morning."

"I prefer to be busy," he said, excusing the menial chores he'd done for Emma. "Have you no other servants?"

"When the water recedes we'll have two—if it's any of your business. A man and his wife who turn their hands to pretty much everything."

"They were caught away when it flooded?" he asked, again his tone that overly polite one that sent squalls along Jessica's nerves.

"I don't see why I bother to explain, but I sent them away. Mrs. Davies has a nervous nature. She's better off with their daughter in Rye."

"And yourself?" he asked.

She sighed. It was clear the man would not let it be, so she might as well give in. "I may, by the terms of my agreement, be away from here for no more than one night at a time. I lose my home if I contravene that clause."

"Iniquitous, if it includes emergencies such as this."

"I was warned that it does. My landlord's eyes gleamed in an appropriately evil manner when he explained it. I believe it was with the expectation I'd not accept under such terms. Any writer of Gothic romances would have been properly impressed both by his gnashing of teeth and my bravery in facing him down. Spiteful old man," she finished without heat.

"I can't believe anyone would be so careless with your life."

"My life? I'm in no danger, my lord."

"Are you not?" He pointed at the kitchen floor. "If the water were to rise only a few more inches, it would be in the back door!"

She chuckled. "The local history goes back a very long way, my lord. Only once in the last hundred years was it high enough to enter the house. This is the highest point of land for miles through the weld."

"Have you looked out this morning?"

"Why no. Do you truly think we're likely to lose our lives?"

"No," he said—reluctantly, it seemed. " 'Tis not so desperate as that, of course, but, since it doesn't look to stop raining any time soon, we should, I think, take precautions. If you do not object, I'll carry the available wine and ale and a store of water upstairs. Also food. Likewise coal and tinder." He explained: "I learned in the Peninsula to be prepared for the worst so that one is not caught at a disadvantage. It would be as well to have things ready if we find we must adjourn to the upstairs."

Jessica finished her morning cup of coffee and rose, going to the windows. As in every room on the ground floor, these were narrow, the sills coming just below her shoulders. She checked the water lapping placidly just inside the hedge at the edge of her property.

Jess had seen it higher twice. Once it had come up to where the path was raised like a dike through the vegetable garden and around the house. Since the water was still holding well back from the path she would not worry yet. On the other hand, the man standing to her back needed occupation. It would not do to have him bored and, for that reason, inclined to mischief.

Jessica turned, found his lordship closer than she'd thought him and, her breath catching, sidestepped around him. She moved to the table where, much against her usual practice, she poured a second cup of coffee! Her hand trembled as she raised the cup to her lips.

How foolish, she thought, to be unsettled by a man's

presence—even one as attractive as Chad Thornton! She must think of something else. She looked at her cup. Coffee. Coffee would be another thing in short supply by the time her unwanted company departed. Perhaps she'd break into her small emergency hoard and buy more. Wine one could do without, but no coffee to start the day? A horrible thought.

"You are the strangest woman," said Adlington, again approaching too near for comfort. "Why do you go off somewhere into your head where I cannot follow? It is most disturbing."

She glanced at him to assure herself he was teasing. He was. At least in part. "I apologize for being so poor a hostess. I've had little practice. Now let me see. You asked about carrying supplies to the upper floor in case we find it necessary to retreat there. I tell you frankly I foresee no need for it. However, assuming you promise to return them all to their proper places, I see no reason why you cannot amuse yourself by carrying them up."

"Thereby indulging me with a high treat," he said. "How generous."

His dry tone drew her eyes. He smiled. She laughed at herself for being so gauche as to tell him why she gave him permission to work like a navvy.

"Ah well. What may one expect of a country mouse such as myself?"

"You don't mind that I find you amusing?"

"Mind? But why should I when I understand so well why you do?"

"As well as beauty, you've an admirable character and are intelligent."

Jessica's smile faded. "Don't feel you must flirt with me, my lord. I abominate false coin."

"I don't offer false coin."

She studied him for a long breath-catching moment and then bent to hide her confusion in her cup. It was empty.

"May I fill that for you?"

"Fill it? No, thank you, my lord. I've had enough." She

198

looked blankly around the kitchen. The blasted man was getting through her defenses and that must not happen. She had no place in his life beyond this short interlude during which it was essential she remember that such as he would never be for her. This conversation must, therefore, be ended. At once. Rudeness? She'd give it a try. "I'll fill a tray which you may carry up to your, hmm, *sister.* We cannot totally disrupt our schedule for the two of you."

"I do not ask it." Chad immediately selected a tray from where they were stored between the old country chest and an enclosed cupboard. Deftly, he filled it. "Please tell me what time you serve a luncheon."

"Luncheon?" Jess pretended shock. "My good man, not only are you in the *country,* but you're in the home of the raggle-taggle gentry rather than that of the aristocracy—you *were* warned, my lord."

"Ah." He didn't sigh, but Jess thought he wished to do so. "Then might you be pleased to inform me when you expect to serve dinner?"

"Sometime between three-thirty and four."

"Thank you," he said with polite disinterest.

Again Jess couldn't forbear studying his harsh features. He was having obvious difficulty, she thought, controlling what he must perceive as a perfectly reasonable irritation. "We have a fairly substantial tray later in the evening—in case you become peckish, my lord," she added, wondering if he worried that he'd starve while forced to remain here. But he just grinned at her before disappearing into the hall with the breakfast tray, so she decided it couldn't have been that.

An hour or so later Jess found Rose standing, disconsolately, in the hall. For a moment she was tempted to pass the young woman by with no more than a polite word and go on about her business, but the girl looked so sad and lost she found she could not do it. "Bored, my dear? We get that way when forced to remain in the house day after day. Do you read?"

Rose threw a suspicious look toward Jessica, her chin rising as if she feared she was being mocked. "I do, ac-tu-ally." Rose thought about it and added, "But not sermons. I won't read sermons."

"I'm glad you don't require them," said Jessica with carefully composed features. "I fear there's not one book of sermons in the house. Isn't that a terrible admission?" She turned toward the door across the hall from the sitting room. It was not a room into which she invited guests. When Rose crowded in after her, however, Jessica, once again, couldn't bring herself to hurt the woman and didn't push her out.

"Whatever do you do in here?" asked Rose.

"Any number of things. Over there is my loom. I weave, you see."

"Cloth?"

What else? thought Jessica. She said, "Woolen shawls, mostly." Bundles of herbs hung from the beams and a table held supplies and the equipment necessary to a still room. "I make simple remedies for some of the locals who wouldn't think to consult a doctor and can't afford to go into Rye to the 'pothecary for every little thing. *Here,*" she added, moving across the room, "is where I shelve the books I have sent out from the lending library." *Which, like coffee, is another extravagance in which I should not indulge!*

Rose moved toward the pile of shawls Jessica had woven during the last few months from hand-spun and home-dyed thread. "Do you sell 'em — *them?*"

"Yes." Jess closed her mouth tightly. She hated admitting to anyone that the trifling income from the sale of her weaving gave her that little bit extra that allowed her the small charities her father had taught her were a necessary part of life and a few luxuries, such as the library membership.

Rose held up the top shawl. "Maybe Chad would buy me one and I could embroider it." She fingered down through the pile, touching each, running her hand into the folds of one or another and lifting the top of the stack when she

200

wanted a better look at the soft dyes. "They'd be extra pretty with colored flowers all over them."

So they would, thought Jess. "Do you sew?"

"Oh yes. I don't like *plain* sewing, but I rather like fancy work. It's sort of ladylike, don't you know?" asked the girl wistfully.

After tucking away the feeling Rosy might be better bred than her present occupation would indicate and thinking it was better the girl be busy than whining, Jessica told her guest to choose one of the shawls.

While Rose dithered between three or four she liked, Jessica found a book she thought her guest might enjoy. There were lengths of yarn left over from threading the loom, odds and ends from past dye lots. She set aside the basket in which the leftover lengths were kept and found a needle with a large eye and scissors. Carrying the basket and the book, she led Rose across the hall to the sitting room and settled the girl before the fire.

Then Jessica wondered what to do with herself. She could, she supposed, help Chad move supplies upstairs. Then again, the less she saw of that fine gentleman, the better off she'd be. She was no light skirt to travel with his lordship and pretend to be his sister—no matter that the thought was tempting beyond belief! Oh dear. She really must stop thinking such things.

So what to do? She wandered to the window and wondered if it was her imagination or the sky had actually lightened slightly. Morosely, she decided it was her overactive imagination. Turning, she looked to where Rose bent over a pale primrose shawl. Already the form of a large flower in various shades of violet was appearing under her busy fingers. It would be a rather good representation of a morning glory when Rose finished with it.

Jessica searched her mind for what she'd be doing at this hour if she had no company. Distracting company. Exceedingly distracting company.

Spinning? Very likely. Weaving? Not when the light was so bad and she couldn't afford work candles. Reading?

201

This early in the day? Not likely. Working with her herbs? Nothing appealed. She didn't know what she wanted to do.

Or she *did* know, but refused to allow herself to indulge such an undisciplined urge. She couldn't afford to find Adlington so interesting, so intriguing, so exciting—the epitome of all those hopes and fears and joys and what-have-yous she'd had to give up when her father died from influenza and she'd found herself penniless.

Bless Peter for hunting for and finding her, making it possible for her to avoid a life of drudgery as a poor relation in her aunt's home. If only his father were not such a curmudgeon. *Oh, Peter* . . . A surge of sadness engulfed her, and her hand clenched the curtain. *Why did you have to die?*

Jessica shook her head, trying to dispel demons from her past. She had a good life. A far better life than she'd had any reason to expect from the moment her father's death made her a pauper. The settlement Peter had been able to make her was small, true, but it was more than a lot of women had.

Jessica noted the golden head of her young guest and wondered if she, too, might have come to Rose's way of life if Peter hadn't discovered her plight that time he'd come home on medical leave from the Peninsula. Probably not. Most likely she'd not have had the nerve—nor have known how to go about it!

Dear Peter. Dear darling Peter. They'd grown up running wild together, she and fun-loving Peter, who escaped his tutor and came to the vicarage to find her and run off with her on adventures. Patient Peter who taught her to ride. He'd learned to swim when he was nine and had, against all rules of propriety, proceeded to teach her that, too. Loyal Peter, who'd grown older and been sent away to school, but, unlike most boys his age, hadn't forgotten the little nuisance of a female back home; his first friend. During vacations he'd taught her other things—to drive his first team, for instance.

But later he *hadn't* taught her something he'd had every

right to add to her list of accomplishments. Dear darling Peter, the almost-brother she'd loved, the might-have-been-lover who wouldn't . . . hadn't . . . No. She mustn't think of that. Generous Peter, who had married her out of hand and then proceeded in his loftiest manner to inform her it would be a marriage in name only because he didn't love her that way, nor she him, and someday one or the other of them *would* love the proper way and they need only have an annulment in order to part and go to their own true loves.

Jessica sighed, remembering how he'd finished that discussion and wondering if he'd felt a twinge of foreknow-ledge as, in more Peter-like tones, he'd added, *Or far more likely, my little wifey, I'll take a fatal wound in battle and leave you a widow.* Surely he'd had no notion of just how soon that would happen. Moreover, he'd believed it when he'd told her in that comfortable way he had, *You'll be all right, m'dear, and that's what I want. I've seen that you'll be taken care of.*

Which he'd done. In a way. Lord Sutton abided by the letter of Peter's will, if not the spirit. She prayed Peter, wherever he was now, would never know how the earl stinted her! The roof his father supplied was one at which he'd believed she'd turn up her nose, and he allowed her to remain beneath it under conditions which were very nearly criminal. But Jess had a reason for accepting them. If she didn't honor every single one of them, however, and his lordship discovered it, he'd evict her, chortling gleefully all the while his men dumped her belongings into the road.

The earl would *love* to be rid of her. Then he could forget her existence, an existence which reminded him of the son he wished to forget. So why didn't she let him get on with it? It must, she supposed, be cross-grained stubbornness on her part that she refused to give the man the surcease to his conscience for which he longed. *Someone* had to remind him now and again he'd once had a son who should be re-membered with admiration and love and pride, *not* erased from the family Bible and forbidden mention!

So, among other things, Jess was careful to keep the

hedge trimmed, to keep the garden neat, and, most important of all, keep close to the house. She'd do nothing which would lose her her home. Besides, although it was possible she might rent rooms in one of the minor spas and *barely possible* she could keep Emma and herself in some sort of comfort on the income from Peter's settlement, Knoll House was far better, the extra space more agreeable — except for the fact that she must never spend but one night in a row away from it.

Oh, it must be the weather, she thought, that I allow such depressing thoughts into my head.

Jessica had sworn never to feel self-pity. She'd count her blessings as she used the hand spinner to spin rough wool for the vests Emma knitted. Emma had recently complained she was nearly out of yarn, and she did enjoy knitting in the evening while Jessica read aloud. Besides, Emma sold her work to the same man who bought Jessica's shawls. So, yes. She'd spin.

Adlington found the two young women cozily sitting together when he quietly entered the sitting room sometime later. Neither heard him. The one had her improbably blond head bent over a pale yellow length of material, sewing neat stitches with a dark green wool. From where he stood he couldn't get a clear view of what Rose was up to, but it surprised him that she appeared to be doing something so practical as sewing. Rose? Sewing? He shook his head, and the movement caught his hostess's eye. She turned slightly and looked at him.

What was *she* doing? he wondered. One of her hands swept back and forth, the other carefully feeding something into the process. Wool? Miss Jessica was *spinning?*

Suddenly Chad felt totally out of his depth, unsure of himself as he never was. The ladies he knew wouldn't occupy themselves with something so workaday as spinning. Yet he knew from her voice and graceful ways that Miss Jessica had not risen from ungenteel beginnings. Could her plight be such that she found it necessary to spin and weave her own cloth?

What a horrible thought. If true, he and the others must be a terrible charge on her . . . Well, that was easily enough dealt with: He'd remember to leave a handful of guineas behind. Then, once he'd stopped at Deep End Grange and fulfilled his promise to Peter to discover whether his friend's "little wifey" was well cared for and not unhappy living with the old man, he could get on with his life and forget this handsome woman.

An amazing woman, really, Miss Jessica . . . so, would he forget? Chad had a sinking feeling his thoughts might, for a long time to come, be wound up in this tall graceful woman who sat comfortably and without embarrassment in the same room as his mistress, her small dog at her feet. Such thoughts shouldn't be. It was not at all proper. Not if Jessica were, herself, as untouched by scandal as he'd assumed.

Now *there* was a thought! Perhaps he worried about nothing. Perhaps her isolation here at the end of nowhere was because she'd made herself a social outcast at some point in her young life. What intriguing possibilities *that* thought brought to mind! He eyed her speculatively. She'd suit him far better than Rose ever had!

"Are you coming in or are you going out, Lord Adlington?"

He stepped farther into the room. Rose, he noted, bundled up her material and stuffed it out of sight beside her chair, her face flaming. "I see you've found something with which to occupy yourselves." He stared at Jessica who continued to ply her hand-held spinning device. How could she do so and not feel the embarrassment Rose should *not* be feeling? After all, he'd never seen such devices except in the hands of country women who sat by their doors in the sun, spinning as they watched the world go by. "Well, Rose," he asked a trifle gruffly, "why did you stop your work? May I not see it?"

" 'Tisn't nothing, m'lord," she mumbled.

He couldn't believe it. Rose, delightfully uninhibited Rose, was still blushing—and only because he'd caught her doing something so lacking in dash as sewing? "Show me," he insisted.

Rose looked to Jessica for help. Jessica had been astonished by the design her unexpected and, it must be said, unwanted, house guest produced. "Do show him, Rose. It's quite lovely, I believe, but we should ask an expert's opinion, should we not?"

Reluctantly the girl spread out her work. "I ain't about done yet. There's more leaves to do here. And that stem should come on down this way. And I think maybe another big posy right there and a bud or two. . . ."

"Rose is something of an artist, is she not, Lord Adlington?"

"I wish you'd call me Chad. All my friends do."

"I don't believe I qualify, my lord," said Jessica, dismissing the dangerous but seductive invitation to intimacy even as she hid her disappointment that she must. "You haven't said how you like Rose's design."

"I'm pleasantly surprised. I didn't know you had such talent, Rose."

"You're bamming me," she accused.

"Jesting? Certainly not. That will be a beautiful shawl once you've finished it. Where did you get the material?"

"Oh. I forgot . . ."

"No, Rose," interrupted Jessica. "Please. *Don't.*"

The woman ignored her hostess, and Jess ground her teeth as Rose demanded of Adlington: "You pay Miss Jessica." Rose held Chad's gaze. "She's been nice to me and treated me like a lady, which she hadn't no need to do, and I like 'er—*her*, I mean. She weaves them shawls to sell, so you pay her good, you hear?" The young woman spoke quickly and with a certain fierceness.

"Lacking in tact, Rose, but beautifully frank. How much do I owe you for the shawl and embroidery wool," he asked, turning laughing eyes on Jess.

For a moment Jess felt choked with pride. False pride, she reminded herself and forced herself to relax. "Nothing for the thread. That is no more than leftover bits I'm too miserly to throw away. For the shawl — eight shillings would be a more than fair price, my lord. That is, I believe, what Mr. Wardon gets for them in his shop in Rye."

Which means, he thought, that you get less than that for the weaving of them. Is it worth it? he wondered. Poor puss.

He pulled a guinea from his pocket, handing it over.

Jessica rose to her feet. "I'll come right back with your change."

"Let Rose choose another shawl. We'll call it even."

"But that would be ten and a half shillings per shawl. That's too much."

"I'm not going to haggle over a few shillings, and besides, shawls of the same quality would cost far more in London." Jessica shook her head. "Enough. You'll take the guinea for two shawls, my dear, and there's an end of it. The subject bores me." Jessica's chin rose a notch. He wasn't certain if it was because he'd called her 'my dear' without thinking or because she was too proud to take the shillings.

The chin dropped as Jess thought of the dwindling coffee supply. She sighed. "Thank you, my lord. Rose, do remember to choose another shawl."

"I'd like that," said Rose smugly, her pleasure that she'd helped her hostess obvious. "They're nice soft wool and *warm.*"

Rose's eyes met Jessica's still stormy gaze. There was a plea in hers for understanding, and Jess softened. She'd encouraged Rose to talk while they worked, and her father's teachings had once again proven true. Rose was deserving of understanding, not censure. She, a wealthy farmer's daughter, had been seduced by the squire's son for no more than a bit of pleasure, and thereby ruined. Jessica once again reminded herself to count her blessings.

"Are you ignoring me?" asked Adlington, half laughing and half irritated.

"Ignoring you, my lord?" Jessica looked up, blankly. "Ah. You've finished your self-imposed tasks? That means

207

you need occupation, does it not? Well, I believe we can find something for you to do. Read to us, my lord, while we work!"

Charles Hilbert Adam Dudley Thornton, fourth earl of Adlington, didn't *quite* boggle at his hostess' treating him like a small boy in need of diversion, but he came near to it. He took the book she held out to him, his gaze never leaving her demure expression. He cleared his throat. After one more suspicious look, he began, " 'The family of Dashwood had been long settled in Sussex. Their . . .' "

Another day and still more water. Jessica looked out the kitchen window and wondered how she might occupy her guests today to keep them from mischief. Yesterday Rose had sewed a bit more before putting aside her work to listen, raptly, to Miss Austen's tale. She could continue her embroidery or read and likely be content. But Chad—Lord Adlington, that is—what of him? He'd stayed up late the night before. She suspected he'd finished Miss Austen's novel. She had another, a Gothic tale, at which, she felt certain, he'd turn up his aristocratic nose. Beyond that were her tomes on herbs and cures which would not interest his lordship. Drat the man.

Peter would know what to do with him. But she was not to think of Peter. Peter was dead and she mustn't dream of his returning, of his making things right for her once again as he'd done, often, in the past. Wedding her was his most important rescue, but he'd started saving her groats when she was a mere child. There'd been the time he'd found her up a tree, for instance, and unable to get down, or what about that long-ago summer day when she'd poled their homemade raft down the canal and found she hadn't the strength to pole it back again against the sluggish current? She chuckled.

Then she frowned. Oh dear. There she went again, living on memories from the long-lost past. She must not do that.

A rapping at the back door broke her abstraction. Jess set down her cup, going to open it for Adlington's man, as she thought, only to find the young son of her nearest neighbor grinning at her. "Well, Martin. And how did you manage to fly across all that water?" Remembering her rafting experience, her look sharpened. "You haven't been boating alone, have you?"

"Yes, o'course, missus. M'da said you'd be running low on food, most like, after all the rain." The lad lifted a basket which Jess hadn't noticed from the step and set it down in the kitchen. "Eggs, missus, and Da killed an extra fowl and sent along a side o' bacon we won't be needing."

Now that last, thought Jess, is an outright lie.

Martin's family was not badly off, but they weren't rolling in guineas. "I thank your father very much. We'd not be in need, but we've guests. You know the bridge is out?"

The boy nodded and informed her word had been taken up to the Grange, but that they didn't expect much, 'o'course,' from Lord Sutton.

Jessica grinned at what was obviously the father's mature opinion on the son's young lips. "Did you find it difficult, coming here?" He pooh-poohed the idea so she asked, "Is your mother's dairy still producing? We ran out of milk yesterday and are low on butter. More eggs, if possible, and . . . oh, I don't know, but I'd like to buy what I can."

The boy tipped her a worried look. "Don't know as how da'll *sell* to ye, Missus Jess. Not after all you done for us, a saving Sueanne's life and all. He'll *give* you what he can, o' course."

"I know he would, but I would not be happy receiving so much charity." Jess turned as the boy's eyes widened and a soft "Cooee" escaped his lips. Drat, she thought, staring at Adlington. How much had the blessed man overheard?

"You have a boat, lad?" asked Adlington.

"Yes sir—m'lord-sir." Martin's thatch of hair flopped against his forehead as he nodded vigorously.

"How far is it to your father's land?"

"Not m'da's land, m'lord-sir."

Jess hid a grin as Chad bit back a biting retort and drew in a deep breath. He tried again. "How far to where you live, then?"

"About two miles as the crow flies—m'lord-sir."

"Or," said Jess softly, "as the fish might swim it."

The boy grinned at her, but turned back to Adlington when his lordship said, "I'd like to go back with you and have a word with your father."

Jess stepped forward at that, her hand raised. "Now just a minute, my lord. No one asked you to interfere with my household arrangements!"

Adlington looked down a nose Jessica had already stigmatized in her mind as far too aristocratic. Without conscious thought he drew a mantle of authority around himself, one that derived from knowing that generations of ancestors, each as haughty as himself, were in his background. Jessica pinched her lips tightly together. "Exactly so, my dear," he said softly. "It never pays to argue with me." He turned back to the boy. "Wait here. I'll be with you shortly."

"Cooee," repeated Martin when Adlington disappeared. "Who's that? I'll bet *he'd* strip to advantage!"

Jess felt herself blushing at the notion of Adlington stripped and posed for a prize fight. The thought of those broad shoulders and well-muscled arms revealed to her gaze was almost more than she could bear. She controlled her voice. "He's Lord Adlington, an old friend of Peter's. You remember Peter, do you not?"

" 'Course I do," said the boy, his disgust obvious. *"Everyone* 'members Lord Peter. 'Twere a sad day when a bullet came by with *his* name on it."

"Yes, it was. A very sad day." Jessica, always one to bash her head against the wall—as evidenced by her determination that Peter not be forgotten by his father—marshaled arguments against Lord Adlington's going with Martin. When his lordship returned to the kitchen, she opened her mouth to speak her mind—and shut it again, her anger punctured when he held out her own heavy woolen cape for her to don. "My lord?" she asked. "You wish me to go as well?"

"Yes, of course you must. Do you think I could convince your friends of your welfare without you? They'd be more likely to incarcerate me in a byre until the water went down and then take me before the nearest magistrate for daring to intrude on you. Come along now."

When she didn't move he came to her, swinging the wrap around her, and pulling it together at the neck. For a minute Jess was caught by the heated look in his eyes. For even less time than that, as his fists tightened in the cloth at her throat, she thought he was going to pull her closer, kiss her. . . .

"You tie it," he said, huskily. His tone was gruffer than normal when he turned and asked, "Where did you leave your boat, boy?"

"Just out by the front gate, m'lord-sir."

"I'll take Miss Jessica out the front rather than carry her around." He winked at the boy and added, "She's too much of an armful to carry so far."

"You, my lord, are a dreadful tease. Ah, Emma dear, we are off to Nine Acres. What, besides dairy products, do we need?" asked Jess.

"Coffee? We'll need more soon," said Emma, her forehead creased. "I don't know how we can have gone through so much in just a couple of days."

Bright red spots appeared on Adlington's cheeks. "I'm afraid that's my fault. I drink far too much, and I've been into the beans, Emma."

Jess stalked across the kitchen to where the coffee was kept, took the tin down from the shelf and, even before she opened it, had a sinking feeling. She looked in and raised her head to glower at her guest. "Drat."

"That bad?"

"You don't really think the Clays will have coffee, do you Emma?"

"Well no, but one may hope."

"We're about out."

"Yes."

"Drat and drat again."

211

"Would you," asked Adlington, wavering between amusement and chagrin, "like me to teach you stronger words which might do more toward relieving your irritation with me?"

"I'm familiar with such language. I am merely too well bred to use it." Jessica, her swirling cape flowing out behind, stalked toward the front door, which she then began to unlock. Adlington reached over her shoulder to push at a particularly stubborn bolt. He lifted the bar for her, too, his arms around her. For a moment neither of them moved. Jessica barely breathed. What, she wondered, would happen if she leaned back? If she turned just a little? If she raised her face . . . ?

The moment passed and his lordship stepped away to allow her to turn the key. He lifted the latch and pulled open the heavy door which squawked more loudly than it had the night he'd arrived. They looked out into the drizzle.

Adlington turned to find an umbrella in the brass stand and handed it to her. "You'll need this."

"I'll not melt, my lord," she said, although she wondered if that were true. The heat in her veins caused by his proximity refused to recede, and she thought it likely she might turn into a puddle right there on the hall floor. Particularly if he didn't stop looking at her that way! "I'll not need that."

"A couple of miles in an open boat and even that mizzle will leave you soaked, Miss Jessica. You'll carry it."

"You, my lord, are a bully."

"I, my dear, am concerned for your health. Which, given your isolation, you, too, should have a care for."

Jess sighed. The dratted man was right again. Must he always be so? She brightened. He hadn't, yet, been right about the flooding. She was certain they needn't concern themselves about that — although the water *had* risen, here and there, to lap at the base of the barrier walk around the house.

"Shall we go?" he asked. Jessica turned on her heel, but this time she wasn't allowed to walk away from him. He lifted her easily into his arms and strode down the flagged walk, his boots splashing through the shallow water. Jess automatically threw an arm around his neck and then embarrassment immobilized her. "Relax," he said.

"Tell me how and I'll do so," she said through gritted teeth. Other sensations were following on embarrassment: bewilderment, mortification—and a sense of *belonging,* which horrified her. She shouldn't feel as if she fitted into his arms, shouldn't wish to stay there. The other emotions faded as a desperate fear for her future, alone, without Chad, engulfed her.

Oh Peter, she thought, how right you were that someday I'd meet The One—but you forgot to warn me the feeling might not be mutual!

The water reached Adlington's ankles as they neared the gate and the boat tied to it. Jessica looked over her shoulder at the shallow-draft craft—more a small barge than a boat. "In you go," he said and set her down. Taking the umbrella from her, he opened it and handed it back. "Now keep that over you. I need you to introduce me to Mr. Clay, but you mustn't come down with a chill as a result."

"Yes, m'lord-sir," said Jess, mimicking their young guide.

Adlington only grinned before stepping into the back of the boat and lifting the pole. "Now, m'lad," he asked the boy, "which way?"

The drizzle worsened before they reached the Clays', and Jessica noted a rather grim look around Chad's jaw as he carried her toward the burly farmer sloshing through shallow water to meet them. Once the introductions were completed Mr. Clay looked at her from under rough eyebrows. "Missus? Be all right with you?" He glanced at Adlington.

"I'm fine. Emma is pleased we've company, but she's quite distracted, worrying about feeding us all. Can you help?"

"Enough," interrupted Lord Adlington. "Mr. Clay, I'll take my hostess into the house. You and I will come to terms more quickly without the interference of the most stubborn young lady I've ever met." His brows rose in a quizzical expression, inviting the farmer to enjoy the joke. When Jess would have spoken he shushed her. "I will be indebted to no one," said his lordship sternly. "You'll find I get my own way in this in the end, so do not waste our time arguing." Chad took her into the kitchen and set her gently onto her feet.

Jessica reached for a stool and sat, fearing her knees wouldn't hold. "Ah, Sueanne, m'chuck!" said Jess as the Clay's youngest came into the kitchen. "How's my sweetings?"

The four-year-old turned worshipful eyes up to her goddess and held out thin arms to be taken into Jessica's lap. The child turned her face into Jessica's shoulder and sniffed loudly. Worried, Jess turned the little face back, wondering if the child were crying. Sueanne tipped her little head and gave her a questioning look.

"What troubles you child?" asked Jess. The little girl raised curious eyes to look at Jess and blinked. Jess added, "Why were you snuffling? Were you crying, or have you a chill?"

"You jest smell good." The simple answer was followed by the child's putting her face back into Jessica's lavender-scented clothing where she blissfully returned to inhaling the odor.

Jessica blushed rosily when Lord Adlington laughed. "I've noted your scent myself. How I envy the youngster the freedom to get so close to it."

Mrs. Clay moved behind Jessica, and Mr. Clay took a step toward Lord Adlington.

His lordship blinked. "What have I done *now?*" he asked.

Jessica's laugh burbled up. "You, my lord, should know better than to flirt with a desiccated old stick like me. And bless you, friends," she said to the couple obviously wondering if the fine gentleman were a dangerous predator. "I assure you it is not necessary to defend my honor. His lordship is incapable of talking sense, but his morals are good.

He'll not harm me."

"Ah," said Mr. Clay, nodding. "Just a lot of barking, is it?" But his look warned that Missus Jessica was not without protection.

Later Jessica was carried back out to the boat and set amongst the supplies. They were alone on the trip back to Knoll House, and she wished that Martin were with them. Her feelings for Peter's old friend were growing—getting out of hand, actually. Not his arrogance or bullying ways or even the presence of the man's mistress could give her a disgust for him: quite simply, she wanted to walk into his embrace and never leave it.

How absurd, she thought. The first presentable man to come within ken for over a year and immediately you thlnk you've lost your foolish heart to him!

"Now where have you disappeared to?" asked Chad, his voice shaking her from her musings. A trifle cross-sounding, he added, "I've never before met a woman so wrapped up in her own mind."

"Oh." Jessica drew herself up, "You startled me—my lord-sir."

"Enough of that. I've about convinced young Martin I'll not put up with his lord-sirring me and don't you encourage him by such ridiculous mimicry."

She sighed. "Then tell me why we're keeping the boat. At least I assume we must be, since Martin did not come with us to take it home."

"We will keep it, my curious lady, because we'll need it to transport you women to Deep End Grange."

"Do you still fear we'll be inundated at Knoll House?"

"We won't wait for that." He sighed when she glowered and poled the boat along another stroke or two before he spoke again. "My coachman—the best weatherman I know—predicts another deluge. You'll soon be knee deep in water—especially if they open the sluices up the canal which is something your Mr. Clay predicts will happen. We'll move everything we can upstairs, but then you'll go to Deep End Grange and like it."

Jessica stared at him, her hands tightly clasped around the umbrella. "Mr. Clay truly thinks they'll relieve their flooding by opening the sluices and letting it down on us?"

"He's nearly certain they will—especially if there's more rain."

"In that case, Emma and I'll appreciate the fact you've taken supplies to the upper story, my lord, because we'll *not* leave Knoll House."

"You will if I have to tie you up and carry you off."

"You would do me out of my home?" she asked sweetly.

"Only temporarily."

"Oh no, my lord." Jessica's lips compressed once, before she added, *"Permanently."* Her elbows pressed into her sides protectively, and her knuckles whitened. "You forget, my lord, if I stay away from Knoll House more than one night I lose it. Lord Sutton would be delighted."

"I haven't forgotten, but I'll still take you to his lordship to whom I'll explain the danger in which you stand. He'll agree to make an exception. According to Clay it is only four miles across the fields. Roy and I can manage that easily. He and I'll return for my groom and the horses."

"I suppose you expect to take Rose as well?" she asked.

"Of course. All of you."

"My lord, you are a bigger fool than I thought."

"Miss Jessica, if I'm proved a fool, I'll give you my head for washing. Until then will you stop arguing?"

"What fun," she said, eyeing him. "I'll add a drop or two of dye to the water, I think. Those blond curls would look so interesting with a green tint—or perhaps purple? Purple to match the royal snit you'll be in when I finish? I can hardly wait."

"Jessica . . ."

"Yes, my lord?" she asked.

"Shut up."

"Yes, my lord-sir."

They remained silent the rest of the way to Knoll House, Jessica forming plans to avoid being in the middle of the confrontation between Adlington and her father-in-law.

216

Should she warn Chad about Peter's father's curmudgeonly ways? But surely he knew of them—assuming he and Peter had been half so close as she thought.

But, obviously, Chad could have no idea of how bitter Lord Sutton had become, how much he'd grown to hate his son. Recently, he'd even accused Peter of dying merely for spite. His death, said his lordship, followed naturally after defying his father's edicts that Peter *not* buy a commission. Then, when he *had*, his willfulness in volunteering to carry dispatches to the Peninsula where, once he'd arrived at the front, he contrived to get into active service on General Hill's staff merely added insult to injury. Peter had done that *after* his father had pulled strings to get him kept in London where he'd be safe.

As his father had predicted, Peter was wounded. When sent home to recover from a saber cut to the thigh, Peter discovered Jessica's predicament. By marrying her out of hand, he had given Lord Sutton more ammunition for his ranting: his son had forgotten his duty to his name to the point of marrying a penniless woman of no account who hadn't even the grace to be delivered of an heir. In Jessica, Lord Sutton had a scapegoat on whom to blame all his son's many errors, and since he was miserable himself, he did his best to make her miserable as well.

Lord Adlington stared at his passenger's bowed head and wondered, for about the hundredth time, it seemed, what was going on in her mind. Women had always been easy for Chad. They fell into one of several categories and, once fit into their proper place, never surprised him again in any way. Miss Jessica simply would not fit into any of the places he tried to fit her. Much to his surprise, she seemed to be an entirely new type altogether which, he thought, surely wasn't possible. . . .

He knew from her speech, from things Emma let drop, and from allusions the young woman made to things about which the normal chit knew nothing, that Miss Jessica was better educated than other women he'd met—except for his Aunt Bliss, a bluestocking to end all bluestockings. But

Jess was nothing of *that* nature.

Nor did she fit the category of poor relation. True, she wasn't wealthy—in fact, he thought living as she did stretched her income to the maximum. But she didn't have that downtrodden air of the indigent. Nor could she be of the class *his* class stigmatized for being cits—there wasn't a sign of that in either her taste or her conversation: he'd never yet known a cit who didn't give himself away very quickly. So what else, he wondered, was there?

Would she hide it if she were the impoverished daughter of a peer? If her father died under the hatches and she'd escaped the disgrace of poverty with what funds she could pull together? Or perhaps she'd been jilted and her isolation was due to an unwillingness to face the scandal? No, Chad decided. That couldn't be it. No man in his right mind would jilt Miss Jessica: once having her in hand, a man would be a fool to let her escape.

It occurred to his lordship that that was a strangely possessive notion, and he returned to his earlier idea that Jessica had, on her own, put herself beyond the pale and fled society's scorn. That might also explain that ridiculous clause in her lease: was it, perhaps, Lord Sutton's attempt to control her . . . er . . . *extraordinary* behavior? Chad sent another speculative glance at Jessica's bent head.

So. Did he think the notion plausible because it *was* or because he *wished* it to be? Chad very much feared it was the latter. Unfortunately, from his point of view, Miss Jessica gave off none of the signals he wished to receive from her, those signals a woman of loose morals gave a man without consciously planning to do so.

Angry with himself for even thinking such things about a woman he suspected was entirely virtuous, Chad set the pole and pushed. Hard. And lifted it barely in time to avoid being dragged from the craft, and ignobly wound around the pole—an embarrassing position which would necessitate wading through the muck to catch the boat. It *hadn't* happened, but there was a lesson there: now was not the time for attempting to unravel the mystery which was Miss

Jessica. If only she weren't so entirely intriguing. If only her sense of humor didn't make him want to . . .

Once again Chad barely retained control of the pole. This time he lectured himself firmly: he was not to think about the woman who was slowly driving him crazy—not until he'd carried her inside and they were dry and warm again!

As it turned out there was no time for thinking when they returned to Knoll House. Almost immediately it started to rain heavily, and they spent the remaining hours of that day and all the next moving as much of the contents of the lower floor to the upper as could be shifted.

Jessica, warned by Mr. Clay's fears, cooperated with no more argument. At one point she straightened her back and, hearing a noise, turned to discover Rose carefully putting books into a crate the groom had brought in from the barn for the purpose.

"Rose, you're a guest and don't need to do that."

"I don't *need* to, but I don't know why I shouldn't help if I want."

"Do you want?"

The girl tossed her curls. "And why not? There aln't— *amn't* much else to do, is there, with Chad busier'n a bee in the thyme and you worrying and working harder'n anyone else. Not very agreeable company, any of you—are you?— and the sooner we get it done, then the sooner we can all go up to the big house Chad wanted to go to in the first place and maybe I won't be bored to tears no more. Besides," she added, with a trace of bravado, "I rather like doing it. Makes me feel part of a family again for a bit . . . you know?"

Jessica's soft heart was torn. It had never occurred to Jess to wonder if a woman who chose Rose's occupation— or had it thrust upon her—was happy or lonely or lacking anything. Perhaps all women should be forced to share a house with a trollop: it might teach them humility and leave them satisfied with their own life!

"Rose," said Jess slowly, "Lord Sutton isn't a particularly

agreeable man, and if he learns of your relationship with Adlington, he'll throw us out. Would you object to being introduced as my friend? Could you pretend?"

"I like you and wouldn't have to pretend: how could anyone *not* like you? You're the most ladyish lady I ever saw. A *real* lady. You've no business even talking to the likes of me, but you do and just as if I were as good as you. Which I ain't—amn't, that is. Not that I wouldn't 'a been if that Gerald Bointyn hadn't gotten hot for me, and me fool enough to believe him when he said we'd marry and live at the big house and all," she finished defiantly.

"You don't have to explain. You'd no choice but to find a protector."

Rose blushed. "Well, I did and all."

Jessica's eyebrow rose.

"I could have gone for a housemaid somewhere. And I knew all about dairy work because I ordered ours and kept the records and all. I *could* have gone for a dairymaid."

"Yes, but the notion you'd be just a maid must have been very difficult since you'd once ordered your own maids about."

Rose looked at her in wonder. "I don't see how you understand so well."

"My father was once the vicar here, Rose. He was a good man, but with no money sense. When he died we found he'd given away all we had. I was sent to live with an aunt who despised me. I wasn't very good at playing the humble, grateful, poor relation."

Rose tut-tutted, but then chuckled. "You, a vicar's daughter?"

"Yes. What's wrong with that?"

"I don't believe you. Vicar's daughters don't have laughing eyes."

Jessica's mouth dropped. After a moment she closed it. "Don't have *what?*" she asked.

Adlington's voice, coming from the hall, explained. "Eyes that show you are laughing inside. I've noticed it myself."

"And how long, my fine lord, have you been listening at keyholes?"

"No keyholes, my equally fine lady. The door is open. How could I help but overhear? Rose, I think you could help Emma if you would?"

"Why don't you just say you want to talk to Miss Jess? You don't need to go being tactful and all with the likes of *me*."

"He most certainly does if you're going to be my friend, Rose. Remember what we discussed."

"Ah well, then! M'lord, you just go 'n' treat me like a real lady. I think I'd like that," she added, wistfulness making her almost beautiful. It didn't last though. She flirted her skirts quite dreadfully and winked at Lord Adlington as she passed him on her way to the kitchen. Silence reigned until the door at the back of the hall slammed.

"What's this about a friendship between the two of you?" he asked, stern and disapproving.

"There is no other way to introduce Rose into the Grange." Chad muffled a groan. "It won't be so bad. She's lost that rather brittle manner she had when you arrived, and she tries to watch her speech. Besides," Jess added, as defiant as Rose had been, "she doesn't deserve to be scorned. She didn't ask that some idiot seduce her or that her father throw her out when the boy left her or that the world treat her as if it were *her* fault men are beasts!"

"Do I hear an accusation in there somewhere?"

"If the shoe fits, my lord-sir . . ."

"If you mean I've used her as men use women, then yes, I have. She sold and I bought," he said, more crudely than he would have done if he weren't so angry. "I suppose I'm to blame?"

"*Yes.* Men may do as they please, and no one thinks the worse of them. Except some, like me, who feel you're as sinful as she."

"Damn and blast your beautiful eyes. How dare you presume to judge me? What right have you . . . ?"

"The same right to judge you as you have to order me

around in my own home. None!" She turned away from him. "Oh drat and drat again. Go away and let me get on with this." She lifted a bunch of dried thyme from its hook and laid it gently into the basket in which she was putting her herbs.

"You're crying," he accused, unsettled that she would.

"I don't like losing my temper. It makes me *angry*."

He struggled to subdue a chuckle, but couldn't: he chortled.

Jess turned, hands on hips. "You laugh? You think it *humorous* I've a badly controlled temper?"

"I think it hilarious that *losing your temper* makes you *angry*." He raised a quizzical eyebrow.

She was nearly too far down in the dumps to catch the joke. Finally she did and her eyes widened, her mouth rounding into an O, and then she too chuckled. The chuckle turned to a laugh, and soon they were both laughing freely.

"Oh dear," she said. "I am not usually so illogical. Truly I'm not."

"I know. May we go back and discuss that thing you said without *quite* so much passion?"

"If you mean my offer of friendship to Rose, I'll try to explain. Lord Sutton has become very nearly *peculiar* in the year or so since his son died. On top of that he would love to do me an injury. If he knew I'd acquiesced to allowing a . . . a . . ."

"Soiled dove?" asked Chad with pretended innocence.

"That will do," she said, with a repressive look. "Anyway, my allowing *one of those* under my roof and the fact I'd actually spoken to her at length — well! He'd have found an excuse for running me out of the county, let alone one for evicting me from my home. And don't think I could ask aid from the vicar or from some local family. I am believed past praying for because I live here with only Emma to provide propriety. As my old nurse, she isn't considered sufficient, *especially* as several ladies have indigent relatives they would love to thrust upon me in her place!"

222

"I see. All right," he said slowly. "I will go along with your ploy, but I do not approve. I wish to high heaven I'd not brought her with me on this journey."

"They say hindsight is always better than foresight—my lord-sir."

He grinned. "Am I being top-lofty again? I'm sorry. You might like to know the parlor has been stripped and we are proceeding with the pantry. You are coming along well here. With luck we'll be off early tomorrow—with a picnic basket, perhaps, for sustenance on our way to the Grange."

"Four miles. It will be heavy going, poling all of us for such a ways."

"Surely we'll reach high ground long before that and walk the rest of the way?"

"Thanks for the reminder. It'll be muddy. I must find pattens for Rose."

"Rose!" Jessica's spaniel yipped at the sharpness in Adlington's tone. His lordship reached down and picked Amigo up. "Will you stop thinking of Rose for a minute?" he asked.

Jess was startled by an undertone in his voice. It was reminiscent of Sueanne when she wanted Jessica's full attention and wasn't getting it. She stared at him. "Lord Adlington?" she questioned.

"And that's another thing. Why must I be Lord Adlington when you call *her* by her first name?"

Jess grinned, her eyes twinkling. "Finally. Something I can answer! I don't *know* another name for her, and I refuse to call your *er . . . sister* by *your* family name."

"Call me Chad, Jess." She made a movement as if to shake her head in a negative way, and he held out his hand to her. "Please?"

Chad Thornton saying please? Almost begging? Jess blinked. "Certainly *not* where Lord Sutton might overhear us," she scolded.

"Aha. That means you will where he will *not*. Very good." He grinned at her. "Oh, by the way, Emma thought it would be only a minute or two until we ate. Shall we go?"

he added, looking as if it hadn't been *him* keeping *her* there talking. He offered his arm and, with a glance which told him exactly what she thought of him for not delivering the message immediately, they walked into the kitchen.

Lord Sutton scowled. Most of Lord Sutton's acquaintances backed down at that dark look, but not Lord Adlington. "Oh all right," said Sutton with bad grace, but he added, "It's blackmail, though, and you cannot know what that woman has—"

"Enough. The lease is iniquitous. That you agree she shall not lose her home—assuming she still has a home once the flooding is over—will be sufficient." Chad finished on a gentler note. "Thank you for taking in the ladies."

Lord Sutton glared, but under Adlington's steady gaze, his look softened. "I know. I know. I was worrying about them down there at Knoll House. . . . That friend of Jessica's—pretty woman, that," he added casually.

"Very."

"You have an interest in her?"

"I haven't had time to think of such things."

Sutton's knaggy brows rose. "You? I don't believe it. You've always got a woman in tow," he said with something very like jealousy.

"I assure you. We carried everything from downstairs to upstairs before abandoning Knoll House, and frankly I'm tired. My lord," he added, suddenly serious, "I've not conveyed to you my sincere condolences on Peter's death. I lost a very good friend, but you lost your son."

"Harrumph. Don't speak to me of the boy! I'll not have it. He was no son to me: disobedient, disobliging, and disloyal! That's all he ever was."

Chad stiffened, his features rigid. "Your son loved you. He was sad you couldn't understand his need to have a go at Boney—a patriotic need *you* instilled in him. As for obedience to duty, he was very well thought of by General Hill, who didn't give praise where it wasn't deserved. Peter was admired by his men as well. And he was the most loyal man I've known, both to England and where friendship was concerned."

When Sutton said nothing, only turned away, Lord Adlington stalked from the library, slamming the door. He met Jessica in the hall.

She gave his anger-filled visage a startled look, glanced at the door through which Chad had come, saw that it was Lord Sutton's favorite room, and nodded understanding. "You've just had a run-in with our host, have you not? I warned you he'd become embittered."

"He talks of Peter as if his son were a damned scoundrel instead of one of the best men who ever walked!"

"Oh, he *was*, was he not? No better ever trod the weld."

Chad's eyes widened. "You knew him? Well?"

"Everyone knew Peter," said Jess, her fondness for Peter obvious. She suddenly recalled she'd decided not to reveal her marriage—although she could no longer quite remember her reasons why.

"You loved him," Chad accused.

"What is it to you if I did?" asked Jess, evasively. Not that she *hadn't* loved Peter—just not with the sort of love implied by Chad's tone.

"He was my friend. He never mentioned you. And he married . . . which reminds me," said his lordship, looking around, "why haven't we met her? Where is she?"

"Where is who? Or do I mean whom?"

"Peter's wife, of course. Do you deliberately wipe her from your mind so that you need feel no guilt for loving a married man?"

Jess gave him a concerned look. "Are you feeling quite the thing, Lord Adlington?"

"You said you'd call me Chad."

"Not while under Lord Sutton's roof, and lower your voice," she scolded.

"I'll be damned if I'll worry about such nonsense," he shouted. "You've not answered my question!"

Lord Sutton opened the door to the wide hall. He glared at Jess. "You! I should have known it'd be you. You always cause controversy and contention, do you not?"

"No. Only amongst foolish men who want to blame anyone and everyone but themselves for their own mistakes and pig-headedness," she said acidly and crossed her arms.

"If you refer to *me,* Jessica Darling, then say so." Lord Sutton thrust out his chin in a belligerent fashion.

"Jessica Rippon to you, Lord Sutton," she said with just as much belligerence, totally forgetting Adlington's presence.

"Wait a minute," said Chad. "Wait just one minute. *You?* You were Peter's *little wifey?*"

Jess blushed. The jig was up—and suddenly she was glad. "That's what he called me, bamming me, you know. Well," she added when Adlington, stunned, still stared up and down her tall form, *"you* know what a joke-smith he was, always jesting about something or other . . ."

"You . . . *you!"*

Sutton beamed. "Good man. You don't like her either."

Adlington turned his glare on Lord Sutton. "Peter said she'd be living with you. He asked that I see you were treating her with the consideration and the respect his wife deserved. Well, I've seen. *And you aren't."*

"Aren't?" Lord Sutton was bewildered by Chad's attack. "Aren't what?"

"Treating Peter's wife decently!" Chad raised his fists to the air and shook them. "Mad. You're both mad as hatters." He glared once again at Jessica before stalking out the front door and slamming it behind him.

"I wonder if we're any more insane than he is," mused Jessica.

"Couldn't be," said her father-in-law, equally bemused and, for once, in agreement with Jess. "Only a madman would walk out into rain like that without his umbrella. Didn't even take his *hat.*"

"For once I think you're on the mark."

Sutton looked at her. "Harrumph. Where's that pretty

little friend of yours? Should be entertaining her, should you not?"

"She asked that I let her rest. It has been a rather tiring few days."

"Harrumph. She'll be down for dinner?" his lordship asked cautiously.

"Of course." Jess gave him a speculative look. "I know we have our differences, my lord, but do you think we might put them aside while Rose is here? She's such a gentle soul, she truly wouldn't understand," added Jess, crossing fingers hidden in her skirts at the prevarication.

"Pretty little thing too," suggested Sutton, as if he hadn't already said that several times.

"Do be nice to Rose, my lord," Jessica begged.

"I'm her host. Of course I'll be nice to her." He turned toward his book-room but, at a thought, turned back. "It is *Miss* Rose, is it not?"

"Hmm. Thinking of getting up a flirtation, my lord?"

"Harrumph!"

"I don't think she'd be very good at a light flirtation," mused Jessica, thinking Rose would likely jump far beyond society's unwritten rules regarding such things. "Not a mere flirtation. What I think is that Rose would make a good wife—and mother." Jess looked up as if she had just re-membered Lord Sutton was staring at her. "Now don't you go raising her hopes if you've no honorable intentions!"

"You mean marry . . . me? What a very odd notion *that* is."

"Is it? You're a perfectly healthy man, are you not? I don't see a cane or dyspepsia or signs of anything more than a very bad temper—which I suppose *is* a sign of grow-ing old, is it not?"

"Marry again . . . ?"

Lord Sutton seemed not to have heard her rather acid comment, and Jessica was glad he either had not or was ig-noring it. She hadn't *meant* to contravene the truce for which she'd asked, but her father-in-law was enough to make a saint stamp a foot in frustration. His lordship turned without another word and, as if in a daze, walked into his library, softly shutting the door.

"Well!" Jess stared at the door. "Well, well, well," she added in an entirely different tone.

This may turn into one of the more interesting visits I've ever made, she thought as she went up the stairs to her room.

But dinner that evening was a bore. Chad was polite but withdrawn. Rose was monopolized by Lord Sutton who made assumptions and stated them as facts. The most astounding was that Rose had been at school in Bath during the year Jess was there and that was where the two had met. Rose had, at that pronouncement, turned to look at Jess. Jess, her fork halfway to her mouth, didn't raise her eyes from her plate, only pausing for a moment in her eating.

Later, when the men joined the women in the drawing room, Chad ignored Rose, but, taking Jess firmly by the elbow, led her to the far windows. "How dare you allow that poor man to believe such things?" he asked, glancing to where Lord Sutton had joined Rose.

"He didn't ask, did he?"

"That's an excuse?"

"Perhaps not, but why should I offer explanations which will only get me into deep water. I thought," she added accusingly, "that avoiding excess water was your reason for bringing us here?"

Chad chuckled before he remembered he was angry with her. "You seem to delight in secrecy, do you not? You did, I presume," he asked politely, "have a good reason for not telling me who you are?"

"*You* didn't ask, either."

"I assumed it would be impolite when you so obviously avoided giving your full name, and why should I forgive you for such stupid trickery? I see no reason whatsoever to avoid telling me you were my best friend's widow when my only purpose for being in this region was to see to your well-being."

Jess stared at him. "And just how was I to know *that?*"

"But why else would I have been on my way to see Lord Sutton?" He glowered at her.

"I presumed to give, in person, your condolences for Peter's death."

Chad was a fair man, and nodded judiciously. "I suppose you might have thought that."

"Good Heavens, what else was I to think? I didn't know if you even knew of my existence." At his astounded look she continued a trifle diffidently: "War is an uncertain thing, Chad, a chancy thing. I couldn't know that you and Peter had been in communication after our wedding."

"He died in my arms, Jess."

"Oh God." She turned away.

"He wasn't in pain," Chad hurried to say. "It was a spine wound and he couldn't move, but he could talk. He was quite peaceful once I'd promised I'd check up on you if— *when*— I finally returned to England. He worried about you. Oh, not that you'd be back in the situation from which he'd rescued you, but that you might be uncomfortable living with his father. He should have known," added his lordship with a touch of bitterness, "that you'd not do anything so sensible as live at the Grange."

"Do I hear criticism, my lord?"

"You do. You've no business living way out there in the weld, far from any sort of protection and without any of the comforts you should expect, without question, to have."

"I am *perfectly* comfortable in Knoll House, my lord."

"I note you say nothing about your safety," he commented, a dry note drawing her attention which had been directed out the windows at the moon-drenched night. "Yes," he added, when she turned a startled look back toward the night sky, "it stopped raining late this afternoon and cleared almost immediately. If they don't open the sluices, your house will very likely stay dry. But you still haven't said anything about your safety."

She sighed. "I don't know what I *can* say. Nor do I see why I am particularly less safe at Knoll House than I would

229

be here."

"Here you are protected by the presence of your father-in-law and any number of servants. What men are there at your house?"

"Mr. Davies is normally there."

"Mr. Davies is, I understand, a man of nearly seventy years."

Jess grinned. "I think you should see him before you discount him. He's almost as tall as you are and in excellent health. He also has a certain presence which can intimidate visitors of whom he disapproves. Emma and his wife have had a life-long rivalry. I wouldn't trust anything she is likely to say about either of them, if I were you."

"You are incorrigible."

"Oh, surely not."

They looked at each other and suddenly Chad remembered he was angry at her. "That is beside the point. I asked you if you intended correcting Lord Sutton's misapprehensions concerning Rose."

"No."

His brows rose.

"He thinks she's pretty." Again their eyes met and understanding passed between them. "I see no reason to spoil his fun."

"Fun."

"And hers." Chad looked shocked. "Well, *you've* ignored her ever since arriving at Knoll House, have you not?"

"What would you expect? That I continue to treat her as I have in the past? While living under your roof?" He glared down his nose at her.

"I'll admit I would not like *that,* but can you not treat her with common courtesy?"

He stared at her. "She's my mistress."

Jessica glared. "She is also a woman and a human being, and deserving of the same courtesy as any other woman and human being of your acquaintance."

He quite literally gnashed his teeth. "You don't know what you're talking about."

She eyed him. "Do I not? I thought I was talking about manners and one's behavior toward those less fortunate then oneself."

"She's beneath your contempt."

"Nonsense. She was seduced by pretty promises and left ruined once her seducer had his sport. She was barely fifteen, my lord, and her father disowned her. He did that even though he'd had a very good notion what was going forward and would have had quite another reaction, of course, if the pretty boy had actually come through with a ring as it was hoped the lad would do. But, since he didn't, poor Rose had to make her way as best she could."

"Barely fifteen?" he asked, turning to look at Rose who was curled up in her chair, her eyes on Lord Sutton. He shook his head. "Drat it, Jess, you shouldn't be talking of such things. You especially shouldn't be talking of such things with Rose."

"You're impossible." Jess turned away. "This is a totally nonsensical discussion in any case."

"So it is. Shall I tell Lord Sutton who she is or shall you?"

"You agreed to allow him to believe her my friend. Don't go back on your word."

His mouth compressed. "I didn't realize he'd take her up as he has. I don't see how I can honorably allow him to continue with his belief that she's a decent woman."

"She's far more decent than Lady Ho—Never mind who! A lady of my acquaintance who has presented her lord with several children he has had no part in fathering. But *she* is considered proper company for Lord Sutton, and Rose, who did not choose her way of life, having had it thrust upon her, is *not*. Such thinking disgusts me."

Chad blinked. He'd never heard such sentiments from a gently bred woman, and this one was not only gently bred but had been reared in a vicarage! Or, he thought, eyeing her speculatively, perhaps that is it; she imbibed too much of the notion of Christian charity. He turned and looked again at Rose who was adding another splashy flower to the

231

shawl as she listened to her host. She had the look of any young woman doing needlework. The difference was that she was no longer chaste. But that wouldn't fadge, would it? He'd heard whispers of any number of young ladies just out of the schoolroom who managed to have their cake and eat it too. Most of them married well, even so.

"A penny for them, my lord."

"I don't think they're worth a farthing. All right. I'll keep m'mummer dubbed—as my coachman would say."

"I *think* that means you'll keep a still tongue in your head?"

"It does, but how do you know that?"

"Peter must have known a coachman akin to yours," she said demurely.

"Peter. Oh yes. Peter." He stared down his nose at her before turning and stalking from the room.

Jess looked after him and sighed. He is the most changeable man, she thought. I do wish he'd forgive me so we could get back to our normal relationship. She considered that and sighed again. It wasn't really their *usual* relationship she missed so much as the intriguing possibility of making their budding friendship something *more*. Her third sigh was so deep Rose came to her, Lord Sutton having left the room when Chad did.

"He acting like he owns the earth again?" asked Rose sympathetically.

"That's just the way he's acting! How did you guess?"

"Because that's the only time I ever felt like sighing—when he started acting lord-of-the-manorish, don't you know?" Rose gave Jess a kind look. "Don't fret about it. He's a good sort, and don't you let me be a stumbling block. You accept his proposal when he gets around to making it." She chuckled at Jessica's expression. "He's wild about you. He'll propose. I haven't counted for nothing from the moment he set eyes on you," she explained.

"Rose . . ."

"No, it's all right. He'll not treat me badly when he tells me I have to go. He's a gentleman, and real gentlemen say

232

goodbye with a nice present."

"How can you accept such things so calmly."

Rose gave her a straight look. "You think I should have hysterics or temper tantrums? You wouldn't like that . . . Neither would the gentlemen," she added after a pause.

"I don't suppose they would." It was Jessica's turn to pause. "Lord Sutton isn't a bad sort either," she suggested.

Rose giggled. "He's a one, he is."

"He needs a son, Rose."

Rose stared at Jess. After a moment she asked, "You ain't suggesting . . . ?"

"I'm not suggesting a thing. Just don't . . . don't . . ."

"Don't let on to him about m'occupation?" Rose giggled. "He would have kittens, wouldn't he?"

"Definitely kittens!"

They smiled at the thought of Lord Sutton in a tantrum. "Well," said Rose with a shrug, "the water will go down in a day or two and we'll be gone then anyway. I guess I can pretend to be a lady for that long."

"Don't deprecate yourself, Rose. You were the daughter of a farmer who did well and rose in the world. That's all his lordship needs to know."

They looked at each other, and the pact was sealed. Rose smiled a trifle sadly, knowing that nothing could really come of their charade, but it was nice that, for a little while, she could pretend to be a proper young woman again. It had only been three years, and she hadn't forgotten how it was to live in a decent home. It'd be nice to feel respected again. And, for a day or two, maybe she could even dream a little. . . .

The next day Jess donned boots and pelisse and, tucking her skirts up a trifle, walked away from the Grange toward a hill overlooking the Knoll's part of the marsh. She climbed steadily and soon reached the top where, to her surprise, she found Chad. "How does it look?" she asked.

"I think everything will be all right in a day or two—assuming no more rain and assuming they keep those sluices closed."

"Would they still open them now the water is beginning to go down?" She stared toward her home. A chimney and a bit of roof were visible where a few ancient trees grew. Trees were not common on the weld and these made an excellent landmark in the huge shimmering mass of flood waters.

"You've lived here for a long time. What have they done in the past?"

"I don't recall that it has ever been as bad as it was this time."

"Your Mr. Clay was truly worried."

"I'd trust Mr. Clay's judgment in such things."

"Then you may still go home to a mud-filled house."

She sighed.

"Lord Sutton will send men to help clear it up." She gave him a straight look. "I'll insist."

"What right have you to insist?"

"The right of being Peter's friend?" he suggested after a moment.

They stared at each other solemnly. "Thank you, my lord," she said, turning to look toward her house.

"Chad. Say it, Jess."

She glanced at him, away. "I assumed that, since you were angry with me, you wouldn't wish me using your name."

"Have I been such an idiot?"

She nodded.

He bit back a laugh. "No pulling of punches with you, is there?" Before she could respond Chad took her hand and lifted it to his lips. "I don't know why I behaved like such a fool, except that I *felt* a fool—as if you'd deliberately duped me and I'd taken the bait like any green lad just come onto the town."

"I've been thinking, and truly I believe I didn't mean to do more than avoid the pity I believed you'd feel for me. I abhor pity."

"I see." Again the long solemn look into each other's eyes. "Jess, may we begin again? Can you forgive me for

234

acting the unmitigated ass?"

She laughed. "I don't think it was that bad."

"It was Rose."

Jess tipped her head, frowning.

He sighed. "It was bad enough introducing her into the home of a decent woman, but — don't ask me why — it seemed *worse* introducing her into the home of Peter's widow. I felt as if I'd besmirched you, as if I'd done Peter a bad turn . . . I don't know. It was irrational, as you'd be the very first to tell me. But I still feel that I should have done something differently." Suddenly he glared at her. "What's more, you'd no business accepting the situation so complacently!"

"You'd rather I'd had a whole series of hysterics and taken to my bed?"

He choked back a chuckle. "Am I once again showing myself a fool?"

"Perhaps. A trifle," she teased.

Suddenly they both laughed. Chad dropped the hand he still held and put an arm around her shoulders, pulling her close to drop a kiss on her forehead. Jess drew in a sharp breath, held it. Would he kiss her? Really kiss her? He did not. He released her. Abruptly, he backed away.

"I apologize," he said stiffly, his eyes focused somewhere near her left ear.

She sighed. "Apology accepted." Jess started across the hilltop toward the path.

"Where are you going?"

"Back to the house. I've seen all I wished to see and had my exercise. I fear that if I do not start back, I'll be late for the nuncheon Lord Sutton has set out at one and he'll have still another reason to scold me. I do get so tired of his scolds, Chad."

"So I'd think!" He approached and offered his arm. "Here. The path is a mite slick, and you don't want to fall. Muddy skirts would be another black mark against you, would they not?"

"Especially," she said with a sly look, "if I were also

to arrive on *your* arm. Sutton loves to think the worst of one."

Chad's ears turned a bright red, and he looked away from her. Jessica's eyes narrowed. Now why, she wondered, would my teasing discommode him so? Unless he's had thoughts about me which make him feel guilty? Jess grinned to herself. Maybe her affection for Chad was not entirely one sided? Even if he was only a little attracted to her, wasn't that something on which one could build, and might he not come to feel those warmer feelings she wished he'd feel for her? She wondered if she might allow herself, just this once, a dream or two.

Her musings were shattered by a sudden muted but angry roar that went on and on, becoming louder each moment. Startled, she looked up at Chad whose eyes narrowed.

"Wait here, Jess." He took long strides back the way they'd come.

She wasn't about to stand idly by. She picked up her skirts and followed him, reaching his side just as a spreading line of rolling debris-filled water appeared from the direction of the upper reaches of the canal. "Oh no."

"*Now* would you like me to teach you a few new swear words?" When he got no response, he glanced at her. Her eyes were glued to the flood line, her face was white and pinched, her shoulders were slumped. Slowly, so as to avoid frightening her, Chad pulled her to him and gently turned her face into his shoulder. By the time the spreading water reached the trees marking her home its force had slackened, but there was no avoiding the knowledge that it would raise the water level, leaving the lower floor of Knoll House a reeking mess. Chad's arms tightened. He'd have to see that the worst was cleared out before he allowed her to go back. "We'd better go, Jess."

She turned in his arms and took one more look. "You told me it would happen. I was a fool not to believe you."

"You've lived here and know it *doesn't* happen. I'm new and could accept that it might."

"Don't be kind, Chad. I don't think I can take it. Besides, I've told you what I think of pity."

"Then I won't pity you."

"No," she said. "There's no need for pity. It is merely mud which will dry to dirt. It will clean up." She pushed away from his embrace. "We must go, my lord."

"We must go, *Chad*."

Her eyebrows arched. "Now you've taken to talking to yourself?"

He looked bewildered for a moment. His lips repeated his last statement silently before he looked at her. "You're a *tease*, Jessica Rippon."

She grinned, her complexion looking better. "So I am. I learned it from Peter, you see."

"I thought I caught a hint of his methods. Come along now."

As they approached the Grange, Jessica looked up to the windows which had once been Peter's. A faint sadness swept over her. Peter, she thought. You sly old thing. Did you hope something might come of a visit from Chad? If so, you've bats in your belfry, my beloved Peter: did you forget what you once told me about how you and Chad were attracted to the same women? Then how could you think he might be attracted "in that way" to me when you were not? He could have kissed me. We were alone, and he didn't take advantage so he can't have wanted to very badly. . . .

"You are doing it again," said Chad softly as they started up the steps to the door Sutton's butler, Babson, held open while pretending disinterest.

"What? I don't understand."

"You've gone off into your head where I can't follow."

"But why should you wish to?"

Chad looked confused. "I don't know. I just know I don't like it."

Jessica blinked, then grinned. "I'll try to do better, my lord. In this case I was thinking of Peter. That's all."

Chad stared down at her, his face a mask. "I see," he said. He bowed and walked off, leaving her to stare

237

after him.

"Now what," she wondered aloud, "does the idiot think he sees?" She glanced up at the stiffly correct butler. "Babson, you're a man. You tell me."

The butler unbent enough to smile slightly. "I cannot say what Lord Adlington was thinking, but I know what I'd have thought."

"Well, don't just stand there! Tell me."

"I'd have thought you were thinking sad thoughts of the man you loved—and that it would be useless to court you myself."

Jess stared at the stairs up which Chad had disappeared. "Drat the man." She glanced at the butler. "Thank you, Babson. I suppose I'll just have to accept the fact that men jump to conclusions and then haven't the decency to check and see if they are correct."

"If it helps, my lady," said Babson, "I don't think I'd allow that thought to stop me. Not for long. Not if I were serious about the lady, that is."

Jessica, her features as composed as the butler's, thanked him for the information and, happy again, took herself to her room to change from boots and skirts muddied at the hems. Nuncheon was enlivened by Lord Sutton's continued pursuit of Rose, an occupation Chad watched with distaste and Jess with a certain complaisance that riled Chad all over again. He followed her into a small room at the back of the house once lunch was over and again berated her for not telling Lord Sutton the truth about Rose.

"Why would I be so unkind?"

"How can you let him continue to make such a fool of himself? What if he actually asks her to wed him?"

"What if he does?"

"I don't understand you. You know why it cannot be allowed."

"Do I? I don't believe I do."

"She's not a chaste woman," he said through his teeth.

"Are you a chaste man?"

Chad looked startled. "It isn't the same."

238

"You condemn her for that which you take as a right for yourself. I do not like hypocrisy. What is more, I think she would make his lordship an excellent wife."

"That does not make it right," he insisted.

"Hypocrite."

"I tell you it is not the same, what a man does and what a woman does."

"But, Adlington, the man may not do it without a woman, or at least . . ."

He chuckled as she glanced up at him, her cheeks heating. "I see," he said, "that there are still *some* thoughts which embarrass you. And you are right that what we discuss takes two, but I still insist it is not the same for a man."

"Men's natures are such they just cannot help themselves, is that it?"

"Don't be absurd," he said, his ears heating in turn. "Of course they may. It's just that . . ."

"Yes, my lord?"

"Oh, the devil take it." He looked shocked at his own words and asked her pardon for swearing. "You are right," he continued. "I'm a hypocrite." He studied her. "You aren't gloating," he accused.

"Why should I gloat?"

"Because you've bested me in an argument."

"That's a reason for gloating?" she asked.

"The women I know in London would crow at such a win."

"Have those women so little self-esteem they must exult over others?"

"You ask the strangest questions."

"Do I? I suppose it is because I have so little town bronze. I found the *ton* exceedingly strange when Peter took me to London."

"I must be too much of the *ton*. I find you the strange one."

She pouted a trifle coquettishly.

"It's a compliment," he said softly. "You intrigue me."

"Do I?"

He reached for her, gave her a moment to object and then, when she didn't, pulled her closer. He looked down into her bemused face, saw the stars in her eyes. Slowly he lowered his head, taking her lips gently. Sweet lips, untutored lips . . . Untutored? He raised his head in confusion.

"Did I do something wrong?" she asked, worried.

"Wrong? Jessica, you were Peter's wife, yet you have no more notion of kissing than a kitten. How can that possibly be?"

This time she pouted for real and pulled away from him. "I don't wish to discuss it."

"I do."

"I will see you at dinner, my lord."

"Chad!"

"Chad, my lord-*sir!*" She shut the door on his laughter. Later, just before Jessica was to go down to dinner, Rose entered her room, a bemused look to her that had Jess holding her breath. "Rose? What's the matter?"

"He asked me. *Me!*"

"Who asked you what?"

"Lord Sutton. He asked me to marry him. I was lecturing him on how nasty he was about his son, saying that instead of ranting and raving about a dead son, a hero for whom he should feel nothing but pride, he should get on about the business of getting himself a new one—and he said 'Well?' and I said 'What?' and he said 'Well, then, let's get married and get on with it.' And . . . and I said . . .'"

When Rose didn't go on Jess wanted to shake her. "What did you answer?"

"I said yes," breathed Rose, her eyes wide. "Oh, I shouldn't have done it, Jess. I shouldn't have. It isn't *right*, somehow."

"Oh yes it is. He need never know about your past." After a moment Jess asked, "Did you set a date?"

"We thought June. And Jess, that's the reason I wanted to talk to you." Jess nodded encouragement, and Rose spoke in a rush: "He told me I was to spend what I like and have my trousseau made up in Rye. Will you help me? I don't always choose what's real ladylike, and I want to do what's right. So will you? Help me?"

Jess moved to kiss Rose on the cheek. "Gladly," she said warmly.

"Oh. One more thing?" said Rose. "He thought maybe we ought not tell anyone? Not just yet? He didn't want you teasing him, he said."

Jess, dreaming up all sorts of little needles with which she might get a trifling of revenge on her curmudgeonly father-in-law, felt ashamed. "I'll be good, Rose. You may tell him I'm very pleased for the both of you."

Dinner passed off most pleasantly. Lord Sutton was in a mellow mood, Rose shyly happy, Jess on her best behavior, and Lord Adlington, who didn't yet know about the engagement, bemused by the change — but quite willing to help keep the mood going. Afterward he'd had enough, however, and suggested he and Jess stroll in the gardens, which were beautiful under a full moon and pleasantly warm after all the cool wet weather.

Jess was willing. All too soon Chad would be gone. She would, she'd decided, spend every moment with him. They reached a bench sheltered in the shrubbery and Chad seated her. He towered over her, staring down at her very nearly glaring at her! "I've come to the conclusion I cannot let you go until I've some understanding of your mind."

"My lord-sir?"

He chuckled. "I suppose that did sound a little pompous, did it not?"

"*Very* pompous."

He sat beside her and took her hands in his. "The thing is, Jess, I think it may take a lifetime to come to any true understanding of you. Do you think you could put up with me for that long?"

Jess drew in a long slow breath. "Chad, just what are you asking?"

"Bungled it again have I?" He squeezed her fingers. "Jess, will you marry me?"

"Yes."

For a long moment silence reigned. "That's it? Just yes?"

"You'd rather I'd said no?" she asked.

"Good heavens, never that! But I expected more dilly-dallying and maybe the need to urge you or make silly promises or — I don't know — woo you?"

"I think I've wanted to marry you almost since you walked in my door, embarrassed by the need to lie about Rose. You see, I've known about you since you were a boy, Chad, from when you and Peter met at school. It didn't take long for my heart to be involved — so if you wish to wed, then I'd be very pleased to marry you, my lord . . . sir."

"I've heard enough of 'my lord-sir' for one evening, Jess, so I'll *try* to be less top-lofty, but would June be too soon for our wedding?"

"That sounds good. Rose and Lord Sutton wed then too — and don't you dare say a word, Chad Thornton! Unless you still have an itch for her . . . ?"

Chad looked shocked. "Not since the moment I met you. And remember what I said about men and control? You needn't fear I'll stray once we're wed either, Jess. That's a vow."

She had been a trifle worried about that. His promise was, she knew, one he'd keep, and she felt even happier now in her decision to marry him. "It will be a good marriage between Lord Sutton and Rose. She'll make him comfortable and give him children, and she need never again fear being turned off or have the need to look for another protector, or find it more and more difficult as she gets older. She's asked me to help her choose her trousseau, by the way."

For the last time Chad swallowed his objections to Rose's marrying Lord Sutton. "You can order your own while ordering hers. And, Jessica . . . ?"

"Yes?"

"See she doesn't buy anything purple, will you? She has a fatal attraction for purple. It'll be better if Lord Sutton

242

doesn't discover that before they've wed!"

They chuckled, and then Jess said, seriously, "Our Rose deserves a good life, Chad. After all, it was one of your sort who ruined her and left her to make her way as best she could — why shouldn't one of you repair the damage?"

"Are you trying to arouse guilt in me?"

Jess grinned. "Perhaps. Just a little. I keep remembering, that, if it were not for Peter, I might have come to her way of life myself — unable, as I was, to adopt the appropriately humble and grateful attitude necessary to one accepting charity." She looked thoughtful. "I wonder," she said on a teasing note, "if I'd have been successful as a courtesan?"

"You, my darling, will, I hope, never have the opportunity to discover that — unless I train you in the role for my own enjoyment?"

"Now there's a thought," she said, looking at him from the corners of her eyes.

"Come here, my love, for your first lesson in how to please me."

She came willingly.

When he groaned in her ear, she reluctantly roused from the passion he'd induced. "What's wrong? What have I done?"

"Nothing, love. Nothing at all — although," he gave her a hopeful look, "you *are* a widow so we needn't be quite so particular about propriety. May I come to your room tonight?" She turned her head. "Please, Jess . . . ?"

"Peter married me . . ." She looked back, bravely. "That's all he did."

Sudden understanding set Chad's heart to thumping in a completely new rhythm. "A marriage of convenience?"

"*Very* convenient for me," said Jess with a certain dryness, but she added on a sober note, "Peter was very special in my life, Chad, but as a brother, not a lover."

"Now I understand what he meant when, just before he died, he said you were not just in the common way, and that I'd like you. Well," he grinned, "common you certainly are *not* — and I do like you, Jess. Very much. In fact," he added

243

obviously a trifle embarrassed to speak aloud about that tenderest of emotions, "I think I love you. I just wish," he added hurriedly, scowling again, "I understood you."

She smiled mistily. "Ridiculous notion!" she said, pretending to scold. "You are bored by women you understand and I would never wish to bore you."

Chad tipped her face up until he could look into her eyes. "Quiet, woman."

She grinned at him, but sobered as he continued to look serious. "It is impertinent, but I have to ask: are you, then, still a virgin?" He hugged her tightly when she nodded. "I don't know why, but I'm glad."

"And, sir, if I were not?" she asked a trifle belligerently.

"My dear, if you were not I'd not feel it necessary for us to wait until our wedding night before I continued teaching you ways of pleasing me — to say nothing of discovering how I may please you." He smiled a trifle sardonically when he added, "I wonder why I was fool enough to suggest a June wedding? It'll be weeks of this torture before I may begin your education" — He arched one brow — "not in how to please just *any* man, you understand. Only *this* man."

"June will come, my lord."

"Chad."

"Chad. My lord-sir?"

"Grrr."

The days rolled on as days tend to do, and in the fullness of time, this particularly merry month of May reached an end. With its ending, A Springtime Affaire resulted in two June weddings, *one* of which was happy-ever-after.

Actually, the results of the other one weren't too bad. Considering.

A Groom For Juno
by Cynthia Richey

Miss Juno Davis pushed her wheat-colored hair out of her ice blue eyes and decided it was time to return to the stone house in which she had lived all her life. It was an unseasonably warm day for April, and Juno felt she was in danger of melting like butter in the brilliant sunlight.

She laughingly wondered how long it would take her younger sister and the girl's two besotted swains to discover her disappearance. They had scarcely seemed to notice her all afternoon, but since that was nothing out of the ordinary, Juno really did not mind. Generally speaking, the mantel of invisibility served her well in chaperoning her younger sister, Helen, for whose favor, as for her ancient namesake's, men would gladly have fought a war.

As if the thought conjured up the reality, Juno heard the unmistakable sounds of an altercation involving the young gentlemen who had come to call on Helen after yesterday's Assembly Ball. Heated insults, a scuffle in the gravel, and the thunk of a fist striking flesh caused her to catch her skirts in her hand and hurry around the corner before serious damage could be done.

"Gentlemen," she cried, attempting to interpose herself between the two combatants.

Paying her as much attention as they would a stray kitten, they continued to circle about, looking for an opening through which to throw a telling blow. Juno could see by their intense concentration that she needed help if she was to avert a full-blown mill. Turning toward her sister, she ordered, "Helen, go and get Brindle!"

Immediately, the younger girl picked up her skirts and, like the schoolgirl she was, dashed down the pathway toward the house, crying, "Help! Help! Brindle, come quickly!"

Helen's frightened retreat gave one disgruntled buck the chance he was looking for. His opponent turned to ogle the shapely ankles she unconsciously displayed, leaving himself open for an uppercut to the jaw.

Juno never saw the punch. Just as the young man let fly with his fist, she stepped into it. Surprised by the crushing pain that lifted her off her feet, she stared at her attacker, unable to believe what had happened to her, then collapsed, unconscious, to the ground.

Propelling himself toward the fallen lady, Brian Wilton, the Viscount Lancaster, shoved aside the two miscreants standing over her as if they did not quite believe what they had done. "I didn't see her," one of the fools was saying to the other.

"Well, of course you didn't, Ox." His confrere shrugged. *"Nobody* sees Miss Juno."

"I saw her," Lancaster growled as he knelt beside her, his heart contracting painfully at the sight of her closed eyes.

For the first time in his life, the viscount did not know what to do. Not even his experiences on the Peninsula had prepared him for caring for an injured girl. She did not curse as his fellow soldiers had done, but only lay as still as death on the crushed stone. She looked so helpless, it frightened him. He could not help raging against the foolish turn that had laid her low.

There was only one thing to be done. Forcing a calm he did not feel, Lancaster threw a contemptuous look upon the twin idiots who were still attempting to justify the accident. "Go to the village," he said, "Fetch the doctor."

They seemed glad for the errand. As they ran toward the stables to request their mounts be saddled, Lancaster turned back to Juno and gently caressed her left cheek and the delicate line of her jaw. It was already swollen and discolored from the blow, but her pulse was strong and regular and she was breathing normally. Leaning back on his heels, Lancaster inhaled a calming breath.

A veteran of the late wars and of Jackson's Parlor at Thirteen Bond Street, he was no stranger to sparring injuries. Still, he was not prepared for the jealous rage that built up inside him the longer Miss Juno lay unconscious. Why did no one come to help? What if she . . . ?

Steeling himself against such unreasonable fears, Lancaster set about to discover what he might do for her without causing further injury. Running a gentle hand along her neck, he satisfied himself that the blow had not snapped that slim column; then he gathered her in his arms and carried her back to the house.

She weighed no more than a butterfly, he noted, and even in her unconscious state, she curled her uninjured right cheek trustingly against his shoulder, as if she belonged in his arms.

But that, Lancaster told himself sternly, was foolishness. He had only met her last night, and he had come today to pay court to her sister!

The butler and several housemaids met him on the path, but they offered more hindrance than help in getting his burden inside. Finally, concern sharpening his tone, Lancaster growled, "Kindly stand aside or take over."

"This way, your lordship," said Brindle, assuming his proper role with his customary hauteur as he held open the French doors, allowing Lancaster to lay Juno on a sofa near the window.

An astute housemaid hurried forward with a tray, handing Lancaster a compress from which she had wrung icy water. The viscount lay the cold cloth along Juno's injured cheek, expecting her to flinch at the frigid contact. When she lay insensible of his care, his concern deepened. He wished he knew what else to do for her. He wished the doctor would come.

He had not long to wait before the village doctor was ushered into the sunny salon. "Thank God," Lancaster declared involuntarily, propelling himself to his feet and standing aside to let that worthy gentleman examine his patient, which the physician did without comment.

249

Lancaster discovered he was holding his breath apprehensively, and exhaled long and slowly just as Helen burst into the salon. "Oh, Dr. Burns, how glad I am you have come!" Flinging herself dramatically on her knees at her sister's side, she queried, "Is Juno all right?"

Juno heard her sister's teary question, and attempted to relieve Helen's fears. To her horror, she was unable to speak. A cold compress bound her jaw, which ached abominably. If that wasn't bad enough, an unfamiliar masculine voice said, "She'll be fine, Miss Davis, after the swelling goes down."

"Lord Lancaster?"

Juno could not mistake the tenor of dread that tinged Helen's query. Determined to protect her sister from yet another foolish suitor, Juno exerted a concerted effort to open her eyes. A moan escaped her lips as her lids fluttered open, causing the room about her to spin dangerously.

"Junie?" Helen said, clutching her hand desperately. "You gave me *such* a fright!"

"She gave us *all* a fright," Lancaster said fervently. He controlled the urge to take Juno's limp hand from her flighty sister's desperate grasp. To disguise the concern he felt, he took a turn about the femininely decorated room, and was surprised to discover how comfortable he felt among the ribbons and roses. He felt as if he had come home.

Shaking off that uncharacteristic sentiment, he returned to the domestic scene. For a brief moment, he met Juno's pale, confused gaze, and was struck in the chest by an inexplicable pain. He was quick to veil the shock he felt by hooding his cinnamon-colored eyes beneath his prominent brow.

Extending his arm, he said, "I was on my way to pay my respects to you, Miss Helen, when . . ." His explanation stumbled to an uneasy halt as his gaze returned to Juno once more. Her eyes were closed and her pale face turned toward the cushion of the sofa as if the company gave her pain.

Coming to her feet and accepting the viscount's arm, Helen cried, "I cannot think what Peter and Winnie were about, knocking my poor sister into oblivion the way they did." She drew the viscount away from the sofa on which Juno was resting. Lowering her voice to a more confidential tone, she added, "They were just funning, you know."

"No, that I did not know," Lancaster said in disapproving tones. "Gentlemen do not spar for a lady's benefit."

Helen's pert nose crinkled as if she had just ingested a bitter pill. "You sound just like Junie," she said with a pout. "Always quelling a person's joy in life."

Lancaster raised a dark brown eyebrow dubiously, saying "Indeed?" in such a manner as would leave the chit in no doubt as to his opinion of a person whose joy included knocking others about.

"Truly," Helen said, her china blue eyes innocently wide. "It is not easy standing in Juno's shadow; she always knows the right thing to do."

"I see," said the viscount, and indeed, Helen's ingenuous speech had served to open his eyes. Her elder sister had attempted to turn her into a proper lady instead of the spoiled, willful chit who was clinging possessively to his arm. This Helen bore no resemblance to the charming young lady with whom he'd danced last night. She seemed more like a conniving spider weaving a web about him, as did every young miss in London. Suddenly he wanted nothing more than to escape her clutches.

But that would leave her helpless sister at Helen's uncertain mercies, and leave Juno he would not until he was satisfied that someone in this house would see to her welfare.

Glancing toward the sofa on which she reposed so quietly, he doubted whether anyone would take care of her. The doctor had taken his leave, as had the butler and the housemaids who had fluttered so ineffectively around him while he had carried her inside.

Lancaster knew he could not very well invite himself for an extended stay, there being no male in the household to lend his presence a respectable appearance. But there was

251

no reason he could think of not to call while the object of his concern recovered. That way he would assure himself Juno was regaining her health without calling attention to himself.

Though normally practical-minded and sensible, Juno could not quell the knot of disappointment that clenched her heart when the handsome lord offered his arm to her pretty sister. Juno had thought at first that he was worried about *her*, but his quickly averted attention brought that hope to a crashing halt.

Leaning her aching head back on the cushion, she closed her eyes rather than watch the intimate scene that was being played out, and so missed seeing her sister's nose wrinkle the way it always did whenever she rang a peal over the younger girl's head.

It was obvious to the injured girl that her sister had conquered yet another gentleman's heart merely by batting her long, dark eyelashes. That being a talent Juno had never acquired, she had long ago decided that one must be born with long, dark eyelashes to become an effective flirt. But for the first time in her life, Juno was jealous of her sister's youth and beauty.

Helen did not need to fling herself at a man to be noticed. And if ever she did, the man would not have thrown a punch at her. It was more likely he would catch her in a heart-stopping embrace.

Not one who was ordinarily prey to jealous feelings, Juno was ashamed they had taken root in her heart. Her sister was so vivacious, no man could help but fall in love with her. That Lord Lancaster had fallen under Helen's spell ought not to cause Juno such pain. But then she had never been so bemused by a gentleman caller. Even had she not been muzzled, she doubted she would have been able to string words together to communicate a coherent thought.

Still, she had to make the attempt. Drawing the compress off her jaw, she raised herself upon an elbow and inhaled deeply to quell the uncharacteristic dizziness that assailed her before she could say, "If you will give me a moment to catch my breath, I shall ring for tea."

As if oblivious to her sister's frailty, Helen clapped her little gloved hands and exclaimed, "Oh, Juno, that would be lovely!"

Lord Lancaster was not so insensible however, and growled, "Nonsense; we can request tea ourselves." Striding toward Juno, he caught her fingers in an inescapable, but gentle grip and inquired, "Is there anything you'd especially like?"

Juno could only stare up at him. No one, other than her mother, had ever asked such a question, and she was of a sudden choked with an emotion she had suppressed for years. She felt strangely sad and vulnerable, two unaccustomed feelings that left her again speechless.

Helen was not so reticent, however. Laughing gaily, she said, "Ordinarily, Juno likes nothing more than to take her tea with a good book."

Lancaster continued to stare at Juno. "Reading is out of the question," he said. "Tomorrow I shall read to you, if you wish. However, what I meant was what kind of treat would you prefer with tea?"

Juno could not help but blush at the viscount's show of concern, and she blurted out the first thing that came to mind — a childhood favorite. "Thumbprints," she said. Her fiery blush intensified as reason caught up with her tongue. "B-but I doubt if cook has prepared anything so foolish in a long time."

Picking up a bell on the table beside Juno's sofa, Lancaster said, "Then cook can make them today."

"I would not put her to such trouble," Juno stammered, lest he think her the most selfish female alive.

The viscount bestowed a dark, questioning look upon her. What sort of household would consider an employer's request too much trouble to fulfill? But he refrained from pressing the issue, only directed the housemaid to fetch tea for the sisters, and to request that cook make "thumbprints for Miss Juno tomorrow."

If either Juno or Helen thought it odd for a guest to take

over the ordering of the household refreshments, they did not say so. But when Lancaster stoutly maintained that he would return to take tea with them on the morrow, Juno was compelled to protest, "Please my lord, you need not put yourself out on our account."

He raised an eyebrow in a manner that compelled Juno's complete attention. Giving her fingers an almost imperceptible squeeze, he said, "I am not coming solely on your account, but on my own." Smiling boyishly, he added, "I confess I am curious about these 'thumbprints' you remember so fondly."

"I can satisfy your curiosity, sir," Juno said, lowering her gaze self-consciously. Her heart was all aflutter, she thought from the effects of her injury, and she hoped it would settle down when she focused on something less stimulating than their visitor's indulgent smile. That her pulse did not return to its more usual pace while she stared at her pale blue skirts only added to her confusion.

"Do you not wish me to return?" Lancaster inquired in a grieved tone that compelled her to raise her gaze once more to his.

He sounded so disappointed, Juno could not help but reassure him, "You are very welcome, my lord. Only, I hope you will not be dissatisfied with the silly refreshments you ordered. They are nothing more than childhood fancies. We are all grown up, and ought to have put childish things behind us."

Lancaster saw Juno's sister roll her eyes, as if to say There she goes again, before he smiled. "Perhaps, but when one needs comfort, one sometimes returns to childhood pleasures." He winked, adding, "I do not generally admit it, but when I am feeling poorly, I sometimes ask for gingerbread."

It was Juno's turn to press his fingers. "Having shared childhood secrets, we *must* be friends," she said, breathless with a sense of joy that was all out of proportion to her pronouncement.

Lancaster allowed he would have liked it better had she

said she *wanted* to be his friend, but he did not share that secret. Pressing a chaste kiss to the backs of her fingers, he said, "And now I must go. I would not be much of a friend if I did not let you rest."

As the maid entered with the tray, Juno blurted out, "You will not take tea with us?"

"Tomorrow," Lancaster said in a tenderly reassuring tone that gave Juno goose flesh. He directed a compelling look toward Helen, who was pouring tea into cups. She smiled as he said, "I want to see roses in your sister's cheeks."

Juno completely misunderstood him. Thinking he would not be disappointed in Helen's looks on the morrow, she hid her own disappointment and said, "We shall make a special effort to please you."

Not for the first time, Juno wished she had not stepped into Lord Peter's hard fist. She was not accustomed to the light-headed feeling his assault had caused, and she had no patience with this maddening sense of frailty. Despite being exceedingly uncomfortable, it provided too many opportunities for Helen to spend time with Lord Lancaster. They were sharing too many lingering glances, from which Juno was all too aware she was excluded.

She had grown accustomed to feeling as if she were invisible, but she did not want Lord Lancaster treating her as if she were not there. Telling herself he was too old for Helen, Juno attempted to convince herself that she was merely concerned for her younger sister's happiness. And until her sister and Lancaster shared a concern for *her,* Helen had seemed almost to dislike the handsome viscount.

To Juno's surprise, Lancaster pressed her fingers once more, and grinned when she turned her wide-eyed, confused gaze upon him. "I know how capable you are, Miss Juno," he said, exhibiting strong white teeth in his teasing smile, "but you must not attempt to arrange everything to perfection tomorrow." He added in a mesmerizing voice, "You are to rest, let Helen fetch for you until my return. Then I shall take care of everything."

"I think you have already done so," Juno said in dazed,

but happy tones.

After a moment's hesitation during which he seemed taken aback by her unconscious vehemence, Lancaster regained his customary aplomb and replied, "No, you are wrong. I should have liked nothing more than to have spent the rest of the afternoon in the company of two beautiful ladies. But I am expected elsewhere and must go." And so saying, he bowed from the waist and took himself away.

Juno could only smile the next afternoon as Helen flitted about the bedchamber in a girlish attempt to help her elder sister appear to better advantage. She thought Helen's efforts were to no avail, and said so, adding affectionately, "I do not know why you are going to such trouble, goose, when we both know that it is *you* Lord Lancaster is coming to visit." Hearing Helen's piqued sigh, Juno relented. "Oh, very well, since it is so important, let me wear my best."

Her best, a green sprigged muslin with embroidered ivy trimming was discarded out of hand. "No," Helen insisted, laying the pretty gown back in its tissue. "The color clashes with your bruise. I wish you would let me dust your face with pearl powder."

Laughing, Juno allowed herself to be dressed in a gown that belonged to her sister—a pretty mauve-striped jaconet with puffed sleeves trimmed in lace points. She was compelled to admit the warm color of the fabric enlivened her normally pale looks, but she drew the line at painting her face. "No, I thank you," she said, turning away from the mirror so as not to regard the bruise that marred her complexion. "I have no wish to hide behind a mask. I only hope I will not frighten your friend away."

Helen gave her sister a long-suffering appraisal, understanding that Juno thought the viscount was enamored of *her*. But then she would think so, as every gentleman darkening their door had come claiming to call on Helen, even when they were more at ease in Juno's company.

Helen thought men were such foolish creatures not to realize Juno's worth simply because she did not enhance her outward appearance. "Transparent as glass," one of Helen's former suitors had called Juno, thus earning Helen's undying enmity. But he was right in a way—Juno was Juno, clear through. It was just that Juno hid her inner beauty behind a capable, managing mien that discouraged most gentlemen from seeing her in a romantic light.

Given the sidelong looks Lord Lancaster had directed toward her sister yesterday, Helen suspected that he *did* recognize Juno's virtues and her frailties. He was one gentleman who would not be fooled by powder or paint. Nor would he allow Juno to affect a manner that ignored her injuries. They gave her a delicate "damsel in distress" air over which gentlemen invariably seemed to trip. And Helen, the belle of Hampshire at whose feet men fell like cordwood before an ax, decided that the Viscount Lancaster should fall deeply and irrevocably in love with her sister.

Unaware of Helen's thoughts, Juno was giving herself a critical appraisal in the pier glass. She looked surprisingly pretty, in spite of the bruises, but had grown so accustomed to deprecating her looks, that she said, "It will have to do, I suppose." Then turning her eye onto her sister, who was wearing a dove gray frock covered with a voluminous white apron that gave her the appearance of a housemaid, Juno heaved an exasperated breath and said, "Why do you not wear the white book muslin we made this spring? It's such a contrast to your brilliant coloring."

"No, I must run the house and see to your comfort today," Helen said, draping a rose-printed shawl around Juno's shoulders, and placing her on a fainting couch in the sitting room they shared above stairs. "You must let me do my part," she added gently, as if she knew Juno was about to protest her idleness.

And indeed, Juno did protest. "But at least allow me to sit in the morning room," she said, in half-hearted tones which admitted that she did feel in need of a restoring repose away from the bustle of the house.

Kissing her sister's uninjured cheek, Helen smiled and said, "I'll send for you when . . . your friend calls," adding before Juno could further protest, "He did say he wanted to

257

read to you. What shall he read, do you think?"

"He is welcome to read anything but the Marquess of Queensbury rules." Juno laughed, reassuring her sister that she had not lost her customary sense of humor. But as Helen scurried out of the sitting room to direct the staff in their work, Juno admitted she did not feel at all like herself. She felt more like a wilting violet, and she was not comfortable in the unfamiliar role.

"Here she is, my lord," Helen trilled, bursting into the sitting room and putting an end to Juno's nap.

Juno stared sleepily at the viscount, knowing she should protest the impropriety of a gentleman entering a lady's boudoir. But she only blinked as Helen explained, "Juno, Lord Lancaster has kindly offered to carry you down to the gazebo where we are going to take tea."

Struggling upright on the blue sofa, Juno finally found her voice. "There is no need," she said, as she thrust her feet to the floor and attempted to rise. But the sudden change in position caused her to stumble dizzily into Lord Lancaster's arms. "Oh, dear," she stammered as he steadied her against his frame. "I do beg your pardon."

"There is *every* need," he said, supporting her arm in an unconscious instinct to protect her. "You are weak as a lamb. And I am perfectly happy to be of service." Then, without asking permission, he swept Juno off her feet and propelled them both down the stairs.

Helen followed, twittering like a pretty bird, obviously unaware of the feelings that warred within Juno's breast — guilt at allowing such ineligible feelings free rein in her heart battled hope that Lord Lancaster might return a particle of the foolish regard she felt for him.

That he did not was driven home like a stake in her breast, for he carefully placed her on a padded garden chair, and stepped back to gaze tenderly on Helen as she draped the fallen shawl around Juno's shoulders. He smiled on the younger lady, and clasped her fingers as she sighed tremulously and said, "I cannot help but think this is all my doing. Dear Juno, *can* you forgive me?"

"What is there to forgive?" Juno asked, unable to quell the waspish tone induced by the sight of her sister clinging to Lord Lancaster's fingers. Inhaling deeply, Juno brought the burst of jealousy under control and allowed, "You did not incite Lord Peter and Sir Winston to arms yesterday. I only beg you, stop treating me as a hopeless invalid. I am merely bruised."

"She's not well, you know," Helen said, turning toward the viscount with an apologetic smile. "And completely unaccustomed to being idle. Perhaps you could entertain her while I see to our refreshments. I took the liberty of setting out several of Juno's books."

Juno hoped Helen had not laid out *A Clergyman's Advice to His Daughter,* or other edifying tomes with which she ordinarily began her day. But as the viscount let go of Helen's fingers and reached for the top volume which rested on the teakwood table, she breathed a sigh of relief. He was turning over the pages of Miss Austen's *Sense and Sensibility.*

"Ah," he said, placing himself in a chair beside Juno. "Shall I read to you now or later?"

"I leave it to you to decide," Juno said in a voice that sounded like a breathless stranger's.

"Oh, no," he teased, wagging a playful finger at her. "I am here to entertain you. Your wish is my command."

Blushing, Juno said, "Then I wish you would simply talk with me. I fear I cannot quite follow a story line right now." Her confession caused his dark eyebrows to knit together suspiciously, and she was quick to add, "I am all right, truly. Please, my lord, do not render me any unusual service, only treat me as you would any lady."

"If you mean we should speak of the weather and fashion," he said, grinning infectiously, "I think I can do better than that."

Juno's heart soared as she allowed herself to float on a flight of fancy, wondering what the viscount had in mind.

She did not have long to await a delcaration of his intentions. Leaning forward, Lancaster said in confidential tones, "Friends need not speak of such mundane matters."

Juno's hopes plummeted to earth as an involuntary sigh drove all the air from her breast. Lord Lancaster wanted her to stand as his friend in his suit with Helen.

Forgetting her own wish to call him friend, Juno felt as if her heart was being squeezed by disappointment. Why did gentlemen only seem to want her as a "friend"? Was something the matter with her that no one could see her in a romantic light?

Of a sudden her parents' penchant for bestowing classical names on their daughters seemed the height of folly, at least in regard to herself. Juno was the patron goddess of marriage, and she, Juno Davis, was the most unmarriageable female in all of England. She doubted she would ever meet a bridegroom at the altar.

Such bitter ruminations made it difficult for her to frame an agreeable reply, but she mustered all her strength and presented what she hoped was an amiable smile as she said, "Of course, my lord. One can never have enough friends."

Lancaster met Juno's wary smile with a careful one of his own, outwardly agreeing with her cautious assertion. But he was aware of the protective wall she had thrown up between them—the averted gaze, the overbright smile, the hand clutching her shawl like a shield.

Why had she gone stiff with him? Was it something he had done or said?

He racked his brain. Juno had allowed him to carry her down the stairs and outside, and seemed willing enough to spend a few moments unchaperoned in his company.

Perhaps, he thought on an inspiration, she was hesitant to enter into an intimate relationship with him, despite her earlier wish to call him friend. He knew it was not the custom between ladies and gentlemen to enjoy comfortable relations. And having enacted the part of chaperone for her sister, Juno Davis was, after all, a modest young lady whose dealings with gentlemen had of necessity been more formal than those most ladies enjoyed. She took her responsibilities as guardian to her sister quite seriously.

Of a sudden Lancaster realized he had never met a lady like her. Juno Davis was capable and possessed a modesty far exceeding that of every debutante to whom he had been introduced. Moreover, she seemed completely unaware that she was pretty, which only increased her appeal.

Lancaster had grown wary of the unending marital lures cast at him by hopeful young ladies the past ten years. It was refreshing, for a change, to be the pursuer.

However, until Juno felt more comfortable in his company, he knew he would have to go slowly in his quest. He did not want to frighten her into prohibiting future visits.

Smiling and concealing his true feelings, Lancaster opened the volume and began reading.

Juno enjoyed the sound of his voice, a mellow baritone that soothed like warm honey. Relaxing under the sensual spell of his voice as it rose and fell in the pleasant cadence of Miss Austen's prose, Juno chided herself for liking it entirely too well, for she was certain his heart was set on wooing Helen.

Before he had read long enough to suit her, Juno saw her sister returning down the crushed stone walk. She was not alone, but was accompanied by a housemaid bearing a tea tray, as well as Lord Peter Oxley. He seemed to be making a desperate case for himself, pleading for Helen to take his arm. When the couple stepped into the gazebo, Lord Lancaster set the book aside and directed a disgruntled look upon them.

Of course, Juno thought it was because he wanted Helen for himself, and was confirmed in her opinion when he smiled grimly as the girl hissed, "Oh, Peter, how *could* you?"

Lord Peter threw up his hands. Juno could do nothing but dodge his frustrated swing, which set her head to aching again. "I beg you to forgive me, Miss Juno," said the repentant fool, shoving his dangerous hands into his pockets. "Didn't mean to plant you a facer, after all."

"No," Juno said, in weak tones she despised, "You

261

meant to draw Sir Winston's claret."

"Not with an uppercut, ma'am," Sir Peter corrected. "Meant to pop him one under the chin," adding by way of explanation, "Winnie has a glass jaw. I say, so do you!"

Juno blushed, the tinge of pink darkening the bruise that marred her jaw and cheek. She was about to concede the point when Lord Lancaster cleared his throat emphatically and said, "That is beside the point, Oxley, as you well know. And if you have anything else to say to Miss Davis, I should suggest you make short work of it. She's not half glad to see you."

"No, well, shouldn't blame her if she threw me off the grounds," Lord Peter said. "Helen, if I apologize, will you speak to me again?"

The pretty brunette sniffed in reply, crossing her arms and turning her shoulder on the repentant man. He ran a hand through his ruffled auburn hair, looking as if he had lost his last friend. "I *am* sorry, Miss Juno. Know I'd never have hit you if I'd . . ." He'd been on the verge of saying seen you, but thought better of it and, scratching his head to stimulate his brain, he concluded with, "If I'd had better control of my temper."

Juno knew that Lord Peter Oxley was not in the habit of striking ladies, even when he was possessed of a fury, and was about to absolve him of guilt. But Lord Lancaster did not know the young man as well, and said, "If you think that makes it all right, you are sadly mistaken."

"I know it doesn't make it all right," said Lord Peter in tones of desperation. "Didn't ask her to forget it. Couldn't if she tried. Hit her too hard."

"Yes, you did," Juno said on a note of laughter as she cradled her aching jaw in protective fingers. "Have you been sparring with the Gentleman?"

"Yes," came the enthusiastic confession. Lord Peter insinuated himself into the chair beside her. "Capital fellow. Taught me that very move. Of course he did not let his guard down the way you did. . . ."

"Ah," said Juno, trying to sound appreciative. Then, seeing that he was eyeing Helen in the manner of a whipped spaniel, she said, "Would you like to take tea with us?"

"Glad to," he said, moving immediately to Helen's side.

"Ought to have sent the puppy packing," Lord Lancaster said in irritated tones that Juno thought made him sound like a dog guarding a bone.

"But he did say he was sorry," she replied. "I think he was about to make an offer."

"Shouldn't accept it," counseled the viscount.

Juno could not help feeling that someone had suddenly squeezed all the breath out of her. Convinced that Lord Lancaster meant to steal a march on the unhappy young man, she was unable to reply. Indeed, it looked as if the viscount might be right, for Helen was pointedly ignoring her erstwhile suitor as she went about pouring tea. She went so far as to request that Millie, the maid, hand out the refreshments when her unforgiven suitor offered to do that very thing.

Lord Lancaster, being a guest, was served first, but he placed the plate in Juno's shaking fingers. "No, take it," he insisted when she protested. But he appropriated a small biscuit, turning it over in his fingers, asking, "Are these your famous 'thumbprints'?"

"Yes," Juno said, over the rim of her cup as he bit into the crumbly delicacy. "Silly things, aren't they? Cook got the idea when I stuck my fingers in her biscuits. Said they needed a spot of jam to remind her of 'helping hands.' "

"Our cook would have smacked my fingers with his wooden spoon, had I been so careless as to destroy his masterworks," Lancaster said, savoring the sweet jam treat.

"That's dreadful," Juno said, feeling as her own the pain Lancaster must have endured. Then, thinking the viscount might interpret her distress as criticism of the way a grand home was run, she explained, "At Breakstone Cottage, children were given the run of the house. Mama believed helping as much as we could was the best way to learn how to keep a household running smoothly."

"No," marveled the viscount in teasing tones. "And did

you carry coal and sweep carpets?"

Convinced he thought less of her for being actively involved in seeing to her family's comfort, Juno lowered her eyes self-consciously, hoping her confession would not give him an unalterable disgust. "Yes, if it needed doing."

"Remarkable," he breathed out, in awe. Unable to keep his feelings to himself, he exclaimed, "I have never met anyone quite like you."

Not comprehending that he spoke in tones of the utmost respect, Juno shrugged. "I know it is not fashionable, my lord, but I believe our work is a great reward."

Lord Peter laughed in derisive tones. "Don't say such things, Miss Juno. Papa's been trying this age to convince me to 'apply myself' to honest work. But what should I do? Go into the law or the church? They're no better than tradesmen, hawking their wares, and not as well paid. Rather raise horses."

"No one's stopping you," snapped Lancaster before Juno could reply.

"Oh, but you're wrong, my lord," Juno replied in gentle but reproachful tones. "Lord Peter is a second son."

And Helen chimed in, in tones of bold, yet breathless outrage, "Peter is a very good judge of horseflesh. Only, he does not inherit, and it is so . . . unfair!"

Allowing that the law of primogeniture was patently unjust, Lancaster suggested that Lord Peter invest his quarterly allowance in a good horse farm instead of squandering it on boxing lessons. In truth, he wished the two younger people would take themselves away, to allow him a few more unchaperoned moments with Juno. She seemed to be tiring quickly, and he was reluctant to let her out of his sight.

To her own disappointment, Juno was fading rapidly. Usually, her stamina knew no end, but today she felt despicably weak. And when Lord Lancaster suggested he carry her back to the house where she might rest out of the sun, she fought back tears of useless fury. Protesting that she did not wish to be taken away, she was overruled by his gentle determination, which gave rise to fears that he no longer wanted to be in her company.

Biting her tongue as he stated he would return on the morrow, Juno rebuked herself unreservedly on his departure. How could she have been so stupid as to suggest that she, a giddy country mouse, knew better than a viscountess how to manage a grand household? She must have sounded to the viscount as if her brain had been rattled, admitting that she carried coal like any housemaid.

No wonder he wanted to, as he had said in that carefully solicitous voice, 'see how she did.' He was probably worried that she would turn violent and harm Helen.

As Lancaster returned to the inn at which he was staying, he marveled at Miss Juno's ingenuous confidences. That she was not above turning her hand to whatever needed doing marked her as a remarkable person in his circle of acquaintances. "Work as a great reward," he mused aloud, drawing rein at the top of a rise to overlook Juno's Breakstone Cottage.

Made of brick instead of half timbers, and roofed in slate rather than thatch, it was actually more the size of a manor house. But it felt cozy, like a cottage wherein love resided, and he knew its warmth and charm were due to Juno. Even the foolish Lord Peter was welcome.

Of a sudden Lancaster felt a twinge of jealousy. Juno had encouraged the clunch entirely too vehemently to merely consider him a friend, yet that was the name she chose to grace their relationship.

Still smarting under his unhappy suppositions, Lancaster wondered how he could wrest Juno out of the influence of Lord Peter's Turkish treatment. Other than his companions on the Peninsula, he had never felt such protective instincts toward another living being as he did for Juno Davis. He wanted to be with her, to protect and cherish her. And he longed to see how The Keep would fare under her gentle influence.

His inheritance, a gray stone fortress built as an abbey,

had always felt more to him like a prison than a home. Since succeeding to his title, he had visited as seldom as duty required. But if Juno lived there, she would warm its cold halls with her sunny smile, and soften the stony hearts of the army of servants he had employed to keep the old pile inhabitable.

He could scarcely wait until tomorrow to return to Breakstone Cottage, to ask her if she would take care of his household as her own.

"I beg your pardon?" Juno asked, after Lord Lancaster had made his heart-stopping request. He had taken her hand in his, pressing it in an urgent manner that did not correspond with his unemotional proposition. Retrieving her fingers, she inquired, "Am I to understand you want me to come to The Keep to manage your staff?"

He looked stupidly at her, wondering what had gone wrong with his proposal.

"I am not in such desperate straits as to go into service," she was saying in constricted tones that betrayed her complete misunderstanding.

Of a sudden it struck him; she thought he wanted her as his housekeeper.

"You know I am not ashamed of the work I am called to do," Juno added. "But you cannot expect me to give up my hopes by taking a position in a gentleman's household."

"No, no," Lancaster blurted out. How could she have mistaken his offer for one of employment? "I spoke too quickly. We scarcely know one another. If we did, I should have known how you might react to my . . . proposal."

"To be sure," Juno agreed, stifling an embarrassed giggle. "I believe you will realize how ineligible your offer was, when you discover the lady who will someday be your wife."

"I hardly think we need worry about that," he said, ruffling his fingers through his dark brown hair, as he wondered what he could to do convince Juno that she was the lady he wanted for his wife.

But Juno did not wait for him to mount an explanation, and he began to worry that her injury had addled her brain, for at that moment, she burst into tears.

"My lord, how can you be so heartless?" she cried, her voice a shocked whisper, as she flung herself from the sofa.

"What did I say?" he demanded, coming to his feet and capturing her arms in a gentle grasp. "I did not ask you to be my . . ." The horrible thought intruded that she had misread his interest in an insulting manner, and he was forced to choke out, "Mistress. . . ."

"No, of course you did not," Juno said, allowing him to draw her into a reassuring embrace. She leaned her cheek against his firm chest, and sighed as he brushed her hair with his jaw. They seemed to fit together, as if they had been made to support one another in this way.

This was heaven, Juno thought, inhaling his clean fragrance of musk and lime. The essence seemed to envelop her until everything was tinged with its vigor. She sighed in disappointment. If only he had asked her to marry him.

But that, reminded the cold voice of cruel reality, was a vain hope. Lord Lancaster had asked her to be his housekeeper not his wife, yet she was reposing in his arms with all the eagerness of a . . . mistress.

Disentangling herself from his embrace, Juno fled to the far end of the sofa and lay cold hands on her flaming cheeks. "Please forgive me, Lord Lancaster," she said, hiding the furious blush that betrayed her complete humiliation. "I shan't mistake you again."

Subsiding on the other end of the couch, he replied, "I should hope not," in stiff, offended tones. Her refusal hurt him far more than he had thought possible. He crossed his arms so as to restrain himself from touching her again.

Having spent all his adult life avoiding the parson's mousetrap, the Viscount Lancaster did not realize how deeply one oblivious miss could affect him. He was tempted to take himself far away before she could fire another round into his heart.

But to withdraw would leave her open to the dubious and

probably violent advances of Lord Peter Oxley, and that Lancaster vowed he would not do.

"Oh, there you are, Junie," cooed Helen as she peered into the library. Turning to someone behind her, she said, "Your concern is touching, sir, but see, she is coming along very well."

Lord Peter stuck his head through the door. "Had to see for myself." Striding into the room, he said, "Be glad to know, Juno, that I've told Father my hopes."

"That is good news, Peter," Juno said in enthusiastic tones that encouraged him to seat himself beside her on the sofa. "And what did he say?"

"Agreed with me; said I must find a good horse farm if I am to succeed in other matters. 'First things first,' y'know." Juno did not miss the significant look he shot Helen as she seated herself on a solitary chair at her sister's elbow.

"Yes," growled Lancaster, glaring at Oxley beneath knotted brows. "Don't let us keep you from your task."

"Oh, I'm in no hurry," said Lord Peter, smiling as if he were aware of the viscount's frustration. "Wouldn't have plucked up the courage to lay it before the old man, had you"—turning to Juno—"not urged me to."

"What a nice thing to say," Juno breathed, laying her hand in his. She had done nothing that she could recall, but his confidence buoyed her spirits.

"And completely unnecessary," grumbled the viscount. He did not like the way Juno gave the lout her hand in so trusting a manner. "You ought to have known a word to your father would stand you in good stead. Now I suppose you'll be wanting a few moments alone."

"Well, now you mention it," Peter said, darting a red-faced glance toward Helen before turning his eyes on Juno in a pleading manner. "I would."

Lancaster crossed his legs at the knees and slumped against the sofa cushion. Giving Oxley an unchaperoned visit with Juno Davis was the last thing he intended to do. "Don't mind me," he said ungraciously.

The four sat in uncomfortable silence for several moments. Juno was mortified to realize that her hand remained suspended in Lord Peter's, and Helen and Lord Lancaster were glaring furiously upon them. Of a sudden, she reclaimed her fingers and shot to her feet. "Forgive me, gentlemen, Helen; I . . ." she began, stumbling to an embarrassed silence.

Normally she would have pleaded the tyranny of her work to excuse herself, but since Helen had taken over her duties, Juno had nothing with which to occupy herself. Moreover, the tension of the past minutes had left her feeling drained and unhappy, and suspecting she was an unnecessary member of the company. She cringed as she confessed, "I am suddenly tired. Would you excuse me?"

As one, Helen and Lord Peter arose. Draping a solicitous arm around her sister, Helen uttered sympathetic sounds as she ushered Juno into the hallway. Peter followed like a love struck calf.

Only his wish not to seem ridiculous on the heels of his thwarted proposal kept Lancaster in the library. But when the thought intruded that Oxley might have the opportunity of carrying Juno above stairs, he thrust himself toward the departing trio.

"I say, Oxley," he said, as Juno paused on the bottom step of the staircase. Commanding himself not to grin like a Cheshire cat at having foiled the young man's plans, he inquired, "Would you take a look at my mount? Took a stone bruise on the road this afternoon." Paladin had done nothing of the sort, but Lancaster wanted Oxley out of Juno's way.

"Glad to, my lord," said the handsome younger man. "If you'll excuse me, ladies?" Intent on easing the animal's pain, he hurried off, without hearing Helen's suggestion that she accompany him to the stables.

Left alone with the viscount and expecting him to soon follow Helen in order to spite Lord Peter, Juno leaned heavily on the balustrade in an attempt to muster the strength to climb the stairs. Her sister was already hurrying off, saying she would be glad to lend Lord Peter a hand if he would tell

269

her what needed to be done, and Juno did not want to recall her from her pursuit merely to be helped above stairs.

She wondered whether she would ever be herself again. It had been three days since her introduction to fisticuffs; time enough, she thought, to have regained strength in body and mind. Yet the slightest exertion left her feeling as if she had climbed to the top of Box Hill with a fully loaded haversack.

"Will you sit?"

Juno's heart leapt into a panicked flight at Lord Lancaster's query. Pressing a hand to her bosom, she drew a shaky breath and attempted to make light of her startled reaction. "Oh, are you still here?" she asked. "I thought you would go after Helen."

"Why would you think such a thing?" he demanded in disgruntled tones as he drew her from the staircase and settled her into a chair in the hallway.

"I am no fit company for a guest," she replied wearily, sinking onto the soft cushion without resistance.

Thinking Lord Peter's sudden departure was to blame for Juno's low spirits, Lancaster felt a jealous thrust to his midsection. "I don't know what you see in him," he said in pettish tones that raised her puzzled gaze to his. "Oxley," he said by way of edification. "Kindly explain his attraction."

"Oh," she said, assuming the viscount wondered what Helen saw in the young man. "I know you will not believe me, after his foolish assault, but Lord Peter really is quite nice. He is a devoted friend and cannot do enough for . . . Helen and me. His family lives adjacent to Breakstone Cottage, you know. Very convenient."

That would explain Juno's faint praise, Lancaster thought. The two had grown up together; she was too familiar with Lord Peter's faults to overstate his virtues. She did not sound like a woman in love, but the viscount had to be certain that her heart was not engaged. Drawing a courageous breath, he inquired, "Would you welcome his offer?"

"Oh, yes," Juno said, wanting to be honest with him. It

would do no harm for the viscount to know she preferred Helen to marry Lord Peter. "He has always seemed like a part of our family; it would be no hard thing to . . . Lord Lancaster, have I said something to offend?"

The viscount did not think her confession would hurt him, but it did. It was a blow to his pride to think the lady who inspired his protective instincts thought so little of herself as to prefer a man who excused himself from hitting a lady by saying he hadn't good control over his temper. Lancaster felt he ought to go and never return.

But the mere thought of leaving Juno incited such a pain between his eyes he could only stroke his forehead. He simply could not leave her at the mercy of Oxley's uncertain temper.

"Please, my lord," she repeated, "I hope I may not have hurt your feelings."

"No," he said, when at last he could speak. "You are only being honest. Well, I must also speak the truth."

"I hope you will," Juno said, although her heart pounded so hard within her breast, she almost hoped he would spare her any more truth.

"I cannot like him," Lancaster said, not knowing how to soften his blunt declaration.

"Well, of course you do not," she replied, suppressing the stab of jealousy that his statement occasioned and hoping she did not sound as breathless as she felt. Why did men have to be such fools over beauty? "You look upon Lord Peter as a rival. I could not expect you to think of him kindly."

Rather than being taken aback by her astute perception, Lord Lancaster discovered he was able to agree with her. "You're right," he confessed with a self-deprecating grin. "But I have hopes of eventually winning the disputed lady's heart."

Sighing as she acknowledged the hopelessness of her attraction to the viscount, Juno drew upon her love for Helen to say, "I wish you success; however, the lady may prove stubborn."

She knew it was more likely, given Helen's sweet nature and eagerness to please, that her sister would accept the viscount's hand simply to avoid hurting his feelings. But she did not want Lord Lancaster to think he should have an easy courtship, even though her conscience gave her no end of trouble for the deception. It was neither ladylike nor the Christian thing to do, but she could not help herself. But it was all for the best; Helen would not be happy marrying Lord Lancaster.

However she rationalized her part in this coil, Juno felt she did not deserve to enjoy the pleasure of his company. Excusing herself to go above stairs, she fretted the remainder of the afternoon away, regretting her rudeness and berating herself for not discovering whether the viscount meant to return on the morrow.

Despite the rain that had fallen all morning, making the roads slippery and dangerous, Lancaster returned to Breakstone Cottage by noon. Juno was polishing silver upon his arrival and bore his gentle remonstrance against overexertion with breathless good humor. "I have never thought that a little occupation did one serious harm," she laughed, taking up another spoon. "Besides, inactivity weighs more heavily on my hands than does my family silver."

Agreeing inwardly that the joy in her quiet work imparted a glow to her normally too-pale beauty, Lancaster took up a cloth and began to rub the polishing compound into an antique teapot. It was not a chore with which he had much experience or aptitude, but he liked being engaged in such an intimate domestic task with her. It gave him a warm feeling within his heart. Happy in her company, he began to whistle.

As the viscount rubbed the teapot with far more vigor than necessary, Juno fell uncomfortably silent. He obviously did not wish to converse with her since he had begun to whistle almost immediately. But the tune was cheerful, and the homely task she had assigned herself gave her a purpose. Juno was glad he had not begun to grill her about

Lord Peter and Helen. Before long, she was absently humming along, and then she remembered the words to "Sumer Is A-Cumin' In", which they sang as a round.

Lord Lancaster's warm baritone gave her no end of pleasure. His voice made her nerve endings tingle as if in anticipation of a rare treat.

Flustered, Juno felt a blush steal over her features. Lord Lancaster had given her no reason for giddy romantic hopes. Indeed, he seemed completely unaware that he was melting her heart by his friendly manner and honeyed voice.

Juno could not tell him how he affected her, fearing such an admission on her part would propel him into Helen's company. Applying her cloth to a silver vase, she told herself that only a green girl would confess her feelings to a gentleman who was so obviously infatuated with another lady. As it was, she was wearing her feelings for all to see. She was ashamed that she possessed so little self-control.

Her sister knew better than to wear her heart on her sleeve, but she was more accustomed to flirtations, and did not set much store in a gentleman's attention.

Sighing, Juno wished she knew what to do about her hopeless attraction to the viscount. She supposed she would know what to do if she had been the object of as many suitors as Helen had been. Flirtation had made Helen bold enough to pursue the man she wanted. But instead of acting courageously, Juno only began the round again, leaning toward Lord Lancaster as they sang, the better to hear the harmonious blend of their voices, the better to gaze upon his handsome face, the better to pretend that his smile was for her.

Lingering on the last note, their voices blended to perfection. Juno felt as if she were floating on Lancaster's earnest gaze and harmonic suspension. She did not want to end their melodic flirtation.

But end it she must. She was becoming light headed from spinning out the last tone, even though their voices had faded to an almost imperceptible pianissimo. But Lancaster seemed unaffected by the sustained chord.

Drawing an enormous breath, Juno laughed off her lack of breath control. "We have very little opportunity to engage in musical afternoons at Breakstone Cottage," she said, lowering her gaze to his enticing mouth. It was still pursed as if he intended once more to sing "cuckoo." But no sound did he utter. Indeed, his jaw tensed as if he suddenly found her company distasteful, and he seemed to have turned to stone.

When she'd drawn that shaky breath, Lancaster's gaze had been drawn, against his better intentions, to the rise and fall of her bosom. So soft and round, he thought, and made for him. If only he could persuade her to forget her dangerous affection for Lord Peter Oxley. The dread of allowing her to submit to Oxley's passions set his jaw tensely. There was only one way to save her from the beast. Before he quite realized what he was doing, Lancaster advanced his suit.

⟨ Juno wondered what she could have done for Lord Lancaster to have gone so stiff in her company, and was about to inquire if he wanted a glass of water. But as she opened her mouth to speak, he dropped a kiss on her lips.

It was only a feather-light brush of his mouth against hers, but she was so surprised, she dropped the vase she had been polishing.

The ensuing clatter broke them apart like a pair of guilty lovers. Stunned, Juno clapped a hand over her bosom, compelling her racing heart to cease its frantic pace. Lancaster stared at her as if he were seeing her for the first time, and he looked as if he did not like what he saw. Mortified, Juno lowered her gaze to the fallen vase which lay between them. Then, as one, they knelt to retrieve it.

In a romance Juno had once read, the hero and heroine had reached for a book of poetry at the same time. Their hands had inadvertently touched, and they had reacted as if a spark had ignited tinder.

It was a sad truth that reality was not a friend of romance. Instead of clasping fingers, Juno and Lancaster bumped heads.

Juno saw stars. Lancaster thought he heard bells. He caught her in an instinctive embrace that was more heated than protective.

"Please, my lord," she said, pressing a hand to her forehead until her world stopped spinning. But she was compelled to cling to him for support, even while she protested, "I am not hurt, I promise you."

"Thank God for that," he exclaimed. Still supporting her, he uttered profuse apologies for his presumption, then sat her at the table so that he could pick up the accursed vase. Then, muttering, "I am no better than Oxley," he strode out of the room, his hands clenched into fists at his side.

Lancaster felt like a benighted fool. He had intended to kiss her again, but had bungled the attempt in the clumsy manner of a green cub. Too embarrassed to excuse himself, he wandered about the sodden garden, wondering how he could make up with Juno without seeming even more callow.

His sudden retreat made Juno think she had imagined the embrace, but the furious blush coloring his handsome features told her she had not. He had kissed her. Her lips still burned from the brief caress. And her heart ached for the lost opportunity.

Their clumsy encounter over the vase did not surprise her. It was what she might have expected to happen. But Lancaster had kissed her in broad daylight. That she would never have expected.

Had she been prepared, Juno would have kissed him back to make him forget her sister, to make him want her as much as she wanted him. If only she hadn't been so startled. To her everlasting mortification, she had jumped back the way only a confirmed spinster might have done.

Juno felt like weeping. She had ruined her only chance for romance.

But looking forlornly onto the garden, wherein Lord Lancaster had taken himself, she noted sadly that her sister would not prove so hopeless. Helen was gliding toward the viscount, her hands outstretched becomingly. And Lancaster seemed to be welcoming her with a degree of enthusiasm that had been missing from his unfortunate encounter with Juno.

Lancaster was relieved that Helen had come out to the garden without her pesky escort, Oxley. Without thinking, he took her hand in his and allowed the young lady to direct their steps around the clipped hedges, too miserable to enjoy her beauty.

"What is the matter, my lord?" Helen inquired, pulling him down on a bench after another heavy exhalation escaped his lungs. "Did you and my sister quarrel?"

"No," Lancaster grumbled. "I kissed her."

"Oh," said Helen in awful tones. Knowing Juno, she probably flew into hysterics. Helen waited for the viscount to go on, but when he did not enlighten her, she said, "I hope she did not slap you."

He shook his head. "No, she didn't have to. She dropped a vase."

Helen nodded sagely, although she did not understand why a kiss should cause her sister to throw pottery. "She did not injure you, did she?"

"No," he allowed in melancholy tones. Then, sighing and rubbing his temple, he added, "At least not very badly. She hit my head."

Reacting automatically, Helen took hold of his head to survey the damage, saying, "And your head was harder than the vase, I suppose," when she could see no outward sign of harm.

"No, rather I think my head is harder than hers," Lancaster said, propelling himself to his feet as a misty rain began to fall. "Indeed, I should see how she does, Miss Helen. We bumped heads, picking up the vase."

"That is not very romantic," Helen allowed, following him up the path toward the house.

"No," he agreed, in tones of the deepest dejection. He held the door open for her, and followed her into the hall. Brushing the rain off his shoulders, he said, "I have not got a romantic bone in my body. Oh, I know how to please, except with Juno. With her, I feel as though I am a callow youth—or a horrible rake."

"I have heard you do not lack experience," Helen said, frowning on his last pronouncement. "But I should hope you are not a rake. Juno is . . ." Helen thought better of telling him that her sister would welcome his courtship. It would not do to allow him to think he did not have to woo her. So, she concluded by saying, "My sister is unused to rough handling, sir."

He flinched before her implied accusation, and bit back a self-justifying rejoinder. Instead, he vowed, "I would not willingly harm her, Miss Helen. It is only, my feelings are, to my surprise, rather violent where she is concerned."

Helen's lips formed a silent O, and he hastened to assure her, "I have never felt this way toward another woman," just as Juno stumbled into the hallway.

"I beg your pardon, my lord, Helen," she said, in broken tones, as she propelled herself above stairs. She was too late. He had already asked for Helen's hand.

"No, wait, Juno, you are not interrupting," Helen called, perceiving the cause of her sister's distress. "I daresay Lord Lancaster would like to read to you now."

"I cannot," Juno said, fleeing above stairs. "Too busy to read now."

As Juno disappeared, Lancaster scowled at Helen. "What have you got her doing now?" he demanded. "Airing linen? Scrubbing floors? I won't have her exhaust herself."

"Do you think I made Juno polish the silver?" Helen retorted. "I should like to see anyone make her stop! She has been champing at the bit for two days, frantic to keep herself occupied—to keep from thinking, I dare say."

He looked as if he was going to offer a typically male rejoinder about the female thought process producing little more than smoke, so Helen offered her own set down. "Do not consider men superior because ladies are occupied with the mundane affairs of life, while you concern yourself with Parliamentary matters or Napoleon's Guard. If we did not take a thought to what you might eat, or have a care to your comfort, you would not like it at all."

Taken aback by the vehemence of her defense, Lancaster could only stammer, "Of course. That is, I did not mean to imply your concerns were less worthy than ours. Oh dear, Miss Helen. I did not intend to deprive your sister of her purpose. Only, she is not, as you say, accustomed to Turkish treatment, and must allow herself to recover."

"But Juno is not the sort who can abide inactivity for long," Helen said. "And I am too busy now to entertain her."

"Then it must devolve to my shoulders," Lancaster said in what sounded to Helen like grudging tones. "Would you kindly ask her whether I might engage her in a game of piquet."

Bestowing the look of a disapproving chaperone on the viscount, Helen said, "I am sure she would prefer to rest now. Tomorrow is Sunday, when we go to church."

Knowing he sounded like a love-struck calf and despising himself for it, Lancaster could not help saying, "I could return in the afternoon. . . ."

"I fear not," Helen said, shaking her head so that her ebony curls bounced. "We are engaged tomorrow afternoon. But if you like, you may call on Monday."

Lancaster wanted to recall Juno immediately and discover whether she wanted him to leave or stay, but the injured look in her gaze as she had stumbled upon the couple in the hallway discouraged him. "Very well," he said, glancing above stairs despairing of her interest. "If you will tell Juno I mean to return, I'll go now."

"Have a nice evening, my lord," Helen said. Her smile widened ingenuously as she added, "We'll see you tomorrow in church."

As she had seen him to the door, Lancaster had had no choice but to jam his hat on his head and make for the stable, attempting to avoid the mud puddles that marred the path between the house and its outbuildings. For all the care the Davis ladies took of their home and garden, it seemed they had not given much attention to the grounds. Breakstone Cottage needed a man's hand, much as The Keep needed a woman's touch.

Lancaster spent the evening more pleasantly than he had anticipated, planning improvements on a property that was not his to improve. In time, he would win Juno's wary heart, and then, when he had the right, he would care for her belongings as tenderly as he hoped to care for her.

Because he wanted her to think well of him, the viscount made sure he was counted among the faithful at church the next day. But owing to his rank, he was ushered to the very front of the sanctuary where he could not gaze on Juno Davis. He was compelled to assume a ramrod stiff posture in an effort to resist the temptation to find her during the interminable service.

Unfortunately, his attempt to appear attentive must have given him an arrogant and unfriendly aspect, for as the vicar invited him to stand with him at the door after the benediction, the communicants filed silently past. Lancaster could scarcely meet their uneasy gazes, so intent was he on finding Juno and inviting himself to her table.

But she was not among the line of worshippers, and he began to despair that she had suffered a relapse overnight. It was all he could do not to tear himself away and gallop off to Breakstone Cottage. Then, out of the corner of his eye, he caught a glimpse of Juno walking arm in arm with Helen and that pest, Oxley. They must have slipped outside through a side door.

Begging pardon as the last of the parishioners filed past, Lancaster propelled himself toward the trio just as Oxley handed the ladies into a closed carriage.

Skidding to a halt on the party's heels, Lancaster inquired in a breathless voice, "Going home?"

"No," said Juno, intent on smoothing her maroon cashmere skirts to save herself the pain of gazing upon the viscount. "We are invited to dine with Peter's family." Juno was too hurt to look at him and did not see the abject disappointment in his eyes.

But Helen did note the viscount's misery and decided he should suffer a little more. Whispering a plea for assistance into Lord Peter's ear, she smiled as her beau placed himself at Juno's side in the carriage.

Juno played into her sister's hands nicely, glancing upward in confusion as she felt the pressure of a male thigh against hers. To Helen's delight and Lancaster's dismay, she blushed, but did not draw away from their family friend.

"You're looking exceptionally pretty today," Peter said, earning a radiant smile which did not fade even when he said, "Almost forget you got in my way the other day. By the way, Winnie regrets that you took the blow meant for him."

"What a pretty apology," Lancaster growled, locking his gaze with the clumsy lordling. "If he were any kind of man, he'd offer his own regrets."

Juno's gaze slid from Lord Peter to fall upon the viscount. He was scowling in a manner that reminded her of a bantam rooster strutting about the hen house. How foolish it was of him to begrudge Lord Peter's attempts to mend fences. She certainly bore neither gentleman any ill will. "I rather think you frightened him away with your black looks," she said.

"I'm not saying Winnie's a coward," said Lord Peter in conciliatory tones, "But he did suddenly recall an engagement in Town that he had come here to avoid." He chuckled as if he appreciated the irony in leaping out of the frying pan of Mortal Combat into the fire of Social Engagements. "Heard he's unwittingly committed to a Diamond he had no intentions of courting. But recollecting her vast fortune and his debts convinced him there was nothing for it but to accept his lot."

"We should all be so prudent," grumbled the viscount.

"We should all be so fortunate," amended Lord Peter with a raised eyebrow that left Lancaster feeling as if the younger man were mocking him. He was confirmed in his suspicions when Lord Peter drawled, "And I have the good fortune of escorting two lovely ladies to dinner. If you will excuse me, m'lord." Then tipping his hat to the viscount, he signaled his driver forward.

Lancaster stood back as the carriage rolled down the road. When he turned to go, he was compelled by the sudden lull in the congregations' conversations to pass a startled look around the church yard. Everyone, it seemed, was staring at him as if he were some sort of circus freak.

Striding toward his horse, he chided himself for making a fool of himself. He was certain they would chew his lovesick behavior thoroughly over Sunday dinner. That the villagers thought he pined for Miss Helen Davis was made abundantly clear over his lonely dinner at the Bell and Star Inn. The good wife who set the platter before him clucked sympathetically and said she thought he would do better to fall in love with Miss Juno, as she was just plain enough to care about a man's comfort. "But will the gentlemen spare a second look for her?" she asked rhetorically. "No, their heads be turned by a pretty face."

Lancaster turned a questioning look on the innkeeper's wife. Of a sudden he wanted nothing more than to live a private life, uninspiring to the curiosity of others. That desire caused him to speak more harshly than he would normally have done. "Have I perhaps given you the impression that I was courting your opinion?"

The good woman clucked as if she knew his ill humor was due to disappointment in love, and went on unhindered. "Beggin' your pardon, but I hope you won't let beauty break your heart, my lord."

"There is very little chance of that," he said in lofty tones that implied that he was above the designs of a country miss. This rejoinder succeeded in sending the woman off in a huff, leaving him to savor his dinner in peace. But the steaming roast beef, boiled potatoes, asparagus, and Yorkshire pudding settled uneasily in his stomach. He was compelled to endure a miserable evening in the private parlor he had engaged at the inn, suffering dyspepsia and imagining his Juno fending off the aggressive embraces of Lord Peter Oxley.

Juno suffered none of the indignities that plagued Lord Lancaster's peace; however, she did admit a lack of appetite when Lady Oxley pressed more roast lamb on her at dinner.

"Ah," said her hostess. "Only one thing suppresses a young person's appetite: unrequited love."

"Doubt it," drawled Peter over a second slice. "Miss Juno ain't the sort to fall in love."

Sighing, Juno realized no one would believe her if she confessed that she was deeply in love, so she said, "It is merely a foolish complaint which does not merit telling."

"See what I mean?" Peter said. "A lovesick miss would not hesitate to speak."

"A lot you know, you great Ox," snapped Helen. "A lady never tells."

"Never?" blurted out her beau in surprise. All the ladies of his acquaintance, well perhaps they were not "ladies" in the polite sense of the word, but all the females with whom he had dealt were quite open in their affection. But of course he did not confess such indelicate information as might distress the lady he wished to make his wife.

"A lady suffers in silence until a certain gentleman makes a declaration of the heart," Helen replied. "Even if she longs to please herself."

"There is where ladies and gentlemen differ," said Lady Oxley. She had married to please her family, because they needed a generous settlement to maintain their style of living. "A gentleman may please himself to his heart's content, but a lady is happiest when pleasing others."

Even to Juno's sensible ears, Lady Oxley's assertion sounded hollow, and she said so. "One cannot please everyone all the time, ma'am. It is a very false way to go on," she added solemnly. Then, heaving a frustrated sigh, she confessed, "I own that I am not as unselfish as I could be, but for once I wish I could please myself without feeling as if I am stealing someone else's joy."

"La, child," chuckled the elder lady. "One would think you meant to throw contentment to the wind and tread the boards."

"No," Helen said fervently. "My sister knows what she owes to our name. She would not be so foolish as to run away to the stage."

"She might very well take to the stage," said Lady Oxley. " 'Tis more anonymous than hiring a post chaise."

Helen eyed Lord Peter ominously so that he said, "Don't be a goose, mother. Juno ain't going to become an actress. We were talking of 'romance.' "

"I was not speaking of romance," Juno hedged. She cut into her apricot tart with a desultory hand. "And it would please me greatly if you would pick another topic to pieces."

Helen met Lord Peter's gaze over Juno's head and nodded when he mouthed the words, "Lovesick miss." But when he added a shrug and mouthed, "Who?" she shook her head. Reminding herself that a lady never tells even to please someone, she turned the subject to the uncommon heat wave that had hastened Spring along.

Juno was walking down the lane the next morning when Lord Lancaster came to visit. She saw him approaching, and thought about hiding until he passed, for it almost seemed as if she had come to meet him. "Might as well throw myself at him," she grumbled. But it was too late to conceal herself behind a hedge, for as he crested the rise leading toward Breakstone Cottage, he paused and waved.

Resigning herself to wait for him, she strode forward, clinging to her bonnet when the wind threatened to tug it from her head. The brim, trimmed with rose-colored silk, reflected becoming color on her pale face, and she was glad she wore it. Although praised universally for her modesty, she was just vain enough to wish to appear at her best.

"I wondered if I should find you at home today," Lord Lancaster said as he reined in his mount.

"I was, but the weather called me out of doors," she replied, self-consciously raising her gaze to his. "You will be disappointed if you are looking for Helen, though."

The viscount did not care what Helen was doing this morning; he was determined to share the day with her sister. Allowing his horse to turn across the lane so that Juno could not flee from him, he asked politely, "Why is that, Miss Davis?"

"She has gone to the village to assist the ladies aid society in 'doing good works,' " Juno said.

"Don't tell me." He laughed, out of gladness he would have Juno all to himself. "She has taken your place today."

Juno blushed and lowered her face in shame. Agreeing to let Helen assume her customary responsibility made her seem like the most selfish soul alive. She found it very difficult to speak. But his query deserved an honest reply, so she mustered her courage to say, "Yes, my lord. Helen did stand in for me today. I own that our visit with the Oxleys tired me out more than I expected." How paltry her excuse sounded! She felt compelled to explain further. "Only the weather turned so fine, I could not remain within doors. And I am not completely heedless of my responsibility; since I felt the need to come outside, I thought I should carry a basket to the chimney sweep's family. He fell off a roof last month and broke his leg."

Juno seemed so flustered, Lancaster wondered whether she had made an assignation with Lord Peter this morning. If she had done so, he was determined she would not keep it. Reaching down from his height, he commanded, "Give me your hand; I shall carry you on your errand of mercy, then take you home."

Arrested by his outstretched hand, Juno shot a horrified gaze up toward him. Really, the man had no sense if he thought she would allow him to take her up before him. That would only set tongues to wag. She did not say that his gallant offer would fuel the gossip mill, for having her name linked romantically with his would bind him to her in ties that could only tighten like a noose. Not wishing to trap him in a relationship that he did not want as much as she, Juno backed away, saying, "I . . . do not ride, my lord."

"I did not ask if you rode," Lancaster said in quelling tones. "I said I shall carry you about your business."

"There is no need," Juno said, backing futilely toward her gate which was too far away to offer her protection from him. Glancing about, hoping to find a convenient break in the hedges that enclosed the fields on either side of the road, her gaze met only with a tangle of briars. She was hemmed in on all sides.

Lancaster dismounted and caught her arm in a grasp that was born of desperation to keep her at his side, regardless of the consequences. But she turned on him a disbelieving, frightened gaze that struck him a solid blow on the heart, and he was seized in the grip of a protective instinct that compelled him to moderate the tight hold on her sleeve, without releasing her.

As soon as he touched her, Juno ceased her flight, for all strength seemed to ebb from her bones. She wanted to please him above all things, but she had not lost her pride or her principles. She could not entrap him. Bestowing a beseeching look upon him, she breathed, "Please let me go, my lord."

"You ask so prettily, but what would it hurt?" he cajoled as he drew her into his arms where she belonged.

Juno was possessed of a most irrational longing to remain where she was, even though they were embracing on a public road. But the viscount's teasing query reminded her of the fragile nature of a lady's reputation. It was not so with a gentleman; he could embrace whomever he liked, wherever he liked, and let the consequences fall squarely on the lady's shoulders.

"It would hurt us both," she said, placing her basket squarely between them.

Lancaster tilted his head to one side, savoring her attempt to save him from the masculine version of a fate worse than death—marriage. "You are a remarkable woman," he said in laughing tones. "No one else I know would be so concerned about my reputation or preserving my blessed single state."

Juno shook her head, convinced he did not understand the gravity of their situation. "It is no difficult matter to soil a lady's good name, my lord. I am more concerned that you not have to pay the piper for an indiscreet flirtation."

"Why?" he asked.

"Because," she said, clamping her lips together before she told him that she wanted him to offer for her because he loved her, not because he needed a housekeeper or was compelled by an overriding sense of honor to silence neighborhood tattle mongers. Instead, she only confessed, "I don't want you to marry unless your heart is fully engaged."

"Remarkable," he said once more. Then, shaking his head as if to clear it, he urged, "Come, Juno; it would please me to do this for you," in gentle tones that melted her heart but not her resolve.

"I would like to please you," she said, her eyes wide with wonder. Turning toward the horse, she added, "However, I will not mount that animal."

"Then I shall walk at your side," Lancaster said, offering his arm. For a moment, Juno looked as if she would like to decline even this gallantry, and he felt constrained to appeal to her conscience. "Surely you would not deny me this opportunity to do a good work."

"No," she said, eyeing him hesitantly. "Only I cannot believe you want to do it."

"Why not?" he asked. "Haven't I already benefited from visiting the sick?"

"I cannot say," she said uneasily, knowing he referred to his visits with herself. She did not like thinking of herself as a charity case.

"No?" Lancaster tucked her fingers around his arm. Drawing her down the lane, he said, "Then allow me to present the evidence to convince you. Before meeting you, I was an indolent son of the nobility. I would never have put another's comfort above my own, and I thought work was a curse inflicted on those who had displeased their Maker."

Juno blushed at his tongue in cheek confession. Though gently given, it sounded to her burning ears as if it were a blistering condemnation of her creed. How presumptuous she had been to offer such wisdom to someone born to the privileges which the viscount enjoyed.

But he seemed not to notice. "In the past few days," he said, directing their steps toward the village, "I have seen how occupation has benefited your sister, and am convinced that it will in time turn Lord Peter into a paragon worthy of a certain lady's hand."

"Yes," Juno sighed. "Peter is reformed. He will make an admirable husband."

But not for you, Lancaster grumbled inwardly as he kicked a stone down the lane. Connecting with his errant sense of fair play, he choked down the resentful thought and said fervently, "I can only hope the lady discovers the same of me."

It was Juno's fervent hope that Lord Lancaster would cease pining for her sister. But instead of saying so and giving him the opportunity of putting to rest her misapprehensions, she breathed a dejected sigh and said, "I am sure she understands your admirable qualities, my lord."

"If I were confident of the lady's good opinion," he ventured, "I would not hesitate to reveal my feelings in a most indisputable manner."

This sent Juno's spirits into a plummeting spiral. Aside from the avowal she had overheard, she had seen no overt display of affection on the viscount's part toward Helen, and despised herself for wanting that state of affairs to continue. But that would not be fair to Helen if her feelings inclined toward the handsome young lord. Juno's conscience pricked at her until she repeated the opinion she had voiced at the Oxley's table. "You must pluck up your courage, my lord. A lady is not likely to reveal her heart until you make your feelings known."

It was Lancaster's experience that ladies did not hesitate to make their feelings known, and he felt comfortable enough in Juno's company that he did not hesitate to say so. This forwardness of manner was one reason, he said, that he had absented himself from Town this spring. With a self-deprecating grin turned upon her, he added, "It is become too difficult at my age to avoid the marital coils of conniving young ladies and their mothers."

Juno felt she would melt under his heated, mocking stare. Did he think she was a conniving young lady with marriage on her mind? Mortified, she fell silent, enduring his company as a penance for her ineligible hopes. But she could not resist the thrill of pleasure that warmed her as he kept her tucked close to his side during the rest of their journey to the sweep's house, nor could she suppress the glow of admiration that warmed her gaze as he bore with amazing good humor the familiarity of a private conversation with the injured sweep. He might have been visiting a peer, so cordial was his manner.

It quite wrung her heart. She did not deserve the affection of such a man. But she did not let her dejection show until Lord Lancaster made their excuses. Fearing that he would deliver her home straightaway, she allowed her shoulders to slump wearily, and uttered only the mildest complaint when he tossed her upon the back of his horse and mounted behind her.

"You are completely undone," he said, giving her no further opportunity to protest as he tucked her safely against his chest. "I shall take you home as soon as we have had a bite." But instead of taking her within the common room of the inn, he commanded a maid to fetch them a basket appropriate for a private repast *al fresco*.

That done, Juno clasped the requested basket to her heart, scarcely daring to believe that the viscount wanted to prolong their outing. He was merely playing the good Samaritan once more, she told herself. After he had fed her, he would return her home with the strict admonition to recruit her strength. Then he would resume his pursuit of her prettier sister.

But after they had enjoyed a filling but homely repast of cheese, bread, apples, and wine, Lancaster lay back on the blanket, his hands clasped behind his head. "So," he said in amused tones as he stared at the blue sky, "you don't ride."

"No," Juno said. "Helen is an accomplished horse-woman. But I . . ." Am afraid of the beasts, she finished inwardly.

"You," he concluded gently, "Had no time or leisure to learn the art, and probably recall youthful tumbles with the dread of repeating them."

Juno stared in wonder at the viscount, that he should understand her so well. Once, while attempting a jump beyond her ability, she had fallen disastrously from her mount and broken her arm. By the time her bone had healed, she seemed to have lost her spirit, for the thought of remounting that gentle but barrier-shy horse terrified her.

Too stunned by his perception to deny her craven heart, she said, "You will probably think me the most poor-spirited person of your acquaintance, my lord. But I am afraid to ride."

"There is nothing to it," he said in bluff tones that did not conceal a smile. "As long as you do not attempt fences that your horse might refuse to take."

"Oh, my lord," Juno said, allowing her relief to echo in the awestruck tones of her voice. So admiring was she, she could not contain herself but gushed on impulsively, "You seem to know me by heart."

Lancaster's gaze darkened as he returned her adoring one. Would that he could know her so intimately, he thought. But she seemed oblivious of his desire, even as she revealed her own. Stumbling over an avowal, he said, "I was only recalling my own abysmal first attempts." Immediately his first proposal leapt to mind. Fearing she might read his thoughts, Lancaster raised his gaze once more to the sky as if the cloud formations were more fascinating than the ice blue eyes that never failed to melt his heart.

"They say one's technique improves with practice," Juno murmured, disappointed that the viscount had averted his gaze. Then she fell into an embarrassed silence. What if he thought she was criticizing his kiss?

To her surprise, Lancaster propelled himself to his feet, holding out a hand as he said, "Of course. That is what we shall do: improve your technique." Before she knew what he meant, he was pulling her toward an ancient oak tree whose lower branches spread parallel to the ground. "That is what a friend would do."

A thrill of laughter tickled Juno's stomach, and she did not repress the joyous sound as it bubbled forth. "If you say so, my lord, who am I to dispute it? But how will I learn to ride without a suitable mount?"

Lancaster placed a hand along a sturdy oak branch, saying in laughing tones, *Voilà, votre cavalerie, mademoiselle.*

"I beg your pardon," she protested, wondering if perhaps Lord Lancaster was slightly near-sighted. "That is a tree."

"I know," Lancaster replied, spanning her waist to lift her upon the branch. The feel of her unfettered frame inspired his heart to thump giddily, and he was forced to calm himself. "An oak, to be precise," he said. "I promise, you will be perfectly safe; this mount will not shy off or run away."

Eyeing him suspiciously, Juno allowed him to toss her gently onto the branch, which swayed under her weight like a skittish steed. She inhaled a startled breath, and clutched his shoulders to retain her balance when he made as if to release her. "Please, my lord. This high-blooded steed might not prove as trustworthy as you believe her. Do not, I pray, let me go."

"I would not dream of it," he said, releasing her waist and taking her hands one at a time in his. She was seated precariously sidesaddle style upon the sturdy branch, grasping his fingers with the viselike grip of the terrified. "Relax, Juno," he admonished. "I shan't let you fall."

A breeze in combination with her weight caused the branch to dip and rise unexpectedly. She gasped and dropped her gaze to the ground. "One would think you did not trust me," he chided, knowing that her toes nearly brushed the grass.

Juno wished she could believe him. But he was standing on terra firma, at arm's length from her, with the most tenuous grip on her fingers. She was the one swaying in the breeze, with nothing to depend on except the hope that this branch which had survived centuries would sustain her until she could manage to climb down. "Please, my lord," she said in breathless tones. "Set me down. I am becoming quite dizzy."

'Twas not the height or rhythmic movement that made her feel so giddy. 'Twas Lancaster's touch. Juno feared she would swoon like one of those foolish misses who laced their stays too tightly, if he did not release her immediately.

But instead of setting her feet on the ground, Lancaster brought himself to her side, and encircled her waist. "Is that better?" he asked.

Juno looked into his warm, cinnamon brown eyes. Despite the flurry of excitement his nearness inspired, she felt perfectly safe. Relaxing under his tutelage, she murmured, "Much better," hoping he would forget all about her sister, hoping he would kiss her again.

Recalling the confusion of emotion his first, unexpected kiss had aroused, Juno was unable to resist dropping her gaze to his mouth.

Immediately the corners of his mouth raised as if he knew just what she was thinking. Juno felt her cheeks glow in embarrassment, and she forced her gaze to meet his.

"Thank you, my lord," she said. "No one has taken the time to teach me how to ride."

Lancaster's heart soared at her confession, but he compelled himself to stay cool as he asked, "Not even Lord Peter?"

"It would not cross his mind that anyone could not ride. He sat a horse before he could walk."

"But if he is to be"—Lancaster clenched his teeth—"a part of your family, would he not—"

Juno giggled. "I don't see why you should expect him to."

"Don't you?" he asked, wondering whether he had been mistaken in thinking Juno possessed tender feelings for Oxley. Wanting Juno to depend only on him, he settled her more securely within the circle of his arms and pressed the branch, setting it to rocking gently. To his delight, she did not shy away, but met his regard expectantly.

Surrounded by Lord Lancaster's strong arms, and caught in the spell of his intense gaze, Juno swayed comfortably on her wooden mount. But wondering why her companion was staring at her, she nervously moistened her lips. His heated gaze was most exciting, and for a moment, she allowed herself to imagine that he desired her as much as she loved him.

But she pouted in frustrated longing as she reminded herself that he wanted Helen. The only reason Lord Lancaster was holding her, was to . . . teach her how to ride.

That it did not seem like a very good reason came home to roost like a flock of ravens, all screeching at once. Laying her hands on his shoulders, Juno frowned down at him. "My lord," she began in the serious tones of a chaperone.

"Juno," he said at the same time, then motioned her to continue. "No," he added when she hesitated, "you go first."

"Very well," she said, suddenly uncertain of how to go on. "I am most grateful for your kindness of the past few days."

Grateful, he thought beneath lowering brows. The last thing he wanted from this sweet miss was gratitude. He wanted to show her what it was he wanted of her, but he suppressed the almost violent urge and allowed her to continue.

"I have seldom been the best of company," she said, wishing she could speak of what was in her heart. But ladies guarded their feelings. Trying to be brave in her silence, she added, "And I know you have more profitable affairs to conduct."

Lancaster waved away this last. Had he not told her he had left London to evade the match-making mothers and their conniving offspring? "I have enjoyed myself immensely," he said. "Much better than Town parties." He clenched his jaw, thinking he could have sounded a little more romantic. After all, he wanted to spend the rest of his life with this woman, doing whatever it was they did in the country.

Juno blushed. "I doubt that, my lord. But it is kind of you to say so." Dropping her gaze self-consciously, she recruited her courage before tilting her head to the side and inquiring, "I almost hesitate to ask this of you, but I must know: what are your intentions?"

Lancaster was so surprised his chin dropped to his chest. He had always thought a father or chaperone would demand to know his intentions. Never had he expected to hear from his beloved's own lips such a query. But then Juno was a straightforward miss who did not play coy games or flirt like her sister. Heartened by her bold confrontation, the viscount said, "Why, I thought you knew, Miss Davis. . . . Marriage."

But instead of submitting joyously to his embrace as he longed for her to, Juno slid to the ground, evading his encircling arms by hastily collecting the remains of their luncheon. He watched, hoping she would hold out her hand and invite him to share the blanket they had spread on the ground, but he was disappointed. Shaking the coverlet with a resounding snap, she stretched both arms wide and folded it in half, and then in half twice more, before tucking it within the basket.

He strode toward her, inquiring, "Did you not hear me, Juno?"

Brushing off her skirts, she looked dazedly up at him and said, "Yes. I thought so. Well, there's my answer." Then, to his horror, she took off across the field at a run.

"Wait, my dear," he called, striding after her. His long

legs soon brought him even with her, but she did not stop until he took hold of her elbow and drew her to a halt. Swinging her around to face him, he demanded, "What's the matter?"

"I . . ." Breathless from the unaccustomed exertion, not to mention the shock of the viscount's profession, Juno shook her arm free and hugged herself until she could breathe without feeling as if someone had stuck a knife in her side.

How could she tell him she wanted him to say that he wanted to marry *her?* But he had replied to her honest query in the tones of a suitor surprised by an irate guardian. What better proof did she need that he wanted her sister? "I must speak with Helen," she said, backing away from him. "She will know what to do."

Lancaster did not understand why Juno needed to speak with her sister. After all, he had asked *her* to marry him. Twice. But the girls were close, and if Juno wanted to tell Helen before she gave him her answer, what harm could it do? Nodding, he said, "By all means, dearest; speak with your sister. You are concerned for her happiness, after all."

"Yes," Juno choked. She wanted to tell him she did not think Helen could be happy with him, but she could not betray her sister. It hurt too much to know once more that she was the unwanted sister, that Lancaster had merely taken advantage of her to court Helen. "Pray, excuse me," she said, as he drew her back to his mount. "I must go home."

"Yes, I'll take you," he said, leading her back to his mount and lifting her into the saddle. But rather than mount himself, he took the reins in hand and led the steed toward the road.

Juno clung to a handful of the horse's mane, and pressed her lips together to control herself. Lancaster did not act like a giddy suitor, no inquiring about his lady love's likes and dislikes, no waxing poetical about her many charms. Perhaps he only wanted Helen to serve as his hostess or to beget handsome children.

294

Children. The thought of Helen bearing children for the man she loved struck Juno as the worst of all possibilities. She could not have felt worse if Lancaster had doubled his large fist and hit her the way Lord Peter had done. Unable to help herself, she uttered a forlorn sigh.

Lancaster wondered why Juno was not behaving the way an ecstatic young lady ought after receiving a hoped-for proposal of marriage. Could he have read her wrong? Did she still prefer Lord Peter, even though he had hit her and meant to operate a horse farm? How could she? She was terrified of the beasts.

Turning to regard her as she clung to Paladin's mane, he asked, "Juno? Are you all right?"

"Please do not stop, my lord," she said between clenched teeth. "I can think of nothing except getting safely home and away from this monster."

Lancaster grinned. "I would not say that last too often, my dear. Paladin is rather sensitive, and might take your poor opinion to heart." As if in agreement, the beast tossed his head and snorted.

Juno released one hand and stroked the animal's shoulder. "I did not mean to insult you, Paladin." At the sound of his name, the horse turned to eye his rider. To Juno's surprise, she felt an unusual affinity with the beast. Leaning forward, she whispered, "You are really quite handsome."

"Thank you," said the viscount.

Juno did not know quite what to say to that, but stammered, "You're welcome, my lord."

Having arrived at Breakstone Cottage, Lancaster handed Juno down, keeping his hand at her waist a little longer than necessary. Leaning over her ear, he said, "My name is Brian."

Brian.

Juno turned his name over in her mind, imagining how it would taste on her lips. But that privilege belonged to his fiancée. Regarding him sadly, she mounted the steps, saying, "I shall tell Helen."

"Fine, tell Helen," he said gruffly as he watched the tantalizing sway of her trim hips. "I'll be in the garden awaiting your answer." It was fortunate for the roses that they had not yet started to bloom, for in the mood that plagued him, he would have pulled off their blossoms and strewn the petals about to discover whether Juno loved him or loved him not.

Finding Helen in the still-room mixing healing herbs, Juno said, "I've been looking for you."

"Oh?" said Helen. Bestowing an affectionate smile on her elder sister, she said, "I thought you were going to rest this morning while the ladies and I did good works."

"I decided to go out," Juno said. "But that is not why I came looking for you." She crushed a handful of chamomile flowers into a bowl. "Well, it is the cause of it, I suppose. Lord Lancaster found me, and—"

"You need not explain, my dear," Helen teased. "It is no concern of mine."

Sighing, Juno confessed, "I think it must be; Lord Lancaster is ready to make an offer of marriage."

Helen embraced her. "I am so happy. If I were you, I would accept at once."

"I think it is too soon," Juno said. "He has been known to us only a week."

"Time is of no consequence when one is in love," Helen said. "And our friends say he is highly regarded in Town."

"That may mean anything," Juno said repressively. "He may be a three-bottle man, or a gambler, or . . . or do any number of scandalous things that are perfectly acceptable in the ranks of the Corinthian set but that would shock us."

"Juno," Helen laughed. "Listen to yourself. Can you honestly believe Lord Lancaster can present one, handsome face here, and another, monstrous one in London?"

In her heart, Juno knew the Viscount Lancaster was the perfect gentleman, and she could not pretend otherwise, even if she did want to dissuade Helen from accepting his proposal. Shaking her head sadly, she said, "No, dear. He has been the soul of kindness here. I am sure he is just what he appears."

"Just what he appears . . ." Helen directed a narrow eyed stare toward her sister and inquired, "Just what did you tell the viscount when he made his offer?"

"That I should speak to you," Juno said.

"You mean you gave him no answer?" Helen's voice rose in shrill accusation.

Juno tried to impress upon Helen that she was the elder sister and was owed a little more respect than was evident in her junior's waspish tone. But Helen only crossed her arms over her bosom and demanded, "Tell me you said yes."

"Of course I did not," Juno said in self-righteous tones. "I did not think it was wise."

"Not wise?" Helen echoed. "You ought to stop being so wise."

"One of us must be," Juno insisted in brave tones that wavered despite her rigid control. Taking a deep breath, she attempted to persuade her sister of the seriousness of the step she had been asked to consider. "Marriage is a lifelong commitment. I shouldn't want to answer too hastily."

"But Juno, what if he does not ask again?"

"There will be other proposals," Juno said, knowing that Lord Peter at least would be making Helen an offer very soon, one with which she would be infinitely happier. Beating down the pricking conscience that reminded her she wanted to keep Lord Lancaster for herself, Juno snapped, "Anyway, it is not necessary to agree to marry the first man who asks."

"You goose!" Helen retorted. "Lord Lancaster is wealthy, and stands to inherit even more. You'd have to be a fool to turn him down."

Juno was shocked. She had never dreamed her sister would turn out to be such a mercenary miss. "I thought you were happy with our annuity," she said in frigid tones.

"Well, I am," Helen responded. "But what is Breakstone Cottage and five hundred a year compared with — "

"Love," said Juno as she moved toward the door. "Love is the only reason to marry, Helen. I am convinced you would be miserable as the Viscountess Lancaster."

"Me?" gasped Helen. She clutched Juno's hand in an arresting movement. "He asked for *my* hand?"

Juno stared at her sister, wondering whether she had been out in the sun too long without her bonnet, before saying at last, "Who else would he want?"

Rather than reveal the true recipient, Helen chose to censure the looby whose proposal seemed to have left so much to be desired. "I cannot understand why he should think I would marry *him*."

"But you said you would accept at once," Juno said.

"If I were *you*, I would." Unable to believe she had such a lackwit as a sister, Helen sadly shook her head. How could any lady not realize she was the object of a gentleman's affection?

"That is beyond the point," Juno snapped. Clapping a hand to her head, she confessed, "I am so confused. He said he meant to speak of marriage. What else was I to think except that he had fallen head over heels in love with you, as have most of the county at one time or other."

"Perhaps he has fallen in love with you," Helen said in thoughtful tones.

"Me?" Juno cried in disbelief. Nothing would make her happier, however she knew the truth, and bitter as it was, she confessed it, "I am not the sort of lady men fall in love with."

"I have heard you repeat that so many times, I fear you have come to believe it," Helen said in grim tones.

Juno hung her head, saying, "I do not wish to believe it, Helen, but Lord Lancaster has given me no reason to doubt it."

"Foolish man," Helen said. It would serve the viscount right if she did accept his offer, or at least lead him to think she meant to accept. But that would tear Juno apart, and she could not bear to hurt her sister.

Juno had given up so much for her; this was one thing Helen could do for her. Knowing the couple would only beat around the bush without coming to a happy conclusion unless she intervened, she asked, "Would you like me to tell him?"

For the first time since she had found her sister, Juno smiled. "Would you, please? I cannot."

"Just leave it to me, my dear," Helen said, pouring her sister a cup of soothing chamomile tea. "I know what needs be said."

Juno placed a restraining hand on Helen's sleeve. Regarding her pleading look, Helen said, "Don't fret, Junie. I promise I shan't hurt the man if it means so much to you."

"Thank you," Juno said, stirring honey into her cup as her sister strode into the garden.

Lancaster had not expected to see Juno's sister making her way toward him, a battle light glowing in her eye. He supposed that meant Juno did not want to marry him.

"Hello, my lord," said Helen, seating herself on a stone bench. Patting the seat beside her, she said, "You look as if you are expecting bad news."

"Is that not why you have come to speak with me?" he asked, stiffly placing himself on the stone.

"I have come to tell you that you may have what you long for," Helen said.

"Well, that is a relief," Lancaster exclaimed, leaping to his feet. "But why cannot Juno give me her own answer?"

Helen tapped her toe in a display of irritation. Really, she thought, men could be so stupid! "Because, you looby; she believes you offered for *me!*"

The viscount shook his head as if he had taken a blow to the temple, then demanded, "Why would she think such a thing?"

"My lord, Juno is the most sweet-natured woman I know," Helen said in an attempt to explain. "But she is completely unaware of her appeal. Fully half of the gentlemen who came to call at Breakstone Cottage came on her account. But she was convinced I was the magnet that attracted them."

"I originally came on your account," he mumbled.

"Just so," Helen said without a trace of self-conscious-

299

ness. "Their problem was that they were rather too indirect with her, complimenting her on the refreshments, the floral arrangements, household matters—not that men know anything about such things.

"But they did not limit their flattery to Juno," Helen went on. "They told me how becoming I looked, how charming I was, how I lifted their spirits by coming into a room."

"I don't quite understand," Lancaster said after a long moment of silence attempting to make sense of Helen's confession.

Sighing, she once more thought how thick-headed men could be. Then, in gentle tones, Helen said, "They told me the sorts of things a young lady likes to hear—that I was pretty and gay. What they said to Juno they might have said to a favorite aunt or their beloved's mother." Helen stared up at him with an innocent smile lighting her countenance, then added, "But the worst thing anyone has ever said to her was, 'Would you care for my castle as your own'?"

Clasping his head in his hands, Lancaster groaned, "I am the king of fools."

"Yes," Helen agreed. "What are you going to do about it?"

He arose from the judgment seat and looked despairingly across the garden. "The only thing I can do," he said. "I must go away."

Helen leapt to her feet and lay a forbidding hand upon his sleeve. "That would break Juno's heart."

"Naturally, I have no wish to do that," he said. "But she cannot want to marry me after my clumsy attempts to propose."

"But that is precisely what she does want!" Helen insisted.

He turned upon her a look that ought to have melted any resistance and asked, "Will you speak for me?"

"Certainly not," Helen snapped. "But I will tell you what to do. You must kiss her again."

"Oh, no," groaned the viscount. He ran his fingers de-

300

spairingly through his hair as he recalled their only kiss. "I don't think she liked the first one very much."

"Oh, she liked it," Helen said with an affirming nod. "You listen to me, Lord Lancaster. You had better propose to my sister, and make sure you do it right. If you don't, I promise you, she will have *us* married, and that would not suit me at all. For once, I mean to please myself and marry Peter Oxley!" So saying, Helen hurried back to the kitchen, where she told Juno she had done what she had to do. "Now," she added in calculating tones, "I think Lord Lancaster wishes to say a few words to you."

"Oh dear," moaned Juno, as the viscount strode into the kitchen. But to her surprise, he did not appear angry or disappointed. Bestowing a hopeful gaze upon her, he bowed at the waist and begged to speak with her in the book-room before striding off.

"Oh dear," Juno echoed, turning her anxious gaze upon her sister. "Whatever can he want?"

"Only one way to find out," said Helen. She held open the kitchen door. "Ask him."

Recruiting her courage, Juno hurried after the viscount.

He was staring out a window, his hands clasped behind him in a manly pose, and she felt her heart catch in her throat. How handsome he was.

He must have heard her involuntary intake of breath, for he turned to gaze upon her as she glided into the room. "Juno," he said, taking her hand in his. "Has anyone ever told you how beautiful you are?"

She blushed in protest of his flattery. "No, my lord," she said, when she was capable of speaking. "Helen is beautiful."

"Yes, I am sure she is," he said, gazing deeply into Juno's eyes. "However I do not wish to discuss your sister." He drew her into the circle of his arms, still bestowing upon her that tender, awestruck gaze. "You, Juno, possess an inner beauty that outshines the sun."

Her heart longed to believe him, but the reflection in the mirror behind him told her the truth. She was not beautiful. She was so pale as to fade into insignificance. The only color on her face was a greenish tinged bruise that gave her a misshapen appearance. Certain he was mocking her, she said, "Don't my lord. It isn't true, and it isn't kind."

"It is true, Juno," he said, tightening his gentle grip on her slender waist. When she ceased her useless struggles, he tipped up her chin and said, "How long can you keep mistaking my interest?"

"You mistake *me,*" Juno said. She had no wish to hurt him, but it would be better than to allow him to think Helen was going to marry him. Speaking quickly, so as not to lose her courage, she said, "I knew all along that you preferred Helen, and I have tried, really tried not to mind. But I am afraid I cannot give my permission for you to wed her, as I am persuaded my sister doesn't return your regard."

"The devil take it," he growled, holding her face in a gentle, but inescapable grip. "I don't want Helen; I never wanted the girl." Then, goaded beyond the limits of his patience, Lancaster swooped down to plant a kiss upon Juno's startled lips.

She felt as if she were melting, and feared that if he did not let her go soon, she would become nothing but a puddle on the floor so watery did her limbs grow. But he did not release her, only deepened the kiss to plunder with his tongue the soft inner recesses of her mouth.

It was not the kiss of a brother for his sister-in-law. It was the kiss of a man for the woman he loved.

Emboldened by hope, Juno flung her arms about him and entangled her fingers in the long brown hair that curled over his starched cravat. Having that which she longed for with all her heart, she was reluctant to let him go. But the prolonged kiss was making her dizzy, and when she broke away to catch a shaky breath, he chuckled, low in his throat. She could feel the rumble against her breasts and in her stomach, but she did not place a more proper distance between them, even when he asked, "What I want to know, Juno, is whether *you* can return my regard."

Blushing, Juno attempted to drop her chin to her chest, but Lancaster would not allow her to avert her gaze. And though she longed to confess her feelings, she had not lost all sense of propriety; she would not compel Lancaster to make a declaration.

"My dear," he said. "I know you would rather die than force my hand. So, I must declare myself."

"You need not," Juno said in constricted tones that betrayed her despair at feeling he was constrained to speak.

"Hush," he said, kissing her lips in a tantalizingly brief caress that left her breathless with longing. "I love you, Juno Davis. Do you think you could possibly love me too?"

"Oh, yes," Juno said, her eyes sparkling wetly. "Yes, Brian. I do love you."

His name tasted as sweet on her lips as his kiss.

"Oh, dear," she sighed, in an attempt to silence such unladylike thoughts. "You must think me the most forward female the way I cling to you. Only, I like your kisses excessively. Do you think I could have another one?"

"With pleasure, my love," Lancaster said, obliging her with another heart-swelling kiss. Then, he teased, "You are the most retiring, self-effacing female I have been ever been privileged to meet. Also the most maddening. I was beginning to despair of your interest."

"Were you?" she asked in wonder. "I feared the same of you."

Releasing her only to fall to one knee, Lancaster held her hand in a reverent grip, saying, "Dear Juno, lest you doubt my affection ever again, would you do me the honor of becoming my wife so I might prove my good intentions every day?"

"But I am not a lady," she reminded him. "I carry coal — and sweep carpets."

"Yes, I know," he said. "You turn your hand to whatever needs doing. But there are other chores you could take on." Squeezing her fingers urgently, he said, "I need someone to love me."

"I do love you, Brian. That is no chore," she said, blushing again. "And I will marry you, to keep house for you, and"—her blush intensified as she giggled—"to love you."

"That is the part I shall like best," he said, coming to his feet and kissing her again. "Loving you."

Juno could scarcely believe him, even when the vows hàd been said on a June morning six weeks to the day after the viscount's proposal. Brian Wilton, the sixth Viscount of Lancaster was the most handsome gentleman of her acquaintance, and she, as she reminded him after the last guest had wished them well at their wedding breakfast, she, in her wedding finery, was so pale as to be almost invisible.

Determined that she should never again think of herself in such disparaging terms, the viscount bestowed a lingering kiss upon her hungry lips. "You, Lady Lancaster" he said fervently, "Are no more invisible than a diamond." He kissed her once more, because he wanted to, and because she wanted him to. Then, raising her hand, he kissed her fingers, one at a time before wrapping them possessively within his. "And I mean for you to sparkle as brilliantly as this ring I put on your finger."

Blushing becomingly as she always did under his compliments, Juno protested, "I have no idea how to 'sparkle,' my lord husband."

"No?" he queried, raising a dark eyebrow in a rakish manner that made Juno melt in his arms. "Then you must place yourself unreservedly in my hands, for I know what must be done."

And the shimmering look Juno bestowed upon him as he carried her above stairs proved him right.

A Charmed Engagement
by Monette Cummings

The wedding was to be held at St. George's, Hanover Square, for it was difficult to consider that a *ton* wedding would be held anywhere else in London. Some, of course, might be held at St. Margaret's, but only because the other church would not be available for them.

Both families had been city-bred, but deserted London a score of years ago for country life, choosing to settle in the Lambourn area, although none of them were interested in racing. Still, they would return to the City to celebrate the union of the Warne heir to the Pierce heiress.

The marriage was set for June—quite early in the month because after the Regent had left for his summer pavilion in Brighton, London would be thin of important company. And it was beyond belief that a marriage between the Warne and Pierce families should not be attended by everyone who mattered.

Neither of the young people who were involved needed— or expected—to give any thought to the arrangements. Their mothers had seen to everything.

Lorna and Stacy had always accepted the fact that they would have everything managed for them. Such details as the sort of service which would be held were unimportant; all they needed to know was that they would soon belong to one another. They had grown up on neighboring estates, and neither of them had ever looked at anyone else. But now . . .

At one and twenty, Stacy Warne had come to London, ready for a young man's fling. Sixteen-year-old Lorna

Pierce was to make her come-out that year, with the wedding to follow before the end of the Season, but the sudden death of an aunt had thrown the family into mourning.

Stacy had generously offered to delay his own journey to London until she could join him. "What difference does a year make?" he asked. "Next year, we can go together. I shall enjoy it more when you are there, too."

"I love you for saying that, but you must not be foolish," Lorna told him. "You have wished for years to see London. As long as I can remember, you have talked of it. And you have already given up Oxford and the army to remain here and manage the estate while your papa was so ill. Now that he has recovered, you must go to London and enjoy yourself before you are tied down as a married man."

Stacy laughed at the idea of marriage to Lorna tying him down, since they agreed on everything. Then he grew serious. "How can I truly enjoy myself when you are not with me?"

The tender words made her want to weep, but, as she had reminded him, she knew how much this journey meant to him. "I should be but poor company for you if you remain here at home. You know I cannot attend even the smallest party for some time. I would spoil your fun."

There was further argument that there would be no fun for him without her to share it. At last, however, Stacy bowed to her wishes and went off to London, to find that there were many things which could be enjoyed, even without the presence of his beloved. When he came home at the end of the Season, eager to be reunited with Lorna, it was to learn that she had been taken off to visit an aunt and several cousins in Cornwall and would be away from home for several months.

Disappointed, he returned to London for the Little Season, then, receiving word of his father's further improvement in health, stayed in the city during the winter.

Until the Spring Season arrived, Lorna had moped at the weeks spent without him, and she looked forward so eagerly to seeing Stacy again that the horses seemed to lag on the journey. At last, however, she and her mother were settled in their London house and word had been sent to Stacy that they were awaiting his call.

In their earlier days, Stacy would have called her name the moment he entered the house. Lorna would have run down the stairs, thrown herself at him; he would have caught her in his arms, whirled her about and kissed her soundly, whether anyone else could see them or not.

However, she could scarcely recognize the modishly dressed young man who came through the front door, and she slowed her steps. When they stood face to face, he bowed and kissed her hand, then, receiving an encouraging nod from her mother, kissed her cheek as well.

When he had taken his leave, after promising Mrs. Pierce that his mother, who was expected to arrive in London on the morrow, would call upon her at the first opportunity to discuss the arrangements for the wedding, Lorna said, "I do not think I should have known Stacy, had I met him at a ball or somewhere. He has become a complete fop."

"Oh, I think you are being too harsh with him, my dear," her mother said soothingly, well aware of her daughter's flights of fancy. "You must remember that Stacy has had the benefit of a year in London. He is quite the same young man as he always was, only his manners are perhaps a bit more polished."

"That is what I said—a fop."

Stacy would have been highly insulted had he known his betrothed considered him a fop. He could don his modish coat without needing several footmen as well as his valet to fit it on him. Its shoulders were not wadded with buckram, nor were its buttons the size of coppers. He did not wear shirt collars so high that he could not turn his head, nor did he deck himself out with a dozen fobs or rings, carry a quizzing glass, or douse himself with scent.

Had he been asked, he would have described himself as a Corinthian. He regularly attended Gentleman Jackson's saloon, sometimes being permitted to exchange blows with the master himself; with the pistols he had obtained at Manton's, he had become a much better shot than he had been at home; he could outride and outdrive most of his fellows. And sometimes, after several rounds of Blue Ruin, they would roam the streets, boxing the watch—all exercises which would have been shudderingly avoided by the fops.

"What else is a man to do in London?" he would have asked, had anyone ventured to condemn him for the sort of life he had been leading this past year. Many of his friends had been with Wellington's forces on the Peninsula or were now fighting in the Americas, but as the only son—in fact, the only child—and heir to a great estate, he had yielded to his father's pleas not to risk his life in the army which had been responsible for so much damage to the health of the elder Mr. Warne.

There was no disloyalty to Lorna in his wish to join the army. She had known that, like every young man of spirit, he had yearned for adventure, for an opportunity to display his courage.

He adored Lorna, had done so since they were children. And not even a war could have kept them apart for long. Because of her, however, he had been more willing to accede to his father's wishes not to seek a commission.

How often he had dreamed of the day she would join him in London. He would catch her eager form in his arms, kissing her as he had done so often at home. But when he had seen the puzzled expression in her brown eyes, which he had often thought were like those of a startled fawn, and had realized he must greet her under her mother's eye, he had stiffened, becoming totally unlike himself.

It seemed to him that Lorna, too, had changed in some way since he had seen her last. Anyone hearing their conversation and not being privy to their thoughts would have thought them strangers.

"Welcome to London, my dear." *Oh, how I have missed you.*

"Thank you. I have been looking forward to the visit. Have you enjoyed being here?" *What has happened since I saw you last?*

"It will be better, now that you have come. How was your journey?" *My dear one, has this last year changed you so very much as this?*

"Some of the roads are bad, as you know, but we had good weather. And we stayed at the posting houses you recommended." *How can you talk like this, as if I were someone you had only met five minutes ago?*

"Good, good. Some of the places are not fit for travelers, and I would not have wished you to stop in those. I missed you last summer when I was home." *Why could you not have waited till I came?*

"Yes—we visited Aunt Maude. She misses her sister so much. But we hoped we would see you last winter." *Do you know what it was like to spend an entire winter without so much as a word from you?*

"I decided to remain in London. Had I known that you would be home . . ." *I would have walked the entire distance just to be with you for a day.*

"Oh, we understood why you did not come. London must be more exciting than the country." *But I never thought it would be so exciting that you would not miss me.*

After several more moments of such banal talk, having no idea that her thoughts were as chaotic as his, and with an almost brotherly kiss on her cheek, Stacy excused himself, wondering what had gone wrong. He loved Lorna as much as he had always done and was certain that she loved him.

She did still love him, did she not? She could not have changed so much in only a year, could she? Perhaps when she had settled into the regimen of life here, she would not look at him as if he were someone she did not know.

Then there was the matter of Muriel to be considered. She seemed to depend solely upon him now; he hoped Lorna would understand about that. He would have liked to consult his father about the matter, but under the circumstances, he could say nothing. He knew, however, what the old man would probably say: "You must do what is right." Well, he was trying to do just that, but there were problems.

There had never been the slightest doubt that Lorna would receive a voucher for Almack's. In fact, at least half the Patronesses vied with one another to be the first to make the offer. In addition to being well bred—and wealthy, although wealth counted for little in comparison with other attributes—she was reported to be beautifully behaved, the sort of young lady on whom they could depend to do nothing which might cause a raised eyebrow.

"In these days," Mrs. Drummond Burrell said grudgingly, as if loath to give any young lady of the present generation so much as a single kind word, "that is greatly in her favor."

"Yes, indeed," Lady Sefton agreed. "I have checked upon her credentials, and I am certain Miss Pierce would never waltz without being given permission—or do anything else that is not entirely proper."

"Quite a pattern-card, in fact," the other stated.

Even before her arrival in London, Lorna had been eagerly looking forward to her first appearance at this most important of all meeting places of the *ton*. Her mother had often spoken about it, laughing over the fact that there were those who referred to it as the Marriage Mart. "I suppose that is true enough for young ladies who have no prospects. Not that *you* need concern yourself about that, of course, since you and Stacy have already made your plans."

Now that the occasion was at hand, however, Lorna began to worry that she would not be able to get through the evening successfully. The Patronesses were said to be very strict about the behavior of those who entered those all-important doors—especially that of the young ladies.

Furthermore, she was not at all familiar with London

ways; what if she should make some horrible *faux pas,* causing people to look askance at her? What if — horror of horrors — she was asked to leave the hall? Farewell to any chance of having her wedding in London; she would have to creep home in disgrace.

Mrs. Pierce continually reassured her that she would face no problems. After all, Lorna *had* been in company before — not London company, to be sure, but she knew how to behave properly. "Just remember, my dear, these are merely people, after all, just like those you have been seeing for most of your life."

"But they live by different rules, I have heard."

"Not at all. I have told you how it will be. Be your sweet self, and all will be well."

"But is my gown all right?" Lorna asked nervously for at least the dozenth time.

"It is beautiful, my dear. After all, Celeste is in the habit of making gowns for members of the *ton.* You can trust her to see that you are properly attired for any occasion. And you look lovely."

Lorna was indeed lovely, although she would never have recognized the fact. She would have preferred golden ringlets to her soft brown hair, and she thought her brown eyes nothing out of the common run. Mrs. Pierce blamed Stacy's childhood teasing for her daughter's present insecurity about her looks. He had not teased the girl for several years, had often praised her instead, but memories of his earlier remarks remained, leaving Lorna unsure.

"I am thankful, at least," Lorna remarked, "my skin is clear enough that I may wear white." Several of her friends had such sallow complexions that white did not become them.

Her gown for this evening was simply made, with a faint tracery of green leaves about the square neckline, the design repeated more boldly at the hem. Her satin slippers were also touched with green, and the color was used discreetly on the fan she carried.

If she had any doubt about the effect of her appearance,

it was banished by the frank admiration in Stacy's eyes when he arrived to escort them to Almack's. There was no sign that he remembered having ever teased her. Instead, he assured her that she would be the belle of that night's ball.

For her part, however, Lorna took one look at him and began to giggle.

"Is something amiss?" Stacy demanded, looking down at his apparel.

"No—nothing at all. You look wonderful!" To her, Stacy's appearance was always perfect. She had been happy that his features were not the classical ones so admired on statues. Those seemed to Lorna to be as cold and hard as the material of which they were made.

Stacy's nose was slightly snubbed, with several freckles across it, his mouth wide, showing strong teeth when he smiled, and his chin was firm. His eyes always seemed a brighter blue beneath that mop of hair which was too red to be called golden. She could not know he had adopted the fashionable Windswept look because he was unable to train his hair into any other style without overapplication of pomade. To her, Stacy's hair looked as it always had, which made his choice of garments so unusual.

"It is only," she confessed, "that I remember how you have always declared that you would never be the sort to rig yourself out—"

"Like a man-milliner," he finished, also laughing. "Nor is it my favorite mode of dress, even now. But if I were to garb myself otherwise, the doors would be closed against me this evening."

"It may not be what you would choose, but you should always be dressed so," Lorna declared, gazing with admiration at his broad shoulders smoothly fitting beneath the long-tailed evening coat of midnight blue, at the buff knee breeches and white silk stockings which showed the strength of his thighs and calves.

She thought back to her first impression upon meeting him in London—her dismay at his foppish appearance. Now, seeing him in clothing so much more elegant than he had worn on that occasion, she did not find anything amiss with his appearance. "Do you not think so, Mama?"

"Oh, Lorna, you cannot mean that." He could not help being pleased, even while he flushed with embarrassment. "Just think what would happen if I decided to wear this rig out into the fields at home. Not only would I frighten all the crows, I would send the cattle fleeing for safety, as well."

"And the neighbors would set their dogs on you for making a disturbance," Lorna agreed.

The earlier restraint between them vanished as they bantered, and they clung to one another, whooping with laughter, while Mrs. Pierce said with mock severity, "I do not know what all this hilarity is apropos of. Stacy looks very nice tonight—but then he always does. I am certain you will be the handsomest pair in the room this evening."

This sent them into further laughter and Stacy, after wrapping the evening cloaks about mother and daughter, offered each an arm and led them to the waiting carriage.

Having heard much about the wonders of Almack's in the short time she had been in London, Lorna was expecting to see a ballroom suitable for the royal palace. When Stacy escorted them through the doors, she looked about at the unadorned room, then at her companion, wondering if this was a jest on his part. The Stacy of old would not have been above taking them to some old warehouse and attempting to convince her it was where she was supposed to attend a fashionable ball.

He grinned down at her, knowing what she must be thinking, having had much the same experience the first time he had come here, and said in an undertone, "No. This is it, I assure you—the most important spot in all of London."

"But . . . but the village hall at home looks better than this."

"My dear girl, Almack's is Almack's. There is no need for any sort of ornamentation."

"If you say so," she retorted doubtfully, as she looked about her. Her mother did not appear to see anything amiss but stood still, drawing in deep breaths, as if there was an air about the place that she remembered.

No one else appeared to notice that anything was less than perfect. In fact, all the other white-clad young ladies, their mothers or sponsors, and the brightly dressed gentlemen who circled about them—looking, she thought, much like gaily plumaged male birds showing off before their paler mates—appeared well pleased that they were permitted to come here.

Always somewhat shy in crowds, especially among strangers, Lorna edged slightly behind her mother and peered around her at the assemblage. Aside from Stacy, there was no one here with whom she was acquainted, of course, but she did see one or two other ladies she thought it would be nice to know, and some others of whom she was less certain.

Several young ladies seemed as shy as she; others nervously tugged at their ribands or poked their fingers through their hair, receiving whispered orders to behave properly, while one or two frankly ogled the gentlemen in attendance.

"Is Aunt Alice here tonight?" Lorna asked. She had always called Stacy's mother "Aunt," although there was no relationship between them.

"No. Mother does not care for these 'do's,' as she calls them. You must remember that she seldom accompanied us when we went about at home."

"Oh yes." Lorna could not prevent a slight twinge of disappointment, for she would have welcomed at least one more familiar face in this crowd of strangers. But at least she could depend upon Stacy for companionship, she reminded herself.

He offered one arm to her and the other to her mother and led them across the room to a rather large lady who was gazing through her lorgnette at the throng. Her expression was one of deep dissatisfaction, as if she expected to see something amiss.

"Mrs. Drummond Burrell," he said, "may I have the honor of introducing Mrs. Pierce and Miss Pierce, who have just recently come to London? I do not believe you have met them."

The lorgnette was turned in their direction, and after a long examination of the pair, the scowl softened into what might have been a smile of welcome. "No, I have not had the pleasure, although I have heard a great deal about you. Nothing," — the smile became genuine — "that was not most gratifying. I trust you will enjoy our little affair."

Both ladies assured her that they knew they would enjoy every moment of it, then the Patroness subjected Mrs. Pierce to another severe scrutiny and queried, "Have we met previously?"

"Oh, you could not remember me, ma'am. I have not been here since my marriage. My husband and I do not reside in London."

"Oh, yes . . . I believe you were one of the Millham gals, were you not?"

"Millbank, Mrs. Drummond Burrell."

"Ah, that is correct. I never forget a name or a face," the older woman declared, ignoring the fact that she had just been in error. Aware of the Patroness' reputation, Mrs. Pierce only smiled, and she and Lorna permitted themselves to be dismissed with a nod, while the formidable lady looked about her for possible misconduct. Stacy took several steps, then turned back.

"And I suppose you are now about to request permission to waltz with Miss Pierce," Mrs. Drummond Burrell said in a tone of disapprobation. "You know that I disapprove of the dance — think it vulgar and almost indecent. But I suppose if I refuse to consent, you will merely go to one of the other Patronesses . . . so I may as well give you permission."

"Th-thank you, ma'am," Lorna said, curtsying; then she turned away to walk back to the chairs at the far side of the

317

room. "I do not believe she is really so fierce as she wishes people to think," she whispered to Stacy.

Mrs. Pierce merely shook her head, but Stacy said, "You may take my word for it, Lorna, she is quite as bad. A frown from her can do more to ruin a young girl's future than . . . than even a snub from Beau Brummell."

"Why should a gentleman's opinion do any harm to a young lady's future if she does not even know him?"

"Believe me, Lorna, it could do grave damage, indeed."

"Surely he cannot make up tales about people he does not know?"

"No . . . but he contrives to know everyone. Everyone of any importance, at least. And what the Beau thinks, many others are certain to agree with if they are wise."

"In my day," Mrs. Pierce put in, "it was Mr. Nash who was known as the Beau. Bath was his . . . one might almost call it his kingdom. I confess I should like to see this new arbiter of the *ton's* habits."

"I doubt if you would care much for him, Aunt Ellen." Like Lorna, Stacy had always referred to his future mother-in-law as "aunt." "However, it does not seem that he is here this evening. At any rate I am certain that he would approve wholeheartedly of both you and Lorna. He could not fail to do so. If he should object to anyone, it would be to me."

"To you?"

"Yes. The Beau has decreed that the only proper evening garb for a gentleman must be black. Not that many of us heed him in the matter, much as we may copy him at other times. You can imagine how an entire room full of black coats would appear."

"They would look like a gathering of crows, would they not? I do not think I should like it at all, and I am happy that you do not wish to follow his example." Lorna squeezed the arm on which her hand rested. "For I like you exactly as you are."

"And your opinion means more to me than any dozen Beaux. But listen, they are playing a waltz. And since we have been given permission . . ." Stacy seated Mrs. Pierce in one of the gilt chairs, bowed to her, and led Lorna into the circling dancers. She attempted to draw back.

"I . . . I have never done the waltz—except at home with my cousins," she protested.

"You are not supposed to have done it," Stacy reminded her with a grin. "To have waltzed in public before receiving permission from one of the Patronesses would label a young lady as being fast."

"How odd. Why should what they say make so much difference as that?"

He shrugged. "London has its own rules. But you will have no trouble in waltzing. It is simple. You have only to follow my lead."

"Since I have been doing that since I was three years old," she told him, laughing and yielding herself to his embrace, "no matter what sort of mischief you were planning, I should be able to follow you now."

She found the music exhilarating, and the familiar feel of Stacy's arm about her waist made the dance as simple as he had said it would be. When the music ended, he led her back to where her mother was chatting with several new acquaintances while looking about in search of people she might have known when she was last in London. All of the ladies complimented Lorna upon her gown and upon her dancing, which made her feel more shy than before.

Several of Stacy's friends approached and he introduced them one by one. All asked her to dance, and after a glance at her betrothed for his approval, Lorna agreed to the requests of several gentlemen. However, no matter how often she was urged to do so, she would not waltz with any of them. The dance was too intimate, she felt, to be done with anyone except the man she was to marry.

When the musicians struck up another waltz, Lorna looked about for Stacy, only to see that he was already upon the dance floor. One glance at his partner was enough to make Lorna want to hide; the lady was no newcomer to Society, Lorna was certain. She was chatting gaily with Stacy as they moved about and seemed to know him very well.

Easily the most beautiful person in the room, Stacy's partner had copper-colored hair intricately arranged high on her head, with several tendrils allowed to hang loose, to swirl about her face as she was whirled about in the dance. Her gown of brilliant green—another sign that she was no newcomer this Season—was made of some soft material designed to display an excellent form, and her jewels glistened in the light of the chandeliers.

At the end of the dance, Stacy came to where Lorna was sitting beside her mother, the lady clinging to his arm—much more tightly than was necessary, or so Lorna thought. "Mrs. Pierce, Lorna," he said, "I should like you to meet a friend of mine, Mrs. Liveredge."

Mrs. Pierce greeted the new arrival and indicated the seat at her side while Lorna murmured an acknowledgment of his words. If this was Mrs. Liveredge, she wondered, Where was Mr. Liveredge? Why was he not at his wife's side, so that she need not attach herself to another's betrothed? The sight of this . . . this creature clinging to Stacy gave Lorna a chilled feeling such as she had never known.

"I thought you would be enjoying this dance," Stacy said, wrapping a strand of Lorna's hair about his finger. It was a habit of his, one she usually enjoyed, but now, with this red-haired *parasite* at his side, it seemed too much the sort of gesture one might make to a small child.

"I did not wish to do so." Not without you, she thought, but she would not say the words aloud before this beautiful stranger who acted as if Stacy were *her* property. "In fact, I have been feeling rather tired."

"Certainly you could not be weary already, not this early in the evening," Mrs. Liveredge said, making it sound, Lorna thought, as if she were chiding a baby for remaining awake past her bedtime.

"I needed only a moment to rest and catch my breath; the dances follow one another so quickly. But no longer, for I have promised this dance to Mr. Calvert."

Lorna hoped that Stacy would protest that he wished her to dance with him, which would have been enough to make her forget any other promises, but he only said, "That is good; I am happy that you are enjoying the evening."

"Very much," Lorna prevaricated, watching the red-haired lady link her arm with Stacy's.

"Since your friend is taken for this dance, Stacy, why should we not enjoy it, as well?"

She might as well have purred, Lorna thought; her satisfaction at keeping Stacy as a partner was so evident.

Stacy allowed her to draw him away, but glanced over his shoulder to say, "Remember to save the next waltz for me, Lorna."

Recalling that he had not come to her for the last one, she said as brightly as she could manage, "Oh, I fear you are too late. I did not know you would wish me to save it, and it is already promised to . . . to . . ." Why could she not think of another name quickly?

"Oh, I had thought . . ." He sounded disappointed that she should choose to dance with another, but had he not done just that? As he walked away she sank into the chair at her mother's side, hoping that *someone* would request the dance, so that Stacy would not see that she had been untruthful.

"Did you really promise these dances to other gentlemen?" her mother inquired. The sympathy in her tone made Lorna blink back tears.

"Of course I have not done so—although Mr. Calvert did ask for this one. But I would not promise the waltz, at any rate. I had thought to save every one of them for Stacy. Since he clearly prefers to dance with . . . with *her*, I felt I must say something."

Mrs. Pierce patted her hand. "Now, you must not be jealous, Lorna. Remember that Stacy may have made a number of friends in the past year. Doubtless, he feels an obligation to give them a part of his time."

Lorna nodded. How could she say what she was thinking—that on their first appearance together in public,

Stacy owed her the greater part of his attention. After all, they were betrothed. Or had he forgot that as well?

At that moment Mr. Calvert came to claim the dance she had promised to save for him, and Lorna rose, wishing that she had never come to London.

She need not have worried about obtaining a partner for the next waltz. Several gentleman were beside her the moment the music began, begging the right to lead her to the floor. They were all people Stacy had presented to her earlier, but she could scarcely tell one of them from another.

She did not remember the name of the partner she chose, a tall young man with shirt points so high that he could not turn his head and was forced to look down his nose at her while he uttered slighting comments about people whose names she did not know. Lorna tried as well as she could to appear interested in his conversation, while she peered around him for a glimpse of Stacy. She caught sight of his erstwhile companion, but Mrs. Liveredge was in the arms of another gentleman.

When Lorna's partner returned her to her mother, Stacy was seated beside Mrs. Pierce. He rose when Lorna appeared, placing a hand upon her arm. "Thank you for your kindness to my betrothed," he said stiffly to the other gentleman.

Oh, then you have remembered. Lorna bit back the words as her dancing partner hastily bowed and took his leave, fearing the wrath of a gentleman larger than himself.

"I thought it was the habit at such balls to exchange partners now and then," she said innocently, hiding a smile. Stacy behaved as if he was jealous, resentful of the other man's attention to her! Perhaps now he understood how she had felt when the beautiful Mrs. Liveredge was twirled about in his arms.

"It is, of course. Even in our case, when everyone knows we are to be married, we are not expected to have too many dances together—at least, not here, lest we set a bad example for others who are not yet promised. But I thought you

322

would save your waltzes for me. I confess I dislike the thought of another holding you."

"Had I known that, I should not have accepted his offer." *And how do you think I felt when you held that red-haired creature?* But it appeared that he saw no comparison between the two cases. Lorna sighed, then smiled brightly at him, placing a hand upon his arm.

"I shall save the others just for you."

"I knew you would do so, if you understood my feelings. No one has ever understood me as well as you, my dear girl. Now, shall we join the set just forming? 'Tis only a country dance, but we shall be able to touch hands now and then."

As he bade Lorna and her mother good night, Stacy assured them that he would call for them on the morrow. "That is, if you think you might enjoy a drive in the park," he offered. "It is all the thing to make the rounds, visiting with everyone one knows."

"Only I know no one—or almost no one." Lorna had been introduced to a number of people at Almack's, but she could not actually say that she knew any one of them well enough to greet as a friend. Except for that red-haired Mrs. Liveredge—and Lorna knew she would never consider her any sort of friend. Not a woman who clung so tightly to Stacy and who seemed to think of him as *her* property. Lorna had never met anyone like Muriel Liveredge and was totally unprepared to handle the sort of emotions the woman aroused in her.

Stacy had no idea that anything was amiss. "You will make friends quickly, my dear one, for everyone will wish to know you," he told her.

Mrs. Pierce had preceded them into the hallway, so he bent quickly and brushed his lips across Lorna's. Not the sort of kiss they had shared so often at home, but although he knew her mother had been aware of their exchanged caresses, it seemed a completely different matter when she was watching them. "And soon you will be all mine," he whispered.

"All yours," she echoed, feeling that everything would come right for them, that there would be no more trouble from Mrs. Liveredge. Lorna was smiling as she followed her mother into the house.

Stacy sauntered away, feeling a fool to be walking abroad in these clothes, although by London standards it was still early in the night, and others were similarly clad. There were friends who would welcome his company, but as he had bade her adieu, Muriel had said in a low tone, "I *must* see you. It is most important."

What could she have to say to him that could not have been said at the ball? There were moments during the dance when a few words could have been exchanged. Still, he knew Muriel was a fanciful creature and doubtless had what she would consider to be an excellent reason for summoning him secretly. He hailed a passing hackney and climbed in, giving her address.

In the days that followed, London life seemed to Lorna an unending whirl, much like being on a carousel. There were visits to be made, breakfasts — to her amazement, these were always held after noon, frequently extending into the evening hours — and routs and balls of all kinds.

"I vow," she told her mother, "I cannot always tell a rout from a ball. I thought a rout did not include dancing, yet at Marietta Colom's, we danced most of the evening."

"Yes, it does get confusing at times. I do not believe even the hostesses know what sort of affair they are arranging. But you are enjoying all of them, are you not?"

"Well, yes, of course. But there is so *much* expected of one. I begin to yawn before the last party of the evening — if one can call midnight evening."

"Yes, dear. But one's first Season comes only once, so you must enjoy it to the fullest."

Lorna tried to obey, and in most cases, was fully able to

find enjoyment in the affairs they attended, particularly when Stacy was their escort. At other times, she and her mother were the guests of friends her mother had known many years ago. All of these had sons and daughters around Lorna's age—and she had heard several mothers lamenting the fact that she was already promised. A young lady of her expectations, especially one who was not yet accustomed to London life, would make an ideal choice for an impecunious son.

Still, it seemed to Lorna that, wherever she might go, there was a familiar red-haired lady among the guests. Sooner or later, she would drift to Stacy's side, linking her arm in his or engaging him in conversation.

Lorna did not know how she should deal with this situation. At home, everyone had accepted the fact that Stacy was hers, and they were always included in all amusements as a pair. She had never felt that she was being pushed aside by a more attractive—if older—woman, and this worried her.

"Look, Mama," she would say, tugging at Mrs. Pierce's arm. "There she is again, clinging to Stacy like—like a *leech*."

"What a thing to say," Mrs. Pierce would reply absent-mindedly. "You should not be selfish, my dear. Stacy must certainly have other friends—as you do."

"But mine do not cling to me in that fashion." Lorna said this beneath her breath, not wishing another reproof. But *what* should she do about the lady?

What *could* she do?

"Please, Lorna, you must hurry," Mrs. Pierce said. "You know that Celeste has so many orders at this season one must be prompt or the fitting time will be given to someone else."

"Yes, Mama, I know how important it is." Lorna was pulling on her gloves as she descended the stairs. "And I am ready. Where is Polly?"

"Here, miss." The maid scuttled to her mistress' side. Lorna was to go for her fitting this morning, accompanied only by the servant. Mrs. Pierce did not approve of young ladies going about alone, but there was a good reason for her doing so this time.

Mrs. Warne, Stacy's mother, had sent word, asking if it would be convenient for her to call, and Mrs. Pierce had replied that it was, forgetting that she had already scheduled an appointment for Lorna's fitting. The two mothers had the difficult task of choosing Lorna's attendants from among the many cousins in both families, hopefully not offending the ones who were omitted.

Lorna did not envy them their chore. She only hoped, however, that they would not include her cousin Sophronia. Sophronia was a giggler. To be sure, there was nothing truly wrong in a certain amount of giggling; Lorna was guilty of doing the same at times.

However, as she confided to Polly, who nodded, knowing the young cousin almost as well as Lorna did, "The trouble with Phronie is she giggles when there is nothing to giggle about. I should not doubt she would begin giggling during the prayers, oversetting everyone."

Lorna very much wanted to include Esther in her wedding party, and it would be impossible to include Esther without having her sister as well, for if she had even a faint suspicion that she was being slighted, Sophronia would wail. Loud and long. Instead of giggles during the prayers, there would be the sounds of her cousin's wailing.

Lorna wondered if Stacy had cousins who were as difficult as hers. Probably he did, for she knew at least one or two she hoped might not be included in the wedding party. But after all, Mama and Mrs. Warne would be the ones to make the final decisions about the attendants, as they had about everything else. All she and Stacy need do was be present at the proper time.

Except for several minor alterations on the wedding gown, all of Lorna's bridal clothes had been finished. Still, she was informed that this final visit was not an occasion which could be hurried.

Cicely Tompkins had been born within sound of Bow-bells, was the third of ten children, and at fourteen had been apprenticed to a seamstress. Within a short time, it was evident that her work was much finer than that of her mistress—so much so that the woman had quickly found excuse to dismiss her without giving her a penny.

Fortunately for Cicely it was done before one of the seamstress's more important clients, who immediately set the young woman up in a shop of her own. Advised by him, Cicely changed her name to Celeste, adopted a French accent, and before she was three and twenty had repaid her sponsor's loan and had become *the* couturiere of fashion-able London.

No gown ever left her shop without having received the wholehearted approval of the owner. It mattered not at all to her how important her customers might be or what they might wish, it was Celeste who decided what they must wear. This did not mean that she was always completely satisfied with the results she achieved, but that was because she could only design the clothing, not the one who wore it.

Too often, the clients with the most money had deplor-able taste—Celeste could deal with this and did so ruth-lessly—and deplorable figures. Faced with the latter, she struggled to turn out respectable gowns.

It had been a pleasure to design the bridal clothing for Lorna Pierce. The young lady was neither short and dumpy nor tall and ungainly, as were a good many who were mak-ing their come-outs this Season. Nor was she afflicted with spots or with protruding teeth, either of which detracted from the appearance of the gowns. Celeste was able to give advice about the control of the spots, but was helpless to do anything about a client's teeth.

Of course the ensemble must be white, but there was so much that a designer with Celeste's flair could do with such gowns. There were embroidered skirts, bodices laced with ribands of various colors, bunches of flowers scattered hither and thither across the material, and any number of ways to make the most of the client's good complexion and figure.

Lorna made an exclamation of pleasure when she saw what had been done for her. She gave orders to have everything sent home when the wedding gown was done, but found she could not escape so easily.

"Not just yet, *mademoiselle*," Celeste ordered. "First we must see that everything is *you*."

"I . . . I do not know what you mean. These are the gowns Mama and I chose."

"True. But Celeste does not permit her work to be skimped. By the wearer, as well as by the worker. You will put on each of the gowns — then we shall see if they are right."

"But what is there to see? They have all been fitted to me. A number of times. Everything should be — "

"You will not argue. Quickly now. I cannot waste time with you. If you wish the gowns — "

"Oh, I do." Faced with the implied threat that these beautiful gowns might be withheld, Lorna obediently allowed each of the garments to be slipped over her head, then turned about until Celeste had pronounced herself satisfied with the way each hung, the manner in which it moved with the wearer. At last, Lorna made her way out onto Bond Street with a feeling that she had done a day's work and had accomplished a great deal.

"Why, Miss — It is Miss Pierce, is it not?"

Lorna spun about to see a beautiful red-haired lady descending from a carriage as she spoke.

"Mrs. Liveredge." She had no doubt who this was, nor did she think Muriel Liveredge had any doubt about her name.

Ignoring the coolness in Lorna's tone, the other lady said, "It seems I am early for my appointment. It is almost as bad to be early for an appointment with Celeste as it is to be late. And I do not see your carriage about. Will you not share a cup of chocolate with me while you wait?"

"I am certain Morris will arrive soon." Let him come at

once, Lorna said to herself, so that I need not remain with this woman a moment longer than necessary.

"Doubtless he will do so. But it is so difficult to know exactly how long you must wait for him, and you must not stand in the street, to be ogled by passersby. Not on so busy a thoroughfare as this, especially. And there is a shop at hand where you can be comfortable. Come with me; your maid can summon you when he arrives."

Lorna was reluctant to go with Muriel Liveredge, even to speak with her, but she was forced to admit that the invitation was cordial enough. She could scarcely refuse without being downright rude. And, little as she liked the other lady, she had been taught to be polite—especially to her elders, she told herself with some malice. Too, Mrs. Liveredge spoke no more than the truth about the glances they were receiving from strange gentlemen. "Thank you, that would be nice. Wait here, Polly, and tell me when Morris comes."

As Polly murmured an assent, the two went into the shop and were shown at once to a table near the window. "Good," Mrs. Liveredge said. "Now we can see when your carriage arrives. They have very good cakes here. Will you not have some with your chocolate?"

"Thank you, no. The chocolate will be enough." Lorna hoped her driver would come at once so that she would not even have to accept the chocolate.

Her red-haired companion laughed. "Well, I think you are wrong to abstain from something so tasty as these. Doubtless, you are wiser than I, for I shall certainly indulge myself. I always do so, given the opportunity. That is why I am here. I must have a seam let out on one of my gowns. Unless I am careful, I shall soon grow fat—and I do not think my husband would approve of that."

There must be many ways this lady indulges herself of which her husband would not approve, Lorna thought, such as her habit of clinging onto the arm of an attractive young man. She almost asked if the gentleman was in London at present, but Mrs. Liveredge was busying herself in choosing several small cakes.

As she thrust a fork into one of them, she said, "I was certain it was you when I saw you coming out of Celeste's shop. She is a wonder, is she not?"

"Yes. It is not surprising that she is so busy at this time of year." Especially if she took as much time over every customer as she had just done with Lorna.

"Ah yes, everyone needs new gowns for the Season. This is your first, is it not?"

"As you might judge by my white gown," Lorna said with a smile. "How I envy anyone who can wear colors—especially, as effectively as you do." Even though she did not like the other woman, she would not refrain from admiring her splendid clothing.

"Yes, indeed. I remember, although my first Season was some time ago. Three years, in fact."

"You must have been quite young then." Lorna would have thought it much longer ago than that. Or else Muriel had been much older than most when making a come-out. She must have seen her twentieth bithday some years ago.

Unaware of the other's thoughts, Muriel Liveredge patted her hand. Lorna found it difficult not to snatch her hand away and place it in her lap. "Yes, I was quite young. But how kind of you to say it as you did. I thought you would be someone I should like to know when Mr. Warne introduced us. And I have seen you together often."

As I have seen you, Lorna said to herself.

"You are very good friends, are you not?"

"More than merely good friends. In fact, we are to be married next month." What would she have to say to *that?* Lorna wondered, recalling how the redhead had clung to Stacy at every opportunity whenever they met. She was certain that *he* had not mentioned his betrothal or the woman would have behaved more discreetly. Mrs. Liveredge, however, did not appear to be even slightly disturbed by the information, so Lorna decided that perhaps she was mistaken.

"You are?" she exclaimed happily. "How wonderful!

330

Stacy deserves someone as nice as you. He is so kind. I do not know how I should have managed all last winter here in London if I had not had him to lean upon."

Before Lorna could think of a reply to this stunning remark, Polly thrust her head through the doorway and signaled that the carriage had come. Snatching up her reticule, Lorna said, "My driver has arrived. I must thank you for . . ." She allowed the rest to die away as she hurried from the shop and took refuge in the carriage.

No wonder Stacy had not returned to the country last winter—not when that beautiful red-haired creature was "leaning upon" him, with all that those words implied. It was surprising that he'd even recalled he was to be married soon. Or had he? Perhaps he was seeking an excuse to end their engagement.

Still, Mrs. Liveredge had said she had a husband. So she did not expect to marry Stacy. Perhaps he intended to go through with his marriage and continue the *affaire* at the same time.

"But that will never happen. Not if I have anything to say about it—and I shall," Lorna said aloud, causing Polly to stare at her.

"What did you say, miss?"

"Oh . . . nothing at all. I was merely thinking."

By the time they had returned home, however, Lorna's thoughts of preventing Muriel Liveredge from snatching her betrothed had taken a different turn. If Muriel wanted him—and he wanted her—so be it. "Mama," she cried as soon as she entered the parlor, "I want to go home."

"Home? Why should you wish to do that? Your Papa has assured me that he will be here in time for the wedding, and he will remember. There is no need for one of us to fetch him. Now, what did Celeste say about your gowns?"

"She made me model all of them. Even the ones I had worn for her before. And she approved of each of them, I am relieved to say. Everything is ready but the wedding gown, and it will be finished by tomorrow. But that is just it—"

331

"Splendid! And we have chosen your bridesmaids. There is just one thing . . ."

"Sophronia, of course." Her mother's foreboding tone had diverted her for a moment.

"Yes, we could not see any way of leaving her out. I know you had hoped we could do so. . . ."

"It does not matter. What I have been trying to tell you, Mama, concerns that Mrs. Liveredge."

"Yes. Thank you for reminding me of her. I must remember to add her name to the list of invitations."

"But you do not understand. She was here in London last winter — with Stacy."

Mrs. Pierce laughed. "You make that sound so serious, dear. No doubt there were a number of people who remained here, although I do not know why anyone should wish to do so. London in the winter must be rather a dreary place — unless, of course, there happens to be an ice fair."

"Mama —"

"But they do not have them every year, I believe. Only when it is cold enough to freeze the Thames so that they can set up shops and bazaars. That must be exciting, although I think I should be afraid to go out on the ice."

"Mama!" Lorna despaired of bringing her mother's thoughts to the subject most important to her. "I am trying to tell you, Mrs. Liveredge said that she did not know how she could have gone on, except that she was able to lean upon Stacy last winter."

"I doubt she meant that literally. If she needed help, I am certain Stacy would have done everything possible to aid her. You know how kind he is."

"Yes, but . . ." How could she explain this so that her mother would understand? Mama would be much more overset to think her daughter knew of such things than to hear that Stacy had been indulging in an *affaire*. Gentlemen were expected to sow some wild oats, but their female acquaintances or relatives were not supposed to know of such matters — as if there were any way of keeping such secrets. Still, it would be impossible to con-

332

vince her of the truth.

"If you are worried," Mrs. Pierce said practically, having understood far more than her daughter suspected, "why don't you simply ask him about his acquaintanceship with the lady? You and Stacy have never had any secrets; he would tell you everything."

"That is exactly what I shall do. We are driving this afternoon. That will be an excellent time to bring everything into the open."

It was, however, a more difficult task than Lorna had thought it would be. How did one ask one's betrothed if he had an inamorata? One could scarcely blurt out such a question. It would sound too insulting. Too inquisitive. Would it make her seem fast even to know of such things? What was the best way to approach it?

When Stacy arrived at the house, it seemed that he had not recalled that he had included Mrs. Pierce in yesterday's invitation to go driving. Of course he had invited her often, but she had seldom accepted, feeling they deserved some time alone.

On this occasion, he had definitely not expected her company. His newest acquisition, a black curricle with huge yellow wheels, drawn by a pair of matched blacks, would be most uncomfortable for three, especially when one of the party was as robust as Mrs. Pierce. She had not, however, intended to accompany them, thinking it would be best if Lorna had an opportunity to allow him to explain the matters that seemed to disturb her. There was so little time for the two of them to talk at the affairs they both attended. Today they should be able to clear the air.

When Lorna, in a white cambric walking dress and a pink spencer, matching ribands trailing from her white hat, joined Stacy, he scarcely spared a moment to admire her new gown, but asked at once, "What do you think of that?"

Accustomed to sitting beside him in a gig, she eyed the new vehicle somewhat dubiously. "Is it not rather . . . dashing?"

"Oh, very much so. All the crack, in fact. I thought you would like it."

"Oh, I do," she said quickly. "It was merely that I was not expecting . . . this."

"Well, one can hardly poke about London in a gig."

"And this — a curricle, is it not; I have heard of them, although I have never seen one at home — I suppose it is considered the *dernier cri* among your set?"

"I suppose you might call it that." He helped her to the seat, adding, "Of course, this would not do for making calls at home. We might drive it occasionally to astonish our neighbors, but I have already sent home a carriage with a proper team for every day use. You will like them, I know. They are gentle enough for you to drive, although I know you can handle any cattle that I drop my lines across. I understand the stables are finished."

"The stables and the house as well."

"And do you approve?"

"Oh, certainly. How could I do otherwise? Our parents have been most generous."

Where the two estates adjoined, Mr. Warne and Mr. Pierce had each contributed a section of property to supply a home for their children. "I suppose that, in time, you may wish to live elsewhere," Mr. Warne had said when their plans were announced, "but for now, I think this will do very well for you. But you need not think you will be overburdened with visits from either set of parents."

It was no doll's house they had built, but a substantial place of red brick with pillars in front, a miniature Palladian structure. This was Mr. Pierce's idea; the two fathers had argued about the proper setting for the newlyweds, but had eventually agreed, Mr. Pierce, as was his custom, getting everything his own way.

There were rooms for half a dozen servants, and eight family bedchambers — one of which, to Lorna's embarrassment, Mrs. Warne had insisted upon fitting out as a nursery. Still, no one knew how many times during the past winter Lorna had crept up to that room and sat, rocking the cradle with her toe, while she dreamed of a tiny Stacy lying in it, as his father had done years earlier.

Each family had also contributed various items with which to furnish the house, making the result something of a hodge-podge. "I was, at least, permitted to choose the draperies," Lorna told him.

"All alone?" Stacy teased. "Without waiting for me to come and help you?"

"Well, you were not there to give me your opinion." This was the nearest she came to mentioning his absence during the winter, and she was careful to keep any note of complaint from her voice. "And after all, I should know what you would like after all these years."

"That you should, and in any case, I shall like whatever you chose."

At the moment, the road on which they were traveling was empty of other vehicles, so he slipped an arm about her and Lorna leaned her head against his shoulder. It was true: she and Stacy knew each other's minds so well. How could she have doubted him for an instant?

"We shall have to purchase *some* furniture in addition to what we have been given, but there is quite enough for us to begin with." The thought of that well-furnished nursery made her blush again. She told herself it was foolish to feel strange at the thought of the children she and Stacy would have some day, and she placed a hand confidingly over the broad one which held the lines above the horses' backs. He drew her closer and she could feel his breath upon her cheek as he whispered, "Happy?"

"With you, my dear one, always."

"And I. But you cannot know how often I have thought that if it had not been for your mourning, you and I would have been wed nearly a year by now and long ago settled in our home."

The drive continued in companionable silence, and when Lorna ran into the house, after waving Stacy farewell from the steps, Mrs. Pierce asked, "What did Stacy have to say about his friendship with that Mrs. Whatever-her-name-was?"

"Nothing at all," Lorna said indignantly. "We never spoke of her. Why did you think we should do so? Even if she needed his help, you know that Stacy would never do anything that was not right."

Mrs. Liveredge was not to blame if she found Stacy attractive, Lorna decided. Her husband, clearly, was not in London; doubtless, he was much older than she and her life was dull. Perhaps that was what she meant when she said she had needed to "lean on" Stacy.

"That is what I told you."

"Yes, Mama, you did." Why should her mother continue to talk about something which did not matter? "Did you see Stacy's new curricle?" Lorna asked.

"No, I did not watch you. I hope he was careful. I have heard of drivers who have had serious accidents with those vehicles because they can overturn so easily."

"Not drivers like Stacy," Lorna retorted and hurried to her room to select a gown for Mrs. Armbruster's ball that evening. With so many from which to choose, it was a problem, but at last, she settled on a gown embroidered all over with green leaves and flowers made of pearls. She hoped that Stacy would like it as much as she did.

Mrs. Armbruster, in an effort to copy the Prince Regent's taste in things Oriental without expending such vast sums, had draped her enormous ballroom in swaths of brilliant gold satin, and had searched the markets for figures she fervently hoped would be mistaken for imports from China. Between the figures, banks of hothouse flowers made the air so heavy with their scent that several guests remarked that they could almost taste it.

It must have been more than an hour, Lorna told herself, since Stacy had relinquished her to another partner, who had brought her back to her mother, and who had been followed by several others. She was happy that he had so many friends who were willing to be kind to her for his sake, but hoped that he would return to her soon.

The last nameless young man, whose dancing abilities did not equal his verve in whirling about the floor, had trod heavily upon her hem and she'd heard cloth tearing before she stopped herself from moving away from him. Red-faced, he apologized for his clumsiness and Lorna assured him that it was nothing, although this was one of her favorite gowns, Stacy had given it his whole-hearted approval, and she liked its clusters of blossoms and buds made of different-sized pearls. Now it was doubtless ruined.

Perhaps not. She hurried away to an empty room and busied herself with pins, fastening the rent. It was not nearly so bad, she found, as it had seemed at the time. She felt the pins would hold the flounce in place for the balance of the evening.

She could hear the musicians beginning a waltz and quickly tucked her remaining pins into her reticule. Surely Stacy would be searching for her by now, remembering the promise she had made at Almack's to save all her waltzes for him. Hurrying along the hall, she stumbled against a door, which swung open silently so that the pair within were unaware of the intrusion.

As if frozen to the spot, Lorna pressed both hands against her mouth to hold back the gasp provoked by the sight of Muriel Liveredge weeping against Stacy's shoulder.

"Now, now," Stacy was saying, "there is no need for tears. Not now."

"But—"

"And no need for you to worry, Muriel. I shall see to everything."

Lorna backed away from the door, then raced toward the ballroom, remembering only to slow her steps, lest someone ask her what was amiss. How could she explain without beginning to scream out accusations at the guilty pair?

She went directly to her mother and said in a low, desperate tone, "Mama, I must leave at once. I have a horrible migraine."

Mrs. Pierce could tell at once that something ailed the

337

girl. If only Lorna could learn to be more temperate in her feelings, rather than being in alt at one moment, in the depths an instant later. Now, however, she seemed to be more overset than usual. Perhaps she was truly ill. "Very well. I shall have someone find Stacy and—"

"No, no!" After what she had witnessed, Lorna knew she could not face him without bursting into tears. "Stacy has . . . has things to do. We can leave a message for him. But I must go—*now.*"

Bewildered, Mrs. Pierce sought her hostess, explained her daughter's indisposition and left a message to be delivered to Mr. Warne. By the time the carriage had been called, Lorna's migraine was a reality, brought on by the effort to hold back her tears. No one, not Mama or *anyone,* must know what she had overheard.

She resisted her mother's efforts to minister to her illness and at last, having almost convinced Mrs. Pierce that all she needed was rest, was able to close her bedchamber door. She dismissed Polly, as well, then allowed the pent-up tears to fall, burying her sobs in her pillow so that she could not be heard. How could Stacy betray her in such a fashion—and almost on the eve of their wedding!

She awoke next morning with a true migraine, the result of her bout of tears, but with her mind made up. She would do what she should have done yesterday—force Stacy to tell her the truth. Bathing her face in cold water in an attempt to remove the stains of last night's tears, she sat at her desk and penned a note, telling Stacy it was most important that he call upon her without delay.

"Call Alfred. Have him take this to Mr. Warne at once," she bade Polly, who curtsied, took the message, and summoned the footman to deliver it to the gentleman's residence immediately. While she awaited his reply, Lorna went over and over last night's scene in her mind, wondering what sort of excuse Stacy could possibly offer for such behavior.

338

Somewhat later Harrow could be heard calling for Alfred and complaining about his nonappearance, so Lorna confessed that she had sent him on an errand. She could not help feeling that the butler disapproved of her and did not relish her giving orders to a lower servant without first telling him about it.

"And I have no doubt he is frittering away his time in some low spot. It will be hours before we see him again," the butler said so sharply that Lorna was forced to state that Alfred was on an errand for *her*, which did little to soothe Harrow's anger.

It was midafternoon before the footman returned. "Well," Lorna demanded, feeling that Harrow had been correct in complaining about him, after all, "What did Mr. Warne say?"

Alfred shook his head. "Nothing, miss. That is to say, I could not find him."

"Could not find him?"

"No, miss. I tried the clubs and everywhere I could think of. Then I went back and told Mr. Warne's man that it would be to his advantage to give me a straight answer. He got quite huffy with me and said he could not tell me where Mr. Warne might be at the moment, making it sound that he would not tell me even if he could, but that Mr. Warne had left London early this morning—or rather, late last night—along with a red-haired lady. They were on their way to Dover, as he understood."

"Dover? Red-haired lady?"

"Yes, miss. That was what he told me. He could have done it hours ago, if he hadn't been so stiff-rumped about it. If you'll forgive my saying so, miss."

"Yes," she said dully. "Thank you."

"Sorry it took me so long to find out."

"You could not help that." The man may have loitered a trifle, but if Stacy had left before dawn, Alfred could not have found him at home.

"If he had said so at once, I could have followed Mr. Warne and delivered your message to him instead of leav-

339

ing it with that —" He broke off, thinking his description of the fellow would not do for a lady's ears.

"No, Mr. Warne would not have wanted it." She turned and went up the stairs to her mother's parlor. "Mama, I am going home," she announced.

Mrs. Pierce looked up from her needlework with some exasperation. "Now, Lorna, please do not begin that again. I have told you that brides frequently feel as you do. You have only a case of nerves. Sit down here with me and we can read over the list of wedding guests."

"There will be no wedding."

"Are you going to begin that again? Of course the wedding will take place as scheduled. You have planned this for more years than I can count."

"But there can be no wedding without a bridegroom — and Stacy will not be here."

"I think you must be in hysterics. Where did I leave my vinaigrette?"

"I am *not* in hysterics. And Stacy has left London. He has run off with Muriel Liveredge."

"That pretty red-haired lady he introduced to us at Almack's?"

"The one who has been clinging to him at every affair we have attended since then. And how long before we came, no one knows."

"I remember. And yesterday, if *you* remember, you were telling me some nonsense about her, and I told you to ask Stacy about your imaginings. You should have done so at once, so that you could forget all this."

"Yes, I should have asked him about her, but I wonder if he would have told me the truth. Yesterday, he allowed me to think —"

Mrs. Pierce shook her head. "Yesterday, you returned from your drive saying that you ought to have known better than to doubt Stacy for an instant, which I could have told you. Now, you are beginning to imagine —"

"Mama, please. I am *not* imagining things. Last night at Mrs. Armbruster's ball, I saw Stacy in a room away from

340

the ballroom."

"Why were you wandering about?"

"I had gone to pin up my flounce. What does that matter? Stacy was holding that . . . that creature in his arms and telling her she need not worry, that he would see to everything. Today, I sent Alfred with a message asking him to come to me — and Alfred came back with word that Stacy and Mrs. Liveredge had left London, were on their way to Dover."

"No," Mrs. Pierce said with decision, folding her piece of needlework and tucking it into her bag. "It is not hartshorn you need. I am putting you to bed with a dose of laudanum. Tomorrow, we can talk about this sensibly."

"Tomorrow," her daughter said with equal decision, "I am leaving London, whether you go with me or not. And the first thing I am going to do when I get home," she added viciously, "is go up to the nursery in our new house and smash that cradle into splinters."

Polly wept as she packed Lorna's gowns. "Only the ones I brought with me," her mistress ordered. "Leave the wedding gown and all the new ones. I shall never want to see any of them again."

The maid sniffled. "And stop sniveling! You need not go with me if you do not wish to do so."

"What'd I do here, with you gone?"

"Help Mama's dresser, I suppose."

"Oh no, miss. She wouldn't like that, nor would I. It'd be best for me to go with you. Alfred just has to wait — if he will."

"Oh, you should have told me." Lorna forced a smile, one she was far from feeling. "I should not wish to be responsible for spoiling your romance, just because mine has failed. I shall ask Mama to find something for you to do, so that you may remain here with Alfred."

"Thank you, Miss Lorna." Instead of stopping, Polly's tears flowed more freely at this bit of kindness. "But if your

341

Mama decides to go with you?"

"Then we should close this house. There will be no need to keep it open, as I, for one, will not be returning to London. Oh well, we can find something for Alfred to do — unless he prefers to remain in London and seek other employment. The two of you must work that out."

Lorna slowly walked downstairs, drawing on her gloves. She would make one more attempt to convince her mother to leave London with her. If she remained adamant, Lorna would go alone, although she had never traveled anywhere alone. The butler was crossing the hall, and she asked, "Have you seen my mother, Harrow?"

"In the drawing room, miss. I was about to send for you."

Lorna nodded and then entered the drawing room, wondering why her mother should be there. Mrs. Pierce was not alone. With her were Stacy, Muriel Liveredge, and a strange young man.

Stacy bounded to his feet at sight of her, and the other man started to rise, only to be pushed back onto the sofa by Muriel.

"Lorna, my dear, I should like to make you known — "

"I do not think we have anything to say to each other, Stacy. I do not know why you have come."

"Not come to you? Of course I should do so at once. When I returned home this morning, I received your message — and discovered that dunderhead of a man of mine never had mine sent to you."

"Your . . . message?"

"Yes, explaining that I had to take Muriel to Dover to meet . . ." He caught her hand, and because she had no wish to make a scene before a stranger, especially before Muriel Liveredge, Lorna permitted him to draw her across the room. "This is my friend — the best friend a man could have. Lorna, may I present James Liveredge? Captain Liveredge, I should say."

The stranger struggled to his feet, and this time Muriel rose beside him, her arm about him as if in support. It was evident that the captain was quite weak. There was a bandage about his head, and he had one arm in a sling.

"Yes, Lorna," her mother was saying, "Stacy has just begun telling us the most exciting thing. Oh, here are Harrow and the maids with tea and biscuits. But would you not prefer that I have breakfast prepared for you?"

"Oh no, thank you, Mrs. Pierce. We ate at a little inn somewhere along the way. At about dawn."

"At least, Captain, you must sit down."

"Oh yes," Lorna exclaimed, coming forward as she suddenly realized the gentleman's condition. "You are tiring yourself. Stacy, you ought not to have dragged the captain about without letting him rest, especially if he has come all the way from Dover."

"He has come much farther than that." There was some acerbity in Mrs. Liveredge's tone. "Dover was only his most recent stopping place. But nothing would deter Stacy from rushing over here without allowing us to stop at my hotel."

"Guilty," Stacy said with a grimace. "When I reached home and found that you had been urgently asking for me—and that you had no way of knowing where I had gone—my only thought was to come to you at once. James made no objection, realizing what you must mean to me, and I merely ignored Muriel's insistence that I allow them to go home."

"Of course, my husband had no choice but to agree with him."

"I had every choice," Captain Liveredge said. "But we—or at least, I, for Muriel has already met you—was anxious to meet the young lady who has caused my friend to rhapsodize in every communication I have had from him. Since he was out of short coats, I believe."

Lorna could feel herself blushing furiously, but Stacy placed an arm about her shoulders and said, "Now, can you blame me?"

"Certainly not," his friend said gallantly. "If I were not already happily married, I might also have been overcome with feeling for the young lady. As it is, of course, I can see no one but my Muriel."

"And if you do not sit down at once," his Muriel said sternly, "you will collapse again and not be able to see me at all."

"Oh yes, Captain, you must sit down at once," both Lorna and Mrs. Pierce cried, for the officer did appear to be very pale. Both feared that Muriel was correct and that he might collapse.

However, he only said, "Perhaps I should do that, for I own that I have traveled far. And I would be grateful for a cup of your delicious-smelling tea."

Lorna quickly poured the tea and carried it to him, but he remained standing until Mrs. Pierce had seated herself. Only then did he sink back against the sofa cushions and raise the cup to his lips while Muriel took the saucer and the serviette. Seeing the lady's concern for him, one would never have suspected she was the same creature who had flitted so gaily about at all the *ton* affairs.

"When we leave here," Captain Liveredge told them, "I *must* make a call at the War Office."

"Not before you have had some rest," Muriel protested.

"Yes. I will make a full report *after* I have rested. They must first know, however, that I have returned."

"Now that you have come back, may I tell our friends what you have been doing?" Stacy asked, smiling at Lorna as she refilled his teacup.

"It seems I shall be of little further use. Since our enemies seem to know everything there is to know about me, I see no reason why our friends cannot be informed."

"James has been doing some very secret work for our army for some time."

"No details about that," the captain said swiftly.

"Certainly not. Although I can assure you both these ladies can be trusted, I do not know any of the details, and so would be unable to reveal them if I wished to do so."

Captain Liveredge laughed shortly. "You may be certain that the French have a good idea of my work."

"They would not have captured you, otherwise."

Mrs. Pierce gasped at this, and Lorna exclaimed, "You were taken . . . by the French?" From her tone, one might have thought he had been the prisoner of some tribe of cannibals. And in truth, she did think a country that would allow its own monarchs to be executed would be liable to do anything vile.

"Yes. 'Twas not something I care to remember. But I was able to escape. There are some people in France who are not in sympathy with Napoleon's aim to conquer the world. They hid me until I was able to make my way into Spain to our own forces."

"And all this time, we did not know where he was, or even if he was alive. To protect him, to keep anyone from suspecting what he might be doing, I had to go on pretending to a gaiety I was far from feeling, acting as if nothing mattered to me except enjoying the frivolities of the Season or a flirtation with a handsome gentleman. And oh, I am so *very* weary of all that pretense." Muriel bit her lip and dabbed away tears with the serviette she still held, ignoring the mess she was making of her face paint.

Lorna's dislike for the other lady vanished in that moment, and she went on her knees beside the sofa, taking Muriel's hands in hers. "Oh, but you did it so beautifully. I am certain no one suspected the truth. You even fooled *me;* I should not have known you were worried about anything."

"No, you played your part very well," Mrs. Pierce assured Muriel, placing a hand on her daughter's head and thinking that Lorna had matured a great deal in these last moments. She thanked her stars that Lorna had not blurted out her true feelings for the other woman. "You must be quite proud of your wife," she said to the captain.

James Liveredge placed his uninjured hand over his wife's and squeezed it hard. "I am, madam, more proud than anyone will ever know. Her part was the difficult one, not knowing where I was or what I was doing, and being unable to share her worries with anyone except Stacy."

"She could not have had a better confidant," Lorna said

loyally. "She knew he would say nothing—even to us."

"No. It was difficult at times to remain quiet, not to tell *you* the story behind our pretense, but we feared word of his endeavors might reach the wrong ears."

"Not from us!" There was indignation in Mrs. Pierce's tone, and she set her teacup upon the table with a force that nearly shattered it.

"Of course not," Stacy was quick to assure her, and Muriel murmured an agreement. "But we have been forced to realize that, even among the members of the *ton,* there are some who will give—or sell—information to the French. The slightest hint of anything wrong would be enough to set the wrong ears twitching."

"Unfortunately, Stacy is correct," Captain Liveredge said. He rose to his feet, Muriel at once giving him her support. "But we must now be on our way. I must make my report—and I am looking forward to spending tonight in my own bed." The look he and his wife exchanged spoke of anticipated intimacies, and Lorna blushed at having seen something she knew was not intended for her eyes.

While Mrs. Pierce was shaking hands with her guests, Stacy said in an undertone, "We must talk."

"Certainly," Lorna agreed. "After you have taken your friends to their destinations." Then she turned from him to bid farewell to Muriel and her husband. "I should like it," she told them, "if you would attend my wedding next week."

"I should like that very much," Muriel said. "I have always said that Stacy deserves the best, and I am certain he will have it when he weds you. However, as soon as the War Office releases my husband, I plan to take him to our home near Bristol for a long recuperation. So I doubt we shall be in London for your wedding. Still, I wish you both every happiness."

"As do I," her husband agreed. He then allowed Muriel and Stacy to help him out to the carriage.

"Captain Liveredge seems a nice gentlemen," Mrs. Pierce said in an innocent tone, though glancing sharply at her daughter's face.

"Yes indeed." The reply was warm. "And so is Muriel—nice, I mean." Now that she was certain the other lady had no designs on Stacy, Lorna was quite prepared to like her, though she was secretly pleased that the Liveredges would not be in London to attend her wedding.

She hurried up the stairs to find Polly folding a last garment into an already bulging case. "What are you doing?" she demanded.

"Packing, miss. Like you said," Polly replied, still sniffling.

"Oh . . . that. Well, you must hang those things away. We are not going. At least, not until after the wedding. That will give you and Alfred time to decide what you wish to do. Now, help me—I must dress before Stacy returns."

Reflecting that her mistress was already well dressed, Polly only sighed and began returning the gowns to the armoire, only to have Lorna take out one after another while she tried to decide which she ought to wear. The unhappiness which had been growing worse during the past days had vanished as if it had never plagued her. All she could think of was that Stacy—*Stacy*—would soon return and she must look her best.

Despite her uncertainty as to which of her gowns was the most becoming, Lorna was seated beside her mother in the drawing room, twisting her handkerchief into knots, when Stacy's curricle halted outside the house and Harrow opened the door to him.

Ignoring both her mother and the servant, Lorna dashed across the room and flung herself into Stacy's arms. As he had so often done in the past, but never since they had come to London, he lifted her off her feet, swung her around until she was almost dizzy, then set her down again, kissing her soundly as he did so.

Harrow had discreetly withdrawn, but not out of earshot, and Mrs. Pierce, murmuring vaguely about instructions to the cook, also left them alone. Neither Lorna nor Stacy were aware of their leaving.

"Oh, Stacy, I do love you—love you—love you," Lorna cried when she had regained her breath.

He grinned down at her. "I always thought that you did—just as I have always loved you. But what is the reason for this particular declaration of your feelings?"

"Everything about you, my love—just as always. But now as I realize how you must have been pretending these past weeks that everything was fine, while you were so worried about your friend—"

"I wanted to try for a commission when James did—you know that."

"I did not know about the captain, of course, but I have always known that you wished to have joined the army. You did not because of your father's pressure, and I, for one, have always been happy you did not go. What if I had been left to wonder about you as Mrs. Liveredge did about James. Or worse, if I had heard you had been wounded . . . or . . ." She shuddered, unable even to say the dreaded word.

Stacy's arms comforted her as he said, "But, my dear one, most soldiers come home unharmed."

"Captain Liveredge did not."

"True enough, but his was an exceptional case. He did not operate as a common soldier, but as an agent behind the French lines."

"As I have no doubt you would have done, if you had had the opportunity."

"You are crediting me with more bravery than I possess," he told her with a laugh.

"Nothing of the kind. I *know* you are brave."

This declaration was rewarded with half a dozen kisses; then Lorna said, "And did it not take a kind of bravery to pretend to London—and to the world—that you had not a care when all the time you were worried about your friend's safety?"

"The only bravery was in daring to allow everyone, and

especially you, to think Muriel Liveredge was important to me. I feared you would be jealous. But you were not, were you?"

Lorna instinctively sensed that if she denied any feeling of jealousy, Stacy would be hurt. It would imply that she was too self-assured to think he might look at another female—and Stacy, of all people, knew her too well for that—or that she did not care what he did.

"Well, yes," she admitted, her arms about his neck, "I *was* somewhat jealous when I saw her clinging to you as she did. After all, she is so very beautiful. But"—behind his head, she crossed the fingers of both hands and then, for luck, crossed her wrists as well—"I never doubted *you*, my dearest one. Not for an instant."

St. George's, Hanover Square, was filled to the last seat with the members of the *ton* who had come to the wedding. Even the Regent and two of his brothers were in attendance, carefully avoiding one another. Candlelight glistened on satins of every color and on several fortunes in jewels.

Lorna saw none of these. Her gaze was fastened upon the dear figure of Stacy, resplendent in a coat of deep forest green above knee breeches and striped stockings. Not for him, she thought, was Beau Brummell's edict that a gentleman should wear only black. Not on this day of days.

For today's occasion, Lorna had put aside the white that was the badge of the newcomer to the *ton*. Her wedding gown was of heavy cream-colored satin, richly embroidered with pearls. Her veil was anchored by a wreath of her favorite blooms, lily of the valley.

"Are you nervous, my dear?" asked her father. He had come to London only yesterday, and it had been so long since he had donned a high collar and snowy cravat that his dark suit felt almost like a suit of armor.

"Nervous? Certainly not," his daughter replied. She had been, until she saw Stacy awaiting her. But no longer.

"Well, I am—nigh as nervous as I was at my own wedding."

"Cheer up," Lorna told him. "Since you have only one daughter, you will never have to do this again."

"As long as this is what you want . . ." There was relief in his tone. Secretly, he had worried that, once exposed to the life of the *ton,* she would wish for a grander alliance. He was pleased to see that she had not changed, that she was still his little girl, content with what life had to offer her.

"It is all I have ever wanted." These last words were whispered as she took her place at Stacy's side. The hand she slipped into his was warm and firm, and as he looked down at her with the same love she had known all her life, her voice was clear as she repeated, "I, Lorna, take thee, Stacy. . . ."

ELEGANT LOVE STILL FLOURISHES —
Wrap yourself in a Zebra Regency Romance.

A MATCHMAKER'S MATCH (3783, $3.50/$4.50)
by Nina Porter

To save herself from a loveless marriage, Lady Psyche Veringham pretends to be a bluestocking. Resigned to spinsterhood at twenty-three, Psyche sets her keen mind to snaring a husband for her young charge, Amanda. She sets her cap for long-time bachelor, Justin St. James. This man of the world has had his fill of frothy-headed debutantes and turns the tables on Psyche. Can a bluestocking and a man about town find true love?

FIRES IN THE SNOW (3809, $3.99/$4.99)
by Janis Laden

Because of an unhappy occurrence, Diana Ruskin knew that a secure marriage was not in her future. She was content to assist her physician father and follow in his footsteps . . . until now. After meeting Adam, Duke of Marchmaine, Diana's precise world is shattered. She would simply have to avoid the temptation of his gentle touch and stunning physique — and by doing so break her own heart!

FIRST SEASON (3810, $3.50/$4.50)
by Anne Baldwin

When country heiress Laetitia Biddle arrives in London for the Season, she harbors dreams of triumph and applause. Instead, she becomes the laughingstock of drawing rooms and ballrooms, alike. This headstrong miss blames the rakish Lord Wakeford for her miserable debut, and she vows to rise above her many faux pas. Vowing to become an Original, Letty proves that she's more than a match for this eligible, seasoned Lord.

AN UNCOMMON INTRIGUE (3701, $3.99/$4.99)
by Georgina Devon

Miss Mary Elizabeth Sinclair was rather startled when the British Home Office employed her as a spy. Posing as "Tasha," an exotic fortune-teller, she expected to encounter unforeseen dangers. However, nothing could have prepared her for Lord Eric Stewart, her dashing and infuriating partner. Giving her heart to this haughty rogue would be the most reckless hazard of all.

A MADDENING MINX (3702, $3.50/$4.50)
by Mary Kingsley

After a curricle accident, Miss Sarah Chadwick is literally thrust into the arms of Philip Thornton. While other women shy away from Thornton's eyepatch and aloof exterior, Sarah finds herself drawn to discover why this man is physically and emotionally scarred.